Praise for

STEPHANIE LAURENS

"Laurens's writing shines."
—*Publishers Weekly*

"Stephanie Laurens is a real find! She combines
outstanding characterization with action and
sensuality, bringing larger-than-life characters to the
page with such skill and talent that they become real.
All I need is her name on
the cover to make me pick up the book."
—Linda Howard

"Ms. Coulter, Quick and Lowell, look out!"
—*Affaire de Coeur*

"Entertaining. For those who like their
Regencies a little less ladylike."
—*Kirkus Reviews*

"Stephanie Laurens's novels take my breath away.
With her vivid, exuberant style and lush sensuality,
she weaves a story that satisfies with every page."
—Lisa Kleypas

STEPHANIE LAURENS

An Unwilling Conquest

MIRA

ISBN 0-7783-2301-3

AN UNWILLING CONQUEST

Copyright © 1996 by Stephanie Laurens.

www.MIRABooks.com

Printed in U.S.A.

An Unwilling Conquest

Chapter One

"Is it the devil we're running from, then?"

The question, uttered in the mildest of tones, made Harry Lester wince. "Worse," he threw over his shoulder at his groom and general henchman, Dawlish. "The matchmaking mamas—in league with the dragons of the *ton*." Harry edged back on the reins, feathering a curve at speed. He saw no reason to ease the wicked pace. His match greys, sleek and powerful, were quite content to keep the bits between their teeth. His curricle rushed along in their wake; Newmarket lay ahead. "And we're not running—it's called a strategic retreat."

"Is that so? Well, can't say I blame you," came in Dawlish's dour accents. "Who'd ever have thought to see Master Jack landed—and without much of a fight, if Pinkerton's on the up. Right taken aback, is Pinkerton." When this information elicited no response, Dawlish added, "Considering his position, he is."

Harry snorted. "Nothing will part Pinkerton from Jack—not even a wife. He'll swallow the pill when the time comes."

"Aye—p'raps. Still, can't say I'd relish the prospect of answering to a missus—not after all these years."

Harry's lips quirked. Realising that Dawlish, riding on the box behind him, couldn't see it, he gave into the urge to smile. Dawlish had been with him forever, having, as a fifteen-year-old groom, attached himself to the second son of the Lester household the instant said son had been put atop a pony. Their old cook had maintained it was a clear case of like to like; Dawlish's life was horses—he had recognised a master in the making and had followed doggedly in his wake. "You needn't worry, you old curmudgeon. I can assure you I've no intention, willingly or otherwise, of succumbing to any siren's lures."

"All very well to say so," Dawlish grumbled. "But when these things happen, seems like there's no gainsaying them. Just look at Master Jack."

"I'd rather not," Harry curtly replied. Dwelling on his elder brother's rapid descent into matrimony was an exercise guaranteed to shake his confidence. With only two years separating them, he and Jack had led much the same lives. They'd come on the town together more than ten years ago. Admittedly, Jack had less reason than he to question love's worth, nevertheless, his brother had been, as Dawlish had observed, a most willing conquest. The fact made him edgy.

"You planning on keeping from London for the rest of yore life?"

"I sincerely hope it won't come to that." Harry checked the greys for a slight descent. The heath lay before them, a haven free of matchmakers and dragons alike. "Doubtless my uninterest will be duly noted. With any luck, if I lay low, they'll have forgotten me by next Season."

"Wouldn't have thought, with all the energy you've put into raising a reputation like you have, that they'd be so keen."

Harry's lip curled. "Money, Dawlish, will serve to excuse any number of sins."

He waited, expecting Dawlish to cap the comment with some gloomy pronouncement to the effect that if the madams of society could overlook his transgressions then no one was safe. But no comment came; his gaze fixed unseeing on his leader's ears, Harry grudgingly reflected that the wealth with which he and his brothers, Gerald as well as Jack, had recently been blessed, was indeed sufficient to excuse a lifetime of social sins.

His illusions were few—he knew who and what he was—a rake, one of the wolves of the *ton,* a hellion, a Corinthian, a superlative rider and exceptional breeder of quality horseflesh, an amateur boxer of note, an excellent shot, a keen and successful huntsman on the field and off. For the past ten and more years, Society had been his playing field. Capitalising on natural talents, and the position his birth had bestowed, he had spent the years in hedonistic pleasure, sampling women much as he had the wines. There'd been none to gainsay him, none to stand in his path and challenge his profligate ways.

Now, of course, with a positively disgusting fortune at his back, they'd be lining up to do so.

Harry snorted and refocused on the road. The sweet damsels of the *ton* could offer until they were blue in the face—he wasn't about to buy.

The junction with the road to Cambridge loomed ahead. Harry checked his team, still sprightly despite their dash from London. He'd nursed them along the main road, only letting them have their heads once they'd passed Great Chesterford and picked up the less-frequented Newmarket road. They'd passed a few slower-moving carriages; most of the gentlemen intent on the week's racing would already be in Newmarket.

About them, the heath lay flat and largely featureless, with only a few stands of trees, windbreaks and the odd coppice to lend relief. There were no carriages approaching on the Cambridge road; Harry swung his team onto the hard surface and flicked the leader's ear. Newmarket—and the comfort of his regular rooms at the Barbican Arms—lay but a few miles on.

"To y'r left."

Dawlish's warning growl came over his shoulder in the same instant Harry glimpsed movement in the stand of trees bordering the road ahead. He flicked both horses' withers; as the lash softly swooshed back up the whiphandle, he slackened the reins, transferring them to his left hand. With his right, he reached for the loaded pistol he kept under the seat, just behind his right boot.

As his fingers closed about the chased butt, he registered the incongruity of the scene.

Dawlish put it into words, a heavy horse pistol in his hands. "On the king's highway in broad daylight—never-you-mind! What's the world a-coming to, I asks you?"

The curricle sped on.

Harry wasn't entirely surprised when the men milling in the trees made no attempt to halt them. They were mounted but, even so, would have had the devil of a time hauling in the flying greys. He counted at least five as they flashed past, all in frieze and heavily muffled. The sound of stifled cursing dwindled behind them.

Dawlish muttered darkly, rummaging about re-stowing his pistols. "Stap me, but they even had a wagon backed up in them trees. Right confident of their haul they must be."

Harry frowned.

The road curved ahead; he regathered the slack reins and checked the greys fractionally.

They rounded the curve—Harry's eyes flew wide.

He hauled back on the reins with all his strength, slewing the greys across the road. They came to a snorting, stamping halt, their noses all but in the low hedge. The curricle rocked perilously, then settled back on its springs.

Curses turned the air about his ears blue.

Harry paid no attention; Dawlish was still up behind him, not in the ditch. Before him, on the other hand, was a scene of disaster.

A travelling carriage lay on its side, not in the ditch but blocking most of the road. It looked as if one of the back wheels had disintegrated; the ponderous contraption, top-heavy with luggage, had toppled sideways. The accident had only just occurred—the upper wheels of the carriage were still slowly rotating. Harry blinked. A young lad, a groom presumably, was struggling to haul a hysterical girl from the ditch. An older man, the coachman from his attire, was hovering anxiously over a thin grey-haired woman, laid out on the ground.

The coach team was in a flat panic.

Without a word, Harry and Dawlish leapt to the ground and ran to calm the horses.

It took a good five minutes to soothe the brutes, good, strong coach horses with the full stubbornness and dim wits of their breed. With the traces finally untangled, Harry left the team in Dawlish's hands; the young groom was still helplessly pleading with the tearful girl while the coachman dithered over the older woman, clearly caught between duty and a wish to lend succour, if he only knew how.

The woman groaned as Harry walked up. Her eyes were closed; she lay straight and rigid on the ground, her hands crossed over her flat chest.

"My ankle—!" A spasm of pain twisted her angular

features, tight under an iron-grey bun. "Damn you, Joshua—when I get back on my feet I'll have your hide for a footstool, I will." She drew her breath in in a painful hiss. "*If* I ever get back on my feet."

Harry blinked; the woman's tones were startlingly reminiscent of Dawlish in complaining mode. He raised his brows as the coachman lumbered to his feet and touched his forehead. "Is there anyone in the carriage?"

The coachman's face blanked in shock.

"*Oh my God!*" Her eyes snapping open, the woman sat bolt upright. "The mistress and Miss Heather!" Her startled gaze fell on the carriage. "Damn you, Joshua—what are you *doing*, mooning over me when the mistress is likely lying in a heap?" Frantically, she hit at the coachman's legs, pushing him towards the carriage.

"Don't panic."

The injunction floated up out of the carriage, calm and assured.

"We're perfectly all right—just a bit shaken." The clear, very feminine voice paused before adding, a touch hesitantly, "But we can't get out."

With a muttered curse, Harry strode to the carriage, pausing only to shrug out of his greatcoat and fling it into the curricle. Reaching up to the back wheel, he hauled himself onto the body. Standing on the coach's now horizontal side, he bent and, grasping the handle, hauled the door open.

Planting one booted foot on either side of the coach step, he looked down into the dimness within.

And blinked.

The sight that met his eyes was momentarily dazzling. A woman stood in the shaft of sunshine pouring through the doorway. Her face, upturned, was heart-shaped; a broad forehead was set beneath dark hair pulled severely back. Her features were well defined; a straight nose and full, well-curved lips above a delicate but determined chin.

Her skin was the palest ivory, the colour of priceless pearls; beyond his control, Harry's gaze skimmed her cheeks and the graceful curve of her slender neck before coming to rest on the ripe swell of her breasts. Standing over her as he was, they were amply exposed to his sight even though her modish carriage dress was in no way indecorous.

Harry's palms tingled.

Large blue eyes fringed with long black lashes blinked up at him.

For an instant, Lucinda Babbacombe was not entirely sure she hadn't sustained a blow on the head—what else could excuse this vision, conjured from her deepest dreams?

Tall and lean, broad-shouldered, slim-hipped, he towered above her, long, sleekly muscled legs braced on either side of the door. Sunlight haloed his golden locks; with the light behind him she could not make out his features yet she sensed the tension that held him.

Lucinda blinked rapidly. A light blush tinged her cheeks; she looked away—but not before she registered the subdued elegance of his garments—the tightly-fitting grey coat, superbly cut, style in every line, worn over clinging ivory inexpressibles, which clearly revealed the long muscles of his thighs. His calves were encased in gleaming Hessians; his linen was crisp and white. There were, she noted, no fobs or seals hanging at his waist, only a single gold pin in his cravat.

Prevailing opinion suggested such severe attire should render a gentleman uninteresting. Unremarkable. Prevailing opinion was wrong.

He shifted—and a large, long-fingered, extremely elegant hand reached down to her.

"Take my hand—I'll pull you up. One of the wheels is shattered—it's impossible to right the carriage."

His voice was deep, drawling, an undercurrent Lucinda couldn't identify sliding beneath the silken tones. She glanced up through her lashes. He had moved to the side of the door and had gone down on one knee. The light now reached his face, illuminating features that seemed to harden as her gaze touched them. His hand moved impatiently; a black sapphire set in a gold signet glimmered darkly. He would need to be very strong to lift her out with one arm. Subduing the thought that her rescue might well prove a greater threat than her plight, Lucinda reached for his hand.

Their palms met; long fingers curled about her wrist. Lucinda brought her other hand up and clasped it about his—and she was airborne.

She drew in a swift breath—an arm of steel wrapped about her waist; her diaphragm seized. She blinked—and found herself on her knees, held fast in his embrace, locked breast to chest with her unnerving rescuer.

Her eyes were on a level with his lips. They were as severe as his clothes, chiselled and firm. His jaw was distinctly squared, the patrician line of his nose a testimony to his antecedents. The planes of his face were hard, as hard as the body steadying hers, holding her balanced on the edge of the carriage doorframe. He had released her hands; they had fallen to lie against his chest. One of her hips was pressed against his, the other against his muscled thigh. Lucinda forgot about breathing.

Cautiously, she lifted her eyes to his—and saw the sea, calm and clear, a cool, crystalline pale green.

Their gazes locked.

Mesmerised, Lucinda drowned in the green sea, her skin lapped by waves of warmth, her mind suborned to sensation. She felt her lips soften, felt herself lean into him—and blinked wildly.

A tremor shook her. The muscles surrounding her twitched, then stilled.

She felt him draw breath.

"Careful," was all he said as he slowly rose, drawing her up with him, holding her steady until her feet could find purchase on the carriage.

Lucinda wondered just what danger he was warning her against.

Forcing his arms from her, Harry struggled to shackle his impulses, straining at their leash. "I'll have to lower you to the ground."

Peering over the carriage side, Lucinda could only nod. The drop was six feet and more. She felt him shift behind her; she jumped as his hands slipped beneath her arms.

"Don't wriggle or try to jump. I'll let go when your coachman has hold of you."

Joshua was waiting below. Lucinda nodded; speech was beyond her.

Harry gripped her firmly and swung her over the edge. The coachman quickly grasped her legs; Harry let go— but could not prevent his fingers from brushing the soft sides of her breasts. He clenched his jaw and tried to eradicate the memory but his fingertips burned.

Once on *terra firma*, Lucinda was pleased to discover her wits once more at her command. Whatever curious influence had befuddled her faculties was, thank Heaven, purely transitory.

A quick glance upwards confirmed that her rescuer had turned back to render a like service to her stepdaughter. Reflecting that at barely seventeen Heather's susceptibility to his particular brand of wizardry was probably a good deal less than her own, Lucinda left him to it.

After one comprehensive glance about the scene, she marched across to the ditch, leaned over and dealt Amy, the tweeny, a sharp slap. "Enough," she declared, as if she was speaking of nothing more than kneading dough. "Now come and help with Agatha."

Amy's tear-drenched eyes opened wide, then blinked. "Yes, mum." She sniffed—then shot a watery smile at Sim, the groom, and struggled up out of the thankfully dry ditch.

Lucinda was already on her way to Agatha, prone in the road. "Sim—help with the horses. Oh—and do get these stones out of the road." She pointed a toe at the collection of large, jagged rocks littering the highway. "I dare say it was one of these that caused our wheel to break. And I expect you'd better start unloading the carriage."

"Aye, mum."

Halting by Agatha's side, Lucinda bent to look down at her. "What is it and how bad?"

Lips compressed, Agatha opened iron-grey eyes and squinted up at her. "It's just my ankle—it'll be better directly."

"Indeed," Lucinda remarked, getting down on her knees to examine the injured limb. "That's no doubt why you're white as a sheet."

"Nonsense—oooh!" Agatha sucked in a quick breath and closed her eyes.

"Stop fussing and let me bind it."

Lucinda bade Amy tear strips from her petticoat, then proceeded to bind Agatha's ankle, ignoring the maid's grumbles. All the while, Agatha shot suspicious glances past her.

"You'd best stay by me, mistress. And keep the young miss by you. That gentleman may be a gentleman, but he's a one to watch, I don't doubt."

Lucinda didn't doubt either but she refused to hide behind her maid's skirts. "Nonsense. He rescued us in a positively gentlemanly manner—I'll thank him appropriately. Stop fussing."

"Fussing!" Agatha hissed as Lucinda drew her skirts down to her ankles. "You didn't see him move."

"Move?" Frowning, Lucinda stood and dusted her hands, then her gown. She turned to discover Heather hurrying up, hazel eyes bright with excitement, clearly none the worse for their ordeal.

Behind her came their rescuer. All six feet and more of him, with a lean and graceful stride that conjured the immediate image of a hunting cat.

A big, powerful predator.

Agatha's comment was instantly explained. Lucinda concentrated on resisting the urge to flee. He reached for her hand—she must have extended it—and bowed elegantly.

"Permit me to introduce myself, ma'am. Harry Lester—at your service."

He straightened, a polite smile softening his features.

Fascinated, Lucinda noted how his lips curved upwards just at the ends. Then her eyes met his. She blinked and glanced away. "I most sincerely thank you, Mr Lester, for your assistance—yours and your groom's." She beamed a grateful smile at his groom, unhitching the horses from the coach with Sim's help. "It was immensely lucky you happened by."

Harry frowned, the memory of the footpads lurking in the trees beyond the curve intruding. He shook the thought aside. "I beg you'll permit me to drive you and your..."

Brows lifting, he glanced from the younger girl's bright face to that of his siren's.

She smiled. "Allow me to introduce my stepdaughter, Miss Heather Babbacombe."

Heather bobbed a quick curtsy; Harry responded with a slight bow.

"As I was saying, Mrs Babbacombe." Smoothly Harry turned back and captured the lady's wide gaze with his. Her eyes were a soft blue, partly grey—a misty colour. Her carriage gown of lavender blue served to emphasise the shade. "I hope you'll permit me to drive you to your destination. You were headed for…?"

"Newmarket," Lucinda supplied. "Thank you—but I must make arrangements for my people."

Harry wasn't sure which statement more surprised him. "Naturally," he conceded, wondering how many other ladies of his acquaintance, in like circumstances, would so concern themselves over their servants. "But my groom can handle the details for you. He's familiar with these parts."

"He is? How fortunate."

Before he could blink, the soft blue gaze had left him for Dawlish—his siren followed, descending upon his servitor like a galleon in full sail. Intrigued, Harry followed. She summoned her coachman with an imperious gesture. By the time Harry joined them, she was busily issuing the orders he had thought to give.

Dawlish shot him a startled, distinctly reproachful glance.

"Will that be any trouble, do you think?" Lucinda asked, sensing the groom's distraction.

"Oh—no, ma'am." Dawlish bobbed his head respectfully. "No trouble at all. I knows the folks at the Barbican right well. We'll get all seen to."

"Good." Harry made a determined bid to regain control of the situation. "If that's settled, I suspect we should get on, Mrs Babbacombe." At the back of his mind lurked a vision of five frieze-coated men. He offered her his arm; an intent little frown wrinkling her brows, she placed her hand upon it.

"I do hope Agatha will be all right."

"Your maid?" When she nodded, Harry offered, "If she'd broken her ankle she would, I think, be in far greater pain."

The blue eyes came his way, along with a grateful smile.

Lucinda glanced away—and caught Agatha's warning glare. Her smile turned into a grimace. "Perhaps I should wait here until the cart comes for her?"

"No." Harry's response was immediate. She shot him a startled glance; he covered his lapse with a charming but rueful smile. "I hesitate to alarm you but footpads have been seen in the vicinity." His smile deepened. "And Newmarket's *only* two miles on."

"Oh." Lucinda met his gaze; she made no effort to hide the consideration in hers. "Two miles?"

"If that." Harry met her eyes, faint challenge in his.

"Well…" Lucinda turned to view his curricle.

Harry waited for no more. He beckoned Sim and pointed to the curricle. "Put your mistresses' luggage in the boot."

He turned back to be met by a cool, distinctly haughty blue glance. Equally cool, he allowed one brow to rise.

Lucinda suddenly felt warm, despite the cool breeze that heralded the approaching evening. She looked away, to where Heather was talking animatedly to Agatha.

"If you'll forgive the advice, Mrs Babbacombe, I would not consider it wise for either you or your step-daughter to be upon the road, unescorted, at night."

The soft drawl focused Lucinda's mind on her options. Both appeared dangerous. With a gentle inclination of her head, she chose the more exciting. "Indeed, Mr Lester. Doubtless you're right." Sim had finished stowing their baggage in the curricle's boot, strapping bandboxes to the flaps. "Heather?"

While his siren fussed, delivering a string of last-minute instructions, Harry lifted her stepdaughter to the curricle's seat. Heather Babbacombe smiled sunnily and thanked him prettily, too young to be flustered by his innate charms.

Doubtless, Harry thought, as he turned to view her stepmother, Heather viewed him much as an uncle. His lips quirked, then relaxed into a smile as he watched Mrs Babbacombe glide towards him, casting last, measuring glances about her.

She was slender and tall—there was something about her graceful carriage that evoked the adjective "matriarchal." A confidence, an assurance, that showed in her frank gaze and open expression. Her dark hair, richly brown with the suspicion of red glinting in the sun, was, he could now see, fixed in a tight bun at the nape of her neck. For his money, the style was too severe—his fingers itched to run through the silken tresses, laying them free.

As for her figure, he was having great difficulty disguising his interest. She was, indeed, one of the more alluring visions he had beheld in many a long year.

She drew near and he lifted a brow. "Ready, Mrs Babbacombe?"

Lucinda turned to meet his gaze, wondering how such a soft drawl could so easily sound steely. "Thank you, Mr Lester." She gave him her hand; he took it, drawing her to the side of the carriage. Lucinda blinked at the high step—the next instant, she felt his hands firm about her waist and she was lifted, effortlessly, to the seat.

Stifling her gasp, Lucinda met Heather's gaze, filled with innocent anticipation. Sternly suppressing her fluster, Lucinda settled herself on the seat next to her stepdaughter. She had not, indeed, had much experience interacting with gentlemen of Mr Lester's standing; perhaps such gestures were commonplace?

Despite her inexperience, she could not delude herself that her position, as it transpired, could ever be dismissed as commonplace. Her rescuer paused only to swing his greatcoat—adorned, she noted, with a great many capes—about his broad shoulders before following her into the curricle, the reins in his hands. Naturally, he sat beside her.

A bright smile firmly fixed on her lips, Lucinda waved Agatha goodbye, steadfastly ignoring the hard thigh pressed against her much softer limb, and the way her shoulder perforce had to nestle against his back.

Harry himself had not foreseen the tight squeeze—and found its results equally disturbing. Pleasant—but definitely disturbing. Backing his team, he asked, "Were you coming from Cambridge, Mrs Babbacombe?" He desperately needed distraction.

Lucinda was only too ready to oblige. "Yes—we spent a week there. We intended to leave directly after lunch but spent an hour or so in the gardens. They're very fine, we discovered."

Her accents were refined and untraceable, her stepdaughter's less so, while those of her servants were definitely north country. The greys settled into their stride; Harry comforted himself that two miles meant less than fifteen minutes, even allowing for picking their way through the town. "But you're not from hereabouts?"

"No—we're from Yorkshire." After a moment, Lucinda added, a smile tweaking her lips, "At the moment, however, I suspect we could more rightly claim to be gypsies."

"Gypsies?"

Lucinda exchanged a smile with Heather. "My husband died just over a year ago. His estate passed into his cousin's hands, so Heather and I decided to while away our year of mourning in travelling the country. Neither of us had seen much of it before."

Harry stifled a groan. She was a widow—a beautiful widow newly out of mourning, unfixed, unattached, bar the minor encumbrance of a stepdaughter. In an effort to deny his mounting interest, to block out his awareness of her soft curves pressed, courtesy of Heather Babbacombe's more robust figure, firmly against his side, he concentrated on her words. And frowned. "Where do you plan to stay in Newmarket?"

"The Barbican Arms," Lucinda replied. "I believe it's in the High Street."

"It is." Harry's lips thinned; the Barbican Arms was directly opposite the Jockey Club. "Ah—have you reservations?" He slanted a glance at her face and saw surprise register. "It's a race week, you know."

"Is it?" Lucinda frowned. "Does that mean it'll be crowded?"

"Very." With every rakehell and womaniser who could make the journey from London. Harry suppressed the thought. Mrs Babbacombe was, he told himself, none of his business. Very definitely none of his business—she might be a widow and, to his experienced eye, ripe for seduction, but she was a *virtuous* widow—therein lay the rub. He was too experienced not to know such existed—indeed, the fleeting thought occurred that if he was to plot his own downfall, then a virtuous widow would be first choice as Cupid's pawn. But he had recognised the trap—and had no intention of falling into it. Mrs Babbacombe was one beautiful widow he would do well to leave untouched—unsampled. Desire bucked, unexpectedly strong; with a mental curse, Harry shackled it—in iron!

The first straggling cottages appeared ahead. He grimaced. "Is there no acquaintance you have in the district with whom you might stay?"

"No—but I'm sure we'll be able to find accommodation somewhere." Lucinda gestured airly, struggling to keep her mind on her words and her senses on the late afternoon landscape. "If not at the Barbican Arms, then perhaps the Green Goose."

She sensed the start that shot through him. Turning, she met an openly incredulous, almost horrified stare.

"*Not* the Green Goose." Harry made no attempt to mute the decree.

It was received with a frown. "Why not?"

Harry opened his mouth—but couldn't find the words. "Never mind why—just get it into your head that you cannot reside at the Green Goose."

Intransigence flowed into her expression, then she put her pretty nose in the air and looked ahead. "If you will just set us down at the Barbican Arms, Mr Lester, I'm sure we'll sort things out."

Her words conjured a vision of the yard at the Barbican Arms—of the main hall of the inn as it would be at this moment—as Harry had experienced it at such times before. Jam-packed with males, broad-shouldered, elegant *ton*nish gentlemen, the vast majority of whom he would know by name. He certainly knew them by nature; he could just imagine their smiles when Mrs Babbacombe walked in.

"No."

The cobbles of the High Street rang beneath the greys' hooves.

Lucinda turned to stare at him. "What on earth do you mean?"

Harry gritted his teeth. Even with his attention on his horses as he negotiated the press of traffic in the main street of the horse capital of England, he was still aware of the surprised glances thrown their way—and of the lingering, considering looks bent on the woman by his side. Arriving with him, being seen with him, had already focused attention on her.

It was none of his business.

Harry felt his face harden. "Even if the Barbican Arms has rooms to spare—which they will not—it's not suitable for you to stay in town while a race meeting's on."

"I beg your pardon?" After a moment of astonished surprise, Lucinda drew herself up. "Mr Lester—you have most ably rescued us—we owe you our gratitude. However, I am more than capable of organising our accommodation and stay in this town."

"Gammon."

"What?"

"You don't know anything about staying in a town during a race-meet or you wouldn't be here now." Lips set in a thin line, Harry shot her an irritated glare. "Devil take it—look around you, woman!"

Lucinda had already noticed the large number of men strolling the narrow pavements. As her gaze swept the scene, she noted that there were many more on horseback and in the sporting carriages of every description thronging the thoroughfare. Gentlemen everywhere. Only gentlemen.

Heather was leaning close, shrinking against her, not

used to being stared at and ogled. She raised hazel eyes filled with uncertainty to Lucinda's face. "Lucinda…?"

Lucinda patted her hand. As she raised her head, she encountered a boldly appraising stare from a gentleman in a high-perch phaeton. Lucinda returned his scrutiny with a frosty glance. "Nevertheless," she maintained. "If you will set us down at…"

Her words trailed away as she glimpsed, hanging above a broad archway just ahead, a signboard depicting a castle gateway. In that instant, the traffic parted; Harry clicked his reins and the curricle shot forward—straight past the archway.

Lucinda swivelled to peer at the sign as they moved steadily down the street. "That's it—the Barbican Arms!" She turned to look at Harry. "You've passed it."

Grim-faced, Harry nodded.

Lucinda glared at him. "Stop," she ordered.

"You can't stay in town."

"I can!"

"Over my dead body!" Harry heard his snarl and inwardly groaned. He closed his eyes. What was happening to him? Opening his eyes, he glared at the woman beside him. Her cheeks were becomingly flushed—with temper. A fleeting thought of how she would look flushed with desire shot through his unwilling mind.

Something of his thoughts must have shown in his face—her blue eyes narrowed. "Are you proposing to kidnap us?" Her voice held the promise of a long and painful death.

The end of the High Street appeared; the traffic thinned. Harry flicked his leader's ear and the greys surged. As the sound of hooves on cobbles died behind them, he glanced down at her and growled, "Consider it forcible repatriation."

Chapter Two

"*Forcible repatriation?*"

Harry shot her a narrow-eyed glare. "You don't *belong* in a race-town."

Lucinda glared back. "I belong wherever *I* choose to stay, Mr Lester."

His face set in uncompromising lines, Harry looked back at his team. Lucinda looked ahead, frowning direfully.

"Where are you taking us?" she eventually demanded.

"To stay with my aunt, Lady Hallows." Harry glanced at her. "She lives a little way out of town."

It had been many years since she'd allowed anyone to order her life. Nose in the air, Lucinda held to dignified disapproval. "How do you know she won't already have visitors?"

"She's a widow of long standing and lives quietly." Harry checked his team and turned onto a side road. "She has a whole Hall to spare—and she'll be delighted to make your acquaintance."

Lucinda sniffed. "You can't know that."

The smile he bent on her was infinitely superior.

Resisting the urge to gnash her teeth, Lucinda pointedly looked away.

Heather had perked up the instant they'd quit town; she smiled when Lucinda glanced her way, clearly restored to her usual sunny humour and unperturbed by the unexpected alteration to their plans.

Feeling distinctly huffy, Lucinda looked ahead. It was, she suspected, pointless to protest—at least, not until she'd met Lady Hallows. Until then, there was nothing she could do to regain the ascendancy. The infuriating gentleman beside her had the upper hand—and the reins. Her gaze flicked sideways, to where his hands, covered by soft doeskin gloves, dextrously managed the ribbons. Long slim fingers and slender palms. She'd noted that earlier. To her horror, the memory evoked a shiver—she had to fight to quell it. With him so close, he would very likely feel it—and, she suspected, would unhesitatingly guess its cause.

Which would leave her feeling embarrassed—and even more deeply disturbed. He evoked a most peculiar response in her—it had yet to fade, despite her irritation at his autocratic interference. It was a distinctly novel feeling—one she wasn't at all sure she appreciated.

"Hallows Hall."

She looked up to discover a pair of imposing gateposts which gave onto a shady avenue lined with elms. The gravelled drive wound gently along a slight ridge, then dipped to reveal a pleasant vista of rolling lawns surrounding a reed-fringed lake, the whole enclosed by large trees.

"How pretty!" Heather looked about in delight.

The Hall, a relatively recent structure in honey-coloured stone, sat on a rise above the drive, which wound past the front steps before curving around the corner of the house. A vine stretched green fingers over the stone. There were roses in abundance; ducks clacked from the lake.

An ancient retainer came ambling up as Harry drew his team to a halt.

"Thought as we'd see you this week, young master."

Harry grinned. "Good evening, Grimms. Is my aunt at home?"

"Aye—that she is—and right pleased she'll be to see you. Evening, miss. Miss." Grimms doffed his cap to Lucinda and Heather.

Lucinda's answering smile was distant. Hallows Hall stirred long-forgotten memories of life before her parents had died.

Harry descended and helped her down. After helping Heather to the ground, he turned to see Lucinda looking about her, a wistful expression on her face. "Mrs Babbacombe?"

Lucinda started. Then, with a half-grimace and a frosty glance, she placed her hand on his arm and allowed him to lead her up the steps.

The door was flung open—not by a butler, although a stately personage of that persuasion hovered in the shadows—but by a gaunt, angular-featured woman a good two inches taller than Lucinda and decidedly thinner.

"Harry, m'boy! Thought you'd be here. And who's this you've brought?"

Lucinda found herself blinking into dark blue eyes, shrewd and intelligent.

"But what am I about? Come in, come in." Ermyntrude, Lady Hallows, waved her guests into the hall.

Lucinda stepped over the threshold—and was immediately enveloped in the warm, elegant yet homey atmosphere.

Harry took his aunt's hand and bowed over it, then kissed her cheek. "As elegant as ever, Em," he said, scanning her topaz gown.

Em's eyes opened wide. "Flummery? From you?"

Harry pressed her hand warningly as he released it. "Allow me to present Mrs Babbacombe, Aunt. Her carriage broke a wheel just outside town. I had the honour of driving her in. She had some idea of staying in town but I prevailed upon her to change her mind and give you the benefit of her company."

The words tripped glibly from his tongue. Rising from her curtsy, Lucinda shot him a chilly glance.

"Capital!" Em beamed and took Lucinda's hand. "My dear, you don't know how bored I sometimes get, stuck out here in the country. And Harry's quite right—you can't possibly stay in town during a meet—not at all the thing." Her blue eyes switched to Heather. "And who's this?"

Lucinda made the introduction and Heather, smiling brightly, bobbed a curtsy.

Em put out a hand and tipped Heather's chin up the better to view her face. "Hmm—quite lovely. You'll do well in a year or two." Releasing her, Em frowned. "Babbacombe, Babbacombe…" She glanced at Lucinda. "Not the Staffordshire Babbacombes?"

Lucinda smiled. "Yorkshire." When her hostess only frowned harder, she felt compelled to add, "I was a Gifford before my marriage."

"Gifford?" Em's eyes slowly widened as she studied Lucinda. "*Great heavens!* You must be Melrose Gifford's daughter—Celia Parkes was your mother?"

Surprised, Lucinda nodded—and was promptly enveloped in a scented embrace.

"Good gracious, child—I knew your father!" Em was

in transports. "Well—I was a bosom-bow of his elder sister, but I knew all the family. Naturally, after the scandal, we heard very little of Celia and Melrose, but they did send word of your birth." Em wrinkled her nose. "Not that it did much good—stiff-necked lot, your grandparents. On both sides."

Harry blinked, endeavouring to absorb this rush of information. Lucinda noticed, and wondered how he felt about rescuing the outcome of an old scandal.

"Just fancy!" Em was still in alt. "I never thought to set eyes on you, m'dear. Mind you, there's not many left but me who'd remember. You'll have to tell me the whole story." Em paused to draw breath. "Now then! Fergus will get your luggage and I'll show you up to your rooms— after a dish of tea—you *must* be in need of refreshment. Dinner's at six so there's no need to hurry."

Together with Heather, Lucinda found herself hustled towards an open doorway—a drawing-room lay ahead. On the threshold she hesitated and glanced back, as did Em behind her.

"You're not staying, are you, Harry?" Em asked.

He was tempted—sorely tempted. His gaze not on his aunt but on the woman beside her, Harry forced himself to shake his head. "No." With an effort he shifted his gaze to his aunt's face. "I'll call sometime during the week."

Em nodded.

Prompted by she knew not what, Lucinda turned and recrossed the hall. Their rescuer stood silently and watched her approach; she steadfastly ignored the odd tripping of her heart. She halted before him, calmly meeting his green gaze. "I don't know how to thank you for your help, Mr Lester. You've been more than kind."

His lips slowly curved; again, she found herself fascinated by the movement.

Harry took the hand she held out to him and, his eyes on hers, raised it to his lips. "Your rescue was indeed my pleasure, Mrs Babbacombe." The sudden widening of her eyes as his lips touched her skin was payment enough for the consequent hardships. "I'll ensure that your people know where to find you—your maids will arrive before nightfall, I'm sure."

Lucinda inclined her head; she made no effort to retrieve her fingers from his warm grasp. "Again, you have my thanks, sir."

"It was nothing, my dear." His eyes on hers, Harry allowed one brow to rise. "Perhaps we'll meet again—in a ballroom, maybe? Dare I hope you'll favour me with a waltz if we do?"

Graciously, Lucinda acquiesced. "I would be honoured, sir—should we meet."

Belatedly reminding himself that she was a snare he was determined to avoid, Harry took a firm grip on his wayward impulses. He bowed. Releasing Lucinda's hand, he nodded to Em. With one last glance at Lucinda, he strolled gracefully out of the door.

Lucinda watched the door shut behind him, a distant frown in her eyes.

Em studied her unexpected guest, a speculative glint in hers.

"AGATHA'S BEEN WITH ME forever," Lucinda explained. "She was my mother's maid when I was born. Amy was an under-maid at the Grange—my husband's house. We took her with us so that Agatha could train her to act as maid for Heather."

"Just as well," Heather put in.

They were in the dining-room, partaking of a delicious meal prepared, so Em had informed them, in honour of their arrival. Agatha, Amy and Sim had arrived an hour ago, conveyed by Joshua in a trap borrowed from the Barbican Arms. Joshua had returned to Newmarket to pursue the repairs of the carriage. Agatha, taken under the wing of the portly housekeeper, Mrs Simmons, was resting in a cheery room below the eaves, her ankle pronounced unbroken but badly sprained. Amy had thus had to assist both Lucinda and Heather to dress, a task at which she had acquitted herself with honours.

Or so Em thought as she looked down the table. "So," she said, patting her lips with her napkin then waving Fergus and the soup tureen away. "You may start at the beginning. I want to know all about you since your parents died."

The sheer openness of the request robbed it of any rudeness. Lucinda smiled and laid aside her spoon; Heather was dipping into the tureen for the third time, much to Fergus's delight. "As you know, what with both families disowning my parents, I hadn't had any contact with my grandparents. I was fourteen at the time of the accident. Luckily, our old solicitor hunted up my mother's sister's address—she agreed to take me in."

"Now let's see." Em's eyes narrowed as she surveyed the past. "That would be Cora Parkes that was?"

Lucinda nodded. "If you recall, the Parkes family fortunes had taken a downturn sometime after my parents married. They'd retired from Society and Cora had married a mill-owner in the north—a Mr Ridley."

"*Never* say so!" Em was enthralled. "Well, well—how the mighty did fall. Your aunt Cora was one of the most intransigent when it came to any question of reconciliation with your parents." Em lifted her thin shoulders. "Fate's revenge, I dare say. So you lived with them until your marriage?"

Lucinda hesitated, then nodded.

Em noticed; her eyes sharpened, then flicked to Heather. Lucinda saw—and hastened to explain. "The Ridleys weren't exactly happy to have me. They only agreed to house me, thinking to use my talents as governess to their two daughters and then to broker my marriage as soon as maybe."

For a moment, Em stared. Then she snorted. "Doesn't surprise me. That Cora was ever out for her own gain."

"When I was sixteen, they arranged a marriage with another mill-owner, a Mr Ogleby."

"Ugh!" Heather looked up from her soup to shudder artistically. "He was a horrible old toad," she blithely informed Em. "Luckily, my father heard about it—Lucinda used to come and give me lessons. So *he* married Lucinda instead." Having done her bit for the conversation, Heather returned to her soup.

Lucinda smiled affectionately. "Indeed, Charles was my saviour. I only recently learned that he bought off my relatives in order to marry me—he never told me."

Em snorted approvingly. "Glad to hear they've *some* gentlemen in those parts. So you became Mrs Babbacombe and lived at…the Grange, was it?"

"That's right." Heather had finally relinquished the soup; Lucinda paused to serve herself from the platter of turbot Fergus offered. "To all appearances Charles was a well-to-do gentleman of moderate estate. In reality, however, he owned a considerable collection of inns up and down the country. He was really very wealthy but preferred a quiet existence. He was close to fifty when we married. As I grew older, he taught me all about his investments and how to manage them. He was ill for some years—the end was a relief when it came—but because of his foresight, I was able to handle most of the work for him."

Lucinda looked up to find her hostess staring at her.

"Who owns the inns now?" Em asked.

Lucinda smiled. "We do—Heather and I. The Grange, of course, went to Charles's nephew, Mortimer Babbacombe, but Charles's private fortune wasn't part of the entail."

Em sat back and regarded her with frank approval. "And that's why you're here—you own an inn in Newmarket?"

Lucinda nodded. "After the will was read, Mortimer asked us to vacate the Grange within the week."

"The blackguard!" Em glared. "What sort of a way is that to treat a grieving widow?"

"Well," Lucinda held up a hand. "I did offer to leave as soon as he wished—although I hadn't thought he'd be in such a hurry. He'd never even visited before—not really."

"So you found yourselves out on your ears in the snow?" Em was incensed.

Heather giggled. "It really turned out most fortuitously in the end."

"Indeed." Lucinda nodded, pushing her plate away. "With nothing organised, we decided to remove to one of our inns—one a little way away from the Grange, a place we weren't known. Once there, I realised the inn was far more prosperous than I would have guessed from the accounts our agent had recently presented. Mr Scrugthorpe was a new man—Charles had been forced to appoint a new agent a few months before he died when our old Mr Matthews passed on." Lucinda frowned at the trifle Fergus placed before her. "Unfortunately, Charles interviewed Scrugthorpe on a day he was in great pain and I had to be in town with Heather. To cut a long story short, Scrugthorpe had falsified the accounts. I called him in and dismissed him."

Lifting her gaze to her hostess's face, Lucinda smiled. "After that, Heather and I decided that travelling the country getting to know our inns was an excellent way to see out our year of mourning. It was exactly the sort of enterprise of which Charles would have approved."

Em snorted—this snort clearly signified her appreciation of Charles's good sense. "Seems to have been a very able man—your father, miss."

"He was a dear." Heather's open face clouded and she blinked rapidly, then looked down.

"I've appointed a new agent—a Mr Mabberly." Lucinda smoothly covered the awkward moment. "He's young but extremely efficient."

"And goes in awe of Lucinda," Heather offered, looking up to help herself to a second scoop of trifle.

"As he should," Em replied. "Well, Miss Gifford as was—you've certainly done your parents proud thus far. A capable lady of independent means at what—twenty-six?"

"Twenty-eight." Lucinda's smile was crooked. There were times, such as today, when she suddenly wondered if life had passed her by.

"A very fair achievement," Em declared. "I don't hold with women being helpless." She eyed Heather's at last empty plate. "And if you've finally finished, miss, I suggest we retire to the drawing-room. Do either of you play the pianoforte?"

They both did and gladly entertained their hostess with various airs and sonatas, until Heather fell to yawning. At Lucinda's suggestion she retired, passing the tea trolley in the doorway.

"Indeed, we've had an adventuresome day." Lucinda sat back in an armchair by the fire and sipped the tea Em had dispensed. Lifting her gaze, she smiled at Em. "I can't thank you enough, Lady Hallows, for taking us in."

"Nonsense," Em replied with one of her snorts. "And you could please me by dropping all the ladyships and just calling me Em, like everyone else in the family. You're Melrose's daughter and that's close enough for me."

Lucinda smiled, a trifle wearily. "Em, then. What's it a contraction for? Emma?"

Em wrinkled her nose. "Ermyntrude."

Lucinda managed to keep her lips straight. "Oh?" she said weakly.

"Indeed. My brothers delighted in calling me all the contractions you might imagine. When my nephews came along, I declared it was Em and nothing else."

"Very wise." A companionable silence settled as they savoured their tea. Lucinda broke it to ask, "Do you have many nephews?"

From under heavy lids, Em's eyes glinted. "Quite a few. But it was Harry and his brothers I had to guard against. A rapscallion lot."

Lucinda shifted. "He has a lot of brothers?"

"Only two—but that's quite enough. Jack's the eldest," Em blithely rattled on. "He's—let me see—thirty-six now. Then comes Harry, two years younger. Then there's quite a gap to their sister Lenore—she married Eversleigh some years back—she must be twenty-six now, which makes Gerald twenty-four. Their mother died years ago but my brother still hangs on." Em grinned. "Dare say he'll manage to cling to life long enough to see a grandson to carry on the name, the cantankerous old fool." The last was said affectionately. "But it was the boys I had most to do with—and Harry was always my favourite. Blessed by the angels and the devil both, of course, but such a good boy." Em blinked, then amended, "Well—a good boy *at heart*. They all were—are. I see most of Harry and Gerald these days—what with Newmarket so close. Harry runs the

Lester stud which, even if 'tis I who say so—and Heaven knows I know next to nothing about horses—such a boring subject—is hailed as one of the premier studs in the land."

"Really?" There was not the slightest trace of boredom in Lucinda's face.

"Indeed." Em nodded. "Harry usually comes to watch his runners perform. Dare say I'll see Gerald this week, too. Doubtless he'll want to show off his new phaeton. Told me when last he was up that he was going to buy one, now the family coffers are full and overflowing."

Lucinda blinked.

Em didn't wait for her to find a subtle way to ask. One hand waving, she airly explained, "The Lesters have traditionally been strapped for cash—good estates, good breeding, but no money. The present generation, however, invested in some shipping venture last year and now the whole family's rolling in an abundance of the ready."

"Oh." Lucinda readily recalled Harry Lester's expensive elegance. She couldn't imagine him any other way. Indeed, his image seemed to have fixed in her mind, oddly vivid, strangely enthralling. Shaking her head to dispel it, she delicately smothered a yawn. "I'm afraid I'm not very good company, Lady—Em." She smiled. "I suspect I'd better follow Heather."

Em merely nodded. "I'll see you in the morning, m'dear."

Lucinda left her hostess staring into the fire.

Ten minutes later, her head pillowed in down, Lucinda closed her eyes—only to find Harry Lester on her mind. Tired, adrift, her memories of the day replayed, her interactions with him claiming centre stage. Until she came to their parting—which left one question to plague her. How would it feel to waltz with Harry Lester?

A MILE AWAY, in the tap of the Barbican Arms, Harry sat elegantly sprawled behind a corner table, moodily surveying the room. A smoky haze wreathed a forest of shoulders; gentlemen mingled freely with grooms and stablemen, tipsters wrangled with bookmakers. The tap was all business this evening; the first races, those for non-bloodstock, would commence the next day.

A barmaid came up, hips swaying. She set a tankard of the inn's finest on the table, smiling coyly, one brow rising as Harry flipped a coin onto her tray.

Harry caught her eye; his lips curved but he shook his head. Disappointed, the girl turned away. Harry lifted the foaming tankard and took a long sip. He'd abandoned the snug, his habitual refuge, where only the cognescenti were permitted, driven forth by the all-but-incessant questioning as to his delectable companion of the afternoon.

It seemed as if all in Newmarket had seen them.

Certainly all his friends and acquaintances were keen to learn her name. And her direction.

He'd given them neither, steadfastly returning their bright-eyed enquiries with a blank look and the information that the lady was an acquaintance of his aunt's he'd simply been escorting to her door.

Those facts proved sufficient to dampen the interest of most; the majority who frequented Newmarket knew of his aunt.

But he was definitely tired of covering the lovely Mrs Babbacombe's tracks, particularly as he was trying his damnedest to forget her. And her loveliness.

With an inward growl, Harry immersed himself in his tankard and tried to focus his mind on his horses—usually an enthralling subject.

"There you are! Been looking all over. What're you doing out here?" Dawlish slumped into the chair beside him.

"Don't ask," Harry advised. He waited while the barmaid, with a fine show of indifference, served Dawlish before asking, "What's the verdict?"

Dawlish shot him a glance over the rim of his tankard. "Odd," came mumbling from behind it.

Brows lifting, Harry turned his head to stare at his henchman. "Odd?" Dawlish had gone with the coachman, Joshua, to fetch the wainwright to the carriage.

"Me, Joshua and the wainwright all thinks the same." Dawlish set down his tankard and wiped the froth from his lip. "Thought as how you should know."

"Know what?"

"That the cotter-pin on that wheel was tampered with—half-sawed through, it was—*before* the accident. And the spokes had been got at, too."

Harry frowned. "Why?"

"Don't know as how you noticed, but there were a curious lot of rocks strewn about that stretch of road where the carriage went over. None before—and none after. Just along that stretch. No way a coachman could miss all of 'em. And they were just round a corner so he couldn't see them in time to pull up."

Harry's frown was intense. "I remember the rocks. The boy cleared them away so I didn't have to drive over them."

Dawlish nodded. "Aye—but the carriage couldn't avoid them—and as soon as that wheel hit, the cotter would have snapped and the spokes after that."

A chill swept Harry's nape. Five mounted men in frieze, with a wagon, hiding in the trees, moving towards the road just after the carriage went down. And if it hadn't been a race-week, that particular stretch of road would almost certainly have been deserted at that time of day.

Harry lifted his gaze to Dawlish's face.

Dawlish looked back at him. "Makes you think, don't it?"

Grim-faced, Harry slowly nodded. "It does indeed." And he didn't like what he thought at all.

Chapter Three

"I'll have y'r team out in a jiffy, sir."

Harry nodded absentmindedly as the head-ostler of the Barbican Arms hurried off towards the stables. Pulling on his driving gloves, he strolled away from the inn's main door to await his curricle in a vacant patch of sunshine by the wall.

Before him, the courtyard was busy, many of the inn's guests departing for a day at the track, hoping to pick a few winners to start the week off on the right note.

Harry grimaced. He wouldn't be joining them. Not, at least, until he'd satisfied himself on the score of one Mrs Babbacombe. He had given up telling himself she was none of his business; after the revelations of yesterday, he felt compelled to brave her dangers—long enough to assure himself of her safety. She was, after all, his aunt's guest—at his insistence. Two facts which undoubtedly excused his interest.

"I'll get along and see Hamish then, shall I?"

Harry turned as Dawlish came up. Hamish, his head-stableman, should have arrived yesterday with his string of thoroughbred racers; the horses would be settling into their stables beyond the racetrack. Harry nodded. "Make sure Thistledown's fetlock's sufficiently healed—I don't want her entered unless it is."

Dawlish nodded sagely. "Aye. Shall I tell Hamish you'll be along shortly to see it?"

"No." Harry studied the fit of his gloves. "I'll have to rely on your combined wisdom this time. I've pressing matters elsewhere."

He felt Dawlish's suspicious glance.

"More pressing than a prime mare with a strained fetlock?" Dawlish snorted. "I'd like to know what's higher on y'r list than that."

Harry made no effort to enlighten him. "I'll probably look in about lunchtime." His imaginings were very likely groundless. It could be no more than coincidence, and two likely females travelling without major escort, that had focused the attention of the men in frieze on the Babbacombe coach. "Just make sure Hamish gets the message in time."

"Aye," Dawlish grumbled. With a last keen glance, he headed off.

Harry turned as his curricle appeared, the head-ostler leading the greys with a reverence that bespoke a full appreciation of their qualities.

"Right prime 'uns, they be," he averred as Harry climbed to the box.

"Indeed." Harry took up the reins. The greys were restive, sensing the chance of freedom. With a nod for the ostler, he backed the curricle preparatory to making a stylish exit from the yard.

"Harry!"

Harry paused, then, with a sigh, drew in his impatient steeds. "Good morning, Gerald. And since when do you arise at this ungodly hour?"

He had spied his younger brother amongst the crowds in the tap the night before but had made no effort to advertise his presence. He turned to watch as Gerald, blue-eyed and dark-haired as was his elder brother Jack, strode up, grinning broadly, to place a familiar hand on the curricle's front board.

"Ever since I heard the story of you escorting two excessively likely looking females who, according to you, are connections of Em's."

"Not connections, dear brother—*acquaintances.*"

Faced with Harry's languidly bored mask, Gerald lost a little of his assurance. "You mean they really are? Acquaintances of Em's, I mean?"

"So I discovered."

Gerald's face fell. "Oh." Then Dawlish's absence registered. Gerald shot a keen glance at his brother. "You're going to Em's now. Mind if I hitch a ride? Should say hello to the old girl—and perhaps to that dark-haired delight you had up beside you yesterday."

For an instant, Harry was shaken by the most absurd impulse—Gerald was his younger brother after all, of whom he was, beneath his dismissive exterior, distinctly fond. He concealed the unexpected emotion behind his ineffable charm—and sighed. "I fear, dear brother, that I must puncture your delusions—the lady's too old for you."

"Oh? How old is she?"

Harry raised his brows. "Older than you."

"Well—perhaps I'll try for the other one then—the blonde."

Harry looked down on his brother's eager countenance—and inwardly shook his head. "She, if anything, is probably too young. Just out of the schoolroom, I suspect."

"No harm in that," Gerald blithely countered. "They have to start sometime."

Feeling distinctly put-upon, Harry heaved a disgusted sigh. "Gerald…"

"Dash it all, Harry—don't be such a dog-in-the-manger. You're not interested in the younger chit—let me take her off your hands."

Harry blinked at his brother. It was undoubtedly true that any discussion of Mrs Babbacombe's situation would proceed a great deal more openly in the absence of her stepdaughter. "Very well—if you insist." Within Em's purlieu, Gerald could be relied on to keep within acceptable bounds. "But don't say I didn't warn you."

Almost gleefully, Gerald swung up to the curricle's seat. The instant he was aboard, Harry clicked his reins. The greys shot forward; he had to exert all his skills to thread them through the traffic thronging the High Street. He let them stretch their legs once free of the town; Em's leafy drive was reached in record time.

A stableboy came hurrying to take charge of the curricle. Together, Harry and Gerald mounted the steps to Em's door. The oak door was set wide open, not an uncommon occurrence. The brothers wandered in. Harry tossed his gloves onto the ormolu table. "Looks like we'll have to go hunt. I expect my business with Mrs Babbacombe will take no more than half an hour. If you can keep Miss Babbacombe occupied until then, I'll be grateful."

Gerald cocked an eyebrow. "Grateful enough to let me tool your greys back to town?"

Harry looked doubtful. "Possibly—but I wouldn't count on it."

Gerald grinned and looked about him. "So where do we start?"

"You take the gardens—I'll take the house. I'll call if

I need help." With a languid wave, Harry set off down one corridor. Whistling, Gerald turned and went out of the main door.

Harry drew a blank in the morning room and the parlour. Then he heard humming, punctuated by the click of shears, and remembered the small garden room at the end of the house. There he found Em, arranging flowers in a huge urn.

At his languid best, he strolled in. "Good morning, Aunt."

Em turned her head—and stared in stunned surprise. "Devil take it—what are you doing *here?*"

Harry blinked. "Where else should I be?"

"In town. I was sure you'd be there."

After a moment's hesitation, Harry conceded with the obvious. "Why?"

"Because Lucinda—Mrs Babbacombe—went into town half an hour ago. Never been there before—wanted to get her bearings."

A chill caressed Harry's nape. "You let her go alone?"

Turning back to her blooms, Em waved her shears. "Heavens, no—her groom accompanied her."

"Her groom?" Harry's voice was soft, urbane, its tone enough to send chills down the most insensitive spine. "The young tow-headed lad who arrived with her?"

He watched as a tell-tale blush spread over his aunt's high cheekbones.

Disconcerted, Em shrugged. "She's an independent woman—it doesn't do to argue overmuch." She knew perfectly well she should not have let Lucinda go into Newmarket this week without more tangible escort, but there was a definite purpose to her ploy. Turning, she surveyed her nephew. "*You* could try, of course."

For an instant, Harry couldn't believe his ears—surely

not *Em?* His eyes narrowed as he took in her bland expression; this was the last thing he needed—a traitor in his own camp. His lips thinned; with a terse nod, he countered, "Rest assured I will."

Turning on his heel, he strode out of the room, down the corridor, out of the door and around to the stables. The stableboy was startled to see him; Harry was merely glad the horses were still harnessed.

He grabbed the reins and leapt up to the seat. His whip cracked and the horses took off. The drive back to town established a new record.

Only when he was forced to slow by the press of traffic in the High Street did Harry remember Gerald. He cursed, regretting the loss of another to aid in his search. Taking advantage of the crawling pace, he carefully studied the crowded pavements from behind his habitually unruffled mien. But no dark head could he see.

He did, however, discover a large number of his peers—friends, acquaintances—who, like himself, were too experienced to waste time at the track today. He entertained not the slightest doubt that each and every one would be only too willing to spend that time by the side of a certain delectable dark-haired widow—not one would consider it time wasted.

Reaching the end of the street, Harry swore. Disregarding all hazards, he turned the curricle, missing the gleaming panels of a new phaeton by less than an inch, leaving the slow-top in charge of the reins in the grip of an apoplectic fit.

Ignoring the fuss, Harry drove quickly back to the Barbican Arms and turned the greys into the loving hands of the head-ostler. The man confirmed that Em's gig was in residence. Harry surreptitiously checked the private parlour and was relieved to find it empty; the Arms was the favourite watering-hole of his set. Striding back to the street, he paused to take stock. And to wonder what "getting her bearings" meant.

There was no lending library. He settled on the church, some way along the street. But no likely looking widow haunted its hallowed precincts, nor trod the paths between the graves. The town's gardens were a joke—no one came to Newmarket to admire floral borders. Mrs Dobson's Tea Rooms were doing a brisk trade but no darkly elegant widow graced any of the small tables.

Returning to the pavement, Harry paused, hands on hips, and stared across the street. Where the devil was she?

A glimmer of blue at the edge of his vision had him turning his head. Just in time to identify the dark-haired figure who sailed through the street door of the Green Goose, a tow-headed boy at her back.

PAUSING JUST INSIDE the inn's door, Lucinda found herself engulfed in dimness. Musty dimness. As her eyes adjusted to the gloom, she discovered she was in a hall, with the entrance to the tap on her left, two doors which presumably led to private parlours on her right and a counter, an extension of the tap's bar, directly ahead, a tarnished bell on its scratched surface.

Suppressing the urge to wrinkle her nose, she swept forward. She had spent the last twenty minutes examining the inn from outside, taking due note of the faded and flaking whitewash, the clutter in the yard and the down-at-heel appearance of the two customers who had crossed its threshold. Extending one gloved hand, she picked up the bell and rang it imperiously. At least, that was her intention. But the bell emitted no more than a dull clack. Upending it, Lucinda discovered the clapper had broken.

With a disgusted grimace, she replaced the bell. She

was wondering whether to tell Sim, waiting by the door, to raise his voice in summons when a large shadow blocked out what little light penetrated from the inn's nether regions. A man entered, burly, brawny—very big. His face was heavy-featured but his eyes, sunk in folds of fat, appeared merely uninterested.

"Aye?"

Lucinda blinked. "Are you Mr Blount?"

"Aye."

Her heart sank. "You're the innkeeper?"

"Nay."

When no more was forthcoming, she prompted, "You're Mr Blount, but you're not the innkeeper." There was hope yet. "Where is the Mr Blount who *is* the innkeeper?"

For a long moment, the burly individual regarded her stoically as if his brain was having difficulty digesting her question. "You want Jake—m'brother," he eventually offered.

Lucinda heaved an inward sigh of relief. "Precisely— I wish to see Mr Blount, the innkeeper."

"Wha'for?"

Lucinda opened her eyes wide. "That, my good man, is a matter for your brother and myself."

The hulking brute eyed her measuringly, then humphed. "Wait 'ere—I'll fetch 'im." With that, he lumbered off.

Leaving Lucinda praying that his brother took after the other side of the family. Her prayers were not answered. The man who replaced the first was equally burly, equally overweight and, apparently, only fractionally less dimwitted.

"Mr Jake Blount—the keeper of this inn?" Lucinda asked, with no real hope of contradiction.

"Aye." The man nodded. His small eyes swept her, not insolently but with weary assessment. "But the likes of you don't want to take rooms 'ere—try the Barbican or the Rutland up the road."

He turned away, leaving Lucinda somewhat stunned. "Just a minute, my good man!"

Jake Blount shuffled back to face her but shook his head. "Yer not the sort for this inn, see?"

Lucinda felt the breeze as the inn door opened. She saw Mr Blount's eyes lift to the newcomer but was determined to retain his attention. "No—I do not see. What on earth do you mean—'not the sort for this inn'?"

Jake Blount heard her but was more concerned with the gentleman who now stood behind her, hard green eyes on him. Gold hair, gently waved at the ends, cut in the latest style, a well-cut coat of light brown worn over buckskin breeches and Hessians so highly polished you could see your face in them, all added up to a persona Blount recognised very well. He didn't need the many-caped greatcoat that swung from the gentleman's broad shoulders, nor the patrician features and hooded eyes nor yet the tall, lean and well-muscled frame, to tell him that one of the bloods of the *ton* had deigned to enter his humble inn. The fact made him instantly nervous. "Aaah…" He blinked and looked back at Lucinda. "Not the sort who takes rooms 'ere."

Lucinda stared. "What *sort* of lady takes rooms here?"

Blount's features contorted. "*That*'s wha' I mean—*no* ladies. Just *that* sort."

Increasingly certain she had wandered into a madhouse, Lucinda stubbornly clung to her question. "What sort is that?"

For an instant, Jake Blount simply stared at her. Then, defeated, he waved a pudgy hand. "Lady—I don't knows wha' you want wi' me but I got business to see to."

He lifted his gaze pointedly over her shoulder; Lucinda drew in a portentious breath.

And nearly swallowed it when she heard a drawling voice languidly inform the recalcitrant Blount, "You mistake, Blount. My business here is merely to ensure you deal adequately with whatever the lady desires of you."

Harry let his eyes meet the innkeeper's fully. "And you're perfectly correct—she is not *that* sort."

The particular emphasis, delivered in that sensual voice, immediately made clear to Lucinda just what "sort" had been the subject of her discussion. Torn between unaccustomed fluster, mortification and outrage, she hesitated, a light blush tinging her cheeks.

Harry noticed. "And now," he suavely suggested, "if we could leave that loaded topic, perhaps we might proceed to the lady's business? I'm sure you're breathlessly waiting to discover what it is—as am I."

Over her shoulder, Lucinda shot him a haughty glance. "Good morning, Mr Lester." She gifted him with a restrained nod; he stood behind her right shoulder, large and reassuring in the dingy dimness. He inclined his head gracefully, his features hard-edged and severe, suggesting an impatience to have her business aired.

Inwardly grimacing, Lucinda turned back to the innkeeper. "I believe you were visited recently by a Mr Mabberly, acting for the owners of this inn?"

Jake Blount shifted. "Aye."

"I believe Mr Mabberly warned you that an inspection of your premises would shortly take place?"

The big man nodded.

Lucinda nodded decisively back. "Very well—you may conduct me over the inn. We'll start with the public rooms." Without pause, she swept about. "I take it this is the tap." She glided towards the door, her skirts stirring up dust eddies.

From the corner of her eye, she saw Blount stare, open-mouthed, then come hurrying around the counter. Harry Lester simply stood and watched her, an inscrutable expression on his face.

Lucinda swept on—into the gloomy, heavily shuttered room. "Perhaps, Blount, if we were to have those shutters wide I might be able to see well enough to form an opinion?"

Blount cast her a flustered glance, then lumbered to the windows. Seconds later, sunshine flooded the room, apparently to the discomfort of its two patrons, one an old codger wrapped in a rumpled cloak, hugging the inglenook, the other a younger man in the rough clothes of a traveller. They both seemed to shrink inwards, away from the light.

Lucinda cast a shrewd glance around the room. The interior of the inn matched its exterior, at least in the matter of neglect. The Green Goose was fast living up to Anthony Mabberly's description as the very worst of the Babbacombe inns. Grimy walls and a ceiling that had seen neither brush nor mop for years combined with a general aura of dust and slow decay to render the tap a most unwelcoming place. "Hmm." Lucinda grimaced. "So much for the tap."

She slanted a glance at Harry, who had followed her in. "Thank you for your assistance, Mr Lester—but I'm perfectly capable of dealing with Mr Blount."

The green gaze, which had been engaged in a survey of the unwholesome room, switched to her face. His eyes were less unreadable than his features, but other than distinct disapproval and a species of irritation, Lucinda couldn't be sure what their expression portended.

"Indeed?" His brows lifted fractionally; his languid tone was barely polite. "But perhaps I should remain—

just in case you and the good Blount run into any further...
communication difficulties?"

Lucinda suppressed the urge to glare. Short of order-
ing him out of her inn, hardly supportive of her ploy to
conceal her ownership, she could think of no way to dispense with his attentive presence. His green gaze was
acute, perceptive; his tongue, as she already knew, could
be decidedly sharp.

Accepting fate's decree with a small shrug, Lucinda returned her attention to Blount, hovering uncertainly by the
bar. "What's through that door?"

"The kitchens."

Blount looked shocked when she waved him on. "I'll
need to see those, too."

The kitchen was not as bad as she had feared, a fact she
attributed to the buxom but worn-down woman who
bobbed respectfully when introduced as "the missus."
The Blounts' private quarters gave off the large, square
room; Lucinda disavowed any desire to inspect them.
After closely examining the large open fireplace and engaging in a detailed discussion with Mrs Blount on the
technicalities of the draw and the overall capacity of the
kitchen, which, by their impatient expressions, passed
over both Blount's and Harry Lester's heads, she consented to be shown the parlours.

Both parlours were shabby and dusty but, when the
shutters were opened, proved to have pleasant aspects.
Both contained old but serviceable furniture.

"Hmm, mmm," was Lucinda's verdict. Blount looked
glum.

In the back parlour, which looked out over a wilderness
that had once been a garden, she eyed a sturdy oak table and
its attendant chairs. "Please ask Mrs Blount to dust in here
immediately. Meanwhile, I'll see the rooms above stairs."

With a resigned shrug, Blount went to the door of the kitchen to deliver the order, then returned to lead the way up the stairs. Halfway up, Lucinda paused to test the rickety balustrade. Leaning against it, she was startled to hear it crack—and even more startled to feel an arm of steel wrap about her waist and haul her back to the centre of the treads. She was released immediately but heard the muttered comment, "Damned nosy woman!"

Lucinda grinned, then schooled her features to impassivity as they reached the upper corridor.

"All the rooms be the same." Blount swung open the nearest door. Without waiting to be asked, he crossed to open the shutters.

The sunlight played on a dreary scene. Yellowing whitewash flaked from the walls; the ewer and basin were both cracked. The bedclothes Lucinda mentally consigned to the flames without further thought. The furniture, however, was solid—oak as far as she could tell. Both the bed and the chest of drawers could, with a little care, be restored to acceptable state.

Pursing her lips, Lucinda nodded. She turned and swept out of the door, past Harry Lester, lounging against the frame. He straightened and followed her along the corridor. Behind them, Blount shot out of the room and hurried to interpose himself between Lucinda and the next door.

"This room's currently taken, ma'am."

"Indeed?" Lucinda wondered what sort of patron would make do with the sad amenities of the Green Goose.

As if in answer, a distinctly feminine giggle percolated through the door.

Lucinda's expression grew coldly severe. "I see." She shot an accusing glance at Blount, then, head high, moved along the corridor. "I'll see the room at the end, then we'll return downstairs."

There were no further revelations; it was as Mr Mabberly had said—the Green Goose was sound enough in structure but its management needed a complete overhaul.

Descending once more to the hall, Lucinda beckoned Sim forward and relieved the lad of the bound ledgers he'd been carrying. Leading the way into the back parlour, she was pleased to discover the table and chairs dusted and wiped. Setting her ledgers on the table before the chair at its head, she placed her reticule beside them and sat. "Now, Blount, I would like to examine the books."

Blount blinked. "The books?"

Her gaze steady, Lucinda nodded. "The blue one for incomings and the red one for expenditures."

Blount stared, then muttered something Lucinda chose to interpret as an assent and departed.

Harry, who had maintained his role of silent protector throughout, strolled across to shut the door after him. Then he turned to his aunt's unexpected acquaintance. "And now, my dear Mrs Babbacombe, perhaps you would enlighten me as to what you're about?"

Lucinda resisted the urge to wrinkle her nose at him— he was, she could tell, going to be difficult. "I am doing as I said—inspecting this inn."

"Ah, yes." The steely note was back in his voice. "And I'm to believe that some proprietor has seen fit to engage you—employ you, no less—in such a capacity?"

Lucinda met his gaze, her own lucidly candid. "Yes."

The look he turned on her severely strained her composure.

With a wave, she put an end to his inquisition; Blount would soon be back. "If you must know, this inn is owned by Babbacombe and Company."

The information arrested him in mid-prowl. He turned a fascinated green gaze upon her. "Whose principals are?"

Folding her hands on her ledgers, Lucinda smiled at him. "Myself and Heather."

She did not have time to savour his reaction; Blount entered with a pile of ledgers in his arms. Lucinda waved him to a seat beside her. While he sorted through his dog-eared tomes, she reached for her reticule. Withdrawing a pair of gold-rimmed half-glasses, she perched them on her nose. "Now then!"

Beneath Harry's fascinated gaze, she proceeded to put Blount through his financial paces.

Appropriating a chair from the table—one that had been dusted—Harry sat by the window and studied Lucinda Babbacombe. She was, undoubtedly, the most unexpected, most surprising, most altogether intriguing woman he'd ever met.

He watched as she checked entry after entry, adding figures, frequently upside-down from Blount's ledgers. The innkeeper had long since abandoned all resistance; out of his depth, faced with a totally unforeseen ordeal, he was now eager to gain approval.

As she worked through the ledgers, Lucinda came to the same somewhat reluctant conclusion. Blount wasn't intentionally neglectful; he hadn't meant to run the inn into the ground. He simply lacked direction and the experience to know what to do.

When, after an hour, she reached the end of her inquiries, Lucinda took off her glasses and fixed Blount with a shrewdly assessing glance. "Just so we are clear, Blount, it is up to me to make a recommendation on whether Babbacombe and Company should retain your services." She tapped her closed ledger with one arm of her glasses. "While your figures are unimpressive, I will

be reporting that I can find no evidence of malpractice—
all seems entirely above board."

The burly innkeeper looked so absurdly grateful Lucinda had to sternly suppress a reassuring smile. "I understand you were appointed to your present position on
the death of the former landlord, Mr Harvey. From the
books it's clear that the inn had ceased to perform well
long before your tenancy."

Blount looked lost.

"Which means that you cannot be held to blame for its
poor base performance." Blount looked relieved. "However," Lucinda continued, both tone and glance hardening, "I have to tell you that the *current* performance, for
which you must bear responsibility, is less than adequate.
Babbacombe and Company expect a reasonable return on
their investment, Blount."

The innkeeper's brow furrowed. "But Mr Scrugthorpe—he's the one as appointed me?"

"Ah, yes. Mr Scrugthorpe."

Harry glanced at Lucinda's face; her tone had turned
distinctly chilly.

"Well, Mr Scrugthorpe said as how the profit didn't
matter so long as the inn paid its way."

Lucinda blinked. "What was your previous position,
Blount?"

"I used to keep the Blackbird's Beak, up Fordham
way."

"The Blackbird's Beak?"

"A hedge-tavern, I suspect," Harry put in drily.

"Oh." Lucinda met his gaze, then looked back at
Blount. "Well, Blount, Mr Scrugthorpe is no longer Babbacombe and Company's agent, largely because of the
rather odd way he thought to do business. And, I fear, if
you wish to remain an employee of the company, you're

going to have to learn to manage the Green Goose in a more commercial fashion. An inn in Newmarket cannot operate on the same principles as a hedge-tavern."

Blount's forehead was deeply creased. "I don't know as how I rightly follow you, ma'am. Tap's a tap, after all."

"No, Blount. A tap is not a tap—it is the principal public room of the inn and as such should possess a clean and welcoming ambience. I do hope you won't suggest that that," she pointed in the direction of the tap, "is clean and welcoming?"

The big man shifted on his seat. "Dare say the missus could do a bit of a clean-up."

"Indeed." Lucilla nodded. "The missus and you, too, Blount. And whoever else you can get to help." She folded her hands on her ledgers and looked Blount in the eye. "In my report, I am going to suggest that, rather than dismiss you, given you've not yet had an opportunity to show the company of what you're capable, the company reserves judgement for three months and then reviews the situation."

Blount swallowed. "What exactly does that mean, ma'am?"

"It means, Blount, that I will make a list of all the improvements that will need to be done to turn this inn into one rivalling the Barbican Arms, at least in profit. There's no reason it shouldn't. Improvements such as a thorough whitewashing inside and out, all the timber polished, present bedding discarded and fresh bought, all furniture polished and crockery replaced. And the kitchen needs a range." Lucinda paused to meet Blount's eye. "Ultimately, you will employ a good cook and serve wholesome meals continuously in the tap, which will be refurbished accordingly. I've noticed that there are few places at which travellers staying in this town can obtain a superior repast. By providing the best fare, the Green Goose will attract custom away from the coaching houses which, because of their preoccupation with coaching, supply only mediocre food."

She paused but Blount only blinked at her. "I take it you are interested in keeping your position here?"

"Oh—yes, ma'am. Definitely! But…where's the blunt coming from for all that?"

"Why, from the profits, Blount." Lucinda eyed him straitly. "The profits before your wages are deducted— and before the return paid to the company. The company considers such matters as an investment in the inn's future; if you're wise, you'll consider my suggestions in light of an investment in your future."

Blount met her gaze; slowly he nodded. "Yes, ma'am."

"Good!" Lucinda rose. "I will make a copy of the improvements I'll be suggesting to the company and have my groom drop it by tomorrow." She glanced at Blount as he struggled to his feet; his expression suggested he was still reeling. "Mr Mabberly will look in on you in a month's time, to review your progress. And now, if there's nothing else, I will bid you good day, Blount."

"Yes, ma'am." Blount hurried to open the door. "Thank you, ma'am." He was clearly sincere.

Lucinda regally nodded and sailed from the room.

Reluctantly impressed, Harry followed close behind. Still inwardly amazed, he waited until they were back on the pavement, she gliding along with her nose in the air as if she had not just taken on Goliath and won, before catching her hand, neatly trapping it on his sleeve. Her fingers fluttered, then stilled. She cast him a quick glance, then studiously looked ahead. Her groom followed two paces behind, her ledgers clutched in his arms.

The young traveller who had been slouching in the tap slipped out of the inn door in their wake.

"My dear Mrs Babbacombe," Harry began in what he hoped was an even tone. "I do hope you're going to satisfy my curiosity as to why a gently reared female, however well-equipped for the task, goes about interrogating her company's employees?"

Unabashed, Lucinda met his gaze; aggravation showed clearly in the green. "Because there is no one else."

Harry held her gaze. His lips thinned. "I find that hard to believe. What about this Mr Mabberly—your agent? Why can he not take on the challenge of such as Blount?"

Lucinda's lips quirked. "You must admit he was a definite challenge." She slanted a deliberately provocative glance his way. "I feel quite chuffed."

Harry snorted. "As you well know, you performed a minor miracle. That man will now work himself to the bone—which will be a distinct improvement in itself. But that," he continued, his tone hardening, "is not the point."

"But it is, you see." Lucinda wondered why she was allowing him to put in his oar. Perhaps because it had been a long time since anyone had tried? "Mr Anthony Mabberly is all of twenty-three. He's an excellent man with the accounts and is scrupulously honest and fair—a far cry from Scrugthorpe."

"Ah, yes. The undesirable Scrugthorpe." Harry cast her a quick glance. "Why was he so undesirable?"

"Fraud. He was appointed by my husband just before his death—on one of his bad days, I'm afraid. After Charles's death, I by chance learned that the books as they were being presented to me did not reflect the actual figures generated by the inns."

"What happened to Scrugthorpe?"

"I dismissed him, of course."

Harry noted the righteous satisfaction that underlaid her tone. Clearly, Lucinda Babbacombe had not approved of Mr Scrugthorpe. "So until recently the agent took responsibility for negotiating with your tenants?"

Lucinda lifted a haughty brow. "Until I reorganised the company's procedures. Mr Mabberly would not know where to start with such as Blount—he's of a somewhat timid disposition. And I consider it appropriate that both Heather and myself are familiar with the inns that form our legacy."

"Laudable though such sentiments might be, Mrs Babbacombe, I do hope—" Harry broke off as she stopped and looked consideringly across the street. "What is it?"

"Hmm?" Absentmindedly, Lucinda glanced up. "Oh—I was just wondering if there was time left to do the Barbican Arms today." She glanced back at the busy inn across the street. "But it looks rather crowded. Perhaps tomorrow morning would be better?"

Harry stared at her, an unwelcome suspicion slowly crystallising in his brain. "Very much better," he averred. "But tell me, Mrs Babbacombe—how many inns do you and your stepdaughter own?"

She looked up at him, an unlikely innocence in her powder-blue eyes. "Fifty-four," she replied. Then added, as if in afterthought, "Up and down the country."

Harry closed his eyes and struggled to suppress a groan. Then, without another word, with no more than a single speaking glance, he escorted her into the yard of the Barbican Arms and, with heartfelt relief, handed her up to Em's gig and watched her drive away.

"SO SHE'S STAYING in Newmarket?"

Mr Earle Joliffe drew a riding crop back and forth through his fingers. A thickset man of undistinguished mien, he sat back in his chair, his pale gaze, as pale as his pasty complexion, fixed on the young roughneck he'd sent into town to track their quarry down.

"As to that, I ain't sure." The youngster took a swig from his tankard.

They were in a rundown cottage three miles from Newmarket, the best they'd been able to rent at short notice. Four men sat about the deal table—Joliffe, the youngster whose name was Brawn and two others—Mortimer Babbacombe and Ernest Scrugthorpe. The latter was a hulking man, rough despite the severe clothes of a clerk; he sat silently glowering into his beer. Mortimer Babbacombe, a slight figure in the attire of a would-be dandy, shifted restlessly; he clearly wished himself elsewhere.

"She got into a gig and drove out eastwards. I couldn't follow."

Scrugthorpe grunted. "See? Told you she'd go to the Green Goose. Couldn't keep away, meddling witch."

He spat contemptuously on the floor; the action made Mortimer even more uncomfortable.

"Ye-es, well." Joliffe transferred his gaze to Scrugthorpe. "Might I remind you that she should, by now, have been in our hands? That but for your lack of foresight, she would be?"

Scrugthorpe scowled. "How was I to know it were a race-week? And that gentlemen would be using that road? Everything went perfect, elsewise."

Joliffe sighed and raised his eyes heavenwards. Amateurs—they were all the same. How had he, who had spent his life thus far successfully extracting a living from the rich, descended to the company of such? Lowering his gaze, his glance fell on Mortimer Babbacombe. Joliffe's lips curled in a contemptuous sneer.

"Ought to mention," Brawn put in, surfacing from his tankard. "She was walking the street with a swell today—right chummy—looked like the same swell as wot rescued them."

Joliffe's eyes narrowed and he sat forward. "Describe this swell."

"Fair hair—like gold. Tall, looked like he'd strip to advantage. One of them bloods with a fancy cape." Brawn grimaced. "They all look the same to me."

Not so to Joliffe. "This blood—was he staying at the Barbican Arms?"

"Seemed so—the ostlers and all seemed to know him."

"Harry Lester." Joliffe tapped a pensive nail on the table. "I wonder..."

"Wonder what?" Mortimer looked at his erstwhile friend and most urgent creditor, his expression that of a man well out of his depth. "Would this man Lester help us?"

Joliffe snorted. "Only to the hangman's noose. But his peculiar talents bear consideration." Leaning forward, Joliffe placed both elbows on the table. "It occurs to me, my dear Mortimer, that we may be involving ourselves unnecessarily here." Joliffe smiled, an empty gesture that made Mortimer shrink. "I'm sure you'd be most agreeable to any way of achieving our aim without direct involvement."

Mortimer swallowed. "But how can Lester help us—if he won't?"

"Oh—I didn't say he won't—just that we needn't ask him. He'll help us entirely for the fun of it. Harry Lester, dear Mortimer, is the rake supreme—a practitioner extraordinaire in the gentle art of seduction. If, as seems possible, he's got your uncle's widow in his sights, then I wouldn't like to bet on her chances." Joliffe's smile grew. "And, of course, once she's demonstrably no longer a virtuous widow, then you'll have all the reason you need to legally challenge her guardianship of your cousin." Joliffe's gaze grew intent. "And once your pretty cousin's legacy's in your hands, you'll be in a position to pay me, won't you, Mortimer?"

Mortimer Babbacombe swallowed—and forced himself to nod.

"So what do we do now?" Scrugthorpe drained his tankard.

Joliffe considered, then pronounced, "We sit tight and watch. If we get a chance to lay hands on the lady, we will—just like we planned."

"Aye—far as I'm concerned, that's how we should do it—no sense in leaving anything to chance."

Joliffe's lip curled. "Your animosity is showing, Scrugthorpe. Please remember that our primary aim here is to discredit Mrs Babbacombe—not satisfy your lust for revenge."

Scrugthorpe snorted.

"As I was saying," Joliffe went on. "We watch and wait. If Harry Lester succeeds—he'll have done our work for us. If not, we'll continue to pursue the lady—and Scrugthorpe here will have his chance."

At that, Scrugthorpe smiled. Lecherously.

Chapter Four

When Lucinda drove into the yard of the Barbican Arms the next morning, Harry was waiting, shoulders against the wall, arms crossed over his chest, his boot against the wall for balance. He had plenty of time to admire the artless picture of mature womanhood seated beside Grimms in his aunt's gig. Elegantly gowned in a cornflower blue carriage dress, her dark hair restrained in a severe chignon thus revealing the delicate bones of her face, Lucinda Babbacombe predictably turned the heads of those still dawdling in the yard. Thankfully, the thoroughbred races were to commence that morning; most of Harry's contemporaries were already at the track.

Grimms brought Em's gig to a neat halt in the centre of the yard. With an inward snort, Harry pushed away from the wall.

Lucinda watched him approach—his graceful stride forcefully reminded her of a prowling tiger. A very definite thrill coursed through her; she avoided smiling her delight, contenting herself with a mild expression of polite surprise. "Mr Lester." Calmly, she extended her hand. "I hadn't expected to see you this morning—I thought you were here for the races."

His brows had risen sceptically at her first remark; on her second, his green eyes glittered. He grasped her hand—for an instant, as his eyes held hers, Lucinda wondered why she was playing with fire.

"Indeed," Harry replied, his habitual drawl in abeyance. He helped her from the carriage, steadying her on the cobbles. "I own to surprise on that score myself. However, as you are my aunt's guest, and at my instigation, I feel honour-bound to ensure you come to no harm."

Lucinda's eyes narrowed but Harry, distracted by the absence of groom or maid—Grimms had already disappeared into the stables—did not notice.

"Speaking of which, where's your groom?"

Lucinda allowed herself a small smile. "Riding with your brother and Heather. I have to thank you for sending Gerald to us—he's entertaining company for Heather—I dare say she would otherwise grow bored. And, of course, that leaves me free to tend to business without having to worry my head over her."

Harry didn't share her confidence—but he wasn't, at this point, concerned with her stepdaughter. His expression hardened as he looked down at her. He was still holding her hand; tucking it into his arm, he turned her towards the inn door. "You should at least have a groom with you."

"Nonsense, Mr Lester." Lucinda slanted him a curious glance. "Surely you aren't suggesting that at my age I need a chaperon?"

Looking into her eyes, softly blue, their expression openly independent, challenging yet oddly innocent, Harry inwardly cursed. The damned woman didn't need a chaperon—she needed an armed guard. Just why he had elected himself to the post was not a point he was willing to pursue. He contented himself with repressively stating, "In my opinion, Mrs Babbacombe, women like you should not be allowed out alone."

Her eyes twinkled; two tiny dimples appeared in her cheeks. "Actually, I'd like to see the stables." She turned to the archway leading from the main yard.

"The stables?"

Her gaze ranging their surroundings, Lucinda nodded. "The state of the stableyard frequently reflects the quality of the inn's management."

The state of the stables suggested the innkeeper of the Barbican Arms was a perfectionist; everything was neat, clean and in its place. Horses turned their heads to stare as Lucinda picked her way over the cobbles, still wet with dew, forced more than once to lean heavily on Harry's arm.

When they reached the earthen floor of the stables, she determinedly straightened. Regretfully withdrawing her fingers from the warmth of his sleeve, she strolled along the row of loose boxes, stopping here and there to acknowledge their curious occupants. She eventually reached the tack room and peered in.

"Excuse me, ma'am—but you shouldn't be in here." An elderly groom hurried out.

Harry stepped out of the shadows. "It's all right, Johnson. I'll see the lady safe."

"Oh!—it's you, Mr Lester." The groom touched his cap. "That's all right and tight, then. Ma'am." With another tug of his cap, the groom retreated into the tack room.

Lucinda blinked, then shot a glance at Harry. "Is it always so ordered? So…" She waved at the loose boxes, each with their half-doors shut. "So exact?"

"Yes." Harry looked down at her as she stopped beside

him. "I stable my carriage horses here—you may rest assured of the quality in that respect."

"I see." Deeming all queries on the equine side of business satisfied, Lucinda turned her attention to the inn proper.

Ushered through the main door, she looked with approval on half-panelled walls, well-polished and glowing mellowly. Sunshine reflected from crisply whitewashed walls; stray beams danced across the flagged floor.

Mr Jenkins, the innkeeper, a neat, rotund person of genial mien, bustled up. Harry performed the introductions, then stood patiently by while Lucinda explained her purpose. Unlike Blount, Mr Jenkins was all gratified helpfulness.

Lucinda turned to Harry. "My business with Mr Jenkins will keep me busy for at least an hour. I wouldn't for the world impose on your kindness, Mr Lester—you've already done so much. And I can hardly come to harm within the inn."

Harry didn't blink. For her, the Arms played host to a panapoly of dangers—namely his peers. Meeting her innocent gaze with an impenetrable blandness, he waved a languid hand. "Indeed—but my horses don't run until later."

Which comment, he noted, brought a flash to her eyes. She hesitated, then, somewhat stiffly, acquiesced, inclining her head before turning back to Mr Jenkins.

Wearing patience like a halo, Harry followed his host and his aunt's guest about the old inn, through rambling passageways and storerooms, to bedchambers and even to the garrets. They were returning down an upper corridor when a man came blundering out of a room.

Lucinda, opposite the door, started; glimpsing the man from the corner of her eye, she braced herself for a collision. Instead, she was bodily set aside; the chubby young gentleman ran full tilt into a hard shoulder. He bounced off, crumpling against the door frame.

"Ouf!" Straightening, the man blinked. "Oh—hello, Lester. Slept in, don't y'know. Can't miss the first race." He blinked again, a puzzled frown forming in his eyes. "Thought you'd be at the track by now."

"Later." Harry stepped back, revealing Lucinda.

The young man blinked again. "Oh—ah, yes. Terribly sorry, ma'am—always being told I should look where I'm going. No harm done, I hope?"

Lucinda smiled at the ingenuous apology. "No—none." Thanks to her protector.

"Good—oh! I'd best be on my way, then. See you at the track, Lester." With an awkward bow and a cheery wave, the youthful sprig hurried off.

Harry snorted.

"Thank you for your assistance, Mr Lester." Lucinda slanted him a smile. "I'm really most grateful."

Harry took full note of the quality of her smile. Coolly, he inclined his head and waved her on in Jenkins's wake.

By the end of her tour, Lucinda was impressed. The Barbican Arms, and Mr Jenkins, were a far cry from the Green Goose and Jake Blount. The inn was spick and span throughout; she had found nothing remotely amiss. Her inspection of the books was a mere formality; Mr Mabberly had already declared the Arms a model of good finance.

She and her host spent a few minutes going over the plans for an extension to the inn. "For we're full to overflowing during race-meets and more than half full at other times."

Lucinda gave her general approval and left the details for Mr Mabberly.

"Thank you, Mr Jenkins," she declared, pulling on her

gloves as they headed for the door. "I must tell you that, having visited all but four of the fifty-four inns owned by Babbacombe and Company, I would rank the Barbican Arms as one of the best."

Mr Jenkins preened. "Very kind of you to say so, ma'am. We do strive to please."

With a gracious nod, Lucinda swept out. Once in the courtyard she paused. Harry stopped beside her; she looked up at his face. "Thank you for your escort, Mr Lester—I'm really most grateful considering the other demands on your time."

Harry was too wise to attempt an answer to that.

Lucinda's lips twitched; she looked quickly away. "Actually," she mused, "I was considering viewing this race-meet." She brought her eyes back to his face. "I've never been to one before."

Harry looked down at her ingenuous expression. His eyes narrowed. "Newmarket race-track is no place for you."

She blinked, taken aback—Harry glimpsed real disappointment in her eyes. Then she looked away. "Oh."

The single syllable hung in the air, a potent testimony to crushed anticipation. Fleetingly, Harry closed his eyes, then opened them. "However, if you give me your word you will not stray from my side—not to admire some view, some horse or a lady's bonnet—" He looked down at her, his jaw setting. "I will engage to escort you there."

Her smile was triumphant. "Thank you. That would be very kind."

Not kind—foolish. It was, Harry was already convinced, the most stupid move he'd ever made. An ostler came running in answer to his curt gesture. "I'll have my curricle. You can tell Grimms to take Lady Hallows's gig back; I'll see Mrs Babbacombe home."

"Yessir."

Lucinda busied herself with the fit of her gloves, then meekly allowed herself to be lifted to the curricle's seat. Settling her skirts, and her quivering senses, she smiled serenely as, with a deft flick of the reins, Harry took the greys onto the street.

The race-track lay west of the town on the flat, grassy, largely tree-less heath. Harry drove directly to the stables in which his string of racers were housed, a little way from the track proper, beyond the public precincts.

Lucinda, drinking in the sights, could not miss the glances thrown their way. Stableboy and gentleman alike seemed disposed to stare; she was unexpectedly grateful when the stable walls protected her from view.

The horses were a wonder. Lifted down from the curricle, Lucinda could not resist wandering down the row of loose boxes, patting the velvet noses that came out to greet her, admiring the sleek lines and rippling muscles of what, even to her untutored eyes, had to be some of the finest horses in England.

Engaged in a brisk discussion with Hamish, Harry followed her progress, insensibly buoyed by the awed appreciation he saw in her gaze. On reaching the end of the row, she turned and saw him watching her; her nose rose an inch but she came back, strolling towards him through the sunshine.

"So all's right with entering the mare, then?"

Reluctantly, Harry shifted his gaze to Hamish's face. His head-stableman was also watching Lucinda Babbacombe, not with the appreciation she deserved but with horrified fascination. As she drew nearer, Harry extended his arm; she placed her fingertips upon it without apparent thought. "Just as long as Thistledown's fetlock's fully healed."

"Aye." Hamish bobbed respectfully at Lucinda. "Seems

to be. I told the boy to just let her run—no point marshalling her resources if it's still weak. A good run's the only way to tell."

Harry nodded. "I'll stop by and speak to him myself."

Hamish nodded and effaced himself with the alacrity of a man nervous around females, at least those not equine in nature.

Suppressing a grin, Harry lifted a brow at his companion. "I thought you agreed not to be distracted by horses?"

The look she bent on him was confidently assured. "You shouldn't have brought me to see yours, then. They are truly the most distractingly beautiful specimens I've ever seen."

Harry couldn't suppress his smile. "But you haven't seen the best of them. Those on that side are two- and three-year-olds—for my money, the older ones are more gracious. Come, I'll show you."

She seemed only too ready to be led down the opposite row of boxes, dutifully admiring the geldings and mares. At the end of the row, a bay stallion reached confidently over the half-door to investigate Harry's pockets.

"This is old Cribb—a persistent devil. Still runs with the best of them though he could retire gracefully on his accumulated winnings." Leaving her patting the stallion's nose, Harry went to a barrel by the wall. "Here," he said, turning back. "Feed him these."

Lucinda took the three dried apples he offered her, giggling as Cribb delicately lipped them from her palm.

Harry glanced up—and saw Dawlish outside the tackroom, standing stock-still, staring at him. Leaving Lucinda communing with Cribb, Harry strolled over. "What's up?"

Now that he was beside him, it was clear Dawlish was staring at his companion, not him.

"*Gawd's truth*—it's happened."

Harry frowned. "Don't be ridiculous."

Dawlish turned a pitying eye on him. "Ridiculous, is it? You do realize, don't you, that that's the first female you've ever shown your horses?"

Harry lifted a supercilious brow. "She's the first female ever to have shown an interest."

"Hah! Might as well hang up your gloves, gov'nor—you're a goner."

Harry cast his eyes heavenwards. "If you must know, she's never been to a race-meet before and was curious—there's nothing more to it than that."

"Ah-hah. So *you* says." Dawlish cast a long, defeated look at the slight figure by Cribb's box. "All *I* says is that you can justify it any ways you want—the conclusions still come out the same."

With a doleful shake of his head, Dawlish retreated, muttering, back into the tack-room.

Harry wasn't sure whether to laugh or frown. He glanced back at the woman, still chatting to his favourite stallion. If it wasn't for the fact they would shortly be surrounded by crowds, he might be inclined to share his henchman's pessimism. But the race-track, in full view of the multitudes, was surely safe enough.

"If we leave now," he said, returning to her side, "we can stroll to the track in time for the first race."

She smiled her acquiescence and laid her hand on his arm. "Is that horse you were talking of—Thistledown—running in it?"

Smiling down into her blue eyes, Harry shook his head. "No—she's in the second."

Lucinda found herself trapped in the clear green of his

eyes; she studied them, trying to gauge what he was thinking. His lips twitched and he looked away. Blinking as they emerged into the bright sunshine, Lucinda asked, "Your aunt mentioned you managed a stud?"

His fascinating lips curved. "Yes—the Lester stud." With ready facility, prompted by her questions, he expiated at length on the trials and successes of his enterprise. What he didn't say but Lucinda inferred, it being the logical deduction to make from his descriptions, was that the stud was both a shining achievement and the very core of his life.

They reached the tents surrounding the track as the runners for the first race were being led to the barrier. All Lucinda could see was a sea of backs as everyone concentrated on the course.

"This way—you'll see better from the stands."

A man in a striped vest was guarding a roped arena before a large wooden stand. Lucinda noted that while he insisted on seeing passes from the other latecomers ahead of them, he merely grinned and nodded at Harry and let them by. Harry helped her up the steep steps by the side of the planks serving as seats—but before they could find places a horn blew.

"They're off." Harry's words echoed from a hundred throats—about them, all the patrons craned forward.

Lucinda turned obediently and saw a line of horses thundering down the turf. From this distance, neither she nor anyone else could see all that much of the animals. It was the crowd that enthralled her—their rising excitement gripped her, making her breathe faster and concentrate on the race. When the winner flashed past the post, the jockey flourishing his whip high, she felt inordinately glad.

"Well raced." Harry's gaze was on the horses and riders as they slowed and turned back to the gates.

Lucinda grasped the moment to study him. He was intent on observation, green eyes keenly assessing, shrewdly calculating. For an instant, she saw him clearly, his features unguarded. He was a man who, despite all other distractions in his life, was totally devoted to his chosen path.

He turned his head at that moment. Their eyes met, their gazes locked. He was standing on the step below her so her eyes were almost level with his. For a moment, he said nothing, then his lips twisted wrily.

Lucinda suppressed a delicate shiver.

With a gesture, Harry indicated the crowded lawns before them. "If you truly want to experience a race-meet, then you have to promenade."

Her own lips curving, Lucinda inclined her head. "Lead on, Mr Lester—I'm entirely in your hands."

She saw his brow quirk but pretended ignorance. On his arm, she descended the steps and exited the private enclosure.

"The Jockey Club maintains the stand for the use of its members," Harry informed her when she glanced back.

Which meant he was a well-known member. Even Lucinda had heard of the pre-eminence of the Jockey Club. "I see. The races are run under their auspices, I take it?"

"Correct."

He led her on a slow perambulation through the milling crowds. Lucinda felt distinctly round-eyed—she wanted to see everything, understand the fascination that drew so many gentlemen to Newmarket.

The same fascination that drove Harry Lester.

He showed her the bookmakers, each surrounded by knots of punters eager to lay their bets. They paraded before the tents and pavilions; again and again they were stopped by some acquaintance of Harry's, keen to exchange a few words. Lucinda was prepared to be on her guard, but she encountered nothing but polite deference in the glances thrown her way; all those who stopped to talk were disarmingly correct. Nevertheless, she felt no impulse to withdraw her hand from the security of her escort's elbow, where he had tucked it, drawing her close. In the press of male bodies, it was unquestionably comforting to have Harry Lester by her side. There were, she discovered, some ladies present. "Some have a real interest in the sport—usually the older ones." Relaxed, in his milieu, Harry glanced down at her. "Some of the younger ladies have a vested interest; their families, like mine, have a long-standing connection with the turf."

Mouthing an "oh," Lucinda nodded. There were other ladies, too, whom he had not seen fit to comment upon, who, she suspected, held dubious right to the title. The race-track, however, was an overwhelmingly male domain—every sub-category of the male population was certainly represented. Lucinda was quite sure she would have neither the courage nor the inclination to attend again—not unless Harry Lester was her escort.

"It's nearly time for the next race. I must speak to Thistledown's jockey."

Lucinda nodded, conveying with a glance her intention of staying with him.

Harry threw her a brief smile then concentrated on forging a path to the mounting yard.

"She seems very lively, sir," the jockey vouchsafed as he settled in the saddle. "But the competition's stiff—Jonquil—that mare out of Herald—is a starter. And Caught by the Scruff, too. And some of them others are experienced racers—it'll be a miracle if she wins, what with her fetlock just come good an' all."

Harry nodded. "Just let her go—let her set her own

pace. We'll consider this a trial, nothing more. Don't cram her—and no whip."

Lucinda left his side to pat the mare's velvet muzzle; a huge, dark brown eye invited her understanding. Lucinda grinned. "Hopeless, aren't they?" she crooned. "But you don't want to listen to them—men are notoriously hopeless at judging women. They should never so presume." From the corner of her eye, she saw Harry's lips lift; he exchanged a glance with the jockey, who grinned. "You just go out there and win the race—then see how they react. I'll see you in the winner's circle."

With a last pat for the mare, she turned and, with divine disregard for the expression on Harry Lester's face, allowed him to lead her back to the stands.

He secured seats in the third row, almost opposite the post. Lucinda leaned forward, eagerly scanning the horses trotting towards the barrier. She waved when Thistledown appeared.

Harry, watching her, laughed.

"She'll win—you'll see." With smug confidence, Lucinda sat back.

But when the horn sounded and the barrier was dropped, she leant forward again, eyes keenly searching the thundering charge for Harry's colours of green and gold. So intent was she that she didn't even notice she rose to her feet, in company with all the other spectators, as the horses rounded the bend. As they entered the straight, a gap appeared in their ranks—Thistledown shot through.

"There she is!" Lucinda grabbed Harry's arm. Only deeply entrenched decorum kept her from jigging up and down. "She's winning!"

Harry was too riveted to answer.

But Thistledown was indeed showing the field a clean pair of heels. Halfway down the straight, her stride lengthened even more—she appeared to be flying when she flashed past the post.

"She won! She won!" Lucinda grasped both Harry's arms and all but danced. "I *told* you she would!"

Rather more accustomed to the delights of victory, Harry looked down at her face, wreathed in smiles and lit by the same joy he still felt every time one of his horses came home first. He knew he was smiling, as delighted as she if rather more circumspect in showing it.

Lucinda turned back to locate Thistledown, now being led from the course. "Can we go and see her now?"

"Indeed we can." Harry took her hand and tucked it tightly in his arm. "You promised to meet her in the winner's circle, remember?"

Lucinda blinked as he steered her out of the crowded stand. "Is it permissible for ladies to enter the winner's circle?"

"There's no rule against it—in fact—" Harry slanted a glance at her "—I suspect the Head of the Committee will be delighted to see you." When she shot him a suspicious glance, he laughed and urged her on. Once out of the enclosure and free of those members keen to press their congratulations, a path cleared before them, leading directly to the roped arena where Thistledown, shiny coat flickering but clearly untired by her dash, waited patiently.

As soon as Lucinda emerged from the crowd, the mare pushed her head forward, dragging on the reins to get to Lucinda's side. Lucinda hurried forward, crooning her praises. Harry looked on indulgently.

"Well, Lester! Another trophy for your mantel—surprised it hasn't collapsed."

Harry turned as the President of the Jockey Club, present Head of the Race Committee, appeared at his elbow.

In his hands, he held a gold-plated statuette in the shape of a lady.

"Remarkable run—truly remarkable."

Shaking hands, Harry nodded. "Particularly as she's just recovered from a strained fetlock—I wasn't sure I'd race her."

"Just as well you did." The President's eye was on the horse and the woman apparently chatting to the beast. "Nice conformation."

Harry knew very well that Lord Norwich was not referring to the mare. "Indeed." His tone was dry; Lord Norwich, who had known him from the cradle, lifted a brow at him.

Glancing at the statuette, Harry confirmed that the lady was indeed decently garbed, then nodded at Lucinda. "It was Mrs Babbacombe who delivered the inspirational address prior to the race. Perhaps she should accept the award on my behalf?"

"Excellent idea!" Beaming, Lord Norwich strode forward.

Shielded by her brimming happiness, the aftermath of fulfilled excitement, Lucinda had succeeded in blithely ignoring the avid interest of the spectators. Lord Norwich, however, was impossible to ignore. But Harry strolled forward to stand by their side, quieting her uncertainties.

Lord Norwich gave a short speech, praising the mare and Harry's stables, then gallantly presented the statuette—to her.

Surprised, Lucinda looked at Harry—he smiled and nodded.

Determined to rise to the occasion, she graciously thanked his lordship.

"Quite, quite." His lordship was quite taken. "Need to see more game fillies at the track, what?"

Lucinda blinked at him.

Harry reached for her elbow and drew her to his side. He nodded at his strapper. "Take her back to the stables."

With a last lingering look for Lucinda, Thistledown was led away. Lord Norwich and the rest of the crowd turned away, already intent on the next race.

Still conscious of the fading thrill, Lucinda looked around, then cast a glance upwards.

Harry smiled. "And you have my heartfelt thanks, too, my dear. For whatever magic you wove."

Lucinda met his eyes—and stopped breathing. "There was no magic." She felt his fingers on hers; she watched as he raised her hand and brushed his lips across the backs of her fingers. A long shiver traced its path down her spine, leaving an odd warmth in its wake. With an effort she veiled her eyes, breaking his spell. Catching her breath, she made a bid for her usual confidence; she raised the statuette and presented it to him, defiantly meeting his eyes.

He took it in his other hand, his gaze steady on hers.

Time lost its meaning; they stood, largely forgotten, in the centre of the winner's circle. Men crowded about, jostling each other but not touching them. They stood close, so close the small ruffle on Lucinda's bodice brushed the long lapel of Harry's coat. He sensed its flutter as her breathing grew more rapid but he was lost in her eyes, in a world of misty blue. He watched them widen, darken. Her lips softened, parted. Her bodice made contact with his coat.

His head had begun its slow descent when sanity awoke—and frantically hauled on his reins.

Great heavens! They were in the winner's circle at Newmarket!

Shaken to the depths of his soul, Harry dragged in a

quick breath. He tore his gaze from her face, from the consternation that was filling her eyes, and the soft blush that
had started to tinge her cheeks, and looked about them.
No one, thank heaven, had seen.

His heart pounding, he took a firm grip of her elbow—
and took refuge in action. "If you've seen enough of the
racing, I should get you back to Em's—she'll be wondering where you are."

Lucinda nodded—the faintly bored drawl left her no
choice. She felt—she didn't know what—shaken, certainly, but regretful, and resentful, too. But she couldn't
argue with his wish to be gone from here.

But they still had the gamut of well-wishers to run—
they were stopped constantly, more than one gentleman
wishing to make an offer for the mare.

Harry faced the hurdles with what patience he could,
conscious that all he wished to do was escape. With her.
But that was impossible—she was his danger, his Water-
loo.

From now on, every time he looked into her face would
be like looking down the barrel of a loaded gun. A weapon
that could land him in painful slavery.

If he was wise, he wouldn't look too frequently.

Lucinda sensed his withdrawal although he cloaked it
well. His urbane charm came to the fore—but he would
not meet her eyes, her puzzled glances.

They finally escaped the crowds and walked back, in
silence, to the stables. He lifted her to his curricle and
swung up beside her, his expression closed.

He drove back to Hallows Hall without a word, his apparent concentration on his horses a wall Lucinda made
no attempt to breach.

But when he drew up before the steps and secured the
reins, then came around and lifted her down, she held her

position in front of him even though his hands fell immediately from her. "Thank you for a most…instructive morning, Mr Lester."

His eyes flicked to hers; he took a step back. "A pleasure, Mrs Babbacombe." He bowed with innate grace. "And now I must bid you adieu."

Surprised, Lucinda watched as he swung up to the curricle's seat. "But won't you stay for luncheon? Your aunt would be delighted, I'm sure."

The reins in his hands, Harry drew in a deep breath—and forced himself to meet her gaze. "No."

The word hung between them—an unconditional denial. Harry saw the understanding in her eyes, sensed the sudden catch in her breathing as his rejection bit home. But it was better this way—to nip it in the bud before it could flower. Safer for her as well as for him.

But her eyes showed no comprehension of that, of the dangers he could see so clearly. Soft and luminous, they looked at him in hurt surprise.

He felt his lips twist in bitter self-mockery. "I can't."

It was all the explanation he could give. With a crack of his whip, he set his horses down the drive—and drove away.

Chapter Five

Three days later, Lucinda was still not satisfied that she understood what had happened. Seated in a wicker chair in a patch of sunlight in the conservatory, she idly plied her needle while her thoughts went round and round. Heather was out riding with Gerald, Sim in close attendance; her hostess was somewhere in the gardens, supervising the planting of a new border. She was alone, free to pursue her thoughts—little good though that seemed to be doing her.

She knew she was inexperienced in such matters, yet deep within lay an unshakeable conviction that something—something eminently to be desired—had sprung to life between herself and Harry Lester.

He had almost kissed her in the winner's circle.

The moment was etched in her memories, frustratingly incomplete, yet she could hardly fault him for drawing back. But he had then retreated, so completely it had left her feeling unexpectedly vulnerable and inwardly bruised. His parting words confounded her. She could not misconstrue the implications of that "No"—it was his "I can't" that truly baffled her.

He had not appeared since; courtesy of Gerald, who now haunted the house, she had learned he was still in Newmarket. Presumably, she was supposed to believe he was so immensely busy with his racers that he had no time for her.

With an inward snort, Lucinda jabbed her needle into the canvas. She was, she supposed, now too much the businesswoman to enjoy being shortchanged. But time was slipping away; she couldn't remain at Hallows Hall forever. Clearly, if she wanted to know just what might be possible, she was going to have to take an active hand.

But how?

Five minutes later, Em entered through the garden door, the hem of her old gardening gown liberally splattered with earth, a pair of heavy gloves in one hand.

"Phoof!" Sinking into the other armchair, separated from Lucinda's by a small matching table, Em pushed back wisps of browny-grey hair. "That's done!" She slanted a glance at her guest. "You look very industrious—quite wifely, in fact."

Lucinda smiled but did not look up.

"Tell me," Em mused, her sharp gaze belying her idle tone. "Have you ever considered remarrying?"

Lucinda's needle halted; she looked up, not at her hostess but through the long windows at the garden. "Not until recently," she eventually said. And returned to her needlework.

Em studied her downbent head, a definite glint in her eye. "Yes—well, it takes one like that. Suddenly pops into your mind—and then won't get out." With an airy wave of her gardening gloves, she continued, "Still, with your qualifications I hardly think you need worry. When you get to London you'll have a goodly selection of beaux lining up to put a ring on your finger."

Lucinda slanted her a glance. "My qualifications?"

Em's wave became a flourish. "Your breeding for one—nothing wrong with that, even if your parents were disowned. Your grandparents could hardly change the blood in their veins—as far as Society's concerned that's what counts." As if just struck by the fact, Em added, "In fact, the Giffords are as well connected as the Lesters."

"Indeed?" Lucinda eyed her warily.

Blithely, Em continued, "And there's your fortune, too—that legacy of yours would satisfy the most demanding. And you're hardly an antidote—you've got style, that indefinable something—noticed it straight off. Once the Bruton Street *mesdames* get a look at you they'll be vying for your custom, mark my words."

"I am, however, twenty-eight."

The blunt comment brought Em to a blinking halt. Turning her head, she stared at her guest. "So?"

Lucinda grimaced and looked down at her work. "Twenty-eight, I suspect, is somewhat long in the tooth to be attractive to town beaux."

For an instant longer, Em stared at her, then hooted with laughter. "*Rubbish*, my dear! The *ton*'s awash with gentlemen whose principal reason for avoiding matrimony is that they cannot stomach the bright-eyed young misses." She snorted. "More hair than wit, most of them, believe me." She paused to study Lucinda's face, half-averted, then added, "It's very common, my dear, for men to prefer more experienced women."

Lucinda glanced up—and met Em's eye. A light blush slowly spread across her cheeks. "Yes, well—that's another thing." Her gaze flicked to the green vistas beyond the window as she dragged in a determined breath. "I'm not. Experienced, I mean."

Em stared. "Not?"

"My marriage wasn't really a marriage at all—it was a rescue." Lucinda frowned, her gaze dropping to her tapestry. "You must remember I was only sixteen at the time—and Charles was nearing fifty. He was very kind—we were good friends." Her voice low, she added, "Nothing more." Straightening her shoulders, she reached for her scissors, "Life, I fear, has passed me by—I've been put back on the shelf without having been properly off it in the first place."

"I…see." Em blinked owlishly at the tips of her half-boots, peeking from beneath her dirtied hem. A broad smile slowly broke across her face. "You know—your…er, inexperience is not really a handicap, not in your case. In fact," she continued, her old eyes lighting, "it could well be a positive advantage."

It was Lucinda's turn to look puzzled.

"You see, you have to think of it from your prospective husband's point of view." Eyes wide, Em turned to face her. "What *he*'ll see is a mature and capable woman, one of superior sense who can manage his household and family while at the same time providing more—" she paused to gesture "—*satisfying* companionship than a young girl ever could. If you make no show of your innocence, but allow him to—" she gestured again as she groped for words "—*stumble* on it in good time, I'm sure you'll find he'll be only too delighted." With a last shrewd glance at Lucinda's face, Em added, "I'm sure Harry would be."

Lucinda's eyes narrowed. She favoured her impossible hostess with a long stare. Then, looking down to tidy her needlework, she asked, "Has he ever shown any interest in marrying?"

"Harry?" Em sat back, a smile on her lips. "Not that I ever heard. But then, he's never had need to—there's Jack before him and Gerald behind. Jack's about to marry—I just got a summons to the wedding. So Harry's thoughts are unlikely to turn to gold rings and white icing—not, that is, unless he's given an incentive to pursue the subject."

"Incentive?"

"Hmm. Often the case with gentlemen in that particular mould—won't have a bar of marriage until the benefits become so blatantly obvious that even they, with their blinkered vision, can see it." Em snorted. "It's all the fault of the light-skirts, of course. Lining up to give them anything they want—whatever their lusts desire—without any strings attached."

"I suspect," Lucinda said, her expression guarded, Harry's "No" echoing in her ears, "that it would take a fairly…powerful incentive to make Harry actively desire to be wed."

"Naturally—Harry's all male to his toes. He'll be as reluctant as the best of them, I don't doubt. He's lived a life of unfettered hedonism—he's hardly likely to volunteer to change." Em brought her gaze back to Lucinda's face. "Not, of course that that should deter *you*."

Lucinda's head came up; she met Em's old eyes and saw in them a wealth of understanding. She hesitated for only a moment. "Why not?"

"Because, as I see it, you've got the most powerful weapon in your hands already—the only one that'll work." Em sat back and shrewdly regarded Lucinda. "Question is, are you game enough to use it?"

For a long moment, Lucinda stared at her hostess—then shifted her gaze to the gardens. Em sat patiently watching her—slim, dark-haired, fingers clasped in her lap, her expression calm and uninformative, a faraway look in her soft blue eyes.

At length, the blue eyes slowly turned back to Em. "Yes," Lucinda stated, calm and determined. "I'm game."

Em grinned delightedly. "Good! The first thing you'll need to understand is that he'll resist for all he's worth. He'll not come to the idea meekly—you can't expect it of him."

Lucinda frowned. "So I'll have to put up with more of this…" It was her turn to gesture as she sought for words. "This uncertainty?"

"Undoubtedly," Em averred. "But you'll have to hold firm to your purpose. And your plan."

Lucinda blinked. "Plan?"

Em nodded. "It'll take a subtle campaign to bring Harry to his knees."

Lucinda couldn't help but smile. "His knees?"

Em gave her a haughty look. "Of course."

Head on one side, Lucinda eyed her unpredictable hostess. "What do you mean by 'subtle'?"

"Well." Em settled in her chair. "For instance…"

"GOOD EVENING, Fergus."

"Good evening, sir."

Harry allowed his aunt's butler to relieve him of his greatcoat, then handed him his driving gloves. "Is my brother here?" Harry turned to the mirror hanging above the ormolu table.

"Master Gerald arrived half an hour ago. In his new phaeton."

Harry's lips twitched. "Ah, yes—his latest achievement." He made an almost imperceptible adjustment to the folds of his crisply white cravat.

"Your aunt will be delighted to see you, sir."

Harry met Fergus's eyes in the mirror. "No doubt." He let his lids fall, veiling his eyes. "Who else is here?"

"Sir Henry and Lady Dalrymple, Squire Moffat and Mrs Moffat, Mr Butterworth, Mr Hurst and the Misses Pinkerton." When Harry stood stock still, green eyes hooded, his expression utterly blank, Fergus added, "And Mrs Babbacombe and Miss Babbacombe, of course."

"Of course." Regaining his equilibrium, momentarily shaken, Harry resettled the gold pin in his cravat. Then, turning, he strolled towards the drawing-room door. Fergus hurried to open it.

Announced, Harry entered.

Her eyes met his immediately—she wasn't experienced enough to cloak her spontaneous reaction. She'd been speaking with Mr Hurst, a gentleman farmer whom Em, Harry suspected, had long had in her matchmaking sights. Harry paused just inside the door.

Lucinda smiled across the room—an easy, politely welcoming smile—and turned back to Mr Hurst.

Harry hesitated, then, languidly urbane, strolled to where his aunt sat ensconced in regal purple on the end of the *chaise.* "Dear Aunt," he said, bowing elegantly over her hand.

"Wondered if you'd come." Em grinned her triumph.

Harry ignored it. He nodded to the lady sharing the *chaise.* "Mrs Moffat." He was acquainted with all those Em had deigned to invite—he simply hadn't expected her to invite them. Tonight was the last night of the race-meet; tomorrow, after the final races in the morning, all the gentlemen would head back to town. His aunt's summons to dinner was not unusual, yet he had thought long and hard before accepting. Only the certainty that Mrs Babbacombe would shortly be returning to Yorkshire, well beyond his reach, while he intended to retire to Lester Hall in Berkshire, had persuaded him to do so. That, and the desire to see her again, to look into her misty blue eyes—one last time.

He had expected to share a table with his aunt, his brother, his aunt's houseguests—and no one else. Theoretically, the current situation, with so many distractions, should have reassured him. In fact, it did the opposite.

With a nod, and a swift glance at Mrs Babbacombe's dark head, he left the *chaise,* drifting to where Sir Henry Dalrymple stood chatting with Squire Moffat. Gerald was near the windows, Heather Babbacombe beside him, both conversing easily with Lady Dalrymple. The Misses Pinkerton, determined spinsters in their thirties, chatted with Mr Butterworth, Sir Henry's secretary.

Harry's gaze lingered on Lucinda, clad in delicate blue watered silk and talking animatedly with Mr Hurst; if she felt it, she gave no sign.

"Ah, Lester—up for the races, I presume?" Sir Henry beamed a welcome.

Squire Moffat snorted good-humouredly. "Precious little else to bring you this way."

"Indeed." Harry shook hands.

"Saw that filly of yours win in the second—great run." Sir Henry's faraway gaze said he was reliving the moment. Then he abruptly refocused. "But tell me, what do you think about Grand Larrikin's chances in the Steeple?"

The ensuing discussion on the Duke of Rutland's latest acquisition took up no more than half of Harry's mind. The rest was centred on his siren, apparently oblivious on the other side of the room.

Lucinda, perfectly aware of the sideways glances he occasionally sent her way, doggedly adhered to Em's strictures and studiously ignored him, prattling on about she knew not what to the loquacious Mr Hurst. He, thankfully, seemed so taken with the sound of his voice—a soothing baritone—that he didn't notice her preoccupation.

Struggling to focus her mind on his words, Lucinda steadfastly denied the increasing compulsion to glance at Harry Lester. Since the moment he'd appeared in the doorway, clad in severe black and white, his hair gleaming guinea gold in the candlelight, every elegant, indolent line screaming his position in the *ton,* her senses had defied her.

Her heart had leapt—Em had warned her that her summons wouldn't bring him if he didn't want to come. But he had arrived; it felt like she'd won, if not the first battle, then at least the opening skirmish.

She was so excruciatingly aware of him that when he left Squire Moffat and Sir Henry to languidly stroll her way, she had to clench her fists hard to stop herself from turning to greet him.

Approaching from behind her, Harry saw the sudden tension in her shoulders, bared by her gown. Beneath his heavy lids, his green eyes glinted.

As he drew abreast of her, he ran his fingertips down her bare forearm to capture her hand. Her eyes widened, but when she turned to smile at him there was no hint of perturbation in her face.

"Good evening, Mr Lester."

Harry smiled down into her eyes—and slowly raised her hand to his lips. Her fingers quivered, then lay passive. "I sincerely hope so, Mrs Babbacombe."

Lucinda accepted the salute with stalwart calm but withdrew her tingling fingers the instant he eased his grip. "I believe you're acquainted with Mr Hurst?"

"Indeed. Hurst." Harry exchanged nods with Pelham Hurst, who he privately considered a pompous ass. Hurst was a year older than he; they'd known each other since childhood but mixed as much as oil and water. As if to confirm he'd changed little with the years, Hurst launched into a recital of the improvements he had made to his fields; Harry dimly wondered why, with a vision like Lucinda Babbacombe in the vicinity, Pelham thought he'd be interested.

But Pelham rambled on.

Harry frowned. It was wellnigh impossible to keep his gaze on Lucinda Babbacombe's face while Hurst kept bombarding him with the details of crop rotation. Grasping a rare moment when Pelham paused for breath, he turned to Lucinda. "Mrs Babbacombe—"

Her blue eyes came his way—only to slide past him. She smiled in welcome. "Good evening, Mr Lester. Mr Butterworth."

Harry momentarily closed his eyes, then, opening them, forced himself to step back to allow Gerald and Nicholas Butterworth to make their bows. Together with Heather Babbacombe they joined their circle.

Any chance of detaching his quarry was lost.

Mentally gritting his teeth, Harry held to his position by her side. He knew he should go and chat to the Misses Pinkerton; he excused his lapse on the grounds that, being what he was, he made them nervous.

The thought gave him pause.

Lucinda felt very like Daniel in the lion's den—not at all sure of her safety. When the first trickle of heat slid down her nape, she didn't immediately register its cause. But when, but moments later, she felt the skin above her breasts tingle, she shot a frowning glance sideways.

Harry met it with a blank green stare—slightly questioning, all innocence. Lucinda raised her brows and pointedly turned back to the conversation. Thereafter, she steadfastly ignored all her senses—as best she could. She greeted Fergus's arrival and his stately pronouncement that dinner was served with considerable relief.

"If you would allow me to escort you in, Mrs Babba-combe?" Pelham Hurst, ineradicably convinced of his self-worth, offered a heavily creased sleeve.

Lucinda smiled and was about to accept when a drawling voice cut off her escape.

"I'm afraid, Hurst, that I'm before you." Harry smiled at his childhood acquaintance, the gesture in no way softening the expression in his eyes. "By days."

On the words, Harry shifted his green gaze to Lucinda's face—and dared her to contradict him.

Lucinda merely threw him an equable smile. "Indeed." She gave Harry her hand and allowed him to place it on his sleeve, turning as he did so to inform Mr Hurst, "Mr Lester has been of great assistance while we've been in Newmarket. I don't know how we would have escaped our upturned carriage if he hadn't happened along."

The remark, of course, led Pelham to enquire in deeply solicitous vein as to their accident. As the Misses Pinkerton had already wandered into the dining-room eschewing all male escort, Hurst was free to stroll on Lucinda's other side as Harry guided her into the dining-room.

By the time he took his seat beside the lovely Mrs Babbacombe, Harry's temper was straining at its leash.

But there were more trials in store. Lady Dalrymple, a motherly soul who had long deplored his unmarried state, took the seat to his left. Even worse, the Pinkerton sisters settled in opposite, warily eyeing him as if he was some potentially dangerous beast.

Harry wasn't sure they were wrong.

Ignoring all distractions, he turned to his fair companion. "Dare I hope you're satisfied with the outcome of your visit to Newmarket, Mrs Babbacombe?"

Lucinda fleetingly met his eyes, confirming that the question was, indeed, loaded. "Not entirely, Mr Lester. I can't help but feel that certain interests must regrettably be classed as unfinished business." Again she met his gaze and allowed her lips to curve. "But I dare say Mr Blount will manage."

Harry blinked, breaking the intensity of his gaze.

With a gentle smile, Lucinda turned away as Mr Hurst claimed her attention. She resisted the compulsion to glance to her right until the second course was being removed. Ineffably elegant, apparently relaxed, Harry was engaged in idly entertaining Lady Dalrymple.

At that moment, Mrs Moffat called upon Lady Dalrymple to confirm some report. Harry turned his head—and met Lucinda's determinedly mild gaze.

Resigned, he lifted a brow at her. "Well, my dear—what's it to be? The weather is singularly boring, you know nothing about horses and as for what I'd prefer to discuss with you—I'm quite certain you'd rather I didn't."

Attack—with a vengeance. There was no mistaking the light in his eyes. Lucinda inwardly quivered—outwardly she smiled. "Now there you are wrong, Mr Lester." She paused for an artful second before continuing, her gaze holding his, "I'm definitely interested in hearing about Thistledown. Is she still in town?"

He sat so perfectly still Lucinda found she couldn't breathe. Then one brow slowly rose; his eyes were jewel-like, crystalline and hard, sharp and brilliant. "No—she's on her way back to my stud."

"Ah, yes—that's in Berkshire, is it not?"

Harry inclined his head, not entirely trusting himself to speak. At the edge of his vision, the Pinkertons, oddly sensitive to atmospherics, were tensing, casting glances at each other, frowning at him.

Lady Dalrymple leaned forward to speak around him. "I'm so sorry you won't be here for my little gathering next week, Mrs Babbacombe. Still, I dare say you're quite right in heading to town. So much to do, so much to see— and you're young enough to enjoy the social whirl. Will you be bringing your stepdaughter out?"

"Possibly," Lucinda answered, ignoring the sudden tension that had laid hold of the body between them. "We'll make the decision once we're in town."

"Very wise." Lady Dalrymple nodded and turned back to Em.

"London?"

The question was quiet, his tone flat.

"Why, yes." Calmly, Lucinda met his green gaze. "I have four more inns to inspect, remember?"

For a pregnant moment, Harry's eyes held hers. "Which are?"

Again his voice was soft, steel cloaked in silk. Very thin silk.

"The Argyle Arms in Hammersmith, the Carringbush in Barnet, the Three Candles in Great Dover Street and the Bells at Wanstead."

"What's that about the Bells?"

Lucinda turned her head as Pelham Hurst butted in.

"An excellent inn—I can recommend it to you, Mrs Babbacombe. Often stay there myself. Don't like to risk my cattle in town, don't y'know."

Harry ignored him completely. Luckily, as a large apple tart was placed in front of him at that moment, Pelham didn't notice. Harry grasped the opportunity as the diners sat up and looked over the dessert course to lean closer to Lucinda. He spoke in a steely whisper. "You're out of your senses! Those are four of the busiest inns in England— they're all coaching inns on the major roads."

Lucinda reached for a jelly. "So I've been told."

Harry gritted his teeth. "My dear Mrs Babbacombe,

your little act of being an inspector might work in country inns—" he broke off to thank Lady Dalrymple for passing the cream which he immediately set down "—but it'll get you nowhere in town. Aside from that, you cannot visit any of those inns alone."

"My dear Mr Lester." Lucinda turned to face him, her eyes wide. "Surely you're not trying to tell me my inns are dangerous?"

He was trying to tell her just that.

But Pelham Hurst, hearing only snippets, put in his oar. "Dangerous? Not a bit of it! Why, you'll be as safe as…as here, at the Bells. Highly recommend it, Mrs Babbacombe."

Glimpsing the goaded expression in Harry's green eyes, Lucinda kept her lips straight and made haste to assure Mr Hurst, "Indeed, sir. I'm sure that wasn't what Mr Lester meant."

"Mr Lester, as you well know, meant that you have as much experience as a green girl and rather less chance of surviving one of your 'inspections' at any of those inns without receiving at least three propositions and a *carte blanche*." Having delivered this clarification through clenched teeth, Harry attacked the custard that had appeared before him.

"Would you care for some cream?" Lucinda, having helped herself to a generous dollop, caught a drip on her fingertip. Her eyes, innocently blue, met Harry's as she lifted her finger to her lips.

For a blind instant, as she lowered her hand, Harry could see nothing beyond her lips, ripe and luscious, begging to be kissed. He heard nothing, was blissfully unaware of the gaggle of conversation about him. Abruptly, he grabbed hold of his reins, fast disappearing. He lifted his gaze and met hers. His eyes narrowed. "No, thank you."

Lucinda simply smiled.

"It's fattening," Harry added but she only smiled more. She looked very like the cat who had found the right jug.

Stifling a curse, Harry applied himself to his dessert. It was no business of his if she insisted on swanning into danger. He'd warned her. "Why can't Mabberly do those inns? Let him earn his keep."

"As I told you before, Mr Mabberly does not have the right qualifications for conducting an inquisition." Lucinda kept her voice low, grateful that Heather had distracted Mr Hurst.

She waited for the next comment—but her neighbour merely snorted and fell silent.

His disapproval lapped about her in waves.

Harry endured the rest of the evening outwardly urbane, inwardly brooding. The gentlemen did not linger over their port, which was just as well for he was no good company. But when they repaired to the drawing room, he discovered that, rather than the general chatty atmosphere which was the norm for Em's dinners, and which he'd been determined to exploit for his own ends, tonight, they were to be entertained by the Babbacombes, Mrs and Miss.

With no good grace, Harry sat on a chair at the back of the room, unmoved by what he recognised as an exemplary performance. The tea trolley appeared as the applause died.

His temper sorely strained, he was one of the last to come forward for his cup.

"Yes, indeed," Em said as he strolled up, nodding to Lady Dalrymple. "We'll be there—I'll look for you. It's going to be such fun to go the rounds again."

Harry froze, his hand half-outstretched.

Em looked up—and frowned. "Here you are!"

Harry blinked—and took the cup, Em's frown reflected in his eyes. "Are you contemplating going up to town, dear Aunt?"

"Not contemplating." Em threw him a belligerent glance. "I'm going. As Lucinda and Heather are set to visit there, we've decided to go together. Much the best thing. I've sent for them to open Hallows House—Fergus is going up tomorrow. It'll be wonderful, being in the swing again. I'll introduce Lucinda and Heather to the *ton*. Marvellous distraction—just what I need to give me new life."

She actually had the gall to smile at him.

Harry forced himself to utter the expected platitudes—under Lady Dalrymple's mild gaze he could hardly give his aunt the benefit of his true conclusions.

After that he beat a hasty retreat—even Squire Moffat and the intricacies of the local drainage system were preferable to farther contemplation of the web he now found himself in. The only one he could be open with was his brother.

"Em's insane. They all are," he growled as he joined Gerald by the window. Heather Babbacombe was chatting to Mrs Moffat. Harry noticed Gerald's smiling gaze rarely left the girl.

"Why? No harm in them going up to London. I'll be able to show Heather all the sights."

Harry snorted. "While London's rakes are attempting to show Mrs Babbacombe their etchings, no doubt."

Gerald grinned. "Well—you can take care of that. None of the others will come near if you hover at her shoulder."

The look Harry bent on him spoke volumes. "In case it's escaped your admittedly distracted intelligence, brother dear, I am currently the principal Lester target in the matchmakers' sights. Having lost Jack to Miss Winterton, they'll redouble their efforts and turn all their guns on yours truly."

"I know." Gerald shot him an insouciant grin. "You've no idea how grateful I am that you're there for them to aim at—with any luck, they won't remember me. Good thing—I haven't a bean of your experience."

He was clearly sincere. Harry swallowed the sharp words that rose to his tongue. Lips compressed, he retired to the safety of Sir Henry's conversation, studiously avoiding any further contact with his fate. His siren. She who would lure him onto the rocks.

The guests left in concert. Harry and Gerald, as family, stood back to let the others take their leave. Em stepped onto the porch to wave farewell; Gerald and Heather were dallying by the drawing-room door. In the shadows by the front door, Harry found himself beside his temptation.

His aunt, he noticed, was in no rush to return.

"Will we see you in London, Mr Lester?"

She cast him an artless glance—Harry couldn't decide whether it was real or not. He looked down at her face, upturned to his, blue eyes wide. "I have no plans to come up again this Season."

"A pity," she said, but her lips curved. "I had thought to repay my debt to you, as we'd agreed."

It took him a moment to recall. "The waltz?"

Lucinda nodded. "Indeed. But if you will not be in town, then this is goodbye, sir."

She held out her hand; Harry took it, shook it, but didn't release it. Eyes narrowing, he studied her open expression, those eyes he would swear could not lie.

She was saying goodbye. Perhaps, after all, escape was still possible?

Then her lips curved slightly. "Rest assured I'll think of you while waltzing through the London ballrooms."

Harry's fingers closed hard about hers—and clenched even harder about his gloves. The eruption that shook him—of anger, and sheer, possessive desire—very nearly broke his control. She looked up, eyes flaring, her lips slightly parted. It was no thanks to her, and the soft, tempting look in her eyes, that he managed to mask his reaction. He forced himself to release her hand; his face felt stiff as he bowed. "I will bid you good night, Mrs Babbacombe."

With that, he walked out, missing the disappointment that clouded Lucinda's gaze.

From the top of the steps, she watched him drive away—and prayed that Em was right.

Chapter Six

She was still praying ten days later when, flanked by Em and Heather, she strolled into Lady Haverbuck's ballroom. Her ladyship's ball was the first of the major gatherings they had attended. It had taken them four days to successfully transfer to Hallows House in Audley Street; the following days had been taken up with the necessary visits to modistes and the fashionable emporia. The previous evening, Em had hosted a select party to introduce both her guests to the *ton*. The acceptances had gratified Em; it had been many years since she had been in the capital. But there had been one who had not responded to the white, gilt-edged card.

Lucinda herself had penned it and directed it to Harry's lodgings in Half Moon Street. But she had looked in vain for his golden head.

"You'll have to let him go if you want him to come back," Em had declared. "He's like one of his horses—you can lead him to the pond but you can't make him drink."

So she had let him go—without a murmur, without the slightest hint that she wanted him.

He had yet to return.

Now, elegantly clad in shimmering blue silk the colour of cornflowers, her dark hair artfully coiffed to fall in soft curls about her brow and temples, Lucinda stood on the edge of the ballroom floor and looked about her.

They were neither early nor late; the room was already well filled but not yet crowded. Elegant gentlemen conversed with fashionable matrons; dowagers and chaperons lined the walls. Their charges, mostly young girls making their come-out, were readily identified by the pale pastel hues of their gowns. They were everywhere, the bolder ones chatting with youthful swains, others, more bashful, clinging to each other's company.

"Oh—look!" Heather clutched Lucinda's gloved arm. "There's Miss Morley and her sister." Heather glanced up at Lucinda. "May I join them?"

Lucinda smiled across the room at the cheery Misses Morley. "Certainly. But look for us when you've done."

Heather flashed her an excited smile.

Em snorted. "We'll be over there." Wielding a lorgnette, she pointed to a *chaise* by the wall.

With a bob, Heather slipped away, a vision in palest turquoise muslin, her golden curls dressed high.

"A most fetching gown—even if 'twas I who chose it," Em declared. She led the way to the *chaise*.

Lucinda followed. She was about to copy Em's descent onto the brocaded seat when young Mr Hollingsworth appeared by her elbow, an older, infinitely more elegant gentleman beside him.

"I say, Mrs Babbacombe—delighted to see you again." Mr Hollingsworth all but jigged with excitement.

Lucinda murmured a polite greeting; they had met Mr Hollingsworth at Hatchard's the day before.

"Beg you'll allow me to present my cousin, Lord Ruthven."

The elegant gentleman, dark-haired and handsome, bowed gracefully. "I am indeed honoured to make your acquaintance, Mrs Babbacombe."

Curtsying, Lucinda glanced up and met his eye; she suppressed a grimace as she recognised the speculative glint therein.

"A rose amongst so many peonies, my dear." With a languid wave, Ruthven dismissed the youthful beauties about them.

"Indeed?" Lucinda raised her brows sceptically.

Lord Ruthven was undeterred. And, as she quickly discovered, his lordship was not the only gentleman desirous of more mature company. Others, largely of similar ilk, strolled up, unhesitatingly claiming Ruthven's good offices to perform the introductions. His lordship, indolently amused, obliged. Remembering her duties, Lucinda tried to retreat, only to have Em snort—indulgently amused—and wave her away.

"I'll keep an eye on Heather. You go and enjoy yourself—that's what *ton* balls are for."

Thus adjured, and reflecting that Em knew rather more about watching over young girls at *ton* balls than she did, Lucinda inwardly shrugged and smiled on her would-be court. In a very short time, she found herself surrounded—by a collection of gentlemen she mentally categorised as Harry Lester's contemporaries. They were, one and all, ineffably charming; she could see no harm in enjoying their company.

Then the music started, lilting strains wafting over the bright heads.

"Dare I claim your first cotillion in the capital, my dear?"

Lucinda turned to find Lord Ruthven's arm before her. "Indeed, sir. I would be delighted."

A smile curved his lips. "No, my dear—it is *I* who am delighted. You will have to find another adjective."

Lucinda met his eyes. She raised her brows. "My mind is a blank, sir. What would you suggest?"

His lordship was perfectly prepared to oblige. "Devastated with joy? In alt? Over the moon with happiness?"

Lucinda laughed. As they took their places in the set, she arched a brow at him. "How about—'so impressed I am unable to find words to express it'?"

Lord Ruthven grimaced.

As the evening progressed, Lucinda found herself much in demand. As she was ranked among the matrons, she did not have a dance-card but was free to bestow her hand on whomever she chose from amongst her assiduous court. Indeed, their assiduousness triggered her innate caution; while Ruthven appeared too good-humoured and indolent to be dangerous, there were others whose eyes held a more intent gleam.

One such was Lord Craven, who strolled into the ballroom late, surveyed the field from the top of the steps, then beat a disguised but determined path to her side. Dragooning Mr Satterly into providing an introduction, his lordship was bowing over Lucinda's hand when the unmistakable strains of a waltz filled the room.

"My dear Mrs Babbacombe, dare I hope you'll take pity on a latecomer and grant me the honour of this waltz?"

Lucinda met Lord Craven's dark hooded eyes—and decided her pity would be more wisely bestowed elsewhere. She let her eyes widen and swept a questioning glance at the gentlemen surrounding her.

They instantly came to her rescue, dismissing Lord

Craven's claim as outrageous, presumptuous and unfair and plying her with any number of alternatives. Laughing lightly, Lucinda withdrew her fingers from Lord Craven's clasp. "I fear you must take your chance amongst the competition, my lord."

His lordship's expression turned distinctly stiff.

"Now, let's see." Lucinda smiled at her cavaliers and was about to bestow her favour upon Mr Amberly, who, despite the appreciation in his eyes, was another more inclined to amusement than seduction, when she felt a stir beside her.

Long, strong fingers encircled her arm, sliding over the bare skin just above her glove.

"My waltz, I believe, Mrs Babbacombe."

Lucinda's breath caught. She swung to face Harry; their eyes met—his were very green, his gaze sharp, oddly intent. Elation swept Lucinda. She struggled to hide it.

Harry's lips curved, their ends lifting in a smile, which turned to a grimace, hidden as he bowed.

When he straightened, his features were impassive.

"I say, Lester! This is dashed unfair." Mr Amberly all but pouted. Others muttered in similar vein.

Harry merely lifted a supercilious brow, his now-hooded glance shifting to rest on Lucinda's face. "As I recall, my dear, you owe me a waltz. I've come to claim it."

"Indeed, sir." Savouring the sound of his deep drawl, Lucinda gave up her fight and smiled her delight. "I always pay my debts. My first waltz in the capital is yours."

Harry's lips twitched but he stilled them. With an elegant gesture he claimed her hand and settled it on his sleeve.

Lucinda slanted a quick, triumphant glance at Em, but her mentor was hidden by her court. "Gentlemen." With a sunny smile and a nod for her disappointed cavaliers, who were shooting disgruntled glances at her unexpected partner, she allowed him to lead her to the floor.

Harry held his tongue until they reached the dance floor but as soon as he had whirled them into the swirling throng, he looked down and trapped Lucinda's blue gaze. "I realise, Mrs Babbacombe, that your experience does not extend to the vagaries of the *ton*. I fear I should warn you that many of the gentlemen presently intent on your smiles should be treated with extreme caution."

More concerned with adequately following his assured lead than with her redundant court, Lucinda frowned. "That's obvious."

Harry's brows slowly rose.

Lucinda's frown grew distracted. "I'm rather more than seven, you know. As far as I can see, there's no reason I shouldn't enjoy myself in their company—I'm hardly so green as to be taken in by their charms."

At that, Harry snorted. For a full minute, he considered the possibility of scaring her with a more explicit warning, then mentally shook his head. She wasn't, he realised, recalling Jake Blount and the Green Goose, easily scared. But he could hardly countenance her court.

Glancing down at her face, he saw she was still frowning, but in an abstracted way. "What's wrong?"

She started—and cast an irritated glance up at him. "Well?"

"If you must know," Lucinda said. "I'm not terribly experienced at waltzing. Charles didn't, of course. I've had lessons—but it's rather different on a crowded floor."

Harry couldn't stop his slow grin. "Just relax."

The look she sent him suggested that she found his humour ill-conceived.

Harry chuckled—and drew her closer, tightening his arm about her so she could more easily sense his intentions.

Lucinda held her breath—then slowly let it out. Their new positions were just this side of decent but she felt immeasurably more secure. When Harry twirled her through a complicated set of turns as they negotiated the end of the room, she followed without faltering. Reassured, she relaxed—only to find her wits almost overwhelmed by her senses. His hard thighs brushed hers as they progressed down the room; she could feel the heat of his large body reaching for her, enveloping her, his strength effortlessly whirling her about. A strange tension gripped her, making breathing difficult. It was matched by the tension in the arm locked about her. From beneath her lashes, Lucinda glanced up. Her gaze found his lips. As she watched, they firmed into a straight line.

It was an uphill battle but Harry strove to push aside all distractions—like the enthralling curves encased in blue silk nestling in his arms, the womanly softness of those curves and the supple planes of her back, like the subtle scent of her that rose to tease his senses, and the graceful curve of her neck exposed by her new hairstyle—and remind his wandering wits just why he had returned to London. "When are you planning to visit your inns?"

Lucinda blinked, and shifted her gaze to his eyes. "Actually, I'd thought to start with the Argyle Arms at Hammersmith tomorrow."

Harry didn't bother asking if she'd arranged a suitable escort. The damned woman was so irrationally sure of herself, so ignorant of the true dangers, so determinedly wilful... His lips thinned. "I'll call for you at nine."

Lucinda's eyes opened wide.

Harry noticed—and frowned at her. "You needn't fear—we'll go in my curricle and I'll have Dawlish along. Perfectly proper, I assure you."

Lucinda swallowed her happy laugh. Em's strictures

replayed in her head. She eyed him consideringly, then gracefully acquiesced. "Thank you, sir. Your company will, I'm sure, make the drive more interesting."

Harry narrowed his eyes, but could make nothing of her serene expression. Stifling a humph, he drew her a fraction closer—and set his mind to enjoying the rest of the waltz.

At its end, he strolled back with her to where her court waited, impatient and eager. Harry read the anticipation in their eyes. He stiffened. Instead of yielding his fair partner up with a flourish and an elegant bow, the prescribed procedure, he covered her hand, resting on his sleeve, with his. And remained, thus anchored, by her side.

Lucinda pretended not to notice. She chatted gaily, ignoring the intrigued glint in Lord Ruthven's perceptive eye and Mr Amberly's disapproving expression. Harry, she noted, made no attempt whatever to contribute to the conversation; she longed to look at him but standing so close, she could not. Not without making her interest obvious. She was somewhat relieved when Mrs Anabelle Burnham, a young matron ambling past on the arm of Mr Courtney, decided to join them.

"I declare, it's going to be yet another crush." Mrs Burnham fluttered her lashes at Lord Ruthven before turning her laughing brown eyes on Lucinda. "You'll grow used to them, my dear. And you have to admit these larger gatherings are…entertaining."

Another laughing glance went Lord Ruthven's way.

Lucinda struggled to keep her lips straight. "Indeed." Nothing loath, she slanted a glance up at her silent partner. "And the entertainment takes so many varied forms, too. Don't you find it so?"

Anabelle Burnham blinked, then her teasing smile

brightened. "Oh, definitely, my dear Mrs Babbacombe. Definitely!"

She bestowed another arch glance on Lord Ruthven, then turned her sights on Mr Amberly.

Lucinda didn't notice—she was trapped in Harry's green gaze. The planes of his face were hard, sculpted, his expression impassive yet growing more forbidding by the second. She saw his eyes narrow slightly; his lips were a thin line. Breathing was suddenly very difficult.

The squeak of the violins saved her—she didn't know from what.

"Mrs Babbacombe—I declare you must, positively you must, bestow this quadrille on my poor self."

With a mental curse, Lucinda glanced to where Mr Amberly stood watching her, entreaty in his eyes. She blinked—and realized that he was begging her to rescue him. She couldn't help but smile.

She glanced up at Harry; gently she withdrew her hand from under his. For an instant, his fingers tensed—then he released her. "I haven't thanked you for my waltz, sir." Lucinda lifted her eyes to his. "It was most enjoyable."

His features were granite. He said nothing but bowed, effortlessly elegant in his severe black and white.

With an inclination of her head, Lucinda turned away and placed her hand on Mr Amberly's sleeve.

To her intense disappointment, Harry was no longer present when, at the conclusion of the quadrille, Mr Amberly returned her to the small group close by Em's chaise. Under cover of the conversation, Lucinda scanned the surrounding shoulders but could not find the ones she sought. She saw Heather, bright-eyed and clearly enjoying herself hugely. Her stepdaughter waved, then turned back to her set—Gerald Lester, the Morley sisters and two other young gentlemen. Feeling distinctly deflated, Lucinda forced herself to pay attention to her cavaliers. The circle around her, which had earlier thinned, now pressed in on her. She could understand why these events were labelled crushes. At least Mrs Burnham hadn't deserted her.

But her enjoyment in the evening had waned; it was an effort to conjure a bright smile and a witty response to the constant flow of repartee.

Somewhat later, the lilting strains of another waltz drifted from the musicians' dais at the other end of the room. Lucinda blinked. She had already danced with all those of her court she considered reasonably safe—she hadn't anticipated another waltz.

She glanced up—to find Lord Ruthven's eyes upon her, a curious glint in their depths. "Well, my dear?" he drawled. "Which one of us will you favour with a second dance?"

Lucinda raised her brows haughtily. And scanned those she had yet to favour at all. Three promptly pressed their claims—one, a rakish dandy a few years older than herself but infinitely more experienced, held the greatest promise. He might have impropriety on his mind but he was, Lucinda judged, manageable. With a serene smile, and a cool glance for Ruthven, she extended her hand. "Mr Ellerby?"

To give him his due, Mr Ellerby behaved with all due decorum on the dance floor. By the end of the dance, Lucinda was congratulating herself, not only on her increasing confidence in the waltz itself but on her accurate assessment of her partner, when Mr Ellerby abruptly reverted to type.

"Quite stuffy in here, don't you find, Mrs Babbacombe?"

Lucinda glanced up and smiled. "Indeed—one could hardly find it not. The room is certainly very crowded."

So crowded she could no longer see Em's *chaise*, concealed by the milling throng. The waltz had landed them at the other end of the room.

"This window leads to the terrace. And Lady Haverbuck's gardens are extensive. Perhaps a stroll through them would cool your cheeks, Mrs Babbacombe?"

Lucinda turned to stare at her erstwhile partner. The gleam in his eyes was unmistakable.

"Wouldn't want you to feel faint, would we?" Mr Ellerby leaned closer on the words, pressing her fingers meaningfully.

Lucinda stiffened. She drew a steady breath and opened her lips, fully intending to advise her importunate partner that her temper rarely induced faintness, when she was saved the necessity.

"I don't think Mrs Babbacombe needs a stroll on the terrace just now, Ellerby."

The drawled yet steely words sent a frisson of excitement through Lucinda; they turned Mr Ellerby sulky.

"Just a suggestion." He waved the point aside, then offered Lucinda his arm, all but glowering at Harry. "It's suppertime, Mrs Babbacombe."

"Indeed," came from beside her.

Lucinda glanced up and saw Harry's green gaze grow coldly challenging. His fingers feathered down her arm, then firmed about her wrist. She quelled a shiver.

Harry looked down at her. "If you wish, Mrs Babbacombe, I'll escort you in."

He lifted her hand and settled it on his sleeve. Lucinda met his eyes—then turned to coolly dismiss Mr Ellerby. "Thank you for an enjoyable waltz, sir."

Mr Ellerby looked as if he wished to argue—then he met Harry's gaze. With a grumpy air, he bowed. "My pleasure, ma'am."

"I'm sure it was," Harry muttered beneath his breath as he turned Lucinda towards the supper room.

"I beg your pardon?" Lucinda blinked up at him.

"Nothing." Harry's lips compressed. "Couldn't you chose a more suitable partner than Ellerby? You had enough real gentlemen about you—or can't you tell the difference?"

"Of course I can." Suppressing her smile, Lucinda put her nose in the air. "But I'd already danced with all of them. I didn't want to appear to be encouraging them."

Harry resisted the urge to grind his teeth. "Believe me, Mrs Babbacombe, you would do better to encourage the gentlemen and avoid the rakes altogether."

Lucinda copied one of Em's snorts. "Nonsense. I was in no danger."

She glanced up to see Harry's face turn to stone.

"Mrs Babbacombe, I have severe difficulty believing you would recognise danger if you fell over it."

Lucinda had to purse her lips to stop her smile. "Bosh!" she eventually returned.

Harry sent her a severe glance—and determinedly steered her to a table. Not one of the small, intimate tables for two in the corners of the large supper-room, but a table to accommodate a small army set close to the buffet in the room's centre. Taking the seat he held for her, Lucinda cast him a puzzled glance.

She was even more puzzled when her court tentatively descended, and Harry forbore to bite. He sat beside her, leaning back in the chair, a champagne flute in one long-fingered hand, and silently monitored the conversation. His brooding presence acted as a most efficient damper, ensuring the jocularity remained strictly within acceptable bounds. Anabelle Burnham, joining them, cast one awed glance at Harry, then caught Lucinda's eye and raised her glass in a silent toast. Lucinda risked a quick grin, then let her gaze slide to Harry's face.

He was watching her, not the others, his lips set in a line she was coming to know well, his green gaze jewel-like and impenetrable.

Lucinda quelled a shiver. Turning back to the table, she forced herself to focus on her less interesting admirers.

AS HE HAD PROMISED, Harry was waiting for her in the hall of Hallows House at precisely nine o'clock the next morning.

Descending the stairs with a dark blue half-cape draped over her bluebell-hued carriage dress, Lucinda watched as his gaze skimmed knowledgeably over her. When she reached the hall and came forward, her hand extended, his gaze lifted to her face.

Harry saw the feminine smugness in her eyes—and frowned. "At least you shouldn't freeze." He took her hand and bowed over it—then considered the sight of her small, slim hand nestling in his much larger one. "Don't forget your gloves."

Lucinda lifted a brow—and drew her gloves from her reticule. "I'll be back for luncheon, Fergus." Dutifully drawing on her gloves, she glanced at Harry. "Will you join us, Mr Lester?"

"No—please convey my regrets to my aunt." Harry grasped her arm and steered her to the door. Em's house was probably safe enough but his clubs would be safer; he no longer trusted his aunt. "I have other engagements."

Lucinda stopped on the top of the steps and glanced up at him. "I do hope I'm not inconveniencing you by claim-ing your escort to my inns?"

Harry looked down at her, his eyes narrowing. She was an inconvenience unlike any he'd ever encountered. "Not at all, my dear. If you recall, I wished this on myself." Why, he refused to consider. "But it's time we were away."

He led her down the steps, then lifted her to his curricle's seat. Avoiding Dawlish's eye, he retrieved the reins. He waited only until his henchman's weight tipped the carriage before giving his horses the office.

Lucinda thoroughly enjoyed her drive through the morning streets, not yet crowded. She saw orange-sellers plying their wares; she heard strawberry girls calling housewives to their doors. The city seemed different, clean and pristine beneath the morning's dew, the dust yet to be stirred by the traffic. The varied greens of the trees in the Park shifted like a kaleidoscope. Harry drove them briskly along the gravelled carriageway, then out of a distant gate. Once they were bowling along the road to Hammersmith, Lucinda turned her mind to business. Harry answered her questions on the inns they passed, occasionally referring to Dawlish. Lucinda noted that Harry's groom seemed uncommonly morose; his dour tones suggested a death in the family.

But she forgot Dawlish and his patent misery when they pulled into the yard of the Argyle Arms.

The Argyle Arms proved to have much in common with the Barbican Arms. The innkeeper, a Mr Honeywell, after one glance at Harry, deferentially escorted her over the large inn, which extended over three interconnecting wings. They were on the ground floor of one of the wings heading back towards the main entrance when Lucinda heard laughter behind a door she had assumed led to a bedchamber.

Visions of the Green Goose flitted through her mind. It had, however, been male laughter. She halted. "What's behind that door?"

Mr Honeywell remained impassive. "A parlour, ma'am."

"A parlour?" Lucinda frowned and looked about her. "Ah, yes—this was a separate house at one time, wasn't it?"

Mr Honeywell nodded and gestured for her to proceed.

Lucinda stood stock-still and stared at the closed parlour door. "That makes four parlours—does the inn's custom necessitate so many?"

"Not directly," Mr Honeywell admitted. "But we're so near town we often rent rooms to groups for meetings."

Lucinda pursed her lips. "I would like to inspect this extra parlour, Honeywell."

Mr Honeywell's expression grew wary. "Ah—this one's currently occupied, ma'am, but there's another just like it in the other wing. If you'd like to see that?"

"Indeed." Lucinda nodded but her eyes remained on the closed door. "Who is currently using this one?"

"Er…a group of gentlemen, ma'am."

Lucinda's brows rose; she opened her mouth.

"But—" Mr Honeywell smoothly interposed his stout frame between Lucinda and the door "—I really wouldn't advise you to interrupt them, ma'am."

Taken aback, Lucinda allowed her brows to rise higher; for a silent moment, she looked down on Mr Honeywell. When she spoke, her tone was chilly. "My dear Mr Honeywell—"

"Who's in there, Honeywell?"

Lucinda blinked. It was the first time in an hour that Harry had spoken.

Mr Honeywell cast an imploring glance at him. "Just a group of young bloods, sir. You'll know the sort."

"Indeed." Harry turned to Lucinda. "You can't go in."

As frigidly imperious as any dowager, Lucinda slowly turned and met his gaze. "I beg your pardon?"

Harry's lips twisted slightly but his gaze did not waver. "Let me put it this way." His tone was peculiarly soft, silky, with an undercurrent that threatened all manner of danger. "You're not going in there."

If Lucinda had had any doubt as to the reality behind the unsubtle threat, it was laid to rest by the look in his eyes, the set of his jaw and the tension that slowly infused his large frame. Despite her rising temper, she was assailed by an instinctive urge to step back—and a totally maniacal impulse to call his bluff just to see what he would do. Ignoring the shiver that squirmed down her spine, she sent him a seething glance, then transferred her gaze, now icy, to Mr Honeywell. "Perhaps you could show me this other parlour?"

The innkeeper's sigh was almost audible.

Shown the second parlour, repeatedly assured that it was virtually identical to the other, Lucinda gave her haughty approval. Stripping off her gloves, she nodded at Honeywell. "I'll examine the books now. You may bring them in here."

Honeywell departed to fetch his ledgers.

Leaving her gloves and reticule on the table, Lucinda slowly walked down the room. Halting by the window, she drew in a steadying breath and swung to face Harry. He had followed in her wake; she watched as he drew near, stopping directly before her, one brow lifting, a challenging look in his eye.

Lucinda returned it in full measure. "It may interest you to know, Mr Lester, that I had no intention of—" she gestured dismissively "—barging into a private meeting. A fact I was about to make clear to Mr Honeywell when you chose to intervene."

The arrested, suddenly defensive expression that flickered in Harry's eyes was balm to Lucinda's temper. She im-

mediately pressed her advantage. "I merely wished to enquire as to the bona fides of the customers using my inn—
a right I'm sure even *you* will agree is mine." She waggled
a finger under his nose. "Neither you nor Mr Honeywell
had any justification for jumping to such a conclusion—
as if I was a child unaware of the proprieties! And *you*, sir,
had no right to threaten me as you did." Turning aside and
folding her arms, Lucinda elevated her chin. "I wish to hear
an apology, sir, for your ungentlemanly behaviour."

Silence greeted her demand. Harry studied her face, his
gaze clear and steady. Then his lips twisted. "I suggest,
my dear, that you refrain from holding your breath. My
behaviour throughout this morning has been gentlemanly
in the extreme."

Lucinda's eyes flew wide. *"Gentlemanly?"* Her arms
dropped as she rounded on him.

Harry held up a hand. "I'll admit that both Honeywell
and I might have jumped to unwarranted conclusions."
His eyes met hers, his expression fleetingly rueful. "For
myself, for that, I apologise unequivocally. For the rest,
however…" His face hardened. "I fear you must excuse
it on the grounds of extreme provocation."

"Provocation?" Lucinda stared at him. "What provocation was that, pray tell?"

The provocation of keeping her safe, shielded, the un-
deniable, instinctive impulse that had him in its grip. The
truth echoed in Harry's head; he struggled to shut his
mind against it. He looked into her eyes; softly blue, they
searched his, then widened. He dropped his gaze to her
lips, full, blush red—a potent temptation. As he watched,
they parted fractionally. About them, silence reigned; between them, the tension grew. Compelled, as aware of her
increased breathing as he was of the deepening thud in his

veins, Harry lifted a finger and, with the lightest of touches, traced her lower lip.

The shudder his touch evoked in her reverberated deep in his marrow.

His breath caught; if he met her gaze, he would be lost.

Desire welled, unexpectedly strong; he fought to shackle it. He tried to draw breath, tried to step away, and could not.

Distant footsteps drew near; in the corridor a board creaked.

Swiftly, Harry bent his head and touched his lips to hers in a caress so brief he barely registered the gentle movement of her lips beneath his.

When the door opened and Honeywell came in, he was standing by the fireplace, some yards from Lucinda. The innkeeper noticed nothing amiss; he placed the heavy ledgers on the table and looked hopefully at Lucinda.

Harry glanced her way but her back was to the window, hiding her expression.

Lucinda hesitated, just long enough to marshall her thoroughly disordered wits. Then she swept forward, plastering an expression of such haughtiness on her face that Mr Honeywell blinked. "Just the figures for this year, I think, Mr Honeywell."

The innkeeper hurried to do her bidding.

Immersed in figures, Lucinda struggled to soothe her tingling nerves, inflamed by that too-fleeting kiss and further abraded by Harry's lounging presence. For one instant, she had felt as if the world had spun wildly; determinedly, she put the memory aside and concentrated on Mr Honeywell's accounts. By the time she was satisfied, half an hour had passed, leaving her once more in control. Quite capable of maintaining a steady flow of artless prattle all the way back to Audley Street.

Other than bestowing on her one, long, unnervingly intent look, Harry made no particular comment, replying readily to any questions, but leaving the conversational reins in her hands. When they drew up at Em's steps, Lucinda felt she had handled them with laudable skill.

She chose the moment when Harry lifted her down to say, "I'm really most grateful for your escort, Mr Lester." With what she considered commendable fortitude, she refrained from further comment.

"Indeed?" Harry arched one brow.

Lucinda fought against a frown. "Indeed," she returned, meeting his gaze.

Harry looked down at her face, at her wonderfully blue eyes, gleaming with feminine defiance—and wondered how long he could hold her, his hands firm about her waist, before she became aware of it. "In that case, tell Fergus to inform me when you wish to inspect your next inn." She felt warm, vibrant, supple and alive between his hands.

Lucinda knew perfectly well where his hands were; she could feel his fingers burning through her gown. But that kiss, so quick it was over almost before it had begun, had been her first intimation that victory was truly possible; despite the unnerving cascade of emotions the fleeting caress had evoked, she was determined not to back down. If she had, albeit unknowingly, breached his walls once, she could do it again. Battling breathlessness, she dropped her gaze to where her fingers rested against his coat. "But I couldn't so impose on your time, Mr Lester."

Harry frowned. He could see her eyes glinting through her lashes. "Not at all." He paused, then added, native caution returning, "As I told you before, given you're my aunt's guest, at my insistence, I feel it's the least I can do."

He thought he heard a disgusted humph. Suppressing

a smile, he glanced up—and met Dawlish's deeply com-miserating gaze.

All expression draining from his face, Harry dropped his hands. Stepping back, he offered his aunt's guest his arm, then gallantly, in open contempt of his henchman's foreboding, escorted her up the steps.

While waiting for Fergus to open the door, Lucinda glanced up—and intercepted an exchange of glances between Harry and Dawlish. "Dawlish seems very dismal—is anything amiss?"

Harry's features hardened. "No. He's just unused to getting up so early."

Lucinda blinked. "Oh?"

"Indeed." The door opened; beaming, Fergus held it wide. Harry bowed. "*Au revoir,* Mrs Babbacombe."

Crossing the threshold, Lucinda looked over her shoulder and threw him a smile—a soft, alluring, siren's smile. Then she turned and slowly headed for the stairs. Utterly mesmerised, Harry stood and watched her go, her hips swaying gently as she crossed the tiled hall.

"Sir?"

Harry came to himself with a start. With an abrupt nod to Fergus, he turned and descended the steps. Climbing into the curricle, he fixed Dawlish with a warning glance.

Then gave his attention to his horses.

Chapter Seven

A week later, Harry sat at his desk in the small library of his lodgings. The window gave onto a leafy courtyard; outside, May bustled towards June while the *ton* worked itself into a frenzy of betrothals and weddings. Harry's lips twisted cynically; *he* was intent on other things.

A tap on the door brought his head up. The door opened; Dawlish looked in.

"Ah—there you be. Thought as how you'd want to know that they're bound for Lady Hemminghurst's this evening."

"Damn!" Harry grimaced. Amelia Hemminghurst had a soft spot for rakes—the fraternity would be well represented amongst her guests. "I suppose I'll have to attend."

"That's what I thought. You going to walk or should I bring the carriage around?"

Harry considered, then shook his head. "I'll walk." It would be twilight by then; the short stroll to Grosvenor Square would help ease the restlessness his self-imposed restrictions seemed to be creating.

With a humph and a nod, Dawlish retreated.

Idly toying with a pen, Harry reviewed his strategy. On quitting Newmarket, he had stubbornly adhered to his plans and gone home to Lester Hall. There he had found his brother Jack, along with his soon-to-be bride, Miss Sophia Winterton and her guardians, her uncle and aunt, Mr and Mrs Webb. While he had nothing against Miss Winterton, with whom his brother was openly besotted, he had not appreciated the considering light that had lit Mrs Webb's silver blue eyes, nor the contemplative expression with which she had regarded him. Her interest had made him edgy. He had ultimately concluded that London, and the dragons he knew, might well be safer than Lester Hall.

He had arrived in town a day in advance of his aunt and her company. Knowing Em, reared in a more dangerous age, travelled nowhere without outriders, he couldn't conceive that Mrs Babbacombe might face any danger on the trip. Besides, the incident on the Newmarket road had to have been due to mere opportunism. Guarded by Em and her servants, Lucinda Babbacombe was safe enough.

Once they had settled in town, however, that had no longer been the case. He had laid low as long as he could, avoiding any unnecessary appearances, hoping thus to leave the dragons and the matchmakers in ignorance of his presence. By spending most of his days at his clubs, at Manton's or Jackson's or similar all-male venues, eschewing the Park during the fashionable hours and driving himself everywhere rather than risk strolling the pavements, a prey to dowagers and fond mamas, he had largely achieved his objective.

And with Dawlish spending most of his time in the kitchens at Hallows House, he had been able to emerge into the bright lights only when absolutely necessary.

Like tonight. He had thus far succeeded in protecting

the damned woman from importunate inn-dwellers and rakes alike, to the total confusion of the *ton*. And with his appearances amongst their gilded flowers thus restricted, and so very patently centred on Lucinda Babbacombe, the dragons and matchmakers had had few opportunities to exploit.

Harry's lips twisted; he laid aside his pen. He knew better than to bask in triumph—the Season had yet to end. Rising, he frowned. He was, he hoped, as capable as the next of behaving like a gentleman until then.

He pondered the point, then grimaced. Squaring his shoulders, he went up to change.

"TELL ME, Mr Lester—are you enjoying the Season's entertainments?"

The question took Harry by surprise. He glanced down at his partner's face, composed in polite enquiry, then looked up to whirl them around the end of Lady Hemminghurst's ballroom. He had arrived to find her already surrounded—by a crop of the most eligible rakes in town. He had wasted no time in extricating her and gathering her into his arms.

"No," he answered. The realisation gave him mental pause.

"Then why are you here?" Lucinda kept her eyes on his face and hoped for a straight answer. The question had grown increasingly important as day followed day and he made not the smallest move to fix her interest. Em's likening him to a horse appeared increasingly apt—he might have followed her to London, but he seemed determined not to pursue her.

He had escorted her to all four Babbacombe inns, remaining by her side throughout her inspections, but he had thereafter shown no interest in driving her elsewhere. All comments about the Park, about the delights of Richmond or Merton, fell on studiously deaf ears. Talk of a visit to the theatre had simply made him tense.

As for his behaviour in the ballrooms, she could only describe it as dog-in-the-manger. Some, like Lord Ruthven, found the situation immensely amusing. Others, like herself, were beginning to lose patience.

Harry glanced down and met her unwavering gaze. He frowned intimidatingly.

Lucinda raised her brows. "Am I to take it you'd rather be with your horses?" she enquired sweetly.

Goaded, Harry narrowed his eyes. "Yes." A mental picture leapt to mind. "I would infinitely prefer to be at Lestershall."

"Lestershall?"

His gaze growing distant, Harry nodded. "Lestershall Manor—my stud. It's named after the village, which in turn derives its name from my family's principal estate." The old manor house was in dire need of repairs. Now he had the money, he would put it to rights. The rambling, half-timbered house had the potential to be a wonderfully comfortable home; when he married, he would live there.

When he married? Harry clenched his jaw and forced his gaze back to his partner's face.

Lucinda captured it with a challenging glance. "Why, then, aren't you there?"

Because it's empty. Incomplete. The words leapt to Harry's conscious mind before he could shut them out. Her misty blue eyes lured him to the brink; the words burned his tongue. Mentally gritting his teeth, he smiled one of his more practiced smiles. "Because I'm here, waltzing with you."

There was nothing seductive in his tone. Lucinda kept her eyes innocently wide. "Dare I hope you're enjoying it?"

Harry's lips thinned. "My dear Mrs Babbacombe, waltzing with you is one of the few compensations my current lifestyle affords."

Lucinda allowed herself a sceptical blink. "Is it such a grind, then, your current life?"

"Indeed." Harry shot her a narrow glance. "My current round is one no rake should ever be forced to endure."

Gently, her eyes on his, Lucinda raised her brows. "Then why are you enduring it?"

Harry heard the final bars of the waltz; automatically, he whirled them to a halt. Her question echoed in his ears; the answer echoed deep within him. Her eyes, softly blue, held him, beckoning, inviting—open and reassuring. It took an effort of will to draw back, to find and cling to the cynicism which had kept him safe for so long. His features hardening, he released her and offered her his arm. "Why indeed, Mrs Babbacombe? I fear we'll never know."

Lucinda refrained from gnashing her teeth. She placed her hand on his sleeve, reflecting that a single waltz, which was all he ever claimed, was never long enough to press his defences. Why he was so intent on denying what they both knew to be fact was a point that increasingly bothered her. "Your aunt was quite surprised to see you in town—she said you would be…pursued by ladies wishful to have you marry their daughters." Did he, perhaps, see marriage as a trap?

"I dare say," Harry replied. "But London during the Season has never been safe for well-born, well-heeled gentlemen." His eyes met hers. "Regardless of their reputations."

Lucinda raised her brows. "So you view the…pursuit as nothing more than a fact of life?"

"As inescapable as spring, although a dashed sight

more inconvenient." Harry's lips twisted; he gestured up the room. "Come—I'll return you to Em."

"Ah…" Lucinda glanced about—and saw the gently billowing drapes hanging beside the long windows open to the terrace. Beyond lay the garden, a world of shadow and starlight. "Actually," she said, slanting a glance at him. "I feel rather warm."

The lie brought a helpful blush to her cheeks.

Harry's eyes narrowed as he studied hers. She was a hopeless liar; her eyes clouded over whenever she so much as prevaricated.

"Perhaps," Lucinda continued, trying for an airy tone, "we could stroll the terrace for a while." She pretended to peer through the windows. "There are some others out-side—perhaps we could investigate the walks?"

It was at times like this that she most felt the deficien-cies of her upbringing. Being married at sixteen had en-sured she had not the smallest clue how to flirt or even encourage a man. When her escort made no response, she warily peeked up at him.

Harry was waiting to capture her attention, his ex-pression that of a deeply irate man aware of the need to remain civil. "My dear Mrs Babbacombe, it would please me immensely if you could get it fixed in your pretty head that I am here, in London, braving all manner of dan-gers, for one—and only one—reason."

Her eyes genuinely wide, Lucinda blinked at him. "Oh?"

"Indeed." With restrained calm, Harry turned her up the room and started to stroll. His fingers, curled about her elbow, ensured she accompanied him. "I am here to en-sure that, despite my inclinations, your inclinations and certainly despite those of your besotted court, you end this Season as you began it." He turned his head to capture her gaze. "As a virtuous widow."

Lucinda blinked again, then stiffened. "Indeed?" Looking forward, she lifted her chin "I wasn't aware, Mr Lester, that I had appointed you to the post of protector of my virtue."

"Ah—but you did, you see."

She glanced at him, denial on her lips—and met his green gaze.

"When you took my hand and let me pull you out of your carriage on the Newmarket road."

The moment leapt to her mind, that instant when she had knelt on the side of the carriage, locked in his arms. Lucinda quelled a shiver—and tilted her nose higher. "That's nonsense."

"On the contrary." The rake beside her appeared unperturbed. "I recall reading somewhere that if a man rescues another, then he takes on the responsibility for that rescued life. Presumably the same holds true if the one saved is a woman."

Lucinda frowned. "That's an eastern philosophy. You're English to your bones."

"Eastern?" Harry raised his brows. "From one of those countries where they cover their women in shrouds and keep them behind locked doors, no doubt. I've always put such eminently sensible notions down to the fact that such civilisations have apparently existed so much longer than ours."

On the words, they reached her court. Lucinda fought the urge to grind her teeth. If she heard one more of his glib excuses for being by her side she would, she felt sure, embarrass herself and Em and everyone else by screaming in fury. She plastered a bright smile on her lips—and let the admiration of her court and their subtle compliments soothe her abraded pride.

Harry stood it for five minutes, then silently relinquished his position by her side. He prowled the room but at no great distance, exchanging a few words with a number of acquaintances before retreating to a convenient alcove from where he could keep his self-imposed burden in view.

His very presence in the room was enough to keep the dangerous blades from her skirts. Those about her were all gentlemen at heart—they wouldn't pounce without an invitation. His interest, of course, was an added deterrent; he was prepared to wager that not one soul amongst all the *ton* understood what he was about.

With a somewhat grim grin, he settled his shoulders against the wall and watched as Lucinda gave Frederick Amberly her hand.

Taking the floor in yet another waltz, an apparent fixation of Lady Hemminghurst's, Lucinda fitted her steps to Mr Amberly's strides, distinctly shorter than Harry's, and let the music take hold.

Three revolutions later, she met her partner's somewhat concerned expression—and sternly reminded herself to smile. Not a spontaneous gesture.

She was distinctly irritated.

Rakes were supposed to seduce women—widows, particularly. Was she really so hopeless she couldn't break down Harry's resistance? Not that she wished to be seduced but, given his natural flair—and her status—she had to face the fact that, for them, that might well be the most sensible first step. She prided herself on her pragmatism; there was no point in not being realistic.

He had come to London; he was dancing attendance on her. But that clearly wasn't enough. Something more was required.

They were coming up the room for the third time when Lucinda's gaze refocused on Mr Amberly. Presumably if, at her advanced age, she wanted to learn how to encourage a rake, she was going to have to arrange lessons.

The waltz, most conveniently, left them at the other end of the room. Lucinda grasped her fan, dangling by its ribbon from her wrist. Opening it, she waved it to and fro. "The room is quite warm, don't you think, Mr Amberly?"

"Indeed, dear lady."

Lucinda watched as his gaze slid to the terrace windows. Hiding a smile, she gently suggested, "There's a chair over there. If I wait there, could you fetch me a glass of lemonade?"

Her cavalier blinked and hid his disappointment. "Of course." He solicitously helped her to the chair, then, with an injunction not to move, disappeared into the crowd.

With an inward smile, Lucinda sat back, languidly waving her fan, and waited for her first lesson.

Mr Amberly duly reappeared, bearing two flutes of suspiciously tinted liquid. "Thought you'd prefer champagne."

With an inward shrug, Lucinda accepted a glass and took a delicate sip. Harry usually brought her champagne with her supper; it didn't affect her faculties. "Thank you, sir." She cast her escort a smile. "I was in dire need of refreshment."

"Hardly to be wondered at, my dear Mrs Babbacombe. Yet another crush." With an idle wave, Mr Amberly indicated the throng about them. "Don't know what the hostesses see in it, myself." His gaze dropped to Lucinda's face. "Reduces the opportunities to chat, don't y'know?"

Lucinda took due note of the gleam in Mr Amberly's eyes and smiled again. "Indubitably, sir."

Without further encouragement, Mr Amberly chatted on, interspersing remarks on the weather, the *ton* and events forthcoming with gently loaded comments. Lucinda found no difficulty in turning these aside. At the end of fifteen minutes, having politely declined an invitation to go driving to Richmond, she drained her glass and handed it to her escort. He placed it on a passing footman's tray and turned back to help her to her feet.

"I'm desolated, dear lady, that my projected excursion fails to tempt you. Perhaps I might yet stumble on a destination that finds greater favour in your eyes?"

Lucinda's lips twitched. She stifled a giggle. "Perhaps." Her smile felt oddly wide. She took a step, leaning heavily on Mr Amberly's arm. Suddenly, she felt distinctly flushed. Far warmer than she had before her drink.

"Ah…" Mr Amberly's eyes sharpened. "Perhaps, my dear Mrs Babbacombe, a breath of fresh air might be wise?"

Lucinda turned her head to consider the long windows—and forced herself to straighten. "I think not." She might wish to learn a few tricks but she had no intention of damaging her reputation. Turning back, she blinked as a glass appeared before her.

"I suggest you drink this, Mrs Babbacombe," came in clipped accents.

The tone suggested she had better do so if she knew what was good for her.

Obligingly, Lucinda took the glass and raised it to her lips, simultaneously raising her eyes to Harry's face. "What is it?"

"Iced water," Harry replied. He transferred his gaze to Frederick Amberly's innocent visage. "You needn't linger, Amberly. I'll escort Mrs Babbacombe back to my aunt."

Mr Amberly's brows rose, but he merely smiled gently. "If you insist, Lester." Lucinda held out her hand and he took it, bowing elegantly. "Your servant always, Mrs Babbacombe."

Lucinda bestowed a perfectly genuine smile. "Thank you for a most...delightful interlude, sir."

Mr Amberly's departing look suggested she was learning.

Then she glanced up at Harry's face. He was eyeing her narrowly.

"My dear Mrs Babbacombe, has anyone ever explained to you that remaining a virtuous widow is conditional on not encouraging rakes?"

Lucinda opened her eyes wide. "Encouraging rakes? My dear Mr Lester, whatever do you mean?"

Harry returned no answer but his lips thinned.

Lucinda grinned. "If you mean Mr Amberly," she continued ingenuously, "we were just chatting. Indeed," she went on, her smile widening again, "I have it on excellent authority that I'm *incapable* of encouraging rakes."

Harry snorted. "Rubbish." After a moment, he asked, "Who told you that?"

Lucinda's smile lit up the room. "Why, you did—don't you remember?"

Looking down into her very bright eyes, Harry inwardly groaned. And hoped Amberly hadn't noticed just how thin the lovely Mrs Babbacombe's skull was. Taking the empty glass from her fingers, he deposited it on a passing tray, then took her hand and placed it on his sleeve. "And now, Mrs Babbacombe, we are going to perambulate, very slowly,. around the room."

Bright blue eyes quizzed him. "Very slowly? Why?"

Harry gritted his teeth. "So you don't stumble." Into another rake's arms.

"Ah." Lucinda nodded sagely. A delighted, distinctly satisfied smile on her lips, she let him lead her, very slowly, into the crowd.

LUCINDA'S HEAD was throbbing when she followed Em into the carriage. Heather tumbled in after them and promptly curled up on the opposite seat.

Settling her skirts, Lucinda decided that, despite her minor discomfort, her evening had been a success.

"Damned if I know what Harry's about," Em stated as soon as Heather's breathing subsided into the soft cadence of sleep. "Have you made any headway with him yet?"

Lucinda smiled into the gloom. "Actually, I think I've at last found a chink in his armour."

Em snorted. "'Bout time. The boy's too damned stubborn for his own good."

"Indeed." Lucinda settled her head against the squabs. "However, I'm unsure how long this chink might take to develop into a breach, nor yet how potentially difficult it might prove to pursue. I don't even know whether, ultimately, it will work."

Em's next snort was one of pure frustration. "Anything's worth a try."

"Hmm." Lucinda closed her eyes. "So I think."

ON MONDAY, she danced twice with Lord Ruthven.

On Tuesday, she went driving in the Park with Mr Amberly.

On Wednesday, she strolled the length of Bond Street on Mr Satterly's arm.

By Thursday, Harry was ready to wring her pretty neck.

"I suppose this campaign has your blessing?" Harry looked down at Em, settled in majestic splendour on a *chaise* in Lady Harcourt's ballroom. He made no attempt to hide his barely restrained ire.

"Campaign?" Em opened her eyes wide. "What campaign?"

Harry gave her one of her own snorts—the one that signified incredulous disbelief. "Permit me to inform you, dear Aunt, that your protégée has developed a potentially unhealthy taste for living dangerously."

Having delivered himself of that warning, he stalked away. Not, however, to join the crowd about Lucinda Babbacombe. He propped the wall nearby, far enough away so that she wasn't likely to see him, and, eyes glittering greenly, watched her.

He was thus engaged when a hearty clap on the shoulder very nearly sent him sprawling.

"There you are, brother mine! Been looking all over. Didn't think to see you here."

Resuming his languid pose, Harry studied Jack's blue eyes; he decided his brother had yet to hear of his preoccupation. "It passes the time. But why are you back in town?"

"The arrangements, of course. All set now." Jack's blue gaze, which had been idly drifting the room, returned to Harry's face. "Next Wednesday at eleven at St. George's." Jack's slow grin surfaced. "I'm counting on your support."

Harry's lips twisted in a reluctant grin. "I'll be there."

"Good. Gerald, too—I haven't found him yet."

Harry looked over the sea of heads. "He's over there—beside the blonde ringlets."

"Ah, yes. I'll catch him in a minute."

Harry noted that his brother's eyes, glowing warmly, rarely left the slender blonde dancing with Lord Harcourt. Their host appeared captivated. "How's Pater?"

"Fine. He'll live to be eighty. Or at least long enough to see us all wed."

Harry bit back his instinctive response; Jack had heard him disparage marriage often enough. But not even his brother knew the reason for his vehemence; *that* had always remained his secret.

Following Jack's gaze, Harry studied his elder

brother's chosen bride. Sophia Winterton was a charming, utterly open and honest woman whom Harry was certain Jack could trust. Harry switched his gaze to Lucinda's dark head; his lips twisted. She might serve him some tricks, as she was presently doing, but her motives would always be transparent. She was open and direct, uncommonly so; she would never seriously lie or cheat—she simply wasn't that sort of woman.

A sudden longing welled within him, followed immediately by the old uncertainty. Harry shifted his gaze, looking once more at Jack. Once he had found his particular Golden Head, Jack had moved very swiftly to claim her. As usual, his brother had been totally confident, assured in his decision. Studying Jack's smile, Harry felt an unexpected twinge of emotion—and recognized it as jealousy.

He straightened from the wall. "Have you seen Em?"

"No." Jack glanced about. "Is she here?"

Harry strolled with him through the crowd until he could point out their aunt, then left Jack to forge his way to her. Then, shackling his temper, he let his feet have their way. They took him to Lucinda's side.

From the opposite side of the large ballroom, Earle Joliffe watched Harry take his place in the select circle about Lucinda. "Odd. Very odd," was his judgement.

"What's odd?" Beside him, Mortimer Babbacombe inserted a pudgy finger beneath his neckcloth and eased the stiff folds. "Dashed warm in here."

Joliffe's glance was contemptuous. "What's odd, my dear Mortimer, is that, if there was ever a rake guaranteed to gain the entrée into your aunt-by-marriage's boudoir, it would be Harry Lester." Joliffe glanced again across the room. "But as I read it, he's holding off. That's what's odd."

After a moment, Joliffe went on, "A disappointment,

Mortimer. But it seems he's disappointed her, too—she's looking over the field, no doubt about that." Joliffe's gaze grew distant. "Which means that all we have to do is wait for the first whispers—these things always percolate from under even the most tightly closed doors. Then we'll get a little hard proof—it shouldn't be too difficult. A few eye-witnesses of comings and goings. Then we'll have your sweet cousin—and her even sweeter legacy—in our hands."

It was a reassuring prospect. Joliffe was over his ears in debt, although he'd been careful to conceal his des-peration from Mortimer. His erstwhile friend was reduced to a shivering jelly just knowing he owed Joliffe five thou-sand pounds. The fact that Joliffe had pledged the money on, with interest, and to one against whom it was never wise to default, would turn Mortimer to a quivering wreck. And Joliffe needed Mortimer, hale and hearty, sound in mind and reputation, if he was ever to save his neck.

If he failed to help Mortimer to Heather Babbacombe's legacy, he, Earle Joliffe, man about town, would end life as a beggar in the Spitalfield slums. If he was lucky.

Joliffe's gaze rested on Lucinda's dark head. Once he had seen her, he had felt a great deal more confident. She was precisely the sort of widow who attracted the most dangerous of rakes. His hard eyes lighting, Joliffe squared his shoulders and turned to Mortimer. "Mind you, Scrugthorpe will have to forgo his revenge." Joliffe's lips lifted. "But then, nothing in life is ever quite perfect. Don't you agree, Mortimer?"

"Er—ah—yes."

With a last worried glance at his aunt-by-marriage, Mortimer reluctantly followed Joliffe into the crowd.

At that moment, the opening strains of a waltz perco-lated through the room. Lucinda heard it; her nerves, already taut, quivered. It was the third waltz of the evening, almost certainly the last. Relief had swept her when, only moments ago, Harry had, at last, materialised by her side. She had not seen him until then although she had felt his gaze. Breath bated, she had welcomed him with a soft smile. As usual, he had not joined in the conversation but had stood, his features hard, his expression remote, beside her. She had slanted a glance up at him; he had met it with an impenetrable look. Now, a smile on her lips as she graciously acknowledged the usual clamour of offers for the dance, she waited, buoyed with anticipation, to hear Harry's softly drawled invitation.

In vain.

The still silence on her left was absolute.

A deathly moment of awkward silence ensued.

Lucinda stiffened. With considerable effort, she kept her smile unaffected. She felt hollow inside but she had her pride. She forced herself to scan those desirous of partnering her. Her gaze came to rest on Lord Craven.

He had not appeared in her circle since that first evening two weeks ago. Tonight, he had been most assiduous.

Smiling brittlely, Lucinda held out her hand. "Lord Craven?"

Craven smiled, a coolly superior gesture, and bowed elegantly. "It will be a pleasure, my dear." As he straightened, he met her eyes. "For us both."

Lucinda barely heard; automatically, she inclined her head. With a gentle smile she acknowledged those she had disappointed but by not so much as a flicker of an eyelash did she acknowledge Harry. Outwardly serene, she allowed Lord Craven to lead her to the floor.

Behind her, she left an uncomfortable silence. After a moment, Lord Ruthven, cool and suddenly as remote as

Harry, with no hint of his habitual good-humoured indolence in his eyes, lifted a brow. "I do hope, Lester, that you know what you're about?"

His eyes like green ice, Harry met his lordship's challenging stare and held it, then, without a word, looked away to where Lucinda was taking the floor in Lord Craven's arms.

At first, his lordship tried to hold her too close; Lucinda frowned and he desisted. Thereafter, she paid him little heed, answering his polished sallies at random, their underlying tone barely registering. By the time the last chords sounded and his lordship whirled her to an elegant halt, her inner turmoil had calmed.

Enough to leave her prey to an enervating sense of defeat.

The emotion was not one she could approve. Straightening her shoulders and lifting her head, Lucinda reminded herself of Em's words: Harry would be no easy conquest but she had to hold firm to her plan.

So…here she was at the far end of the ballroom on Lord Craven's arm. His hand held hers trapped on his sleeve.

"Perhaps, Mrs Babbacombe, we should grasp the opportunity to become better acquainted?"

Lucinda blinked; his lordship gestured to a nearby door, set ajar.

"It's so noisy in here. Perhaps we could stroll the corridor?"

Lucinda hesitated. A corridor did not sound particularly secluded—and it was certainly crowded in the ballroom; her temples were starting to ache. She glanced up—and met Lord Craven's dark eyes and his faintly superior stare. She wasn't entirely sure of him but he was here, offering yet another potential prod to Harry's possessive nature.

She let her senses reach out, and felt the heat of Harry's gaze. He was watching over her; she cast a glance about but, in the dense crowd, could not find him.

Turning back, she met his lordship's gaze. Lucinda drew in a breath. She had told Em she was game. "Perhaps just a quick turn about the corridor, my lord."

She was quite certain her strategy was sound.

Unfortunately, this time, she had chosen the wrong rake.

Unlike Lord Ruthven, Mr Amberly and Mr Satterly, Lord Craven was not a familiar of Harry's and therefore lacked their insights into the game she was playing. They, one and all, had determined to assist her in whatever way they could, intrigued by the prospect of removing Harry from their paths. Lord Craven, however, had concluded that her flittering progress from rake to rake was merely a reflection of dissatisfaction with the distractions offered. Having seen how far the gentle touch had got his peers, he had determined on a more forceful approach.

With brisk efficiency, he whisked Lucinda through the doorway.

On the other side of the room, Harry swore, startling two dowagers gracing a nearby *chaise*. He wasted no time on apologies or speculation but started into the crowd. Aware of Craven's reputation, he had kept a close watch on his lordship and his burden but had momentarily lost them at the end of the dance, sighting them again just before Lucinda cast a glance about—then allowed Craven to lead her from the room. Harry knew very well what that glance had signified. The damned woman had been looking for him—to him—for rescue.

This time, she might need it.

The crowd, dispersing after the dance, milled aimlessly. Harry had to fight an impulse to push people out of his way. He forced himself to rein in his strides; he didn't want to focus any attention on his goal.

He finally broke free of the clinging crowd and gained the garden corridor. He didn't pause but went straight to its end where a door gave onto the terrace. Lady Harcourt had frequently bemoaned the fact that her ballroom did not open onto terrace and gardens, as was the fashionable norm. Silently, Harry stepped onto the flagstones. The terrace was deserted. His features hardening, he reined in his building rage and, hands on hips, scanned the deeply shadowed garden.

Muffled sounds drifted to his ears.

He was running when he rounded the corner of the terrace.

Craven had Lucinda backed against the wall and was trying to kiss her. She had ducked her head, frustrating his lordship's intent; her small hands on his chest, she was trying to push him away, incoherent in her distress.

Harry felt his rage claim him.

"Craven?"

The single word had Craven lifting his head and looking wildly about just as Harry caught his shoulder, spinning him into a punishing left cross that lifted his lordship from his feet and left him sprawled in an untidy heap against the stone balustrade.

Lucinda, her hand at her breast, swallowed a sob—and flung herself into Harry's arms. They closed about her; he hugged her fiercely; Lucinda felt his lips on her hair. His body was hard, rigid; she sensed the fury that possessed him. Then he shifted her to his side, keeping her within the protection of one arm. Her cheek against his coat, Lucinda glanced at Lord Craven.

Somewhat shakily, his lordship clambered to his feet. He worked his jaw, then, blinking, warily eyed Harry. When Harry made no move, Craven hesitated, then re-settled his coat and straightened his cravat. His gaze shifted to Lucinda, then returned to Harry's face. His features studiously impassive, he raised his brows. "I appear to have misread the situation." He bowed to Lucinda. "My most humble apologies, Mrs Babbacombe—I pray you'll accept them."

Lucinda ducked her head, then hid her burning cheeks in Harry's coat.

Lord Craven's gaze returned to Harry's face. Something not at all civilised stared back at him. "Lester." With a curt nod, his lordship strolled carefully past and disappeared around the corner.

Leaving silence to enfold the two figures on the terrace.

Harry held himself rigid, every muscle clenched, his emotions warring within him. He could feel Lucinda trembling; the need to comfort her welled strong. He closed his eyes, willing himself to resistance, to impassivity. Every impulse he possessed impelled him to take her into his arms, to kiss her, possess her—to put an end to her silly game. A primitive male desire to brand her inescapably his rocked him to his core. Equally strong was his rage, his dislike of being so manipulated, so exposed by his own feelings, so vulnerable to hers.

Mentally cursing her for being the catalyst of such a scene, Harry struggled to suppress passions already too long denied.

The moment stretched, the tension palpable.

Trapped within it, Lucinda couldn't breathe; she couldn't move. The arm about her didn't tighten, but it felt like iron, inflexible, unyielding. Then Harry's chest swelled; he drew in an unsteady breath.

"Are you all right?"

His deep voice was flat, devoid of emotion. Lucinda forced herself to nod, then, drawing on her courage, stepped back. His arm fell from her. She drew in a deep breath and glanced up; one look at his face, at his utterly blank expression, was enough. His eyes showed evidence of some turbulent emotion, glittering in the green; what, she couldn't tell but she sensed his accusation.

Her breath tangling in her throat, she glanced away. His arm appeared before her.

"Come. You must return to the ballroom."

His face like stone, a graven façade masking turbulent feelings, Harry braced himself against the moment when her fingers settled on his sleeve.

Through the simple contact, Lucinda could sense his simmering anger, and the control that left his muscles twitching, shifting restlessly beneath her hand; for an instant, her feelings threatened to overwhelm her. She wanted him to comfort her, yearned to feel his arms about her once again. But she knew he was right—she had to reappear in the ballroom soon. Dragging in a shaking breath, she lifted her head. With the slightest of nods, she allowed him to lead her back, into the cacophany of conversation and laughter, back to the bright lights and bright smiles.

Her own smile appropriately bright if brittle, she gracefully inclined her head as, with a curt nod, Harry deposited her at the end of Em's *chaise*. He immediately turned on his heel; Lucinda watched him stride away, into the crowd.

Chapter Eight

"Good afternoon, Fergus. Is Mrs Babbacombe in?"

Harry handed his gloves and cane to his aunt's butler. His expression stonily impassive, he glanced towards the stairs.

"Mrs Babbacombe is in the upstairs parlour, sir—she uses it as her office. Her ladyship's laid down upon her bed. These late nights are greatly tiring at her age."

"I dare say." With decisive stride, Harry headed for the stairs. "I won't disturb her. You needn't announce me." His lips thinned. "I'm quite sure Mrs Babbacombe is expecting me."

"Very good, sir."

The upstairs parlour was a small room at the back of the house. Tall windows looked onto the garden at the rear; two armchairs and a *chaise* plus an assortment of side-tables graced the floral rug by the fireplace while a large daybed filled the space before the windows. An escritoire stood against one wall; Lucinda, a vision in soft blue muslin, was seated before it, pen in hand, when Harry opened the door.

She glanced around, an abstracted smile on her lips—and froze. Her smile faded, replaced by a polite mask.

Harry's expression hardened. He stepped over the threshold and closed the door.

Lucinda rose. "I didn't hear you announced."

"Probably because I wasn't." Harry paused, his hand on the doorknob, and studied her haughty expression. She was going to hear him out, come what may; he wasn't in the mood to tolerate interruptions. His fingers closed about the key; the lock slid noiselessly into place. "This isn't a social call."

"Indeed?" One brow rising, Lucinda lifted her chin. "To what, then, do I owe this honour, sir?"

Harry's smile was a warning. "Lord Craven."

As he stalked towards her, his eyes boring into hers, Lucinda had to quell a weak impulse to retreat behind her chair.

"I've come to demand an assurance from you, Mrs Babbacombe, that you will, as of this moment, cease and desist in this little game of yours."

Lucinda stiffened. "I beg your pardon?"

"As well you might," Harry growled, coming to a halt directly before her, his eyes, glittering green, holding hers. "That little scene on Lady Harcourt's terrace was entirely your own fault. This ridiculous experiment of yours, this habit you've formed of encouraging rakes, has to stop."

Lucinda summoned a haughty glance. "I don't know what you mean. I'm merely doing what many ladies, situated similarly, would do—looking for congenial company."

"Congenial?" Harry lifted a supercilious brow. "I would have thought last night would have been sufficient demonstration of how 'congenial' the company of rakes can be."

Lucinda felt a blush tinge her cheeks. She shrugged and swung aside, stepping away from the desk. "Lord Craven was clearly a mistake." She glanced back to add, "And I have to thank you most sincerely for your aid." Deliberately, she met Harry's gaze, then calmly turned and drifted towards the windows. "But I really must insist, Mr Lester, that my life is my own to live as I please. It's no business of yours should I choose to develop a…" Lucinda gestured vaguely "…a relationship with Lord Craven or anyone else."

A tense silence greeted her statement. Lucinda paused, fingers lightly trailing the high back of the daybed, her gaze fixed, unseeing, on the prospect beyond the windows.

Behind her, Harry closed his eyes. Fists clenched, his jaw rigid, he fought to shackle his response to what he knew to be deliberate provocation, to suppress the clamorous impulses her words had evoked. Behind his lids, a fleeting image took shape—of her, struggling in Lord Craven's arms. Abruptly, Harry opened his eyes.

"My dear Mrs Babbacombe." He bit the words out as he stalked after her. "It's clearly time I took a hand in your education. No rake in his right mind is interested in a relationship—other than of an extremely limited sort."

Lucinda glanced over her shoulder and saw him coming. She turned to meet him—and abruptly found herself backed against the wall.

Harry's eyes trapped hers. "Do you know what we are interested in?"

Lucinda took in his predatory smile, his glittering eyes, heard the undercurrent in his silky voice. Deliberately, she tilted her chin. "I'm not a complete innocent."

Even as the lie left her lips, her breathing seized. Harry moved closer, crowding her against the wall, stopping only when she could retreat no further, her soft skirts caressing his thighs, brushing his boots.

His lips, so fascinating, were very close. As Lucinda watched, they twisted.

"Perhaps not. But when it comes to the likes of Craven and the others—or me—you're hardly experienced, my dear."

Her expression intransigent, Lucinda met his gaze. "I'm more than capable of holding my own."

His eyes flared. "Are you?"

Harry felt barely civilised. She kept prodding the demon within him; he felt barely sane. "Shall we put that to the test?"

He framed her face with his hands and deliberately moved one inch nearer, pressing her against the wall. He felt her draw in a quick breath; a quiver shivered through her. "Shall I show you what we *are* interested in, Lucinda?" He tilted her face to his. "Shall I show you what's on our—" his lips twisted in self-mockery "—*my* mind every time I look at you? Waltz with you?"

Lucinda didn't answer. Eyes wide, she stared into his, her breathing shallow and rapid, her pulse skittering wildly. His brows rose mockingly, inviting her comment; his eyes burned. Then his gaze dropped from hers; Lucinda watched as he focused on her lips. She couldn't suppress the impulse to run the tip of her tongue over the smooth curves.

She felt the shudder that rippled through him, heard the groan he tried to suppress.

Then his head swooped and his lips found hers.

It was the caress she had longed for, planned for, plotted to attain—yet it was like nothing she had dreamed. His lips were hard, forceful, commanding. They captured hers, then tortured them with subtle pleasures, ravishing her senses until she submitted. The kiss caught her up, conquered and willing, and skilfully swept her free of reality, into a place where only his will prevailed. He demanded—she surrendered. Completely.

When he asked, she gave, when he wanted more, she unhesitatingly yielded. She sensed his need—and wanted, deeply desired, his satisfaction. She kissed him back, thrilled to feel the surge of unleashed passion that answered her. The kiss deepened, then deepened again, until she could sense nothing beyond it and the wild longing that swelled within her.

What deep-seated alarm it was that hauled Harry to his senses he did not know. Perhaps the urgent clamouring of rampant desires and the consequent need to arrange their fulfilment? Whatever it was, he suddenly realised the danger. It took every last ounce of his strength to draw back.

When he lifted his head, he was shaking.

Searching for sanity, he stared at her face—her lids slowly rose, revealing eyes so blue, so soft, so glowing with a siren's allure that he couldn't breathe. Her lips, kiss-bruised, gleaming red, ripe and, as he could now testify, so very sweet, drew his gaze. He felt himself falling under her spell again, leaning closer, his lips hungry for hers.

He dragged in a painful breath—and lifted his gaze to her eyes.

Only to see, in the soft blue depths, an awakening intelligence, superseded by a very feminine consideration.

The sight shook him to the core.

Her gaze dropped to his lips.

Harry shuddered; fleetingly, he closed his eyes. "Don't."

It was the plea of a defeated man.

Lucinda heard and understood. But if she didn't press

her advantage now, she would lose it. Em had said he'd be thrilled—but he was so stubborn, if she didn't play that card now, he might not give her another chance.

She lifted her gaze to his. Slowly, she drew her hands from between them and pushed them up over his shoulders. She saw the consternation that filled his eyes; his muscles were locked tight, paralysed. He was unable to deny her.

Harry knew it; restraining his all-but-overpowering desire took all his strength. He couldn't move, could only watch his fate draw near as her arms tightened about his neck and she stretched upwards against him.

When her lips were an inch from his, she raised her eyes and met his tortured gaze. Then her lids fell and she pressed her lips to his.

His resistance lasted all of two heartbeats, as long as it took for desire, shackled, suppressed for so long it had grown to ungovernable proportions, to sear through him, cindering every last one of his good intentions, his rational reasons, his logical excuses.

With a groan that was ripped from deep within him, he drew her into his arms and engulfed her in his embrace.

With all restraint shattered, he kissed her deeply, caressed her, let his desire ignite and set fire to them both. She kissed him back, her hands clinging, her body wantonly enticing.

Desire rose between them, wild and strong; Lucinda abandoned herself to it, to the deep surge of their passions, fervently hoping to thus disguise any false move, any too-tentative response. If he sensed her innocence, all would come to nought—of that she was sure.

His caresses were magic, the response they drew so shattering she would be shocked—if she let herself think. Luckily, coherent thought was beyond her, blocked out by heated clouds of desire. Her senses whirled. His hands on her breasts provoked an urgent, building compulsion unlike any she'd ever experienced.

When one hand dropped low and he drew her hips hard against him, moulding her to him, flagrantly demonstrating his desire, Lucinda moaned softly and pressed closer.

Burgeoning passion left them frantic, hungry for each other, so desperate Harry's head was spinning as he backed her to the daybed. He refocused his will on salvaging some modicum of his customary expertise, bringing it to bear as he divested her of her gown and petticoats, brushing her fluttering hands aside, content enough that she was too befuddled to sensibly assist. Desire urged them on, riding them both; clad only in her chemise, Lucinda flung his cravat to the floor, then fell on the buttons of his shirt with a singlemindedness as complete as his. She seemed fascinated by his chest; he had to pick her up and put her on the daybed so he could sit and tug off his boots.

Lucinda was fascinated—by him, by the sense of rightness that gripped her, by the warm desire flowing in her veins. She felt free, unrestrained by any tenets of modesty or decorum, sure that this was how it should be. He stripped and turned towards her; she wrapped her arms about him, revelling in the feel of his warm skin, burning to her touch. Their lips met; urgency welled, heating her through and through. He drew off her chemise; as their bodies met, she shivered and closed her eyes. They kissed deeply, then Harry pressed her back against the soft cushions. Caught up in the spring tide of their loving, Lucinda lay back and drew him to her.

He lay beside her and loved her but their spiralling need soon spelled an end to such play. Eyes closed, Lucinda knew nothing beyond a deep and aching emptiness, the overwhelming need he had brought to life and only he could assuage. Relief and expectation flooded her when he shifted and his weight pinned her to the bed. She tried to draw breath, to steel herself; his hand slipped beneath her hips and steadied her—with one smooth flexion of his powerful body he joined them.

Her soft gasp echoed in the room. Neither of them moved, both stunned to stillness.

Slowly, his heart thudding in his ears, Harry raised his head and looked down at her face. Her eyes were shut, a frown tangling her brows, her lower lip caught between her teeth. Even as he watched, she relaxed a little beneath him, her features easing.

He waited for his emotions to catch up with the facts. He expected to feel angry, tricked, deceived.

Instead, a shattering feeling of possessiveness, untouched by lust, driven by some far more powerful emotion, welled within him, thrusting out all regrets. The sensation grew, joyously swelling, strong and sure.

Harry didn't question it—or how it made him feel.

Lowering his head, he brushed her lips with his. "Lucinda?"

She snatched in a breath then her lips clung to his. Her fingers fluttered against his jaw.

Harry brought up a hand to gently smooth away clinging tendrils of her hair from her face.

Then, with infinite tenderness, he taught her how to love.

SOME CONSIDERABLE TIME later, when Lucinda again made contact with reality, she discovered herself wrapped in Harry's arms, her back against his chest as he half-sat, propped against the raised head of the daybed. She sighed long and lingeringly, the glory dimming yet still glowing within her.

Harry bent over her; she felt his lips at her temple.

"Tell me of your marriage."

Lucinda's brows half-rose. With one fingertip, she drew whorls in the hair on his forearm. "To understand, you need to realise that I was orphaned at fourteen. Both my parents had been disowned by their families." Using the minimum of words, she explained her past history, one hand moving slowly back and forth along Harry's arm, snug about her, all the while. "So, you see, my marriage was never consummated. Charles and I were close, but he didn't love me in that way."

Harry kept his doubts to himself, rendering silent thanks to Charles Babbacombe for keeping her safe, for loving her enough to leave her untouched. His lips in her hair, the subtle scent of her filling him, Harry made a silent vow to her late husband's shade that, as the recipient of his legacy, he would keep her safe for evermore.

"You'll have to marry me." He spoke the words as they occurred to him, thinking aloud.

Lucinda blinked. The joy that had filled her faded. After a quiet moment, she asked, "*Have* to marry you?"

She felt Harry straighten as he looked down at her.

"You were a virgin. I'm a gentleman. The prescribed outcome of our recent activity is a wedding."

His words were definite, his accents clipped. Lucinda closed her eyes; she didn't want to believe her ears. The last vestige of lingering afterglow evaporated, the promise of the long, inexpressibly tender moments they had shared vanished.

Lucinda stifled a sigh; her lips firmed into a determined line. Opening her eyes, she turned in Harry's arms and looked him straight in the eye. "You want to marry me because I was a virgin—is that correct?"

Harry frowned. "It's what's expected."

"But is it what you want?"

"It doesn't matter what I want," Harry growled, his eyes narrowing. "The matter, thank heaven, is simple enough. Society has rules—we'll follow them—to the general satisfaction of all concerned."

For a long moment, Lucinda studied him, her thoughts chaotic. It was an offer—of sorts—from the man she wanted.

But it wasn't good enough. She didn't just want him to marry her.

"No."

Stunned, Harry watched as she scrambled out of his arms and off the daybed. She found her chemise and pulled it on.

He sat up. "What do you mean—'No'?"

"No—I will not marry you." Lucinda struggled into her petticoats.

Harry stared at her. "Why not, for heaven's sake?" She started towards her gown and nearly tripped over his breeches. He heard a stifled curse as she bent to untangle her feet. Then she flung the breeches at him and continued towards her gown.

With a muttered curse of his own, Harry grabbed the breeches and hauled them on, then pulled on his boots. He stood and stalked over to where Lucinda was pushing her arms through the sleeves of her gown.

Hands on hips, he towered over her. "Damn it—I seduced you! You *have* to marry me."

Eyes ablaze, Lucinda shot him a furious glance. "*I* seduced *you*, if you recall. And I most certainly do not '*have to marry you*'!"

"What about your reputation?"

"What of it?" Lucinda tugged her gown up over her shoulders. Turning to face him, she jabbed a finger in his chest. "No one would ever believe that *Mrs* Lucinda Bab-bacombe, *widow,* had been a virgin until you came along. You've got no lever to use against me."

Looking up, she met his eyes.

And abruptly changed tack. "Besides," she said, looking down to do up the buttons of her bodice, "I'm sure it's not accepted practice for rakes to offer marriage to every woman they seduce."

Harry ground his teeth. "Lucinda…"

"And I have *not* made you free of my name!" Lucinda glared at him. She wouldn't let him use it—he'd whispered it, coupled with every conceivable endearment, as he'd made love to her.

Love—the emotion she knew he felt for her but was determined to deny.

It wasn't good enough—it would *never* be good enough.

She whirled on her heel and marched to the door.

Harry swore. Buttoning his shirt, he started after her. "This is crazy! I've offered for you, you demented woman! It's what you've been after ever since I hauled you out of that damned carriage!"

Lucinda had reached the door. She swung around. "If you're so adept at reading my mind, then you'll understand perfectly why I'm throwing you out!"

She gripped the doorknob, turned it and yanked. Nothing happened. She stared at the door. "Where's the key?"

Thoroughly distracted, Harry automatically reached into his breeches pocket. "Here."

Lucinda blinked, then grabbed the key and rattled it into the keyhole.

Harry watched her in disbelief. "Damn it—I've given you a proposal—what more do you want?"

Her hand on the knob, Lucinda drew herself up and

turned to face him. "I *don't* want to be offered for because of some social technicality. I don't want to be rescued, or…or protected or married out of pity! What I *want*—" Abruptly, she halted and dragged in a deep breath. Then she lifted her eyes to his and deliberately stated, "What I want is to be married for love."

Harry stiffened. His face hardened. "Love is not considered an important element for marriage within our class."

Lucinda pressed her lips together, then succinctly stated, "Balderdash." She flung open the door.

"You don't know what you're talking about!" Harry ran his fingers through his hair.

"I know *very well* what I'm talking about," Lucinda averred. None better—she loved him with all her heart and soul. Glancing about, she spied his coat and cravat by the daybed. She flew across the room and pounced on them.

Harry turned to face her, blocking the doorway as she bustled back.

"There." Lucinda crammed the expensive coat and cravat into his arms. "Now get out!"

Harry drew in a steadying breath. "Lucinda—"

"*Out!*"

Without warning, Lucinda pushed hard in the middle of his chest. Harry staggered back, over the threshold.

Lucinda grabbed the door. "Goodbye, Mr Lester! Rest assured I'll bear your instructions as to the interests of your set in mind in the coming weeks!"

With that, she slammed the door and locked it.

The fury that had sustained her abruptly drained. Slumping back against the door, she covered her face with her hands.

Harry glared at the white-painted panels. He considered forcing his way back in—then he heard a stifled sob.

His heart wrenched—racked by frustration, he stuffed it back behind his inner door and slammed that shut as well. His lips set in a grim line, he turned on his heel and marched down the corridor. He caught sight of himself in a mirror. Abruptly, he halted and shrugged on his coat, then draped the creased cravat about his throat.

It took him three tries before he could achieve anything remotely resembling decency. With a snort, he turned and headed for the stairs.

He had made an offer. She had refused.

The damned woman could go to hell by herself.

He was finished with being her protector.

He was finished with her.

DISCOVERED, two hours later, with dark shadows under swollen red eyes, Lucinda could hardly deny Em her confidence.

Her hostess was stunned. "I can't understand it. What the devil's wrong with him?"

Lucinda sniffed and dabbed her eyes with a lace-edged square. "I don't know." She felt like wailing. Her lips set in a mulish line. "But I *won't* have it."

"Quite right, too!" Em snorted. "Don't worry—he'll come about. Probably just took him by surprise."

Lucinda considered, then wearily shrugged.

"Seems to me that there must be something we don't know," Em mused. "Known him all his life—he's always the predictable one—always good reasons and logical arguments behind his actions—he's not an impulsive man." She grinned, her gaze distant. "Quite the opposite—Jack's impulsive. Harry's cautious." A frown slowly settled over her face. "Has been for a long time, now I think of it."

Lucinda waited, hoping for some reassuring insight, but her hostess remained sunk in thought.

Then Em snorted and shook herself, her stiff bombazine rustling. "Whatever it is, he'll just have to come to terms with it and offer for you properly."

Lucinda swallowed and nodded. "Properly"—by which she meant he would have to tell her he loved her. After today, and all they had shared, she would settle for nothing less.

THAT EVENING, Em took charge and insisted Lucinda remain at home, there to have an early night and recover her composure and her looks.

"The last thing you want to do is show him or the *ton* a face like that."

Having thus overcome Lucinda's half-hearted resistance, Em left the redoubtable Agatha ministering with cold cucumber compresses and, with the effervescent Heather under her wing, strode forth to do battle at Lady Caldecott's ball.

She spied Harry in the throng, but was not the least surprised when her errant nephew showed no disposition to come within firing range. But it was not him she had come to see.

"Indisposed?" Lord Ruthven's cool grey eyes reflected honest concern. "I do hope it's nothing serious?"

Well—it is and it isn't." Em lifted a brow at him. "You're one who's far more awake than you appear, so I dare say you've noticed that she's been endeavouring to bring a certain recalcitrant to heel. Never an easy task, of course. A difficult road to travel—prone to find potholes in one's path. She's a bit moped at present." Em paused to glance again at his lordship. "Dare say, when she reappears tomorrow, she could do with a little encouragement, don't y'know?"

Lord Ruthven studied Harry's aunt with wary fascination. "Ah—indeed." After a moment, in which he recalled the numerous times Harry had cut him out when they'd both had the same ladybird in their sights, he said, "Pray convey my most earnest wishes for a speedy recovery to Mrs Babbacombe. I will, of course, be delighted to welcome her back to our midst—I look forward to her return with uncommon anticipation."

Em grinned. "Dare say you do."

With a regal wave, she dismissed him. Lord Ruthven bowed gracefully and withdrew.

Fifteen minutes later, Mr Amberly stopped by her *chaise.* The instant the formalities were over, he asked, "Wondered if you'd be so good as to convey my regards to Mrs Babbacombe? Understand she's under the weather tonight. She's a distraction sorely missed by us poor bachelors. Wanted to assure her of my continuing support when she once again graces our halls."

Em smiled her approval. "I'll make certain to pass your kind words on, sir."

Mr Amberly bowed and drifted away.

To Em's satisfaction, her evening was punctuated by a succession of similar encounters as, one after another, Harry's close friends stopped by to pledge their aid in furthering Lucinda's cause.

Chapter Nine

Lady Mott's drum bade fair to being the most horrendous crush of the Season. Or so Lucinda thought as she inched through the crowd on Lord Sommerville's arm. About them, the *ton* milled *en masse;* it was difficult to see more than five feet in any direction.

"Phew!" Lord Sommerville threw her an apologetic glance. "Pity the dance landed us so far from your companions. Normally enjoy wandering the room—but not like this."

"Indeed." Lucinda tried to keep her smile bright, no mean effort when she felt like wilting. The heat was rising about them; bodies hemmed them in. "I must confess that I've yet to divine why *such* a crowd, beyond the bounds of sense, should be considered so desirable."

Lord Sommerville nodded sagely.

Lucinda hid a weak grin. His lordship was close to her own age, yet she felt immeasurably older. He was still striving for a position amongst the rakes of the *ton;* in her opinion, he had some developing yet to do before he would rival some she could name.

Harry's image rose in her mind; with an effort, she banished it. There was no point in bemoaning what was well and truly spilt milk.

Ever since she had flung his offer in his teeth, she'd been plagued by doubts—doubts she did not wish to countenance. She hadn't seen him since; he had not returned to go down on bended knee. Presumably, he had yet to see the error of his ways. Or else, despite her firm conviction—and what did she know of the matter, after all?— he did not truly love her.

She kept telling herself that if that was so, then it was all for the best—when he had forced her to put her thoughts into words, she had realised just how much a marriage built on love now meant to her. She had everything else she could want of life—except that—a loving husband with whom she could build a future. And what use was all the rest without that?

She'd been right—but her heart refused to lift, hanging like a leaden weight in her breast.

Lord Sommerville craned his neck to peer forward. "Looks like the crowd thins just ahead."

Her smile growing weaker, Lucinda nodded. The couple immediately in front of them paused to acknowledge an introduction. Trapped, they halted. Lucinda glanced to her left—directly at a gold pin in the shape of an acorn, nestling in the snowy folds of a cravat tied with mathematical precision. She knew that pin—she had pulled it free a little over twenty-four hours before.

A vice tightened about Lucinda's chest. She looked up.

Clear green eyes, the colour of a storm-tossed sea, met hers. Her heart in her mouth, Lucinda searched but could read nothing in his shadowed gaze. His expression was hard, impassive, the planes of his face an impenetrable mask. Defeated there, Lucinda looked at his lips.

Only to see them firm, thinning into a severe line.

Puzzled, she glanced up—and caught a fleeting glimpse of uncertainty in his eyes. She sensed his hesitation.

Five feet and two pairs of shoulders separated them.

His eyes returned to hers; their gazes locked. He shifted, his lips twisted, quirking up at the ends.

"Ah—there we are. At last!" Lord Sommerville turned and bowed, gesturing before them.

Distracted, Lucinda looked ahead and discovered the crowd had eased, leaving a path forward. "Ah—yes."

She glanced at Harry.

Only to see him turn aside to greet an imposing matron with a simpering young girl in tow. He acknowledged the introduction to the chit with a restrained bow.

Battling the constriction in her chest, Lucinda drew in a deep breath and turned away, forcing herself to listen to Lord Sommerville's patter with some semblance of interest.

From the corner of his eye, Harry watched her move away; he clung to the sight of her until she was swallowed up by the crowd. Only then did he give his attention to Lady Argyle.

"Just a *little* soirée—a select few only." Lady Argyle beamed. "So you younger folk can chat and get to know each other better. Not something one can readily accomplish in this crowd, is it?"

Her ladyship's protruberant eyes invited him to agree. Harry was far too old a hand to fall for the trick. His expression coldly impassive, he looked down on her from a very great distance. "I'm afraid, Lady Argyle, that I'm otherwise engaged. Indeed," he continued, languid boredom threatening, "I don't look to spend much time in the ballrooms this Season." He caught her ladyship's suspicious eye. "Pressing matters elsewhere," he murmured. With a smooth bow, he took advantage of a break in the surrounding throng to slip away, leaving Lady Argyle unsure just what, exactly, he had been telling her.

Once free, Harry hesitated, then followed in Lucinda's wake. His declaration that he was finished with her rang mockingly in his ears; he shut off the sound. After trying a number of tacks, he finally located her, at the centre of her inevitable court. Ruthven was there, as were Amberly and Satterly. Harry's eyes narrowed.

Amberly was at Lucinda's side, chatting with his usual facility; he gestured hugely and everyone laughed, Lucinda included. Then it was Satterly's turn; Hugo leaned forward and smiled, clearly retelling some *on dit* or recounting some incident. Ruthven, on Lucinda's other side, glanced down at her. He was watching her face closely. Harry's lips compressed.

Concealed by the crowd, he focused on Lucinda. She smiled at Satterly's tale yet the gesture lacked the warmth Harry knew it could hold. The conversation became general; she laughed and returned some comment but without the assured gaiety she normally displayed. The dangerous tension that had gripped him eased.

She was subdued—very possibly unhappy beneath her calm veneer.

Guilt welled; ruthlessly, Harry stifled it. Serve the damned woman right—he'd offered; she'd refused.

He'd escaped a dangerous situation. Logic suggested he remove himself from further temptation. Harry hesitated, and saw Ruthven offer Lucinda his arm.

"Might I suggest a short stroll about the terrace, m'dear?" Concerned by the wan, haunted look in Lucinda's eyes, Ruthven could think of nothing else that might bring her some ease. Her gaze, dark and shadowed, constantly roamed the crowd. "Some fresh air will help you forget this stuffy ballroom."

Lucinda smiled, aware her brightness had dimmed. "Indeed," she said, glancing around. "The atmosphere is too close for my comfort, but..." She hesitated, then glanced up at his lordship. "I'm really not sure..."

She let the words trail away, unable to put her uncertainty into words.

"Oh—don't worry about that." Mr Amberly waved expansively. "Tell you what—we'll all go." He smiled encouragingly at Lucinda. "Nothing *anyone* could make of that, what?"

Lucinda blinked—and glanced at Lord Ruthven and Mr Satterly.

"Capital notion, Amberly." His lordship again offered her his arm, this time with a gallant flourish.

"Just the ticket." Mr Satterly nodded and stepped back, waving her on.

Lucinda blinked again. Then, realising they were all watching her, waiting, genuine thoughtfulness their only motivation, she smiled gratefully, and even more gratefully relaxed. "Thank you, gentlemen, that would indeed be most kind of you."

"Only too happy," came from Mr Satterly.

"A pleasure, m'dear," from Mr Amberly.

Lucinda glanced up and found Lord Ruthven's eyes ruefully twinkling. His lips twisted in a wry smile.

"Nothing too good for a friend, you know."

More reassured than she had been all evening, Lucinda smiled back.

From the depths of the crowd, Harry watched the little cavalcade head off, Ruthven steering Lucinda in Satterly and Amberly's wake. As the realisation that Ruthven's goal was one of the long windows opening onto the terrace crystallised in his brain, tension gripped Harry anew. He took a step forward—then stopped short.

She was no longer any business of his.

Satterly and Amberly stood aside for Lucinda and Ruthven to pass through the window—then followed. Harry blinked. For an instant, he stared, eyes slowly narrowing, at the gently billowing drapes through which all four had disappeared.

Then his lips curved cynically. With such cavaliers, the lovely Mrs Babbacombe had no need of further protection.

Somewhat stiffly, he turned on his heel and headed for the cardroom.

"AURELIA WILCOX ALWAYS did give the best parties." Em rustled her silks in the dark of the carriage as it rolled down Highgate Hill. After a moment, she diffidently added, "Didn't see Harry tonight."

"He wasn't there." Lucinda heard the weariness in her voice and was glad Heather, curled on the seat opposite, wasn't awake to hear it. Her stepdaughter was thoroughly enjoying her taste of the *ton* in a wholly innocuous, innocent way. If it hadn't been for Heather's undoubted enjoyment, she would be seriously considering removing from the capital, regardless of the fact that such a move would clearly signal defeat.

She felt defeated. Tuesday night had just come and gone, with no sign of Harry. She hadn't seen him since Lady Mott's ball on Saturday evening; since then, he had not even been present at the balls and parties they had attended. His presence was not something she would miss—his gaze had always triggered a certain sensation, quite unique, within her.

A sensation she now missed—dreadfully.

"Perhaps he's already left London?" Her tone was un-inflected, yet the words embodied her deepest fear. She had played her cards and lost.

"No." Em stirred on the seat beside her. "Fergus mentioned that Dawlish is still haunting the kitchens." Softly, Em snorted. "The Almighty only knows to what purpose."

After a moment, Em went on, her voice low, "It was never going to be easy, y'know. He's as stubborn as a mule—most men are over matters like this. You have to give him time to get used to the idea—to let his resistance wear itself out. He'll come around in the end—just wait and see."

Wait and see. As the carriage rattled on over the cobbles, Lucinda laid her head back against the squabs and reviewed her recent actions. No matter how she tried, she could not regret any of them—faced with the same situation, she would act as she had again. But neither dwelling on the past—nor idling through the present—was advancing her cause. But she could hardly seduce Harry again if he didn't come near her.

Worse—he was no longer concerned for her safety, even though Lord Ruthven, Mr Amberly and Mr Satterly had been particularly assiduous in their attentions. Indeed, if it hadn't been for their enthusiastic if totally platonic support, she doubted she could have held her head up over these past nights. The balls, which she had initially found fascinating, had lost their attraction. The dances were boring, the waltzes trials. As for the promenading, the incessant visiting, the constant appearances demanded by the *ton*, she increasingly saw them as a waste of time; her business persona re-emerging, no doubt. If she told true, she now viewed the time she spent in *ton*nish endeavours as a very poor investment.

It was unlikely to render her the return she sought.

Unfortunately, she had no idea what new tack to take, how to realign her strategies to bring her goal back in sight.

Her goal, in this case unfortunately not inanimate, had taken matters into his own hands—which left her with nothing to do but wait—a scenario she found intensely irksome.

Lucinda stifled a snort—Em's habit was catching.

But Em was very likely right—again. She would have to wait—she had played her cards.

It was Harry's turn now.

SOME TWELVE HOURS LATER, Harry lounged in his customary pose, propping the wall in the long ballroom of the Webb residence in Mount Street, idly watching the crowd gathered to celebrate his brother's nuptials. His father, of course, was there, sitting in his chair at the other end of the room. Beside him sat Em, resplendent in deep blue silk. Her principal houseguest had not attended.

Not, of course, that he needed to worry his head over where she was or what she was doing. Not with the way his friends were behaving. Over the past five days, they had taken to squiring her everywhere while coolly regarding him with a pointedly critical air. Ruthven, indeed, with a sublime disregard for the cryptic, had felt moved to tell him he was "being a damned fool". Ruthven—who was six months older than Harry, but had yet to show the slightest sign of bestirring himself enough to find a wife. Ruthven—who had a title to keep in the family. Disgusted, Harry had snorted—and informed his erstwhile friend that if he was so enamoured of the lady then *he* could pay her price.

Ruthven had blinked, then had looked a trifle abashed.

Eyes hooded, Harry took a soothing sip of brandy, the glass cradled in one hand.

Only to be thumped on the shoulder at the most critical moment.

Harry choked. Recovering his breath, he swung to face his assailant. "Damn it—I hope your wife aims to teach you some manners!"

Jack laughed. "Probably—but none, I suspect, that will apply to you." Deep blue eyes twinkling, he raised his brows at Harry. "She thinks you're dangerous. In severe need of the right woman to blunt your lethal edge."

"Indeed?" Harry replied, repressively chill. He took another sip of his brandy and looked away.

Jack was undeterred. "As I live and breathe," he affirmed. "But she's of the opinion it'll take a brave woman—a Boadicea, I gather—to successfully take you on."

Harry rolled his eyes—but couldn't stop his mind supplying an image of Lucinda, half-naked, bedaubed with blue paint, driving a chariot. "Your wife is clearly blessed with a typically extravagant feminine imagination."

Jack chuckled. "I'll let you know after the honeymoon. We're off to Rawling's Cottage for a week. Nice and quiet up in Leicestershire just now."

Harry shook his head, a half-smile on his lips as he took in his brother's bright eyes. "Just don't lose anything vital—like your wits."

Jack laughed. "I think I'll manage—just." His slow grin surfaced as his gaze found his wife at the centre of a crowd near the door. He turned to Harry and put out his hand. "Wish me luck?"

Harry met his gaze. He straightened—and took Jack's hand. "You know I do. And your Golden Head as well."

Jack grinned. "I'll tell her." Poised to leave, Jack slid Harry a sidelong glance. "Take care yourself." With a last nod, he headed for his future.

Leaving Harry to wonder just how much of his current predicament showed in his face.

Fifteen minutes later, at the top of the steps outside the Webbs' house, he watched as the carriage carrying Jack and his bride rounded the corner into South Audley Street and disappeared from view. The assembled throng turned with a sigh and shuffled back indoors. Harry hung back, avoiding Em and his father. He re-entered the hall at the rear of the crowd.

The butler had just returned with his gloves and cane when a cool, calm voice enquired, "But surely you'll stay for just a little while, Mr Lester? I feel we've hardly had a chance to become acquainted."

Harry turned to view Mrs Webb's delicate features—and her silver-blue eyes which, he was quite positive, saw far too much for his comfort. "Thank you, ma'am, but I must away." He bowed elegantly.

Only to hear her sigh as he straightened.

"I really do hope you make the *right* decision."

To Harry's intense discomfort, he found himself trapped in her silver-blue stare.

"It's quite easy, you know—no great problem, even though it always feels as if it is. One just has to decide what one wants *most* of life. Take my word for it." She patted his arm in a motherly fashion, quite at odds with her supremely elegant appearance. "It's quite easy if you put your mind to it."

For the first time in a very long while, Harry was rendered speechless.

Lucilla Webb smiled up at him, utterly ingenuous, then fluttered a delicate hand. "I must return to my guests. But do try *hard* to get it right, Mr Lester. And good luck."

With an airy wave, she glided back to the drawing-room. Harry escaped.

On reaching the pavement, he hesitated. His lodgings? Brook's? Manton's? Frowning, he shook his head and started walking.

Unsummoned, the image of Boadicea returned. Harry's frown faded; his lips twitched, then curved. A fanciful notion. But was he really such a dangerous figure that a woman needs must put on armour to deal with him?

The rake within him was not averse to the analogy; the man wasn't so sure of the compliment. He was sure, however, having had the point proved repeatedly, that Lucinda Babbacombe was not the sort of woman to *recognise* danger, much less actively consider it. She, he imagined, would simply have looked the Roman commanders in the eye and calmly pointed out that they were trespassers. Then waited, arms folded, toe tapping, for them to remove themselves from her land.

Very likely, they would have gone.

Just as he—

Abruptly, Harry shook himself free of his thoughts. Drawing in a breath, he lifted his head—and found he was nearing the end of South Audley Street. Ahead, the leafy precincts of Green Park beckoned.

Without allowing himself to consider, he strode on, then crossed Piccadilly to amble beneath the trees. There were few of the fashionable in sight—it was early yet and most would go to Hyde Park nearby. The gentle lawns about him played host to nursemaids and children, an odd couple or two strolling, like himself, aimlessly down the paths.

He strolled slowly on, letting the peace sink into him, keeping his mind purposely blank.

Until a cricket ball hit him on the side of the knee.

Harry stifled a curse. He stooped and picked up the

ball, then hefted it in one palm as he looked about for its owner.

Or owners, as it happened to be.

There were three of them, one slightly older but even he was barely seven. They sidled around a tree and approached with great caution.

"I—I'm most fearfully sorry, sir," the eldest piped up. "Did it hurt terribly?"

Harry sternly quelled an impulse to laugh. "Horrendously," he replied, lending the word maximum weight. All three faces fell. "But I dare say I'll survive." They recovered—and eyed him hopefully, large eyes fringed with long lashes, faces as innocent as the dawn.

As his fingertips found the ball's seam, Harry gave up the struggle and let his lips lift. He squatted, coming down to their height, and held out the ball, spinning it so that it whizzed like a top between his fingers.

"Oh—I say!"

"How d'you do that?"

They gathered about him, polite reticence forgotten. Harry showed them the trick, a facility learned over the long summers of his childhood. They oohed and aahed and practised themselves, eagerly seeking advice.

"James! Adam? Where on earth have you got to? Mark?"

The three looked guiltily about.

"We have to go," the ringleader said. Then smiled—a smile only a young boy could master. "But thanks so much, sir."

Harry grinned. He stood and watched them hurry around the tree and over the lawns to where a rotund nurse waited impatiently.

He was still grinning when Mrs Webb's words floated through his head. "One just has to decide what one wants *most* of life."

What he most wanted—he hadn't thought of it for years. He had once, more than ten years ago. He had been very sure, then, and had pursued his goal with what had been, at that time, his usual confident abandon. Only to find himself—and his dreams—betrayed.

So he had put them away, locked them in the deepest recess of his mind, and never let them out again.

Harry's lips twisted cynically. He turned away and resumed his stroll.

But he couldn't turn his mind from its path.

He knew very well what he most wanted of life—it was the same now as it had been then; despite the years, he hadn't changed inside.

Harry stopped and forced himself to draw in a deep breath. Behind him, he could hear the piping voices of his late companions as together with their nurse they quit the park. About him, youngsters cavorted and played under watchful eyes. Here and there, a gentleman strolled with his wife on his arm, their children ranging about them.

Harry let out the breath trapped in his chest.

Other lives were full—his remained empty.

Perhaps, after all, it was time to re-examine the possibilities. Last time had been a disaster—but was he really such a coward he couldn't face the pain again?

HE ATTENDED THE THEATRE that night. For himself, he cared little for the dramatics enacted on the stage—and even less for the histrionics played out in the corridors, the little dramas of *ton*nish life. Unfortunately, the lovely Mrs Babbacombe had voiced her wish to experience Edmund Kean; Amberly had been only too happy to oblige.

Concealed in the shadows by the wall of the pit, opposite the box Amberly had hired, Harry watched the little party settle into their seats. The bell had just rung; the whole theatre was abustle as society's blessed took their seats in the tiers of boxes, the girls and ladies ogled by the bucks in the pit, while the less favoured looked on from the galleries above.

Hugging the deep shadows cast by the boxes above him, Harry saw Amberly sit Lucinda with a flourish. She was dressed in blue as usual, tonight's gown of a delicate lavender hue, the neckline picked out with silver thread. Her dark hair was dressed high over her pale face. Settling her skirts, she looked up at Amberly and smiled.

Harry watched, a chill slowly seeping into his soul.

Amberly laughed and spoke, bending closer so she did not have to strain to hear.

Abruptly, Harry swung his gaze to the other members of the party. Satterly was chatting to Em, who had taken the seat beside Lucinda. Heather Babbacombe plumped down in the seat beyond Em; Harry spied Gerald standing behind her, his stance clearly proclaiming how he viewed his fair charge.

Momentarily taken aback, Harry frowned. Gerald's expression was easy for him to read, even at this distance. His brother looked far too intent. He was midway through making a mental note to have a quiet word in his baby brother's ear, when he pulled himself up short. Heather Babbacombe might be young but she was, to his reading, an intensely carefree and honest young girl. Who was he to speak against her?

His gaze drifted back to Lucinda. His lips twisted, more in self-mockery than in humour.

Who was he to argue with love?

What other reason could he give for being here—other than a deep need for reassurance? Even Dawlish had taken to eyeing him with something perilously close to pity. When he had, somewhat irritably, demanded, "What the devil's the matter?" his dour henchman had rubbed his chin, then opined, "It's just that you don't exactly seem to be enjoying yourself—if you know what I mean."

He had glared and stalked into the library—but he knew very well what Dawlish had meant. The last week had been sheer hell. He had thought that cutting Lucinda Babbacombe out of his life, given she had only just entered it, would be easy enough. He was, after all, a past master at leaving women behind him; avoiding relationships was part of a rake's stock-in-trade.

But putting the lovely Mrs Babbacombe out of his thoughts had proved impossible.

Which left him with only one alternative.

As Mrs Webb had so succinctly put it—what he wanted most.

But did she still want him?

Harry watched as Amberly rattled on, gesticulating elegantly. He was a wit of sorts, and a polished raconteur. The possibility that Lucinda, having rejected his proposal, might have set him aside in her heart, decided he was not worth the trouble and turned instead to someone else for comfort, was not a particularly reassuring thought.

Even less reassuring was the realisation that, if she had, he would get no second chance—had no right to demand another, nor to interfere with his friend's pursuit.

A vice closed around Harry's chest. Amberly gesticulated again and Em laughed. Lucinda looked up at him, a smile on her lips. Harry squinted, desperate to see the expression in her eyes.

But she was too far away; when she turned back to the front of the box, her lids veiled her eyes.

The fanfare sounded, erupting from the musician's pit before the stage. It was greeted with noisy catcalls from the pit and polite applause from the boxes. The house lamps were doused as the stage lamps flared. The performers in the farce made their entrance; all eyes were riveted on the stage.

All except Lucinda's.

Eyes adjusting to the darkness, Harry saw she was looking down, not at the stage, apparently staring at her hands, possibly playing with her fan. She kept her head up, so no one in the box behind her would suspect her attention was not focused on the play, as was theirs. The flickering light played over her features, calm but hauntingly sad, reserved but eloquently expressive.

Harry drew in a deep breath and straightened away from the wall. Some of the tightness in his chest melted away.

Abruptly, Lucinda lifted her head and looked around— not at the stage but at the audience, uncaring of who might notice her distraction. Harry froze as her gaze scanned the boxes above him, then shifted further along.

Even in the poor light, he could see the hope that lit her face, that invested her whole body with sudden animation.

He watched it slowly fade.

She blinked, then slowly settled back in her chair, her face composed yet inexpressibly sadder than before.

Harry's heart twisted painfully. This time, he didn't try to shut it away, to blot out the emotion. But as he turned and moved silently to the door along the wall, he acknowledged the joy that came in its wake.

He hadn't been wrong about Lucinda Babbacombe. The damned woman was so ridiculously sure of herself she hadn't even considered the danger in loving him.

Stepping out of the darkness of the pit, he smiled.

Two floors above, in the crowded gallery, Earle Joliffe was very far from smiling. In fact, he was scowling—at Lucinda, and the party in Amberly's box.

"Deuce take it! What the devil's going on?" he hissed.

Beside him, Mortimer Babbacombe returned an uncomprehending look.

Disgusted, Joliffe gestured at the box opposite. "What's she *doing* to them? She's turned a whole gaggle of the worst wolves in London into pussycats!"

Mortimer blinked. "Pussycats?"

Joliffe all but snarled. "Lap-dogs, then! She *is* a damned witch—just like Scrugthorpe said."

"Quiet there!"

"Ssh!" came from all around them.

For a moment, Joliffe contemplated a mill with positive glee. Then sanity intruded; he forced himself to stay in his seat. But his eyes remained fixed on his sacrificial lamb—who had transmogrified into a wolf-tamer.

After a moment, Mortimer leaned closer. "Perhaps they're softening her up—pulling the wool over her eyes. We can afford to give them a little time—it's not as if we're that desperate for the money."

Joliffe stared at him—then sank his chin in his hands. "Rakes don't behave as they are to your aunt-by-marriage when they're hot on a woman's trail," he explained through clenched teeth. His jaundiced gaze rested on Amberly and Satterly. "They're being *nice,* for heaven's sake! Can't you see it?"

Frowning, Mortimer looked across the theatre, studying the silent tableau.

Joliffe swallowed a curse. As for not being desperate—they were—very desperate. An unexpected meeting with his creditor last night had demonstrated to him just how desperate they truly were. Joliffe quelled a shiver at the memory of the odd, disembodied voice that had floated out of the carriage, stopping him in his tracks on the mist-shrouded pavement.

"Soon, Joliffe. Very soon." A pause had ensued. Then, "I'm not a patient man."

Joliffe had heard tales enough of the man's lack of patience—and what usually transpired because of it.

He was desperate all right. But Mortimer had too weak a head to be entrusted with the news.

Joliffe concentrated on the woman seated across the darkened pit. "We'll have to do something—take an active hand." He spoke more for himself than Mortimer.

But Mortimer heard. "What?" He turned to Joliffe, a shocked, somewhat stupid expression on his face. "But… I thought we'd agreed there was no need to be openly involved—to actually *do* anything ourselves!"

His voice had risen.

"Shh!" came from all sides.

Exasperated, Joliffe grabbed Mortimer's coat and hauled him to his feet. "Let's get out of here." He sent a venomous glance across the theatre. "I've seen enough."

He pushed Mortimer ahead of him to the exit.

Immediately they gained the corridor, Mortimer turned on him, clutching his coat. "But you said we wouldn't need to kidnap her."

Jollife eyed him in disgust. "I'm not talking about kidnapping," he snapped, wrenching his coat free. He looked ahead, his features hardening. "For our purposes, there's a better way."

He glanced at Mortimer, contempt in his eyes.

"Come on—there's a certain party we need to see."

Chapter Ten

By the time Em took her seat at the breakfast table on Friday morning, she was considering visiting Harry herself. Not that it would do any good—but she felt so helpless every time she looked at Lucinda's face. Calm and pale, her guest sat toying with a piece of cold toast, her expression distant.

Em swallowed her snort. Feeling dejected herself, she poured a cup of tea.

"Are we going anywhere today?" Heather, seated further down the table, fixed big hazel eyes almost pleadingly on Em.

Em slanted a glance at Lucinda. "Perhaps we'll just have a quiet day today. A drive in the Park in the afternoon. We've Lady Halifax's ball tonight."

Lucinda's smile was perfunctory.

"Greenwich was such fun." Heather struggled to invest her words with conviction. Lord Ruthven had arranged an outing yesterday to the Observatory, hoping to lift Lucinda's spirits. He and Mr Satterly, who had made one of the party, had battled valiantly but to no avail.

Lucinda shifted in her chair. "It was very kind of Lord Ruthven to arrange it. I must send a note around to thank him."

Em doubted Ruthven would appreciate it. The poor man had pulled out all stops but it was clear Lucinda barely saw him. Not that she made reference to what was occupying her mind. Her composure was faultless; those who did not know her would detect nothing amiss. Those who did saw the superficiality of her smiles, which no longer reached her eyes, mistier than ever and distressingly remote. She was naturally reserved; now, despite going amongst them, she seemed to have withdrawn from real contact.

"Perhaps," Heather ventured, "we could go to the museum? We haven't seen Lord Elgin's marbles yet. You said you'd like to."

Lucinda tilted her head. "Perhaps."

Helpless, Heather glanced at Em.

Em shook her head. She had originally thought Heather too young, too immature, to sense Lucinda's silent woe. Over the last few days, she had realised that Heather both saw and understood, but with the confidence of youth had imagined matters would work themselves out somehow. Now, even Heather's confidence was flagging. She was as concerned as Em, which worried Em all the more.

The door opened; Fergus appeared at Em's side and presented a silver salver.

"The mail, ma'am. And there's a letter just hand-delivered for Mrs Babbacombe. The boy didn't wait for a reply."

Em picked up the white, sealed packet, painfully aware of the sudden tension that had gripped Lucinda. One glance at the scrawled direction was enough to tell her it wasn't from Harry. Helpless to do otherwise, she handed it over without comment, trying not to watch as, the seal broken, the expectation that had momentarily lit Lucinda's face died.

Lucinda frowned as she read the short missive, then, grimacing, laid it aside. She looked down at her toast, now stone-cold. With a tiny sigh, she reached for the teapot.

Em was beyond social niceties. "Well?"

Lucinda glanced at her, then shrugged. "It's an invitation to some houseparty in the country."

"Whose?"

Lucinda frowned. "I can't immediately recall the lady." She sipped her tea, glancing down at the note. "Lady Martindale of Asterley Place."

"Martindale?" Em started to frown, then her face cleared. "Oh—that'll be Marguerite. She's Elmira, Lady Asterley's daughter. She must be helping out. But that's wonderful!" Em turned to Lucinda. "*Just* the thing! Some fresh air and genteel fun is precisely what you need. Elmira is one of my oldest friends although we haven't met in ages. She'll be getting on, now. When's this party to be?"

Lucinda hesitated, then grimaced. "It starts later today—but the invitation's just for me."

Em blinked. "Just for…?" Then she blinked again, her face clearing. "Ah—I see!"

Lucinda looked up. "What is it?"

Em straightened. "Just remembered. Harry's a close friend of Elmira's son—Alfred, Lord Asterley. Been thick as thieves since they were at Eton together."

She watched as Lucinda reached again for the note.

"Oh?"

"Indeed." Em's eyes glazed as she considered the possibilities. "Always hand-in-glove in mischief. Got sent down together any number of times." For a moment, she remained sunk in thought, then flicked a glance at Lucinda, busy scrutinising the invitation. "You know," Em said, sitting back in her chair, "it's probably not surprising that the invitation's just for you. I can see how it would have been—Elmira had a last-minute cancellation and asked Alfred if he could suggest someone suitable to fill the gap." Em hesitated, then added, "And Alfred and Harry *are* very close."

The more Em thought of it, the more convinced she was that Harry was behind the unexpected invitation. It would be just like him to manoeuvre to get Lucinda into the country, free of mentors, admirers and stepdaughters, so he could make amends for his behaviour away from all interested eyes. Very Harry indeed.

Em snorted.

The atmosphere around the breakfast table had altered dramatically. Instead of resignation bordering on the morose, speculation now tinged the air. Varying degrees of calculation and decision were reflected in the ladies' expressions.

Pushing her plate aside, Heather put their thoughts into words. "You *have* to go."

"Absolutely," Em agreed. "Heather and I are more than capable of entertaining each other for a few days."

Lucinda, reanimated but still frowning, looked up from the invitation. "You're sure it's acceptable for me to go alone?"

"To Asterley Place? Of course!" Em dismissed the point with a wave. "It's not as if you were a young girl making her come-out. And you'll find plenty there you've already met, I don't doubt. Very fashionable, Elmira's parties."

"*Do* go." Heather leaned over the table. "I'd love to hear all about it. Maybe we'll all be invited next time."

Lucinda glanced at Heather's eager young face. Her hesitation was pure prevarication; if there was any possibility Harry had organised the invitation then she had no choice but to go.

She straightened and drew in a breath—a surge of revivifying hope came with it. "Very well. If you're sure you can manage without me?"

Em and Heather vociferously assured her they could.

AFTER LUNCHEON, Em retired to the morning room, her mood one of pleasant expectation. Sinking onto the *chaise,* she cast a contented glance about her, then relaxed against the cushions and, slipping off her slippers, swung her feet up. Propping her head on a cushion, she closed her eyes and sighed deeply.

And wondered if it was too early to feel smug.

She was deep in dreams of white tulle and confetti when the click of the door latch had her blinking awake.

What was Fergus thinking of?

Prepared to take umbrage, she turned her head—and saw Harry enter.

Em blinked again. She opened her mouth—then caught sight of the white flower in Harry's buttonhole.

He *never* wore buttonholes—except at weddings.

Harry saw her arrested expression and inwardly grimaced; he should have left the buttonhole off. But he had dressed with inordinate care—it had seemed the right touch at the time.

He was determined to do this right. If they'd had the sense to stay at home yesterday, the ordeal would be over by now. Reining in his impatience, he closed the door and turned to face his aunt just as she managed to catch her breath.

"Ah…"

"Precisely," Harry said, no trace of the languid in his tones. "If you don't mind, Aunt, I'd like to see Mrs Babbacombe." He met Em's slightly protruberant eyes. "Alone."

Em blinked. "But she's left."

"Left?" All expression drained from Harry's face. For a moment, he couldn't breathe. "Left to where?"

Em put a hand to her spinning head. "But…to Asterley, of course." Eyes widening, she sat up. "Aren't you going?"

His wits reeling, Harry stared at her. "I've got an invitation," he admitted, somewhat cautiously.

Em flopped against the cushions, a hand at her breast. "Thank heaven for that. Only reason she went." Recalling the point, she turned to glare at Harry. "Not, of course, that that'll prove any use—it's plain as a pikestaff *you* didn't organise to have her invited."

"Organise…?" Harry stared at her as if she'd run mad. "Of course I didn't!" He paused, then asked, "Why the devil did you think I did?"

Lips prim, Em shrugged. "Well, there's no reason you couldn't have—I'm quite sure Alfred could have got another name on Elmira's lists if you'd asked him."

"Elmira?"

Em waved. "I know Marguerite issued the invitations but it'll still be Elmira's party."

Fists clenched, Harry closed his eyes—and stifled the explosive anger building within him. His father was older than Em—and suffered from the same, oddly selective memory. Em clearly recalled his connection with Alfred but had totally forgotten that his mother, Elmira, had been dead some eight years.

The parties at Asterley Place were, these days, rather different from those Em recalled.

Harry drew in a deep breath and opened his eyes. "When did she leave?"

Em frowned somewhat petulantly. "About eleven." She glanced at the clock on the mantelshelf. "She'll be halfway there by now."

Grim-faced, Harry turned on his heel.

Em stared. "Where are you going?"

Harry glanced back, his hand on the knob, his expression hard and unyielding. "To rescue Boadicea from a gaggle of lecherous Romans."

With that, he departed, shutting the door behind him, leaving Em staring in bemusement at the uninformative panels.

"Boadicea?"

HARRY STRODE THROUGH the door of his lodgings, ripping the white gillyflower from his lapel and tossing it onto the hall table. "Dawlish! Where the devil are you?"

"I'm right here," came in mumbles from down the corridor. Dawlish appeared, an apron over his street clothes, silver spoons and a polishing rag in his hands. "Now what's yer trouble? I thought as how you'd gone to settle it?"

Harry ground his teeth. "I had—but apparently I should have made an appointment. The damned woman's gone off for a quiet sojourn in the country—to Asterley Place."

He had rarely seen Dawlish so dumbfounded.

"Asterley?"

"Precisely." Harry shrugged off his greatcoat. "And, no, she hasn't changed her lifestyle. The damned female has no idea what she's blithely heading into."

Dawlish's eyes grew round. "Gawd help her." He took the coat from Harry.

"I sincerely doubt he can." Harry stripped off his gloves

and threw them onto the table with the gillyflower, then turned to the stairs. "Come on—stop standing there like a gawp. We'll need the greys—she's got more than a two hours' start on us."

As Harry pounded upstairs, Dawlish blinked, then shook himself. "With you fired up and the greys in their usual mood, we should be able to cut that in half easily."

Harry didn't hear. He strode into his bedroom; it was the work of a few minutes to throw a selection of clothes into a bag. Dawlish came in as he was shrugging into a bottle-green coat; he had already changed his ivory inexpressibles for buckskin breeches.

"No need to kill y'rself," Dawlish advised, picking up the bag. "We'll make it on her heels."

Frowning, Harry led the way out. "We'll get there a full hour after her," he growled.

An hour in which she, a total innocent, would have to fend for herself in a house full of wolves, all of whom would assume she was willing prey.

LUCINDA DESCENDED from her carriage before the steps of Asterley Place and looked around. The house bore a relatively recent façade, Ionic columns supporting the porch roof, classic geometric lines delineating the long windows. It stood in a large park, directly before a long sloping lawn leading down to the shores of a lake. Glimpses of gardens tantalised on both sides; the subtle scent of roses wafted over a brick wall. Wide stone steps led up to the porch; as footmen came running to assist with the baggage, Lucinda unhurriedly ascended to find her host, hostess and their major-domo waiting.

"Welcome to Asterley Place, my dear Mrs Babbacombe. Can't say how delighted I am to see you here." Lord Asterley, a gentleman of average height with a tendency to corpulence, severely restrained, bowed, then shook Lucinda's hand.

Lucinda smiled in return, recalling now that she had met his lordship during her earlier weeks in the capital. "I must thank you for your invitation, my lord. It was most… opportune—and appreciated." She couldn't suppress the hope that welled within her; anticipation lit her eyes and her smile.

Lord Asterley noticed—and was instantly smitten. "Indeed? Very pleased to hear it, m'dear." He patted her hand, then turned to the lady beside him. "Allow me to present my sister, Lady Martindale. She acts as my hostess at these little gatherings, y'know."

Lucinda turned and was engulfed in a warm smile.

Lady Martindale shook hands, a smile wreathing her pretty face. "Please call me Marguerite. Everyone else who stays does." Her ladyship was some years Lucinda's senior, a buxom blonde, as transparently good-natured as her brother. "I do hope you enjoy yourself whilst here— don't hesitate to let me know if there's anything the least amiss."

Lucinda could feel herself relaxing. "Thank you."

"The others are gathering in the conservatory—once you've had a chance to refresh yourself, do please join them." Marguerite gestured to the house, gathering Lucinda as she turned towards it. "I dare say there are others you already know but we pride ourselves on informality here." She leaned closer to add, "You may be sure there are none present who don't know *precisely* how to behave, so you need have no worries other than deciding with whom you wish to pass the time."

Lucinda returned her smile.

"Now then—we've put you in the Blue Room." Her ladyship glanced at Lucinda's cambric carriage dress.

"Clearly an inspired choice. Melthorpe here will show you the way and see your maid and baggage sent up. We dine at six."

Lucinda thanked her again, then followed in the major-domo's wake. He was a small man, shrunk within his dark clothes, his long nose and hunched shoulders giving him a crow-like appearance.

As they gained the top of the wide main staircase, Lucinda caught his eye. He gestured along one corridor; she followed as he started down it. And inwardly frowned. Why on earth should Melthorpe regard her so severely? He stopped before a door at the end of the corridor, opening it and standing back so she could precede him; Lucinda took a closer look at his face as she passed.

Casting a professionally assessing glance around the room, she approved it with a nod. "Thank you, Melthorpe. If you would send my maid up immediately?"

"As you wish, ma'am."

She watched as, with a frigid air that barely avoided incivility, Melthorpe bowed and withdrew. Lucinda frowned at the door as it shut behind him.

There was little possibility she had misread his manner—she had too many years' experience of servants and underlings. The man had looked at her, treated her, as if... It was a moment before she could correctly place his behaviour. When she did, she was dumbstruck.

The door opened and Agatha appeared, a footman with Lucinda's case immediately behind. Lucinda watched as her maid, dourly severe as only she could be, instructed the footman to place the case by the dressing-table, then closed the door behind him.

"Well!" Agatha turned to face her.

Lucinda noted the speculation in Agatha's old eyes, but did not respond. From experience, she knew she would get more information if she let Agatha deliver it in her own fashion. And she was suddenly very curious about Asterley Place.

Stripping off her gloves, she threw them on the bed—a wide four-poster with a tasselled canopy. Her bonnet followed. Then she spread her skirts and considered them. "Hmm—too crushed. I'll change into my new tea gown, just until dinner."

Agatha humphed as she bent to the case buckles. "I haven't seen much of them yet, but they do seem a stylish lot. A goodly gaggle of snooty gentlemen's gentlemen in the kitchens as I passed—and from the looks of some of the lady's maids I reckon there'll be fights over the curling tongs before nightfall. Best let me do your hair up, too."

"Later." Lucinda glanced at her reflection in the mirror over the dressing table. "There'll be time before dinner."

"Six, they said. Midway between country and town." Agatha pulled an armful of dresses from the case. "Did hear one of them mention that they have it that way so there'll be more of the evening for 'their little games,' whatever that might mean."

"Games?" Perhaps the Asterley household amused themselves with the usual country house parlour games? Lucinda frowned. The vision of Lord Asterley and the buxom Marguerite presiding over such entertainments wasn't convincing. Lips firming, Lucinda stood. "Come—help me change. I want to meet the other guests before dinner."

As she'd been told, they were in the conservatory. It was an unusually large version built on at the back of the house and filled with potted palms to create a leafy grotto. There was a tiled pool at its centre; the guests were gathered about it, some in wicker chairs, others standing chatting in groups.

One glance made Lucinda very glad she had changed. They were indeed a stylish lot, confident, gaily plumed birds nestling within the greenery. She nodded to Mrs Walker, an elegant widow, and Lady Morcombe, a dashing matron, both of whom she had met in town.

"My dear Mrs Babbacombe." Marguerite rustled forward. "Pray let me introduce you to Lord Dewhurst—he's only just returned from Europe and so has yet to meet you."

Lucinda calmly returned Lord Dewhurst's greetings while inwardly gauging her companions. She could detect nothing odd to account for her flickering nerves. "Indeed," she replied to Lord Dewhurst's query. "I've quite enjoyed my time in town. But the balls are becoming a trifle…" She gestured. "Overdone—don't you find it so? So crowded one can hardly hear one's self think. And as for breathing…"

His lordship laughed, a smooth, suave sound. "Indeed, my dear. Little gatherings such as this are much more *convenable*."

The subtle emphasis he placed on the last word had Lucinda glancing up at him. His lordship looked down at her, a warm light in his eyes.

"I'm sure you'll discover, my dear, that at Asterley Place, it's very easy to find both time and place to… think."

Lucinda stared at him. Before she could gather her wits, he took her hand and bowed low.

"Should you find yourself wishful of company, my dear, pray don't hesitate to call on me. I can be exceedingly thoughtful, I assure you."

"Ah—yes. That is," desperate, Lucinda wrestled her

wits into order, "I'll bear your offer in mind, my lord." She inclined her head, somewhat stiffly.

She waited while his lordship bowed again then gracefully strolled away. Then dragged in a quick breath—and cast another, much more critical, look about her.

And wondered how she could have been so blind. Every one of the ladies present was undoubtedly that, but they were all either widowed or married, all of unquestionable breeding yet of an age when, it might be imagined, they might have a very real interest in indulging in discreet liaisons.

As for the gentlemen, they were each and every one of a type she recognised all too well.

Before she had time to think further, Lord Asterley strolled up.

"My dear Mrs Babbacombe—can't tell you how thrilled I was to learn of your interest in our little gatherings."

"My interest?" Lucinda swallowed her amazement and politely if coolly raised her brows.

Lord Asterley smiled knowingly; she half-expected him to wink and nudge her elbow. "Well—perhaps not especially in *our* gatherings, but in the type of entertainment we all find so…" his lordship gestured expansively "…fulfilling." He looked down at her. "I do hope, my dear, that, should you feel so inclined, you won't hesitate to call on me—to help enliven your stay here?"

Clinging to polite form, Lucinda inclined her head; as she could find no suitable words in which to answer his lordship, she left him to think what he would.

He beamed and bowed; to her chagrin, Lucinda found it very hard to feel indignant with one so openly cheery. She nodded and drifted to the pool. There was a seat vacant beside Mrs Allerdyne, a *ton*nish widow who, Lucinda now realised, was probably not quite as virtuous as she appeared.

Mrs Allerdyne turned as Lucinda subsided onto the wicker seat.

"Good afternoon, Mrs Babbacombe—or can I dispense with formality and call you Lucinda?"

Lucinda blinked at Henrietta Allerdyne's charmingly gentle face. "Yes, of course." Feeling as if her eyes had just been opened to yet another aspect of *ton*nish life, Lucinda, somewhat dazedly, glanced about her again.

"This is your first time here, isn't it?" Henrietta leaned closer. "Marguerite mentioned it," she explained when Lucinda switched her gaze back. "No need to feel awkward about it." Henrietta patted Lucinda's hand. "We're all friends here, of course. The very last whisper in discretion—no need to fear any comments once you're back in town." Henrietta glanced around with the air of one entirely at her ease. "It's been like that for years, ever since Harry started it."

"Harry?" Lucinda's breath stuck in her throat. "Harry Lester?"

"Mmm." Henrietta was exchanging none-too-idle glances with an elegant gentleman across the room. "As I recall, Harry was the one who thought of the idea. Alfred simply implemented it to Harry's directions."

Harry—who had sent her here.

For an instant, Lucinda felt as if she would faint—the room receded into a dark mist; a chill spread through her. She swallowed; clenching her fists in her lap, she fought back the dizziness. When she could, she murmured, "I see." Henrietta, engrossed with her gentleman, had not noticed her difficulty—nor her sudden pallor. Her cheeks felt icy; Lucinda grasped the moment to recoup, to let her senses settle. Then, with what nonchalance she could, she asked, "Does he often attend?"

"Harry?" Henrietta smilingly nodded to her gentleman and turned back. "Occasionally—he's perennially invited but one never knows if he'll show." Henrietta's smile turned affectionate. "Not one to run in anyone's harness, Harry."

"No, indeed!" Lucinda ignored the questioning look her tartness invoked. A rage unlike any she had ever experienced was rising within her.

Was her invitation here Harry's way of showing her how he now viewed her? That she had become one with these ladies, dallying with any gentleman who took their fancy? Had he sent her here to experience the "congenial company" she had assured him she was seeking?

Or had he sent her here to teach her a lesson—and was planning to arrive just in time to rescue her from the consequences?

Her jaw set, her hands clenched, Lucinda abruptly stood. She felt like screaming, pacing the floor—*throwing things!*—she wasn't sure which of his possible motives enraged her the most. She dragged in a deep breath. "I hope he comes," she breathed through clenched teeth.

"Lucinda?" Henrietta leaned forward to peer up into her face. "Are you quite well?"

Rigid, Lucinda plastered a smile on her lips. "Perfectly, thank you."

Henrietta didn't look convinced.

Luckily, the gong sounded, sending them to their rooms. Lucinda reined in her impatience enough to accompany Henrietta to her door—then briskly strode down the corridor to the Blue Room.

"What have you heard?" she demanded of Agatha the instant the door shut behind her.

Agatha looked up from the navy blue silk gown she was laying out on the bed. She took one look at Lucinda's face—and answered directly. "Not much—but nothing good. Lots of innuendo "bout what the nobs get up to o'nights. Doors opening and closing at all hours." Agatha sniffed. "An' such like."

Lucinda sat at the dressing table and started pulling pins from her hair. She shot her maid a severe look. "*What* else?"

Agatha shrugged. "Seems like it's the expected thing here—not just the odd couple or so, like happens any-where." The maid grimaced. "Did hear one of the foot-men liken it to a set of coaching inns—one coach pulls in as the last's pulling out."

Lucinda sat back and stared at Agatha in the mirror. "Great heavens," she finally said, somewhat weakly. Then she rallied—no matter what the general practice, she was confident that not one of the gentlemen present would force his attentions on an unwilling lady.

Her gaze fell on the navy silk gown. "Not that one." Her eyes narrowed. "The silk gauze."

Agatha straightened, hands on her hips. "The gauze?"

In the mirror, Lucinda raised haughty brows.

Agatha snorted. "'Tis barely decent."

"For my purposes tonight, it'll be perfect." Lucinda drew out the last word to a literal purr. She wasn't the one who would learn a lesson tonight.

Grumbling beneath her breath, Agatha put away the navy silk and drew out the shimmering silk gauze, its colour a sil-very sky blue. Laying it carefully on the bed, she sniffed dis-approvingly, then came up and started on Lucinda's laces.

Lucinda tapped her comb on the table. "This is a hor-rendous coil." She frowned. "Have you asked after Lady Asterley?"

Agatha nodded. "There isn't one. The last—her as was Lord Asterley's mother—died years ago."

"Oh." Lucinda blinked, then, drawing in a breath, squared her shoulders. "Well—tonight can't be helped—but we'll be leaving tomorrow."

"Aye—so I thought."

Lucinda heard the relief in Agatha's voice. She hid an affectionate grin. "Don't worry—despite all indications to the contrary, they are entirely gentlemen at heart."

Agatha humphed. "So you say—but gentlemen can be very persuasive at times."

Lucinda rose and let her gown fall to the floor. Stepping out of it, she allowed Agatha to help her into the sheath of shimmering blue silk. Only when she was finally ready to descend to the drawing-room did she deign to acknowledge Agatha's last comment.

"As I should hope you know by now," she said, fixing Agatha with a haughty glance, "I'm more than capable of managing any gentleman who might darken my horizon. So just tidy up in here—and let Joshua know that we'll be departing in the morning." Lucinda glided to the door—then paused to look back at her maid. "And don't *worry,* you old curmudgeon!"

With that, she turned and, a scintillating vision in shimmering silver blue, glided out of the door.

The drawing-room quickly filled, the guests eager for each other's company. Now sure of her footing, Lucinda found no difficulty in strolling through the crowd, acknowledging the compliments and the open admiration in the gentlemen's eyes, artfully turning aside their subtle suggestions. She was once more in control—but her nerves were taut, her whole being on edge.

The moment she'd been waiting for finally arrived.

Harry walked into the room, creating, she noticed, an immediate stir. He must have arrived while they were changing; he was dressed in his usual severe black and white, his fair hair gleaming in the candlelight. Marguerite broke off her conversation to sweep forward and greet him—with a peck on the cheek, Lucinda noted. Lord Asterley came up to wring his hand. Other gentlemen nodded and called greetings; many of the ladies prinked and preened, smiling in gracious welcome.

Abruptly finding herself the object of a piercing green stare, Lucinda didn't smile at all. Her heart stuttered, then accelerated; a vice slowly closed about her chest. Her expression studiously remote, she inclined her head fractionally and turned back to Mr Ormesby and Lady Morcombe.

And waited for him to come to her.

He didn't—nor was he about to. That much was made plain within ten minutes. Excruciatingly aware of his gaze, dwelling on her shoulders, bare above the abbreviated neckline of her gown, and on her upper breasts, likewise revealed, Lucinda gritted her teeth and inwardly cursed. What the devil was he up to now?

Cursing her, as it happened—Harry could barely restrain the urge to cross the room, lay hold of one delicate wrist and haul her away. What the deuce did she mean by appearing in such a gown? Of the sheerest silk gauze, it shimmered and glimmered, tantalised and teased. The soft material clung wherever it touched, outlining then concealing her slender form, artfully displaying the graceful curves of hips and thighs and the smooth planes of her back. As for her breasts, they were barely concealed at all—the square neckline had been cut by a miser. Gritting his teeth, he forced his feet to remain still. As all the gentleman were openly captivated, at least he didn't need to disguise his interest.

"Harry, old chap! Didn't think to see you here. Thought

you might be looking to take a leaf out of Jack's book, what?"

Harry bent a look of intense irritation on Lord Cranbourne. "Not my style, Bentley. But who have you got your eye on?"

Lord Cranbourne grinned. "Lady Morcombe. She's a ripe little plum—that old codger of a husband of hers doesn't appreciate her as he ought."

"Hmm." Harry sent another penetrating glance about the room. "Just the usual crowd, is it?"

"All except the lovely Mrs Babbacombe—but you know all about her, as I recall?"

"Indeed." Harry's gaze rested again on Lucinda. Again he quelled the urge to go to her side.

"Your interest lie that way this evening?"

Harry shot Lord Cranbourne a quick glance, but his lordship's question was clearly an idle one. "Not as you mean it."

With a nod, he strolled away—before a puzzled Lord Cranbourne could ask for clarification.

With studied nonchalance, Harry circled the room, watching, assessing. His interest was certainly centred on Lucinda—but his first concern was to determine who had placed her name on the invitation list.

He'd been halfway to Asterley before his mind had cleared enough to see the point. *He* hadn't suggested her—so who had? And why?

He prowled the room, carefully studying, not only Lucinda, but all who approached her, intent on discovering which, of his fellow rakes, felt he had first claim.

By the time dinner was announced, by Melthorpe in sepulchural vein, Lucinda had come to the conclusion that Harry was waiting for something—presumably disaster—to befall her, so that he could come to her aid and take charge of her again. Vowing it would never be so, she smiled graciously on Mr Ormesby as he offered her his arm. "Do you come here often, sir?"

Mr Ormesby gesticulated airily. "Now and then. A peaceful interlude away from the bustle of town, what?"

"Indeed." From the corner of her eye, Lucinda saw Harry frown. Then Marguerite stopped beside him and claimed his arm. Lucinda turned a bright smile on Mr Ormesby. "I will rely on you, sir, if I may, to guide me in Asterley's ways."

Mr Ormesby looked thoroughly chuffed. "A pleasure, my dear."

Lucinda blinked, and hoped she wasn't raising any false expectations. "Tell me—are the dinners very elaborate?"

Tonight's wasn't, but neither was it less than an elegant sufficiency with four full courses and two removes. The conversation, to Lucinda's relief, remained general throughout, with much exchanging of the latest gossip and *on dits*, accompanied by considerable merriment, all in the best of taste.

Indeed, if it hadn't been for the subtle undercurrent, borne on glances and the occasional whispered word, her enjoyment would have been unreserved.

"My dear Mrs Babbacombe." Lord Dewhurst, on Lucinda's left, leaned closer to claim her attention. "Have you heard of the treasure hunt Marguerite has organised for tomorrow?"

"Treasure hunt?" Aware of the growing warmth in his lordship's gaze, Lucinda dimly wondered if such an enterprise, in this company, could possibly be innocent.

"Indeed—and we play a version of Fox and Geese that will, I'm sure, delight you. Needless to say, there's no board involved." His lordship smiled. "We, ourselves, represent the pieces."

Lucinda could just imagine. But she kept her smile serene, grasping the offer of a custard to turn aside without comment. In doing so, she caught Harry's eye. He was seated across the table, some way along. Despite the distance, she could sense his simmering irritation, there in the odd tenseness that invested his apparently relaxed frame, and in the way his long fingers gripped his wine glass. Lucinda summoned a radiantly ingenuous smile—and turned it on Mr Ormesby.

Harry felt the muscle in his jaw ripple; his teeth were clenched tight. He forced his jaw to relax, turning aside as Marguerite waved at him from the end of the table.

Lucinda had hoped to catch her breath, to rest her wits and strengthen her defences, when the ladies retired to the drawing-room. But at Asterley, port was the last thing on the gentlemen's minds; they followed in the ladies' wake, not even glancing at the decanters on the sideboard.

"We generally take things quietly on the first evening," Mr Ormesby informed Lucinda as he joined her by the hearth. "Let people…get to know one another, if you take my meaning."

"Exactly!" Lord Asterley followed hard on Mr Ormesby's heels. "Tomorrow, of course, things will liven up a trifle." He rubbed his hands together and looked over the assembled company. "We'd thought to start by punting on the lake, then move on to the Treasure Hunt. Marguerite's got it all organised—to be held in the gardens, of course." He turned a perfectly innocent smile on Lucinda. "Plenty of quiet nooks to find treasure in."

"Oh?" Lucinda endeavoured to look politely vague.

"Nothing starts till after noon, of course. We generally all meet in the breakfast parlour about then. Gives everyone a chance to catch up on their sleep, don't y'know."

Lucinda nodded, making a mental note to be on the

road shortly after ten. Quite how she was to excuse herself, and on what grounds, she did not know—but she'd think of something by tomorrow morning.

Lord Cranbourne and Lady Morcombe joined them; the conversation revolved about the expected entertainments of the next few days—the communal ones. As for the others, those that remained unspecified, Lucinda was increasingly aware of the speculative glances cast her way, by Mr Ormesby, Lord Asterley and Lord Dewhurst in particular.

For the first time since entering Asterley Place, she began to feel truly uneasy. Not out of fear for her virtue, but from dislike of the potentially embarrassing situations she might soon find herself in. Mr Ormesby and Lord Asterley showed no disposition to leave her side; to Lucinda's relief, they were both summoned by Marguerite to help pass the teacups. She grasped the opportunity to fill a vacant chair by the *chaise*. On its end sat a pretty woman much of an age with herself; Lucinda vaguely recalled being introduced at Almack's.

"Lady Coleby—Millicent." The woman smiled and nodded as she passed a teacup. "Always a pleasure to welcome another to our circle."

Lucinda's answering smile was a trifle weak. She hid it behind her cup. She was beginning to wonder if she should have braved the fuss and left three hours ago.

"Have you made your choice yet?" Over the rim of her cup, Lady Coleby raised a questioning brow.

Lucinda blinked. "Choice?"

Her ladyship gestured about her. "From amongst the gentlemen."

Lucinda looked blank

"Oh—I forgot. You're new." Lady Coleby lowered her cup and leaned closer. "It's all very simple. One just decides which of the gentlemen one likes the best—one, two or more if your taste runs that way—then one lets them know—discreetly, of course. You don't need to do anything more; it's all miraculously well-organised."

Faced with an unwaveringly enquiring gaze, Lucinda swallowed a mouthful of tea. "Ah—I'm not sure."

"Well, don't leave it too long or the best will be taken." Lady Coleby touched Lucinda's sleeve. "I'm after Harry Lester, myself," she confided, nodding to where Harry stood on the opposite side of the room. "He's not attended in an age—not since I've been coming anyway, which is more than a year. But all that excessive elegance, all that lethal grace—" Lady Coleby broke off with a delicate shiver. "Deep waters hold *dangerous* currents, so they say." Her gaze fixed on Harry, she took a sip of her tea. "I never would have believed brash, impetuous Harry would turn out like that. It just goes to show. He's nothing like the fresh-faced young gentleman who offered for me all those years ago."

Lucinda froze. Then, slowly, she set her cup back on her saucer. "He offered for you?"

"Oh, yes! Not officially—it never came to that. Ten and more years ago it was." Her ladyship affected a dewy-eyed look, then giggled. "He was most *terribly* enamoured—well, you know how young men can be." She waved her hand. "Utterly over the moon. Wild, impassioned declarations—it was all so thrilling for he was very handsome, even then."

Lucinda studied Lady Coleby's face as her ladyship studied Harry, engaged in a discussion with a Mr Harding. "But you didn't accept him?"

"Heavens, no! Poor as church mice, the Lesters. Or they were. Mind you…" a speculative glint lit her ladyship's brown eyes "…now that Coleby's dead and gone and the Lesters have suffered a windfall—" Lady Coleby broke off to state, "Positively *enormous*, my dear, so I've heard. Well—" she turned back to survey Harry, anticipation lighting her face "—I really do believe I should renew old acquaintances."

At that moment, Harry and Mr Harding parted. Harry directed a piercing glance across the room.

Her ladyship smiled delightedly and rose, laying aside her teacup. "And it appears there'll be no better time. Do excuse me, my dear."

Lucinda forced herself to incline her head. Picking up both cups, she carried them to where Marguerite sat by the tea trolley, all the while keeping her gaze firmly fixed on her hostess.

Harry's gaze was fixed on her. He hesitated, frowning, his lips set in a firm line. No gentlemen had pressed her; none had displayed any proprietary interest. Three, if not four, were seriously enamoured; another few were watching closely. But none seemed to consider they had first claim—they were all vying for her favours as if she had swanned into their orbit on her own account.

Which left him with the puzzle unsolved. With an inward grimace, he put it aside until the morning. He was about to cross the room, to head off what he knew would be an embarrassing and confusing confrontation, when he felt a touch on his sleeve.

"Harry!" Millicent, Lady Coleby, uttered the word on a long breathy exhalation. She opened wide brown eyes at him, her delicately tinted cheeks aglow.

Briefly, Harry nodded. "Millie." His head rose again as he looked for Lucinda; she was still chatting to Marguerite.

"Dear Harry." Engrossed in artlessly studying his cravat, Millie didn't notice his interest was elsewhere. "I've always carried a torch for you—you do know that, don't you? I had to marry Coleby—you must see that. You're so much older now—you understand the ways of our world." Millie let a knowing smile curve her lips. "I've heard you understand the ways very well, Harry. Perhaps we might…travel a few avenues together tonight?"

Millie glanced up—just as Lucinda nodded to Marguerite and headed for the door. Harry, about to move, was forced to focus on Millie, standing directly in front of him.

"Excuse me, Millie. I've business elsewhere."

With that, he nodded and sidestepped, then halted, his gaze on Lucinda—and the three gentlemen who had intercepted her. Concentrating, he could just make out their words.

"My dear Mrs Babbacombe." Alfred was the first to gain her side. "Dare I hope you've found the evening to your taste?"

"You've proved a most welcome addition to our ranks, ma'am." Ormesby was close behind. "I do hope we can entice you to spend more time with us—I, for one, can think of little I'd like better."

Lucinda blinked; before she could answer, Lord Dewhurst joined them.

He took her hand and bowed low. "Enchanted, my dear. Dare I hope for some time to further our acquaintance?"

Lucinda met his lordship's calm but distinctly warm gaze—and wished herself elsewhere. Heat tinged her cheeks—then, from the corner of her eye, she saw Harry. Watching.

Drawing in a steadying breath, Lucinda smiled at her three would-be *cicisbei*. With what she hoped they understood as a pointed disregard for all they had hinted at, if not said, she calmly stated, "If you'll excuse me, gentlemen, I believe I will retire early."

With a benedictory smile, she swept them a curtsy; they immediately bowed low. Rising, Lucinda headed straight for the door. Confident she had avoided a potential quagmire, head high, she glided from the room.

Harry stared after her.

Then uttered a single, pungent expletive and spun on his heel. He exited the room by the windows to the terrace. At speed.

Millie simply stared—then lifted her shoulders in a baffled shrug—and glided after Mr Harding.

Lucinda climbed the stairs and traversed the corridors, engrossed, not with the details of her imminent departure nor yet imaginings of what she had escaped. Lady Coleby's revelations of Harry's long-ago disappointment filled her mind.

She could imagine, very clearly, how it must have been, how, with the impetuosity of youth, he had laid his love at his chosen one's feet, only to see it spurned. It must have hurt. A great deal. The fact explained many things— why he was now so cynical of love, not marriage itself, but the love needed to support it, the intensity he now harnessed, that certain something which made so many women view him as dangerous—excitingly but definitely so—and his emotionally cautious nature.

Reaching her room, Lucinda shut the door firmly behind her. She looked for a key, grimacing resignedly when she discovered there wasn't one.

Thanks to Lady Coleby, and her lack of what Lucinda felt was any proper feeling, she could now understand why Harry was as he was. That, however, did not excuse his behaviour in engineering her present predicament.

Eyes narrowing as she considered his perfidy, Lucinda glided across the room, lit by a single candelabra on the dressing table, and gave the bell pull a definite tug.

The door opened. Her hand still clutching the embroidered pull, Lucinda turned.

To see Harry slip around the door.

He scanned the room and found her. "There's no point ringing for your maid—the house rules forbid servants the upper corridors after ten."

"What?" Lucinda stared. "But what are you doing here?"

Harry closed the door and looked around again.

Lucinda had had enough. Eyes narrowing, she sailed across the room to confront him. "However, as you *are* here, I have a bone to pick with you!"

Reassured they were alone, Harry brought his gaze to her face as she halted, slender and straight, before him. "Indeed?"

"As you well know!" Lucinda glared up at him. "How *dare* you organise to have me invited to such a gathering as this? I realise you might be somewhat irritated because I did not accept your proposal—" She broke off as the thought occurred that she, like Lady Coleby, might be said to have rejected him. "But the circumstances were nothing like those of Lady Coleby. Or whoever she was then." With an irritated wave, she dismissed Lady Coleby. "Whatever your feelings in the matter, I have to tell you that I view your behaviour in this instance as *reprehensible!* Utterly callous and without justification! It is totally inconceivable to me why you—"

"I didn't."

The steel beneath the words cut through her denunciation.

Arrested in mid-tirade, Lucinda blinked up at him. "You didn't?"

His jaw set, his lips a thin line, Harry regarded her through narrowed eyes. "For a woman of superior sense, you frequently indulge the most remarkable notions. *I* didn't arrange to have you invited. On the contrary." His tone turned conversational, his accents remained clipped; the undercurrent was positively lethal. "When I discover who did, I'm going to wring his neck."

"Oh." Lucinda backed a step as he closed the distance between them. Her eyes met his; abruptly, she stiffened and stood her ground. "That's all very well—but what are you doing here now?"

"Protecting you from your latest folly."

"Folly?" Lucinda coolly raised her brows—and her chin. "What folly?"

"The folly of the invitation you just, all unwittingly, issued." Harry glanced at the bed, then the fireplace. The fire was lit, a smallish blaze but there was plenty of wood by the hearth. An armchair sat before it.

Lucinda frowned. "What invitation?"

Harry's gaze came back to her face; he merely raised his brows at her.

Lucinda snorted. "Nonsense. You're imagining things. I issued no invitation—I did nothing of the sort."

Harry gestured to the armchair. "Let's just wait and see, shall we?"

"No—I want you out of here." Lucinda couldn't tilt her chin any higher. "Your presence is totally improper."

Harry's eyes glittered. "Naturally—that's the purpose of these parties, in case you hadn't realised." His gaze fell to her breasts. "And speaking of improper—who the devil told you that gown was decent?"

"A whole *host* of appreciative gentlemen," Lucinda informed him, belligerently planting her hands on her hips. "And I hardly need you to tell me what the purpose of this little gathering is *but,* for your information, I plan to have nothing to do with it."

"Good—we agree on that much."

Lucinda narrowed her eyes. Harry met her gaze with a stubbornness as unwavering as her own.

A knock came on the door.

Harry smiled coldly. He pointed a finger at Lucinda's nose. "Wait here."

Without waiting for any agreement, he swung on his heel and retraced his steps. He opened the door. "Yes?"

Alfred jumped. "Oh—ah!" He blinked wildly. "Oh—it's you, Harry. Er—I didn't realise."

"Obviously."

Alfred shifted his weight from one foot to the other, then gestured vaguely. "Right-ho! Er…I'll call later, then."

"Don't bother—the reception will be the same."

The words were a dire warning. Harry shut the door on his old schoolfriend's face, before he could think of doing anything else with the vacuously good-natured features.

He swung back—to find Lucinda staring at the door in utter disbelief. "*Well!* What cheek!"

Harry smiled. "I'm so glad you now see my point."

Lucinda blinked, then gestured at the door. "But he's gone now. You told him not to come back." When Harry merely raised his brows, she folded her arms and lifted her chin. "There's no reason you can't leave now."

Harry's smile turned feral. "I can give you two very good reasons."

They came knocking an hour or so apart.

Lucinda gave up blushing after the first.

She also stopped urging Harry to leave; this was not the sort of houseparty at which she felt comfortable.

When the hour after midnight passed and no one else came creeping to knock on the panels of her door, Lucinda finally relaxed. Curled up against the pillows on her bed, she looked across at Harry, eyes closed, head back, sprawled in the big armchair before the fire.

She didn't want him to go.

"Get into bed—I'll stay here."

He hadn't moved or opened his eyes. Lucinda could feel her heart thudding. "There?"

His lips twisted. "I'm perfectly capable of spending a night in a chair for a good cause." He shifted, stretching his legs out before him. "It's not too uncomfortable."

Lucinda considered, then nodded. His eyes looked closed.

"Do you need any help with your lacings?"

She shook her head—then realised and answered, "No."

"Good." Harry relaxed. "Good night, then."

"Good night."

Lucinda watched him for a moment, then settled down amid the covers, drawing them over her. Although it was a four-poster, there were no hangings on the bed; there was no screen behind which she could change. She lay back against the pillows; when Harry made no sound, did not move, she shifted onto her side.

The soft flickering firelight touched his face, lighting the hollows, throwing the strong bone structure into relief, shading his heavy lids, etching the firm contours of his lips.

Lucinda's eyes slowly closed and she drifted into sleep.

Chapter Eleven

When she awoke the next morning, the fire had died. The chair before it was empty.

Lucinda let her lids fall and snuggled down beneath the covers. Her lips curved in a lazy smile; a deep contentment pervaded her. Idly, she searched for the cause—and remembered her dream.

The time, as she recalled, had been very late, deep in the long watches of the night. The house had been silent when she'd supposedly woken—and seen Harry sprawled in the chair before the dying fire. He had shifted restlessly and she had remembered the blanket left on a chair by the bed. She had slipped from beneath the covers, her shimmering gown slithering over her limbs. On silent feet, she had retrieved the blanket and approached the chair by the fire.

She had halted six feet away, stopped by some sixth sense. His eyes had been closed, long brown lashes gilded at the tips almost brushing his high cheekbones. She had studied his face, the angles and planes, austere in repose, the carved jaw and sculpted lips. Her gaze had travelled on, down his long, graceful body, loose-limbed in sleep, the subtle tension that normally invested it in abeyance.

A little sigh had caught in her throat.

And she had felt the touch of his gaze.

Raising her eyes, she had seen his were open, his gaze, heavy-lidded, on her face. He had studied her, not broodingly but with a gentle pensiveness that had held her still.

She had sensed his hesitation, and the instant he put it aside. Lifting one hand, he had held it out, palm upwards, to her.

Indecision had held her, poised, quivering. He said nothing; his hand hadn't moved. She had drawn in a long, deep breath—and placed her hand in his. His fingers had closed gently but firmly about hers, then he had drawn her slowly towards him.

The blanket had fallen from her grasp to lie on the floor, forgotten. He had drawn her nearer, then reached for her, pulling her gently onto his lap.

She had gone very readily, her heart soaring as she felt his heat enfold her, his thighs hard beneath hers. Then his arms had closed about her and she had raised her face for his kiss.

When they had first come together, desire had propelled them into intimacy, leaving no time for the gentler side of passion. In her dream last night they had explored that aspect fully, spending hours before the fire, wrapped in passion's web.

Beneath the covers, Lucinda closed her eyes tight; a long delicious shiver rippled through her.

In her imagination, she could feel Harry's hands upon her, the long fingers experienced, so knowing, his palms hard and calloused from frequent handling of the reins. He had opened the door to a wonderland of sensation—

and conducted her through it, educating her senses until they had been filled with pleasure—and him.

He had stripped her gown from her in tantalising stages after his lips, artfully following the neckline, had made her long to rid herself of it. He had gently eased it down, revealing her breasts, on which he had lavished untold attention. In her mind, she felt again the touch of his hair, soft as silk on her heated skin.

How long she had lain, naked in his arms as he loved her, the dying firelight gilding her in bronze and gold, she couldn't recall. But it had felt like hours before he had lifted her and carried her to the bed.

He had drawn down the covers and laid her on the sheets, then rekindled the candles in the candelabra and placed it on the table by the bed. She had blushed and reached for the covers.

"No. Let me look at you."

His voice had been low, soft and deep. Deep currents, indeed, but these weren't turbulent, dangerous, but deeper still, slow, steady and infinitely strong. They had swept aside her inhibitions, leaving her with no reservations; held in his green gaze, she had lain as he had left her and watched while he undressed.

Then he had joined her on the bed and desire had flared; this time, he had held it harnessed and showed her how to manage the reins. The power was no less strong but, this time, she had appreciated it fully, felt its quality in each long-drawn moment, in each subtle movement, each lingering caress.

The end had been just as glorious but had left a deeper sense of peace, a more shattering realisation of how strong the power that held them now was.

There had been tears in her eyes when, after it was over, she had lifted her lids and looked up into his face.

And had seen therein what she had almost given up hope of ever seeing—resignation, perhaps, but acceptance, too. It had been there in his eyes, glowing beneath his heavy lids, there in the gentler cast of his features. And there most especially in his mobile lips, no longer so hard and severe, but softer, more pliable. He had met her gaze—and hadn't tried to hide his reaction, nor draw back from the reality.

Instead, he had lowered his head and kissed her, long, deeply, lingeringly, then lifted from her and wrapped her in his arms.

A dream—nothing more, her dream, the embodiment of all her hopes, her deepest desires, the answer to her most secret needs.

Lucinda shut her eyes tight, clinging to the deep sense of peace and contentment, even if it was only illusory.

But the day had dawned; light, streaming through the open shutters, played on her lids. Reluctantly, she lifted them—and saw the blanket, half-folded still, sitting on the floor before the hearth.

Her eyes widened. Blinking, she noted the candelabra—on the table beside the bed. Slowly, hardly daring to breathe, she started to turn over. She only got halfway onto her back before she registered the chaos of the covers. Lucinda swallowed, and turned flat on her back. She slanted a glance sideways—and let out the breath she'd been holding. The bed beside her was empty. But the pillow beside hers was deeply dented.

As a final, incontrovertible piece of evidence, a sunbeam, bobbing in, highlighted two fine gold hairs, reposing on the white lawn of the pillowcase.

Lucinda groaned and shut her eyes.

The next instant, she sat bolt upright and flung the covers from her. Only then did she recall she was naked.

Grabbing the covers back, she rummaged amid their confusion and discovered the nightgown Agatha had laid out the night before. Muttering curses, Lucinda struggled into it, then leapt from the bed.

She crossed the room with determined strides and yanked violently on the bell pull.

She was leaving. Now.

IN THE LIBRARY on the ground floor, Harry paced back and forth before the windows. He had dispatched an intrigued Melthorpe to rout out his master, wherever he might be, with a message that his presence was urgently required.

The door latch clicked; Harry swung about as Alfred entered, nattily attired in a check coat over country breeches and high boots. Harry himself was dressed for travelling in his bottle-green coat and buckskins.

"There you are!" With a smile unimpaired by having been summarily summoned from someone else's bed, Alfred strolled forward. "Melthorpe didn't say what the problem was, but you look in fine fettle. Dare say your night was a great deal more exciting than mine, what? Mrs Babbacombe looks set to take the title of most delectable widow of the year—particularly if she can keep *you* entertained, happy as a grig, all night long—"

The last word ended on a strangled note as Harry's fist made contact with Alfred's face.

Harry groaned and put a hand to his brow. "Sorry—sorry." His expression openly apologetic, he extended his hand to Alfred, who was now measuring his length on the rug. "I didn't *mean* to hit you." Harry's jaw hardened. "But you'd be well advised to mute your comments on the subject of Mrs Babbacombe."

Alfred made no move to take his hand, or get up. "Oh?" He was clearly intrigued.

Disgusted with himself, Harry waved him up. "It was just instinctive. I won't hit you again."

"Ah, well." Alfred sat up and gingerly felt his left cheekbone. "I know you didn't *mean* to hit me—nothing's broken, so you must've pulled the punch. Very grateful you did, mind—but if it's all the same to you, I'll just remain here until you tell me what this is all about—just in case, with my usual babble, I inadvertently trigger any more of your instincts."

Harry grimaced. Hands on hips, he looked down at Alfred. "I think someone's been using us." He gestured about him. "The Asterley Place house-parties."

Unexpected intelligence seeped into Alfred's eyes. "How?"

Harry compressed his lips, then stated, "Lucinda Babbacombe should never have been invited. She's a thoroughly virtuous female—take it from me."

Alfred's brows rose. "I see." Then he frowned. "No, I don't."

"What I want to know is who suggested you invite her?"

Alfred sat up and draped his arms over his knees. He blinked up at Harry. "You know, I don't think I like being used. It was a chap named Joliffe—brushed up against him a couple of times at some hell or other but he's generally about town—Ernest, Earle, something like that. Ran across him on Wednesday night at that hell in Sussex Place. He happened to mention that Mrs Babbacombe was looking for a little entertainment and he'd promised he'd mention her to me."

Harry was frowning. "Joliffe?" He shook his head. "Can't say I've had the pleasure."

Alfred snorted. "Wouldn't exactly call it a pleasure. Bit of a loose fish."

Harry's gaze abruptly focused. "You took the word of a loose fish on the subject of a lady's reputation?"

"Of course not." Alfred hurriedly leaned back out of reach, his expression distinctly injured. "I checked—you know I always do."

"Who with?" Harry asked. "Em?"

"*Em?* Your aunt Em?" Alfred blinked. "What's she got to do with it? Old tartar she is—was. Used to pinch my cheeks every time she came visiting."

Harry snorted. "She'll do more than pinch your cheeks if she finds out what you invited her protégée to."

"Her protégée?" Alfred looked horrified.

"You obviously didn't check too hard," Harry growled, swinging away to pace once more.

Alfred squirmed. "Well, you see, time was tight. We had this vacancy; Lady Callan's husband came back from Vienna sooner than she'd expected."

Harry humphed. "So who *did* you check with?"

"The lady's cousin or something by marriage. Mortimer Babbacombe."

Harry frowned and stopped pacing. The name came floating back to him from his first memories of Lucinda. "Mortimer Babbacombe?"

Alfred shrugged. "Innocuous sort, a bit weak, but can't say I've heard anything against him—other than that he's a friend of Joliffe's."

Harry prowled over to stand directly before Alfred. "Let me get this straight—Joliffe suggested Mrs Babbacombe was looking for an invitation to the entertainment here and Mortimer Babbacombe confirmed she liked living life on the racy side?"

"Well, not in so many words. Couldn't expect him to come right out and *say* such a thing of a female relative, what? But you know how it goes—I made the suggestions and gave him plenty of time to deny them. He didn't. Seemed clear enough to me."

Harry grimaced. Then nodded. "All right." He looked down at Alfred. "But she's leaving."

"When?" Alfred struggled to his feet.

"Now. As soon as possible. Furthermore, she's never been here."

Alfred shrugged. "Naturally. *None* of the ladies are here."

Harry nodded, grateful for his own past deviousness. It was his fertile mind that had devised these parties, where married ladies and widows of the *ton* could enjoy a little illicit dalliance without running the risk of any social repercussions. Total discretion was an absolute requirement—all the ladies who attended had the same secret to hide. As for the gentlemen, honour and their peers—and the likelihood of future invitations—were more than sufficient to ensure their silence.

So the damned woman, despite all, was safe—yet again.

Harry frowned.

"Come on—let's have breakfast." Alfred turned towards the door. "Might as well reap the rewards of being so early—we can snaffle two helpings of kedgeree."

Still frowning, Harry followed him to the door.

An hour later, Lucinda swept down the main staircase, Agatha, dourly protective, three steps behind. An incipient frown tangled Lucinda's brows, put there by Melthorpe, who had knocked on her door while they had been packing with a breakfast tray and a message that his lordship would hold himself in readiness to take leave of her whenever she was ready. Then, a few minutes ago, when Agatha had opened her door, it was to discover a footman patiently waiting to carry her bag to the carriage.

For the life of her, she couldn't understand how they had known she was leaving.

It was all most confusing, a situation not helped by the skittering, totally uncharacteristic panic that had laid siege to her confidence.

As she set foot on the last flight of stairs, Lord Asterley strolled out of the dining-room. Harry followed in his wake, a sight that made Lucinda inwardly curse. She switched her gaze to her gloves, tugging them on; when she lifted her face, it was set in determined lines. "Good morning, my lord. I'm afraid I must depart immediately."

"Yes, of course—I quite understand." Alfred waited by the bottom of the stairs, his most charming smile in place.

Lucinda struggled not to frown. "I'm so glad. I have enjoyed my stay, but I'm sure it's for the best if I leave this morning." She avoided looking at Harry, standing behind his host.

Alfred offered her his arm. "We're quite devastated to have you leave, of course, but I've had your carriage brought around."

Beginning to feel distinctly distracted, Lucinda put her hand on his sleeve. "How kind of you," she murmured. From beneath her lashes, she glanced at Harry but could make nothing of his urbane expression.

"A pleasant day for a drive—hope you reach your destination without any fuss."

Lucinda allowed his lordship—expatiating in similar, totally inconsequential vein—to lead her down the steps.

As he had said, her carriage awaited, Joshua on the box. Lucinda paused on the last step, turning to her host as Agatha slipped past. Calmly, she held out her hand. "Thank you, my lord, for a most interesting stay—even if it was so short."

"Delighted, m'dear, delighted." Alfred bowed extravagantly over her hand. "Dare say I'll see you shortly in London." As he straightened, his gaze met Harry's over Lucinda's shoulder. "In the ballrooms," he hastily added.

Lucinda blinked. Then she turned to the carriage, and discovered Agatha, her expression thoroughly disapproving, up beside Joshua on the box.

"Here—allow me."

Before she could do anything about her maid's unexpected position, Lucinda found herself handed into the carriage. Deciding that rapid departure was undoubtedly her wisest course, she took her seat by the window and settled her skirts. She could get Agatha down once they were clear of the drive.

Lord Asterley spoke through the window. "Do hope you enjoyed your stay. We'll look to see you again next—" Abruptly he caught himself up, a comical look on his face. "Ah—no. Not again."

"Quite," came in clipped accents from behind him.

His lordship quickly stepped back. Lucinda, features rigidly impassive, drew breath to farewell her predatory protector—only to see Harry nod to his lordship and calmly climb into the carriage.

Lucinda stared at him.

Harry smiled a touch grimly, saying, *sotto voce,* as he moved past, "Smile sweetly at Alfred—or he'll be even more confused."

Lucinda did as she was told, plastering an utterly fatuous smile on her lips. Lord Asterley stood on the steps and waved until the curve of the drive hid them from sight.

As soon as it did, Lucinda rounded on Harry. "*What* do you think you're doing? Is this another of your forcible repatriations?"

Harry settled his shoulders against the seat. "Yes." He turned his head to look at her, brows rising arrogantly.

"You aren't going to tell me you belonged at Asterley Place—are you?"

Lucinda blushed, and changed tack. "Where are we going?" She had not left Asterley Place in an unfashionable rush solely because of the activities of its guests. After last night, she had no idea how Harry now viewed her, despite what she had sensed, despite what she now hoped. Undermining her confidence was the realisation, the cast-iron certainty, that if he wanted her, she would go to him—without any marriage vows—without any vows at all. She had intended to rush back to the safety of Em's side, where her own weakness would be bolstered by Em's staunch propriety.

She had never before run from anything or anyone—but what she felt for Harry was not something she could fight.

Her heart thumping uncomfortably, she watched, eyes wide, as he sat back, laid his head against the squabs and stretched his long legs before him, crossing his booted ankles. He closed his eyes. "Lester Hall."

"Lester Hall?" Lucinda blinked—not Lestershall, his own house, but Lester Hall, his family home.

Harry nodded, settling his chin in his cravat.

"Why?"

"Because that's where you've been since yesterday. You left town in your carriage and drove there, with your maid and coachman. I followed several hours later in my curricle. Em and Heather will be following in Em's carriage this morning—Em was indisposed yesterday. That's why they didn't accompany you."

Lucinda blinked again. "Why did I go and leave them behind?"

"Because my father was expecting you last night and you didn't want to disappoint him."

"Oh." After a moment's hesitation, Lucinda asked, "*Is* he expecting me?"

Harry opened one eye, studied the delightful picture she made in her blue cambric carriage dress, her hair neatly caught in a chignon, her bonnet framing her face— the whole made distinctly more entrancing by the uncertainty he could see in her misty blue eyes and her slightly stunned expression—then closed his eye again. "He'll be delighted to see you."

Lucinda thought long and hard about that. "Where's your curricle?" she eventually asked.

"Dawlish drove it back last night with a message for Em. You needn't worry—she'll be there by the time we arrive."

There didn't seem anything more to say. Lucinda sat back—and tried to make sense of what she'd learned.

Some miles later, Harry broke the silence. "Tell me about Mortimer Babbacombe."

Hauled from deep contemplation, Lucinda frowned. "Why do you want to know about him?"

"Is he a cousin of your late husband's?"

"No—he's Charles's nephew. He inherited the Grange and the entailed estate when Charles died."

Eyes still closed, Harry frowned. "Tell me about the Grange."

Lucinda shrugged. "It's a small property as such things go. Just the house and enough fields to support it. Charles's wealth derived from the Babbacombe Inns, which he'd bought with the fortune he'd inherited from his maternal grandfather."

Half a mile had passed before Harry asked, "Was Mortimer Babbacombe familiar with the Grange?"

"No." Lucinda let her gaze wander over the lush fields through which they were passing. "It was one of the things

I found particularly strange—that having barely set foot in the place—I believe he had visited for a day the year before Charles and I married—he was so very keen to take up residence."

Another long silence ensued; again, Harry broke it. "Do you know if Mortimer was aware of Charles's wealth?"

Lucinda frowned. It was some moments before she answered. "If you mean did he know Charles was personally wealthy, then yes, I think he must have known. Although he didn't visit while I lived at the Grange, he did appeal to Charles for financial relief. Basically on an annual basis. Charles used to look on it as a pension for his heir, but the sums were often quite large. The last two were for two and three thousand pounds. However..." Lucinda paused to draw breath. She glanced at Harry. His eyes were now open, narrowed and fixed on the carriage seat opposite as he pondered her words. "If you mean did Mortimer know the details of Charles's fortune, then I can't be sure he did. Certainly, in the past ten years, Charles made no effort to communicate such matters." She shrugged. "They were, after all, none of Mortimer's business."

"So he might not have known that Charles's money did not derive from the estate itself?"

Lucinda humphed. "I would have thought any fool could have seen that the Grange could not possibly generate anything like the amounts Charles regularly sent to Mortimer."

Not from London. And they had no guarantee that Mortimer Babbacombe was not, in fact, just such a fool. But Harry kept such observations to himself. He closed his eyes and listened to the rumble of the wheels as his mind juggled the facts. Someone, he was now convinced, was taking an unwarranted interest in Lucinda's affairs—but to what end he couldn't fathom. Mischief, pure and simple, was impossible to rule out, yet instinct warned him that alone was insufficient reason. On the face of it, Mortimer Babbacombe seemed the most likely candidate, but it was impossible to ignore the fact that he was not Lucinda's heir—her aunt in Yorkshire stood nearest in line. And anyway, why send her to Asterley?

Who could possibly benefit by her enjoying a discreet liaison?

Harry inwardly shook his head—and let the matter slide. Time enough to bend his mind to it when they headed back to London. Until then, she was going to be under his eye every minute of the day—and very close, and safe, every minute of the night. Lester Hall and its surrounding acres were the safest place on earth for a Lester bride.

Her eyes on the greenery sliding past the windows, Lucinda decided that she should feel reassured, not only by Harry's manner, but by his efforts to protect her name. She cast a sideways glance at him; he appeared to be asleep. Recalling how he had spent the night, she could hardly feel surprise. She was physically tired herself but too keyed up to relax.

But as the wheels went around and the miles rumbled past and she had more time to dwell on their state, it occurred to her that she had no guarantee Harry had actually altered his stance.

The carriage hit a rut; a strong arm shot out and saved her from falling to the floor.

Lucinda righted herself; Harry's hand fell away. She turned to him—and glared at his still shut eyes. "Lady Coleby was speaking to me yesterday."

Languidly, his brows rose. "Oh?"

Despite his tone, he had tensed. Lucinda pressed her lips together and forged on. "She told me you had once been in love with her."

She could feel her heart thudding in her chest, in her throat.

Harry opened his eyes. Slowly, he turned his head until his eyes, very green, met hers. "I didn't—then—know what love was."

His eyes held hers for a long moment, then he turned forward and closed them again.

The wheels rolled on; Lucinda stared at him. Then, slowly, she drew in a deep breath. A smile—of relief, of welling hope—broke across her face. Her lips still curved, she settled her head against the squabs—and followed Harry's example.

Chapter Twelve

Three days later, Harry sat in a garden chair under the spreading branches of the oak at the bottom of the Lester Hall lawn, squinting through the early afternoon sunshine at the blue-clad figure who had just emerged onto the terrace.

She saw him; she raised her hand, then descended the steps and headed his way. Harry smiled.

And watched his intended stroll towards him.

Her gown of cerulean blue muslin clung to her figure as she walked. Her face was shaded by a villager hat, three blue daisies decorating its band. He had put them there himself, first thing this morning, when their petals had still sparkled with dew.

Harry's smile deepened; contentment swept through him. *This* was what he wanted—what he was determined to have.

A shout, greeted by gay laughter, drew his attention to the lake. Gerald was punting Heather Babbacombe about. Face alight, Heather was laughing up at Gerald, smiling down at her from his place in the stern.

Harry raised his brows, resigned to what he strongly suspected was the inevitable. But Heather was still very young, as was Gerald; it would be some years yet before they realised just what this Season had begun.

He hadn't been at all surprised to see his younger brother drive up to the Hall a bare hour after he and Lucinda had arrived. As he had foreseen, Em and Heather had reached the Hall before them; Em had already had the household in hand.

Other than casting him a curious, almost wary look, Em had forborne to comment on his arrangements. To his considerable satisfaction, after the debacle of Asterley Place, it appeared his aunt was content to run in his harness.

Just as his intended, albeit suspiciously, was doing.

Harry rose as she approached, his smile openly welcoming.

Returning his smile, Lucinda put a hand to her hat as a gentle breeze whipped her skirts about her. "It's such a lovely afternoon, I'd thought to stroll the grounds."

"An excellent idea." The breeze died; Harry claimed her hand and with a calmly proprietorial air, tucked it in his arm. "You haven't explored the grotto at the end of the lake, have you?"

Lucinda dutifully admitted ignorance and allowed him to steer her onto the path skirting the lake's edge. Heather saw them and waved; Gerald hallooed. Lucinda smiled and waved back, then let silence fall.

And waited.

As she'd been waiting for the past three days.

Her sojourn at Lester Hall was proving far more pleasant than her projected stay at Asterley Place could ever have been. From the moment Harry had led her into the drawing-room and introduced her to his father, his intentions had been plain. Everything—every glance, every touch, every little gesture, every single word and thought that had passed between them since—had underscored the simple fact. But not once during their twilight strolls on the terrace, throughout their ambling rides through woods and fields, through all the hours they had spent together out of the past seventy-two, had he said one single word to the point.

He hadn't kissed her either—a fact which was fuelling her impatience. Yet she could hardly fault his behaviour—it was gentlemanly in the extreme. The suspicion that he was wooing her—traditionally, according to all the accepted precepts, with all the subtle elegance only one of his experience could command—had taken firm root in her mind.

Which was all very well, but...

With one hand on the crown of her hat, Lucinda tipped her head up and studied the sky. "The sunshine's been so constant one forgets the days are winging past. I fear we should return to London soon."

"I'll escort you back to town tomorrow afternoon."

Lucinda blinked. "Tomorrow afternoon?"

Harry raised his brows. "As I recall, we're all promised to Lady Mickleham on the following evening. Em, I suspect, will need the rest."

"Yes, indeed." Lucinda had forgotten Lady Mickleham's ball entirely. After a moment's hesitation, she continued, "I sometimes wonder if Em is overtiring herself in our cause. Heather and I would never forgive ourselves if she ran herself aground because of us."

Harry's lips twisted in a reluctant grin. "Fear not. She's a seasoned campaigner; she knows how to pace herself. Moreover, I can assure you the prospect of playing hostess to you both for the rest of the Season is currently providing her with expectations of untold enjoyment." That, he knew, was the unvarnished truth.

Lucinda shot him a glance from beneath her lashes, then looked ahead. "I'm relieved you think so, for I must confess I'm looking forward to rejoining the throng. It seems an age since I was swirling around a ballroom, held in a gentleman's arms."

The look Harry sent her was distinctly dry. "Indeed— I'm quite looking forward to your return to the ballrooms myself."

"Oh?" Lucinda bestowed on him a smiling glance. "I hadn't thought you so enamoured of the balls."

"I'm not."

Wide-eyed, Lucinda looked up at him. "What, then, lures you there?"

A siren. Harry looked down into her soft blue eyes— and raised his brows. "I dare say you'll understand once we're part of the crush again."

Lucinda's answering smile was weak. She looked forward—and concentrated on not gnashing her teeth. It was all of a piece—she wondered if he was actually trying to drive her to some rash act. Like visiting his room late tonight.

It was a measure of her frustration that she actually considered the idea before, regretfully, setting it aside. The initiative was no longer hers; he had claimed it when he'd brought her here. She wasn't at all sure how to wrest it from him—and even less certain that he would let it go.

"Here we are."

Harry gestured ahead to where the path apparently disappeared into a hedge of greenery. They approached; he put out a hand and held aside a curtain of vines and creepers—blooming honeysuckle among them—to reveal white marble steps leading upward into a cool, dimly lit cave.

Enchanted, Lucinda ducked under his arm and went ahead, climbing the steps to emerge onto the tassellated floor of a mock-temple, formed by four marble pillars separating a rockface on one quadrant, with the lake on the other three. The pillars supported a domed ceiling, covered in blue and green tiles, highly glazed, reflecting the sunshine glancing in off the lake in myriad hues from turquoise to deep green. Leafy vines and the apricot blooms of honeysuckle wreathed the arches looking onto the lake, the gentle breeze stirring their shadows.

The temple was built out over the water, the central arch giving onto steps which led down to a small stone jetty. Wide-eyed, Lucinda halted in the very centre of the temple—and discovered one of its secrets. Each of the three open arches gave onto a different vista. The one to her right led the eye over a short stretch of lake then straight down a glade thick with ferns and shrubs. To her left lay a view over a long arm of the lake to a distant shore lined with willows and beech. Straight ahead lay the most charming vista of all—Lester Hall itself lay perfectly framed within the arch, glinting water in the foreground, manicured lawns leading up to the imposing façade, flanked by the shrubbery and wilderness to the left, the rose garden, just coming into bloom, and the formal gardens on the right.

"It's beautiful." Lucinda went to stand by one of the pillars to better appreciate the view.

Harry hung back in the shadows, content to watch the play of sunlight across her face. When she leaned back against the pillar and sighed contentedly, he strolled forward to stand beside her. After a moment, he asked, "Have you enjoyed your Season? Do you look to become a devotee—enamoured of the *ton* in all its glory, the crushes, the never-ending carousel of balls, parties and yet more balls?"

Lucinda half turned to look into his face. She searched his eyes, but neither they nor his expression gave any hint of his feelings. She considered, then answered, "By and large, I find the *ton* and its entertainments amusing." Her lips curved in a self-deprecating smile, her eyes reluctantly twinkling. "But you will have to remember that this is my first exposure to 'the carousel'—I'm still enjoying the novelty." Her expression growing serious, she put her head on one side the better to study him. "But the *ton* is your milieu—have you not enjoyed the balls this Season?"

Harry's gaze touched hers, then he looked down. He took one of her hands in his. Small, slender, her hand nestled in his much larger palm, confidently trusting. Harry closed his fingers about hers, his lips twisting. "There have been…compensations."

His lids rose; he met Lucinda's gaze.

Slowly, she raised her brows. "Indeed?" When he offered nothing more but simply looked away across the lake, she followed his gaze to Lester Hall, basking in the afternoon sun. As at Hallows Hall, Lucinda felt the tug of old memories. She sighed. "However, to answer your question, despite my fascination, I seriously doubt I could stomach a never-ending round of *ton*nish life. I fear I would need a steady diet of country peace to enable me to brave the Season on a regular basis." She slanted a glance at Harry and found him watching her. Her lips quirked. "My parents lived very retired in a rambling old house in Hampshire. When they died, I removed to the Yorkshire moors, which, of course, is as retired as it's possible to be."

Harry's features relaxed, subtly but definitely. "So you're a country miss at heart?" He lifted one brow. Slowly, his eyes on hers, he raised her hand. "Naïve?" He brushed his lips across her fingertips, then turned her hand in his. "Innocent?" His lids fell as he pressed a kiss to her palm.

Lucinda shuddered; she made no effort to hide it. She couldn't breathe, could barely think as Harry's lids rose and his eyes, green and direct, met hers.

His lips twisted; he hesitated, then shifted closer and bent his head to hers.

"And mine?"

He breathed the question against her lips, then captured them in a long, commanding kiss.

Lucinda answered in the only way she could—she turned to him, sliding her arms up and wrapping them about his neck, then kissed him back with a fervour to match his own.

Instinct prompted Harry to edge back, drawing her around the pillar to where the shadows shielded them from inadvertent eyes.

Silence filled the small pavilion. The breeze idly played with the honeysuckle, wafting perfume through the air; a drake hooted from some distant reed-fringed shore. The shadows shifted gently over the figures entwined in the pillar's lee. Spring had blossomed; summer stood in the wings, eager for its day.

"Oh! How lovely—a Grecian temple! Can we go and see?"

Heather's high-pitched tones carried easily across the water, hauling Harry and Lucinda back to their senses. Harry's chest swelled as he drew in a deep breath—then looked down. Lucinda's eyes slowly filled with comprehension; Harry felt his lips firm as he saw his frustration mirrored in misty blue.

Muttering a curse, he bent his head to taste her lips one last time, then drew his hand from her breast and quickly,

expertly, rearranged her bodice, doing up the tiny buttons
with a dexterity equal to that with which he had undone
them.

Blinking, struggling to subdue her harried breathing,
Lucinda straightened his collar and brushed back the
heavy lock of hair she'd disarranged. She had shifted his
cravat; her hands fluttered uncertainly.

Harry abruptly stepped back, long fingers reaching for
the starched folds. "Your skirts."

Lucinda looked down—and swallowed a gasp. She
shot an indignant glare at Harry, which he met with an arrogantly raised brow, then shook the clinging muslin
down, smoothing the folds so that the skirts once more
hung free. She spied her hat lying on the floor; she swiped
it up and set it in place, tangling the ties in her haste.

"Here—let me." Harry deftly separated the ribbons,
then tied them in a neat bow.

Putting up a hand to check on his efforts, Lucinda
threw him a haughty glance. "Your talents are quite astonishing."

Harry's smile was a touch grim. "And extremely use-
ful, you'll admit."

Lucinda tilted her chin, then, turning, plastered a bright
smile on her lips as Gerald's voice floated up from the bottom of the steps.

"Take care! Wait till I make fast."

Lucinda strolled forward into the sunshine at the top of
the steps. "Hello—did you have a pleasant time on the lake?"

Gerald looked up at her and blinked. When Harry appeared from the shadows behind her, Gerald's expression
turned wary.

But Harry only smiled, albeit a touch coolly. "Just in
time, Gerald. Now we can take the punt and you can show
Miss Babbacombe around the temple then stroll back."

"Oh, yes! Let's do that." Heather could barely wait for Gerald to assist her from the bobbing craft. "It's such a lovely spot—so secluded."

"Usually," Harry murmured, so low only Lucinda heard.

She shot him a warning glance but her smile didn't waver. "The tiles on the ceiling are quite splendid."

"Oh?" Heather trod up the steps and into the temple without further encouragement.

Gerald, meanwhile, was staring, mesmerised, at Harry's gold acorn pin, the one his excessively precise brother used to anchor his cravat. The pin was askew. Blinking in bemusement, Gerald raised his eyes to Harry's, only to be met by a languid, distinctly bored green gaze—which he knew very well meant he'd be well advised to quit his brother's presence forthwith. "Ah—yes. We'll walk back."

His expression studiously blank, Gerald nodded to Lucinda and hurried after Heather.

"Mrs Babbacombe?"

Lucinda turned to find Harry, the long pole in one hand, steadying the boat, as he held his other hand out to her. She put her fingers in his; he helped her into the punt. Once she had settled her skirts on the cushions in the prow, he stepped into the stern and poled off.

The dark water glided past the hull; reclining against the cushions, Lucinda trailed her fingertips in the lake— and filled her sight with Harry. He avoided her gaze, concentrating, to all appearances, on their surroundings.

With a small, disbelieving sniff, Lucinda switched her gaze to the shores slipping past.

The ends of Harry's lips lifted; his gaze, falling to her profile, was unusually soft but cynical, too. Hands on the pole, he propelled them through the water; not even the most inveterate rake could seduce a woman while poling a punt. He hadn't planned their recent close brush with intimacy—for once, he was truly grateful for his younger brother's interruption. He had reason enough to marry his siren, and too many excuses he had yet to convince her he no longer needed. Their night at Asterley had only added to the list, lending weight to the social pressures she might imagine had influenced him. Social pressures he himself had foolishly raised in order to hide the truth.

Harry lifted his gaze to the vista before them—the façade of Lester Hall—Jack's home now, no longer his. His gaze grew distant; his jaw firmed.

She had made it plain that it was important for her to know the truth of why he wished to wed her; during the past days, he had realised it was important to him to know that she did. So before they were done, before he again asked her to be his bride, they would have it all clear between them.

His siren would know the truth—and believe it.

LUCINDA OPENED HER EYES the next morning to discover a dusky pink rose unfurling on her pillow. Enchanted, she took the delicate bloom into her hand, cradling it gently. The dew on the petals fractured the sunshine.

Her smile wondering, delighted, she sat up and pushed the covers back. Every morning she had spent at Lester Hall, she had woken to find just such a tribute waiting somewhere in her room.

But on her pillow…?

Still smiling, she rose.

Fifteen minutes later, her expression serene, she glided through the breakfast parlour doors, the rose between her fingers. As usual, Harry's father was not present—he was a semi-invalid and did not stir before noon; Em adhered to town hours so would not rise until eleven. As for Heather and Gerald, they had the night before announced their intention of riding to a distant folly; they would, Lucinda judged, be well on their way by now. Which left Harry alone, seated at the table's head, long legs stretched out before him, his fingers crooked about the handle of a cup.

Lucinda felt his gaze as she entered; with every appearance of unconsciousness, she considered her lover's token, then, with a softly distant smile, tucked it lovingly into her cleavage, making great show of nestling the velvet petals against the curves of her breasts.

She looked up to see Harry transfixed. His fingers had tightened about the handle of his cup, a stillness, like that of a predator about to pounce, had settled over his long frame. His gaze was riveted on the rose.

"Good morning." Lucinda smiled sunnily and went forward to take the seat the butler held for her.

Harry tried to speak, then had to clear his throat. "Good morning." He forced his gaze to Lucinda's; it sharpened as he read her expression. He shifted in his seat. "I'd thought to visit the stud before we head back to town. I wondered if you'd care to accompany me—and perhaps renew your acquaintance with Thistledown."

Lucinda reached for the teapot. "Thistledown's here?"

Harry nodded and took a long sip of coffee.

"Is it far?"

"Only a few miles." He watched as Lucinda spread a muffin with jam. She leant both elbows on the table, the muffin held with both hands, and took a bite; a minute later, the tip of her tongue went the rounds of her lips. Harry blinked.

"Will we ride?" Lucinda didn't think to voice her agreement formally; he had known from the first she would go.

Harry stared at the rose nestling between her breasts. "No—we'll take the gig."

Lucinda smiled at her muffin—and took another bite.

Twenty minutes later, still clad in her lilac walking dress, the dusky pink rose in pride of place, she sat beside Harry as he tooled the gig down a narrow lane. "So you don't spend much time in London?"

Harry raised his brows, his attention on the bay between the shafts. "As little as possible." He grimaced. "But with a venture like the stud, it's necessary to remain visible amongst the *cognescenti,* which is to say, the gentlemen of the *ton.*"

"Ah—I see." Lucinda nodded sagely, the wide brim of her villager hat framing her face. "Contrary to all appearances, you care nothing for the balls, the routs, the parties—and less for the good opinion of the feminine half of the *ton.* Indeed—" she opened her eyes wide "—I cannot understand how you have come by the reputation you bear. Unless—" She broke off to look enquiringly up at him. "Perhaps it's all a hum?"

Harry's attention had left the bay gelding; it was focused on Lucinda, the light in his eyes enough to make her shiver. "My reputation, my dear, was not gained in the *ballrooms.*"

Lucinda kept her gaze wide. "Oh?"

"No," Harry stated—more in answer to the hopeful expression in her eyes than her question. His expression severely reproving, he clicked the reins, setting the horse to a trot.

Lucinda grinned.

The stud was soon reached. Harry tossed the reins of the gig to a groom, then lifted Lucinda down. "I need to talk to my head-stableman, Hamish MacDowell," he said as they strolled towards the stable complex. "Thistledown should be in her box. It's in the second yard."

Lucinda nodded. "I'll wait for you there." The stables were a massive conglomerate of buildings—stables proper, as well as tackrooms and barns housing training gigs as well as what appeared to be quite enormous quantities of fodder. "Did you start it up—or was it already in existence?"

"My father established the stud in his youth. I took over after his accident—about eight years ago." Harry's gaze swept over the stud—the neat, cobbled yards and stone buildings before them, the fenced fields on either side. "Whenever I'm home I offer to drive him over—but he never comes." He looked down, then added, "I think seeing it all—the horses—reminds him of his inability. He was a bruising rider until a fall put him in that chair of his."

"So you're the son who takes after him most in the matter of horses?"

Harry's lips twitched. "In that regard—and, some might argue, his other most consuming passion."

Lucinda glanced at him, then away. "I see," she replied, her tone repressive. "So is this now all yours?" Her gesture took in the whole complex. "Or is it a family concern?"

She looked up at Harry, light colour in her cheeks, but made no attempt to excuse the question.

Harry smiled. "Legally, it's still my father's. Effectively—" He halted, lifting his head to sweep his surroundings, before looking down to meet her gaze. "I'm master of all I survey."

Slowly, Lucinda raised her brows. "Indeed?" If he was her master, did that make her his mistress? But no—she knew very well that was not his aim. "I believe you said Thistledown was in the second yard?" When Harry nodded, she inclined her head regally. "I'll await you there."

Nose in the air, she headed through the archway into

the second yard. Inwardly, she humphed dejectedly. What *was* his reason for delay?

She located Thistledown by the simple expedient of standing in the middle of the square yard and looking about until an excitedly bobbing head caught her eye.

The mare seemed overjoyed to see her, pushing her nose against her skirts. Lucinda hunted in her pockets and located the sugar lumps she'd stolen from the breakfast table; her offering was accepted with every evidence of equine pleasure.

Folding her arms on the top of the stall door, Lucinda watched as the mare lapped water from a bucket. "Can it really be so very difficult to simply ask me again?"

Thistledown rolled a dark eye enquiringly.

Lucinda gestured. "Women are notoriously changeable—in all the novels *I've* ever read, the heroines always said no when first asked."

Thistledown harrumphed and came to nudge her shoulder.

"Precisely." Lucinda nodded and absent-mindedly stroked the mare's nose. "I'm entitled to a chance to change my mind." After a moment, she wrinkled her nose. "Well—at least revise my decision in the light of fresh developments."

For she very definitely hadn't changed her mind. She knew what she knew—and Harry knew it, too. It was simply a matter of the damned man admitting it.

Lucinda humphed; Thistledown whinnied softly.

From the shadows by the tack room, Harry watched the mare shake her head and nudge Lucinda. He smiled to himself—then turned as Dawlish came lumbering up.

"Seen Hamish, have you?"

"I have. That colt of Warlock's looks promising, I agree."

"Aye—he'll win a pot before he's done, I reckon." Dawlish followed Harry's gaze to Lucinda. He nodded in her direction. "P'raps you should introduce the lady to him—get her to have a little chat to him like she did with the mare?"

In mock surprise, Harry stared at his henchman. "Is that approval I detect? From you—the arch-misogynist?"

Dawlish frowned. "Don't know as how I know what a misogynist is, rightly, but at least you've had the sense to find one as the horses like—and who might actually come in handy to boot." Dawlish snorted. "What I wants to know is why you can't get a move on—so's we can all get back to knowing where we are?"

Harry's gaze clouded. "There are a few loose ends I'm presently tying up."

"Is that what you calls them these days?"

"Apropos of which," Harry continued imperturbably, "Did you get that message to Lord Ruthven?"

"Aye—his lordship said as he'd see to it."

"Good." Harry's gaze had returned to Lucinda. "We'll leave about two. I'll take the curricle—you can go with Em."

He didn't wait for Dawlish's grumbling grunt but sauntered after Lucinda. She had left the mare and wandered along the loose boxes to stop at the end where a grey head had come out to greet her.

She looked around as Harry drew near. "Did he win at Newmarket?"

Harry grinned and stroked Cribb's nose. "He did." The horse nudged his pockets but Harry shook his head. "No apples today, I'm afraid."

"When's he racing next?"

"Not this year." Harry took Lucinda's arm and steered her towards the gate. "The Newmarket win took him to the top of his class; I've decided to retire him at his peak, so to speak. He'll stand for the rest of this season. I might give him a run next year, but if the present interest in him as a stud continues, I'd be a fool to let him waste his energies on the track."

Lucinda's lips quirked; she struggled to suppress her grin.

Harry noticed. "What is it?"

Colouring slightly, Lucinda shot him a glance from beneath her lids.

Harry raised his brows higher.

Lucinda grimaced. "If you must know," she said, switching her gaze to the horizon. "I was simply struck by the fact that managing a stud is a peculiarly apt enterprise for…er, one with your qualifications."

Harry laughed, an entirely spontaneous sound Lucinda realised she had not before heard.

"My dear Mrs Babbacombe!" His green eyes quizzed her. "What a thoroughly shocking observation to make."

Lucinda glared, then put her nose in the air.

Harry chuckled. Ignoring her blushes, he drew her closer. "Strangely enough," he said, his lips distinctly curved, "you're the first to ever put it into words."

Lucinda fell back on one of Em's snorts—the one that signified deep disapproval. Disapproval gave way to hope when she realised Harry was not leading her back to the gig but towards a small wood bordering the nearest field. A path led between the trees, cut back to permit easy strolling.

Perhaps…? She never finished the thought, distracted by the discovery that the wood was in reality no more than a windbreak. Beyond it, the path was paved as it ambled about a small pond where water lilies battled with reeds. "That needs clearing."

Harry glanced at the pond. "We'll get to it eventually."

Lucinda looked up and followed his gaze—to the house. Large, rambling, with old-fashioned gables, it was made of local stone with a good slate roof. On the ground floor, bow windows stood open to the summer air. A rose crept up one wall to nod pale yellow blooms before one of the upstairs windows. Two large, leafy oaks stood one to each side, casting cool shade over the gravelled drive which wound from some gateway out of sight down a long avenue to end in a sweep before the front door.

She glanced at Harry. "Lestershall?"

He nodded, his eyes on the manor house. "My house." Briefly, his lips twisted. "My home." With a languid wave, he gestured ahead. "Shall we?"

Suddenly breathless, Lucinda inclined her head.

They strolled on to where their path debouched onto the lawn, then crossed the grassy expanse and ducked beneath the low branches of one of the oaks to join the drive. As they approached the shallow stone steps, Lucinda noticed the front door stood ajar.

"I've never really lived here." Harry steadied her as they scrunched across the gravel. "It had fallen into disrepair, so I've had a small army through to set it to rights."

A burly individual in a carpenter's leather apron appeared in the doorway as they set foot on the steps.

"Mornin', Mr Lester." The man ducked his head, his cheery face lit by a smile. "It's all coming together nicely—as I think you'll find. Not much more to do."

"Good morning, Catchbrick. This is Mrs Babbacombe. If it won't inconvenience you and your men, I'd like to show her around."

"No inconvenience at all, sir." Catchbrick bowed to Lucinda, bright eyes curious. "Won't be no trouble—like I said, we're nearly done."

So saying, he stood back and waved them on into the hall.

Lucinda crossed the threshold into a long and surprisingly spacious rectangular hall. Half-panelling in warm oak was surmounted by plastered walls, presently bare. A mound draped in dust covers in the centre of the floor clearly contained a round table and a large hall stand. Light streamed in from the large circular fanlight. Stairs, also in oak with an ornately carved balustrade, led upwards, the half-landing sporting a long window which, Lucinda suspected, looked out over the rear gardens. Two corridors flanked the stairs, the left ending in a green baize door.

"The drawing-room's this way."

Lucinda turned to find Harry standing by a set of handsome doors, presently set wide; a boy was polishing the panels industriously.

The drawing-room proved to be of generous proportions, although on far smaller a scale than at the Hall. It boasted a deep bow window complete with window seat and a long low fireplace topped by a wide mantel. The dining-room, now shaping to be an elegant apartment, had, as had the drawing-room, a large mound of furniture swathed in dust cloths in its midst. Lucinda couldn't resist lifting one corner of the cloth.

"Some pieces will need to be replaced but most of the furniture seems sound enough." Harry's gaze remained on her face.

"Sound enough?" Lucinda threw back the cover to reveal the heavy top of an old oak sideboard. "It's rather more than that. This is a very fine piece—and someone's had the sense to keep it well-polished."

"Mrs Simpkins. She's the housekeeper," Harry supplied in answer to Lucinda's raised brows. "You'll meet her in a moment."

Dropping the dustsheet, Lucinda went to one of the pair of long windows, presently propped open, and looked out. The windows gave onto a terrace which ran down the side of the house and disappeared around the corner to run beneath the windows of the parlour, which itself gave off the dining-room, as she next discovered.

Standing before the parlour windows, looking out across the rolling lawns, ringed by flowerbeds, presently a colourful riot of spring and early summer blooms, Lucinda felt a deep sense of certainty, of belonging, as if she was putting down roots where she stood. This, she knew, was a place she could live and grow and blossom.

"These three reception-rooms open one into the other." Harry waved at the hinged panels separating the parlour from the dining room "The result's quite large enough to host a hunt ball."

Lucinda blinked at him. "Indeed?"

His features impassive, Harry nodded and waved her on. "The breakfast parlour's this way."

So was the morning room. As he led her through the bright, presently empty and echoing rooms, lit by the sunshine streaming in through the diamond-paned windows, Lucinda noted the dry plaster walls waiting to be papered, the woodwork and panelling already polished and gleaming.

All the furniture she saw was old but lovingly polished, warm oak, most of it.

"There's only the decorating left to do," Harry informed her as he led her down a short corridor running beside the large room he had described as his study-cum-library. There, the bookshelves had been emptied and polished to within an inch of their lives; piles of tomes stood ready to be returned to their places once the decorating was done. "But the firm I've hired won't be in for a few weeks yet—time enough to make the necessary decisions."

Lucinda eyed him narrowly—but before she could think of any probing comment, she was distracted by what lay beyond the door at the end of the corridor. An elegantly proportioned room, it overlooked the side garden; roses nodded at the wide windows, framing green vistas.

Harry glanced about. "I haven't yet decided what this room should be used for."

Looking around, Lucinda found no pile of shrouded furniture. Instead, her gaze was drawn to new shelves, lining one wall. They were wide and open, just right for stacking ledgers. She glanced about; the windows let in good light, an essential for doing accounts and dealing with correspondence.

Her heart beating in a very odd cadence, Lucinda turned to look at Harry. "Indeed?"

"Hmm." His expression considering, he gestured to the door. "Come—I'll introduce you to the Simpkins."

Suppressing a snort of pure impatience, Lucinda allowed him to steer her back down the corridor and through the baize-covered door. Here she came upon the first evidence of established life. The kitchens were scrupulously clean, the pots gleaming on their hooks on the wall, a modern range residing in the centre of the wide fireplace.

A middle-aged couple were seated at the deal table; they quickly got to their feet, consternation in their faces as they gazed at Lucinda.

"Simpkins here acts as general factotum—keeping an eye on the place generally. His uncle is butler at the Hall. Mrs Babbacombe, Simpkins."

"Ma'am." Simpkins bowed low.

"And this is Mrs Simpkins, cook and housekeeper—without whom the furniture would never have survived."

Mrs Simpkins, a buxom, rosy-cheeked matron of im-posing girth, bobbed a curtsy to Lucinda but fixed Harry with a baleful eye. "Aye—and if you had only thought to warn me, Master Harry, I would have had tea and scones ready and waiting."

"As you might guess," Harry put in smoothly, "Mrs Simpkins was once an undernurse at the Hall."

"Aye—and I can remember you in short coats quite clearly, young master." Mrs Simpkins frowned at him. "Now you just take the lady for a stroll and I'll pop a pot on. By the time you come back I'll have your tea laid ready in the garden."

"I wouldn't want to put you to—"

Harry's pained sigh cut across Lucinda's disclaimer. "I hesitate to break it to you, my dear, but Martha Simpkins is a tyrant. It's best to just yield gracefully." So saying, he took her hand and led her towards the door. "I'll just show Mrs Babbacombe the upstairs rooms, Martha."

Lucinda turned her head to throw a smile back at Mrs Simpkins, who beamed delightedly in reply.

The stairs led to a short gallery.

"No family portraits, I'm afraid," Harry said. "Those are all at the Hall."

"Is there one of you?" Lucinda looked up at him.

"Yes—but it's hardly a good likeness. It was done when I was eighteen."

Lucinda raised her brows but, recalling Lady Coleby's words, made no comment.

"This is the master suite." Harry threw open a pair of panelled doors at the end of the gallery. The room beyond was large, half-panelled, the warm patina of wood ex-tending to the surrounds of the bow window and its seat. A carved mantel framed the fireplace, unusually large; a very large structure stood in the centre of the floor, screened by the inevitable dustcovers. Lucinda glanced at it curiously, but obediently turned as Harry, a hand at her back, conducted her through the adjoining dressing-rooms.

"I'm afraid," he said, as they returned to the main chamber, "that Lestershall doesn't run to separate bedrooms for husband and wife." Lucinda glanced up at him. "Not, of course," he continued imperturbably, "that that should concern you."

Lucinda watched as he leaned a shoulder against the window frame. When he merely returned her expectant look with one of the blandest innocence, she humphed and turned her attention to the large, shrouded mound.

"It's a four-poster," she decided. She crossed to lift a corner of the dustcover and peer under. A dark cave lay before her. With thick, barley-sugar posts, the bed was fully canopied and draped with matching brocades. "It's enormous."

"Indeed." Harry watched her absorption. "And has quite a history, too, if the tales one hears are true."

Lucinda looked up from her study. "What tales?"

"Rumour has it the bed dates from Elizabethan times, as does the house. Apparently, all the brides brought back to the house have used it."

Lucinda wrinkled her nose. "That's hardly surprising." She dropped the covers and dusted her hands.

Harry's lips slowly curved. "Not in itself, perhaps." He pushed away from the window and strolled to where Lucinda stood waiting. "But there are brass rings set into the headboard." His brows rose; his expression turned pensive. "They quite excite the imagination." Taking Lucinda's arm, he turned her towards the door. "I must remember to show them to you sometime."

Lucinda opened her mouth, then abruptly closed it.

She allowed him to lead her back into the corridor. She was still considering the brass rings when they reached the end of the hall, having looked in on a set of unremarkable bedchambers along the way.

"These stairs lead to the attics. The nursery is there, as well as the Simpkins's rooms."

The nursery proved to take up one entire side of the commodious space beneath the rafters. The dormer windows were set low, just right for youngsters. The suite comprised five interconnecting rooms.

"Bedrooms for the head nurse and tutor on either end, bedrooms for their charges, male and female and this, of course, is the schoolroom." Harry stood in the centre of the large room and looked around, a certain pride showing in his expression.

Lucinda eyed it consideringly. "These rooms are even larger, relatively speaking, than your bed."

Harry raised his brows. "I had rather thought they would have need to be. I'm planning on having a large family."

Lucinda stared into his clear green eyes—and wondered how he dared. "A large family?" she queried, refusing to retreat in disorder. "Taking after your father in that respect, too?" She held his gaze for an instant longer, then strolled to look out of a window. "Three boys, I assume, is your goal?"

Harry's gaze followed her. "And three girls. To preserve a reasonable balance," he added in reply to Lucinda's surprised glance.

Annoyed at her reaction, and the fluttery feeling that had laid siege to her stomach, Lucinda snorted. And glanced about again. "Even with six, there's room enough to spare."

She had thought that would be the end of that particular conversation but the reprobate teasing her hadn't finished.

"Ah—but I'd thought to leave sufficient space for the odd few who might not come in the correct order, if you take my meaning. Begetting boy or girl is such a random event, after all."

Lucinda stared into impassive green eyes—and longed to ask if he was joking. But there was something in the subtle tension that held him that left the distinct impression he wasn't.

Feeling a quiver—no longer odd but decidedly familiar—ripple through her, Lucinda decided she'd had enough. If he could talk about their children then he could put his mind to the first of the points that came before. She straightened and lifted her head, her gaze holding his.

"Harry—"

He shifted, turning to look out of the window. "Mrs Simpkins has our tea and scones waiting. Come—we can't disappoint her." With an innocent smile, he took Lucinda's arm and turned her towards the door. "It's nearly noon, too—I suspect we should get back immediately after our impromptu feast. We don't want to be late getting on the road this afternoon."

Lucinda stared at him in disbelief.

Harry smiled. "I know how much you're looking forward to getting back to town—and waltzing in gentlemen's arms."

Frustration filled Lucinda, so intense it made her giddy. When Harry merely raised his brows, all mild and innocent, she narrowed her eyes and glared.

Harry's lips twitched; he gestured to the door.

Lucinda drew in a deep, steadying breath. If she wasn't a lady...

Setting her teeth against the urge to grind them, she slid

her hand into the crook of his arm. Lips set in a thoroughly disapproving, not to say disgruntled line, she allowed him to lead her downstairs.

Chapter Thirteen

"So—do you have it clear?" Seated behind the desk in his library, Harry drew an unnibbed pen back and forth between his fingers, his gaze, very green, trained on the individual in the chair before him.

Plain brown eyes regarded him from an unremarkable countenance; the man's attire proclaimed him not of the *ton* but his occupation could not be discerned from the drab garments. Phineas Salter could have been anything—almost anyone—which was precisely what made him so successful at his trade.

The ex-Bow Street Runner nodded. "Aye, sir. I'm to check up on the gentlemen—Mr Earle Joliffe and Mr Mortimer Babbacombe—with a view to uncovering any reason they might have to wish a Mrs Lucinda Babbacombe—the said Mortimer's aunt-by-marriage—ill."

"*And* you're to do it without raising a dust." Harry's gaze became acute.

Salter inclined his head. "Naturally, sir. If the gentlemen are up to anything, we wouldn't want to tip them the wink. Not before we're ready."

Harry grimaced. "Quite. But I should also stress that we do not wish, at any time, for Mrs Babbacombe herself to become aware of our suspicions. Or, indeed, that there might be any reason for investigation at all."

Salter frowned. "Without disrespect, sir, do you think that's wise? From what you've told me, these villains aren't above drastic action. Wouldn't it be better if the lady's forewarned?"

"If it were any other lady, one who would be predictably shocked and content thereafter to leave the matter in our hands, I'd unhesitatingly agree. However, Mrs Babbacombe is not one such." Harry studied his newest employee; when he spoke his tone was instructive. "I'd be willing to wager that, if she were to learn of Babbacombe's apparent involvement with her recent adventures, Mrs Babbacombe would order her carriage around and have herself driven to his lodgings, intent on demanding an explanation. Alone."

Salter's expression blanked. "Ah." He blinked. "A bit naïve, is she?"

"No." Harry's tone hardened. "Not particularly. She's merely incapable of recognising her own vulnerability but, conversely, has infinite confidence in her ability to prevail." The planes of his face shifted, his expression now mirroring his tone. "In this case, I would rather not have her put it to the test."

"No, indeed." Salter nodded. "From what little I've heard tell, this Joliffe's not the sort for a lady to tangle with."

"Precisely." Harry rose; Salter rose, too. The ex-Runner was a stocky man, broad and heavy. Harry nodded. "Report back to me as soon as you have any word."

"I will that, sir. You may depend on me."

Harry shook Salter's hand. Dawlish, who, at Harry's

intimation, had silently witnessed the interview, straightened from his position by the door and showed Salter out. Turning to the windows, Harry stood idly flicking the pen between his fingers, gazing unseeing at the courtyard beyond.

Salter was well-known to the intimates of Jackson's saloon and Cribb's parlour. A boxer of some skill, he was one of the few not of the *ton* with a ready entrée to those *ton*nish precincts. But it was his other skills that had led Harry to call him in. Salter's fame as a Runner had been considerable but clouded; the magistrates had not approved of his habit of, quite literally, using thieves to catch thieves. His successes had not ameliorated their disapproval and he had parted company from the London constabulary by mutual accord. Since then, however, he had established a reputation among certain of the *ton*'s gentlemen as a reliable man whenever matters of questionable, possibly illegal, behaviour needed to be investigated with absolute discretion.

Such a matter, in Harry's opinion, was Mortimer Babbacombe's apparent interest in Lucinda's well-being.

He would have handled the matter himself but was at a loss to understand Mortimer's motives. He could hardly let the matter rest and, given his conviction that it was linked with the incident on the Newmarket road, he had opted for caution, to whit, the discretion and skill for which Salter was renown.

"Well, then!" Dawlish returned and shut the door. "A fine broiling, altogether." He slanted a glance at Harry. "You want me to keep an eye on her?"

Slowly, Harry raised his brows. "It's an idea." He paused, then asked, "How do you think her coachman—Joshua, isn't it?—would take the news?"

"Right concerned, he'd be."

Harry's eyes narrowed. "And her maid, the redoubtable Agatha?"

"Even more so, unless I miss my guess. Right protective, she is—after you took them away from Asterley and organised to cover the lady's tracks, she's revised her opinion of you."

Harry's lips twitched. "Good. Then recruit her as well. I have a feeling we should keep as many eyes on Mrs Babbacombe as possible—just in case."

"Aye—no sense in taking any risks." Dawlish headed for the door. "Not after all your hard work."

Harry's brows flew up. He turned—but Dawlish had escaped.

Hard work? Harry's lips firmed into a line. His expression resigned, he turned back to the greenery outside. The truly hard part was yet to come but he had charted his course and was determined to stick to it.

When next he proposed to his siren, he wanted no arguments about love.

"Oh!" Dawlish's head popped back around the door. "Just remembered—it's Lady Mickleham's tonight. Want me to organise the carriages and all when I see Joshua?"

Harry nodded. The skies outside were a beautiful blue. "Before you go, have the greys put to."

"You going for a drive?"

"Yes." Harry's expression turned grim. "In the Park."

Fergus opened his aunt's door to him fifteen minutes later. Harry handed him his gloves and shrugged off his greatcoat. "I assume my aunt is resting?"

"Indeed, sir. She's been laid down this hour and past."

"I won't disturb her—it's Mrs Babbacombe I wish to see."

"Ah." Fergus blinked, his expression blanking. "I fear Mrs Babbacombe is engaged, sir."

Harry slowly turned his head until his gaze rested on Fergus's impassive countenance. "Indeed?"

He waited; Fergus, to his relief, deigned to answer his unvoiced question without insisting on an embarrassing prompt.

"She's in the back parlour—her office—with a Mr Mabberly. A well-spoken young gentleman—he's her agent, I understand."

"I see." Harry hesitated, then, quite sure Fergus understood only too well, dismissed him with a nod. "No need to announce me." With that, he mounted the stairs, reining in his impatience enough to make the ascent at least appear idle. But when he gained the upper corridor, his strides lengthened. He paused with his hand on the parlour doorknob; he could hear muted voices within.

His expression distinctly hard, he opened the door.

Lucinda was seated on the *chaise,* an open ledger on her lap. She looked up—and broke off in mid-sentence to stare at him.

A youngish gentleman, precise and soberly dressed, was hovering by her shoulder, leaning over to look at the figures to which she was pointing.

"I wasn't expecting you," Lucinda said, shaking her wits into order.

"Good afternoon," Harry replied.

"Indeed." Lucinda's glance held a definite warning. "I believe I've mentioned Mr Mabberly to you—he's my agent. He assists me with the inns. Mr Mabberly—Mr Lester."

Mr Mabberly somewhat hesitantly put out his hand. Harry regarded it for an instant, then shook it briefly. And immediately turned to Lucinda. "Will you be long?"

Lucinda looked him in the eye. "At least another half-hour."

Mr Mabberly shifted, casting a nervous glance from Lucinda to Harry and back again. "Er…perhaps—"

"We have yet to do the Edinburgh accounts," Lucinda declared, shutting the heavy ledger and lifting it from her lap. Mr Mabberly hastened to relieve her of it. "It's that book there—the third one." As Mr Mabberly hurried across the room to retrieve the required tome, Lucinda raised limpid eyes to Harry's face. "Perhaps, Mr Lester—"

"I'll wait." Harry turned, walked two paces to the nearest chair, and sat down.

Lucinda watched him impassively—she didn't dare smile. Then Anthony Mabberly was back and she turned her attention to her three Edinburgh inns.

As Lucinda checked figures and tallies and rates, comparing the present quarter with the last and that of the year before, Harry studied Mr Mabberly. Within five minutes, he had seen enough to reassure him; Mr Mabberly might regard his employer as something of a goddess, but Harry was left with the distinct impression that his admiration was occasioned more by her business acumen than by her person. Indeed, inside of ten minutes, he was ready to swear that Mr Mabberly's regard was entirely intellectual.

Relaxing, Harry stretched out his legs—and allowed his gaze to settle on his principal concern.

Lucinda sensed the easing of his tension—not a difficult feat as it had reached her in waves—with a measure of relief. If he refused to accept she would need to deal with such as Anthony Mabberly, that regardless of all else she had a business to run, then they would face serious hurdles all too soon. But all appeared serene. While waiting for Mr Mabberly to fetch the last ledger, she glanced at Harry to find him regarding her with nothing more unnerving than very definite boredom in his eyes.

He lifted a brow at her but offered no word.

Lucinda turned back to her work—and quickly completed it.

Mr Mabberly did not dally but neither did he run. He very correctly took his leave of Lucinda, then bowed punctiliously to Harry before departing, promising to carry out Lucinda's commissions and report as usual the next week.

"Humph!" Harry remained standing, watching the door close behind Mabberly.

After one glance at his face, Lucinda remarked, "I do hope you're not about to tell me there is any impropriety in my seeing my agent alone?"

Harry bit his tongue; he swung to face her, his gaze distinctly cool. As he watched Lucinda's gaze shifted, going past him.

"After all," she continued, "he could hardly be considered a danger."

Harry followed her gaze to the daybed before the windows. He looked back at her, and surprised an expression of uncertainty, mixed with a readily identifiable longing. They were, once again, very much alone; his inclinations, he knew, matched hers. Harry cleared his throat. "I came to persuade you to a drive in the Park."

"The Park?" Surprised, Lucinda looked up at him. Em had told her Harry rarely drove in the Park during the hours of the fashionable promenades. "Why?"

"Why?" Harry looked down at her, his expression momentarily blank. Then he frowned. "What sort of a ridiculous question is that?" When Lucinda's gaze turned suspicious, he waved a languid hand. "I merely thought you might be bored and could do with the fresh air. Lady Mickleham's balls are notoriously crowded."

"Oh." Lucinda slowly rose, her eyes searching his face

but with no success. "Perhaps a drive would be a good idea."

"Indubitably." Harry waved her to the door. "I'll wait downstairs while you get your coat and bonnet."

Ten minutes later, Lucinda allowed him to lift her into his curricle, still not at all sure she understood. But he was here—she could see no reason to deny herself his company. Reflecting that after yesterday, when he had driven her all the way from Lester Hall to Audley Street in his curricle, she should have had a surfeit of his dry comments, she blithely settled her skirts and looked forward to a few more.

He didn't disappoint her.

As they passed through the heavy wrought-iron gates and on into the Park, bowling along the shaded drive, Harry slanted her a glance. "I regret, my dear, that as my horses are very fresh, we won't be stopping to chat— you'll have to make do with waves and smiling glances."

Engaged in looking about her, Lucinda raised her brows. "Indeed? But if we aren't to chat, why are we here?"

"To see and be seen, of course." Again Harry diverted his attention from his leader, who was indeed very skittish, to glance her way. "That, I have always understood, is the purpose of the fashionable promenades."

"Ah." Lucinda smiled sunnily back at him, not the least perturbed. She was quite content to sit beside him in the sun and watch him tool about the gravel drives, long fingers managing the reins.

He met her gaze, then looked back at his horses. Still smiling, Lucinda looked ahead to where the drive was lined by the barouches and landaus of the matrons of the *ton*. The afternoon was well advanced; there were many who had reached the Park before them. Harry was forced to rein in his horses as the traffic increased, curricles and phaetons of all descriptions wending their way between the carriages drawn up by the verge. Lady Sefton, holding court in her barouche, waved and nodded; Lucinda noticed that she appeared somewhat startled.

Lady Somercote and Mrs Wyncham likewise greeted her, then Countess Lieven favoured them with a long, dark-eyed stare before inclining her head graciously.

Harry humphed. "She's so stiff-necked I keep waiting to hear the crack."

Lucinda smothered a giggle as, rounding the next curve, they came upon Princess Esterhazy. The Princess's large eyes opened wide, then she beamed and nodded delightedly.

Lucinda smiled back; inwardly, she frowned. After a moment, she asked, "Do you frequently drive ladies in the Park?"

Harry clicked his reins; the curricle shot through a gap between a swan-necked phaeton and another curricle, leaving both the other owners gasping. "Not recently."

Lucinda narrowed her eyes. "*How* recently?"

Harry merely shrugged, his gaze fixed on his horses' ears.

Lucinda regarded him closely. When he offered not a word, she ventured, "Not since Lady Coleby?"

He looked at her then, his green glance filled with dire warning, his lips a severe line. Then he looked back at his horses. After a moment, he said, his tone exceedingly grudging, "She was Millicent Pane then."

Harry's memory flitted back through the years; "Millicent Lester" was what he'd been thinking then. His lips twisted wrily; he should have noticed that didn't sound right. He glanced down at the woman beside him, in blue, as usual, her dark hair framing her pale face in soft curls, the whole enchanting picture framed by the rim of her modish bonnet. "Lucinda Lester" had a certain balance, a certain ring.

His lips curved but, her gaze abstracted, she didn't see. She was, he noted, looking decidedly pensive.

The drive ahead cleared as they left the area favoured by the *ton*. Harry reined in and joined the line of carriages waiting to turn back. "Once more through the gauntlet, then I'll take you home."

Lucinda shot him a puzzled glance but said nothing, straightening and summoning a smile as they headed back into the fray.

This time, heading in the opposite direction, they saw different faces—many, Lucinda noted, looked surprised. But they were constantly moving; she got no chance to analyse the reactions the sight of them seemed to be provoking. Lady Jersey's reaction, however, needed no analysis.

Her ladyship was in her barouche, languidly draped over the cushions, when her gimlet gaze fell on Harry's curricle, approaching at a sedate walk. She promptly sat bolt upright.

"Merciful heavens!" she declared, her strident tones dramatic. "I never thought to see the day!"

Harry shot her a malevolent glance but deigned to incline his head. "I believe you are acquainted with Mrs Babbacombe?"

"Indeed!" Lady Jersey waved a hand at Lucinda. "I'll catch up with you next Wednesday, my dear."

Her ladyship's glance promised she would. Lucinda kept her smile gracious but was relieved when they passed on.

She slanted a glance at Harry to discover his face set in uncompromising lines. As soon as the traffic thinned, he clicked the reins.

"That was a very short drive," Lucinda murmured as the gates of the Park hove in sight.

"Short, perhaps, but quite long enough for our purposes."

The words were clipped, his accents unencouraging. Lucinda's inner frown deepened. "Our purposes." What, precisely, were they?

SHE WAS STILL WONDERING when, gowned in hyacinth-blue watered silk, she descended the stairs that evening, ready for Lady Mickleham's ball. Being in constant expectation of an offer was slowly sapping her patience; there was no doubt in her mind that Harry intended making her another, but the when and the why of his reticence were matters that increasingly worried her. She descended most of the stairs in an abstracted daze, glancing up only as she neared their foot. To have her gaze lock with one of clear green.

Eyes widening, Lucinda blinked. "What are you doing here?"

Her astonished gaze took in his severely, almost austerely cut evening clothes, black and stark white as always. The gold acorn pin in his cravat winked wickedly.

She watched his lips twist in a wry grimace.

"I'm here," Harry informed her, his accents severely restrained, "to escort you—and Em and Heather—to Lady Mickleham's ball." He strolled to the end of the stairs and held out a commanding hand.

Lucinda looked at it, a light blush staining her cheeks. She was glad there were no servants about to witness this exchange. As her fingers, of their own volition, slid into his, she raised her eyes to his face. "I wasn't aware you considered it necessary to escort us to such affairs."

His features remained impassive, his eyes hooded, as he drew her down to stand before him.

The door at the end of the hall swung open; Agatha strode through, Lucinda's evening cloak over her arm. She checked when she saw Harry, then merely nodded at him, severe as ever but with less hostility than was her wont, and came on. Harry held out a hand; Agatha readily surrendered the cloak, then turned on her heel and retraced her steps.

Lucinda turned; Harry placed the velvet cloak about her shoulders. Raising her head, she met his gaze in the mirror on the wall. In the corridor above a door opened and shut; Heather's voice drifted down, calling to Em.

If she clung to polite phrases, he would fence and win. Lucinda drew in a quick breath. "Why?"

For a moment, his gaze remained on hers, then dropped to her throat. She saw his lips quirk, in smile or grimace she couldn't tell.

"Circumstances," he began, his voice low, "have changed." He raised his head and his eyes met hers. His brows rose, faintly challenging. "Haven't they?"

Lucinda stared into his eyes and said nothing at all; she wasn't about to gainsay him. But had things truly changed? She was no longer so sure of that.

Heather came skipping down the stairs, followed, more circumspectly, by Em. Amid the bustle of finding cloaks and gloves, Lucinda had no further chance to question Harry's new tack. The short trip to Mickleham House in Berkeley Square was filled with Heather's bright prattle and Em's reminiscences. Lucinda remained silent; Harry sat in the shadows opposite, equally quiet.

The ordeal of the crowded stairway left no opportunity for private converse. Lucinda smiled and nodded to those about them, aware of the curious glances thrown their escort. For his part, Harry remained impassively urbane but as they neared their host and hostess, he bent his head to murmur, very softly, in her ear, "I'll take the supper waltz—and I'll escort you into supper."

Her lips setting, Lucinda shot him a speaking glance. *Take* the supper waltz, indeed! She inwardly humphed, then turned to greet Lady Mickleham.

As Harry had foretold, her ladyship's rooms were full to overflowing.

"This is ridiculous," Lucinda muttered as they forged a path towards one side of the ballroom, hoping to find a *chaise* for Em.

"It's always this bad at the end of the Season," Em returned. "As if building to a frenzy before summer sends everyone home to the country."

Lucinda stifled a sigh as thoughts of the country—the grotto by the Lester Hall lake, the peace and serenity of Lestershall Manor—returned to her.

"Well—there's only a few weeks left to go," put in Heather. "So I suppose we should make the most of them." She glanced at Lucinda. "Have you decided where we'll spend the summer?"

Lucinda blinked. "Ah…"

"I dare say your stepmother feels such decisions are a trifle premature," Harry drawled.

Heather's lips formed an innocent "O"—she seemed perfectly content to accept the uninformative statement.

Lucinda let out a slow breath.

Em found a place on a *chaise* with Lady Sherringbourne; the two ladies promptly fell to exchanging revelations on the alliances forged that year.

Lucinda turned—to find herself all but engulfed by her court, who, as she was rapidly informed, had been awaiting her reappearance with bated breath.

"A whole week you've been away, m'dear. Quite desolate, we've been." Mr Amberly smiled benignly.

"Not that I can't understand it," Mr Satterly remarked. "The crushes are becoming far too real for my liking. Drive anyone away." His gaze rose to Harry's face, his expression utterly bland. "Don't you think so, Lester?"

"Indeed," Harry replied, casting a steely glance about them. With him on one side and Ruthven, equally large, on the other, Lucinda was at least assured of space enough to breathe. The rest of her court gathered before them, creating an enclosure of relative sanity for which, he was sure, they were all rendering silent thanks.

"And where did you go to recoup, my dear Mrs Babbacombe? The country or the seaside?"

It was, predictably, Lord Ruthven who voiced the inevitable question. He smiled encouragingly down at Lucinda; she sensed the subtle teasing behind his smile.

"The country," she vouchsafed. Then, prompted by some inner devil, released, she knew, by the repressive presence on her left, she added, "My stepdaughter and I accompanied Lady Hallows on a visit to Lester Hall."

Ruthven blinked his eyes wide. "Lester Hall?" Slowly, he lifted his gaze to Harry's face. Entirely straightfaced, his lordship raised his brows. "Noticed you were absent from town this week, Harry. Took some time from the frantic whirl to recuperate?"

"Naturally," Harry drawled, clinging to his usual imperturbability, "I escorted my aunt and her guests on their visit."

"Oh, naturally," Ruthven agreed. He turned to Lucinda. "Did Harry show you the grotto by the lake?"

Lucinda regarded his lordship with as bland an expression as she could manage. "Indeed—and the folly on the hill. The views were quite lovely."

"The views?" Lord Ruthven looked stunned. "Ah, yes. The views."

Harry ground his teeth but was too wise to react—at

least not verbally. But his glance promised retribution—only Ruthven, one of his oldest friends, was prepared to ignore it.

To Lucinda's relief, his lordship's teasing, although in no way openly indelicate, was cut short by the musicians. It took a moment or two before it became clear that Lady Mickleham had decided to open her ball with a waltz.

The realisation brought the usual clamour of offers. Lucinda smiled graciously—and hesitated. The room was very crowded, the dance floor would be worse. In cotillion or quadrille, with sets and steps fixed, demanding a certain space, there was little chance of unexpected intimacy. But the waltz? In such cramped conditions?

The thought brought in its wake a certainty that her circumstances had indeed changed. She did not wish to waltz close with anyone but Harry. Her senses reached for him; he was standing, very stiff, intensely contained, beside her.

Harry saw her glance up, unconscious appeal in her eyes. His reaction was immediate and quite impossible to restrain. His hand closed over hers; he lifted it to place her fingers on his sleeve. "My waltz, I believe, my dear."

Relief flooded Lucinda; she remembered to incline her head, and smile fleetingly at her court as Harry led her from their midst.

On the ballroom floor, she relaxed into Harry's arms, allowing him to draw her close with no attempt at dissimulation. She glanced up at him as they started to slowly twirl; his eyes met hers, his expression still aloof but somehow softer. Their gazes held; they communicated without words as they slowly revolved down the room.

Then Lucinda lowered her lashes; Harry's arm tightened about her.

As she had foreseen, the floor was crowded, the

dancers cramped. Harry kept her safe within the circle of his arms; she was very aware that if anything threatened, she had only to step closer and he would protect her. His hard body was no threat—she had never seen it as such. He was her guardian in the oldest sense of the word—he to whom she had entrusted her life.

The waltz ended too soon; Lucinda blinked as Harry's arms fell from her. Reluctantly, she stepped away and placed her hand on his arm, then let him steer her back through the throng.

Harry glanced at her face, his features impassive, concern in his eyes. As they neared her court, he leaned closer to murmur, "If you don't care to waltz, simply plead fatigue." Lucinda glanced up at him; he felt his lips twist. "It's the latest fashionable ploy."

She nodded—and straightened her shoulders as they rejoined her court.

Lucinda was inexpressibly grateful for that piece of advice—her supposed fatigue was accepted without a blink; as the evening wore on, she began to suspect that her earnest court were no more enamoured of dancing in such cramped surrounds than she.

Immovable, repressively silent, Harry remained by her side throughout the long evening. Lucinda greeted the supper waltz with a certain measure of relief. "I understand Mr Amberly, Mr Satterly and Lord Ruthven are particular friends of yours?"

Harry glanced fleetingly down at her. "Of a sorts," he reluctantly conceded.

"I would never have guessed." Lucinda met his sharp glance with wide eyes. Harry studied her innocent expression, then humphed and drew her closer.

At the end of the waltz, he led her directly to the supper room. Before she could gather her wits, Lucinda found herself installed at a secluded table for two, shaded from much of the room by two potted palms. A glass of champagne and a plate piled high with delicacies appeared before her; Harry lounged gracefully in the seat opposite.

His eyes on hers, he took a bite of a lobster patty. "Did you notice Lady Waldron's wig?"

Lucinda giggled. "It nearly fell off." She took a sip of champagne, her eyes sparkling. "Mr Anstey had to catch it and jiggle it back into place."

To Lucinda's delight, Harry spent the entire half-hour regaling her with anecdotes, *on dits* and the occasional dry observation. It was the first time she had had him to herself in such a mood; she gave herself up to enjoying the interlude.

Only when it ended and he led her back to the ballroom did it occur to her to wonder what had brought it on.

Or, more specifically, why he had put himself out to so captivate her.

"Still here, Ruthven?" Harry's drawl hauled her back to the present. He was eyeing his friend with a certain, challenging gleam in his eye. "Nothing else here to interest you?"

"Nothing, I fear." Lord Ruthven put his hand over his heart and quizzed Lucinda. "Nothing as compares with the joys of conversing with Mrs Babbacombe."

Lucinda had to laugh. Harry, of course, did not. His drawl very much in evidence, he took charge of the conversation. As the languid, distinctly bored accents fell on her ear, Lucinda realised that he never, normally, drawled at her. Nor Em. When he spoke to them, his accents were clipped. Apparently, he reserved the fashionable affectation for those he kept at a distance.

With Harry holding the reins, the conversation predictably remained in stultifyingly correct vein. Lucinda, smothering a yawn, considered an option that might, conceivably, assist her cause while at the same time rescuing her poor court.

"It's getting rather warm, don't you find it so?" she murmured, her hand heavy on Harry's arm.

He glanced down at her, then lifted his brows. "Indeed. I suspect it's time we left."

As he lifted his head to locate Em and Heather, Lucinda allowed herself one, very small, very frustrated snort. She had intended him to take her onto the terrace. Peering through the crowd, she saw Em deep in discussion with a dowager; Heather was engaged with a party of her friends. "Ah…perhaps I could manage for another half-hour if I had a glass of water?"

Mr Satterly immediately offered to procure one and ploughed into the crowd.

Harry looked down at her, a faint question in his eyes. "Are you sure?"

Lucinda's smile was weak. "Positive."

He continued to behave with dogged correctness—which, Lucinda belatedly realised, as the crowds gradually thinned and she became aware of the curious, speculative glances cast their way, was not, in his case, the same as behaving circumspectly.

The observation brought a frown to her eyes.

It had deepened by the time they were safely in Em's carriage, rolling home through the now quiet streets. From her position opposite, Lucinda studied Harry's face, lit by the moonlight and the intermittent flares of the streetlamps.

His eyes were closed, sealed away behind their heavy lids. His features were not so much relaxed as wiped clean of expression, his lips compressed into a firm, straight line. Seen thus, it was a face that kept its secrets, the face of a man who was essentially private, who revealed his emotions rarely if ever.

Lucinda felt her heart catch; a dull ache blossomed within.

The *ton* was his milieu—he knew every nuance of behaviour, how every little gesture would be interpreted. He was at home here, in the crowded ballrooms, as she was not. As at Lester Hall, here, he was in control.

Lucinda shifted in her seat. Propping her chin in her palm, she stared at the sleeping houses, a frown drawing down her fine brows.

Free of her scrutiny, Harry opened his eyes. He studied her profile, clear in the moonlight. His lips curved in the slightest of smiles. Pressing his head back against the squabs, he closed his eyes.

AT THAT MOMENT, in Mortimer Babbacombe's lodgings in Great Portland Street, a meeting was getting underway.

"Well—did you learn anything to the point?" Joliffe, no longer the nattily attired gentleman who had first befriended Mortimer, snarled the question the instant Brawn ambled through the door. Heavy-eyed from lack of sleep, his colour high from the liquor he had consumed to calm his nerves, Joliffe fixed his most junior accomplice with a dangerous stare.

Brawn was too young to heed it. Dropping into a chair at the parlour table about which Joliffe, Mortimer and Scrugthorpe were already seated, he grinned. "Aye—I learned a bit. Chatted up the young maid—no mor'n a bit of a thing. She told me a few things before that groom—yeller-haired lot—came and fetched her orf. Heard him giving her what for 'bout talking to strangers, so I don't think I'll get any more by that road." Brawn grinned. "Pity—wouldn't ha' minded—"

"Damn you—get on!" Joliffe roared, his fist connecting with the table with enough force to set the tankards jumping. *"What the devil happened?"*

Brawn shot him a look more puzzled than frightened. "Well—the lady did go orf to the country that day—just like you'd planned. But seemingly she went to some other house—a place called Lester Hall. The whole household went up the next day—the maid said as she thought it'd been planned."

"Damn!" Joliffe swilled back a mouthful of porter. "No wonder I couldn't get any of the crew who'd gone up to Asterley to say they'd seen her. I thought they must've been practising discretion—but the damned woman hadn't gone!"

"Seems not." Brawn shrugged. "So what now?"

"Now we stop playing and kidnap her." Scrugthorpe lifted his face from his tankard. "Like I said from the first. It's the only way of being sure—all this trying to get the rakes to do our job for us has got us precisely *nowhere*." He spat the last word, his contempt bordering on the open.

Joliffe held his eye; eventually, Scrugthorpe looked back at his mug.

"That's what I say, anyway," Scrugthorpe mumbled as he took another swallow.

"Hmm." Joliffe grimaced. "I'm beginning to agree with you. It looks like we'll have to take an active hand ourselves."

"But...I thought..." Mortimer's first contribution to the conversation died away as both Joliffe and Scrugthorpe turned to look at him.

"Ye-es?" Joliffe prompted.

Mortimer's colour rose. He put a finger to his cravat, tugging at the floppy folds. "It's just that...well—if we do do anything direct—well—won't she know?"

Joliffe's lip curled. "Of *course* she will—but that's not to say she'll be in any hurry to denounce us—not after Scrugthorpe here has his revenge."

"Aye." Scrugthorpe's black eyes gleamed. "Jus' leave her to me. I'll make sure she ain't in no hurry to talk about it." He nodded and went back to his beer.

Mortimer regarded him with mounting horror. He opened his mouth, then caught Joliffe's eye. He visibly shrank, but muttered, "There must be another way."

"Very likely." Joliffe drained his tankard and reached for the jug. "But we don't have time for any more convoluted schemes."

"Time?" Mortimer looked confused.

"Yes, *time!*' Snarling, Joliffe turned on Mortimer. Mortimer paled, his eyes starting like a frightened rabbit's. With an effort, Joliffe reined in his temper. He smiled, all teeth. "But don't you worry your head over it. Just leave everything to Scrugthorpe and me. You do your bit when asked—and everything will work out just fine."

"Aye." Brawn unexpectedly chipped in. "I was thinking as you'd better get a different plan. From what the maid told me, seems like the lady's in expectation of 'receivin' an offer,' as they says. I don't know as I understand these things rightly, but seems pretty useless making her out to be a whore if she's going to marry a swell."

"*What?*" Joliffe's exclamation had all of them starting. They stared at their leader as he stared—in total stupefication—at Brawn. "She's about to *marry?*"

Warily, Brawn nodded. "So the maid said."

"*Whom?*"

"Some swell name of Lester."

"Harry Lester?" Joliffe calmed. Frowning heavily, he eyed Brawn. "You sure this maid got it right? Harry Lester's not the marrying kind."

Brawn shrugged. "Wouldn't know about that." After a moment, he added, "The girl said as this Lester chap had called this afternoon to take the lady for a drive in the Park."

Joliffe stared at Brawn, all his certainties fading. "The Park," he repeated dully.

Brawn merely nodded and cautiously sipped his beer.

When Joliffe next spoke, his voice was hoarse. "We've got to move soon."

"Soon?" Scrugthorpe looked up. "How soon?"

"Before she's married—preferably before she even accepts an offer. We don't need any legal complications."

Mortimer was frowning. "Complications?"

"Yes, damn you!" Joliffe struggled to mute his snarl. "If the damned woman marries, the guardianship of her stepdaughter passes into her husband's hands. If Harry Lester takes the reins, we can forget getting a farthing out of your lovely cousin's estate."

Mortimer's eyes widened. "Oh."

"Yes—oh! And while we're on the subject, I've a little news for you—just to strengthen your backbone." Joliffe fixed his eyes on Mortimer's wan countenance. "You owe me five thousand on a note of hand. I passed that vowel on, with one of my own, to a man who charges interest by the day. Together, we now owe him a cool twenty thousand, Mortimer—and if we don't pay up soon, he's going to take every pound out of our hides." He paused, then leaned forward to ask, "Is that clear enough for you, Mortimer?"

His face a deathly white, his eyes round and starting, Mortimer was so petrified he could not even nod.

"Well, then!" Scrugthorpe pushed his empty tankard away. "Seems like we'd best make some plans."

Joliffe had sobered dramatically. He tapped the table-top with one fingernail. "We'll need information on her movements." He looked at Brawn but the boy shook his head.

"No good. The maid won't talk to me again, not after the roasting that groom gave her. And there's no one else."

Joliffe's eyes narrowed. "What about the other women?"

Brawn's snort was eloquent. "There's a few o'them all right—but they're all as sour as green grapes. Take even you till next year to chat 'em up—and they'd likely refuse to talk even then."

"Damn!" Joliffe absentmindedly took a sip of his porter. "All right." He set the tankard down with a snap. "If that's the only way then that's the way we'll do it."

"How's that?" Scrugthorpe asked.

"We watch her—all the time, day and night. We make our arrangements and keep all in readiness to grab her the instant fate gives us a chance."

Scrugthorpe nodded. "Right. But how're we going to go about it?"

Joliffe sent an intimidating glance at Mortimer.

Mortimer swallowed and shrank in his chair.

With a contemptuous snort, Joliffe turned back to Scrugthorpe. "Just listen."

Chapter Fourteen

First nights later, Mortimer Babbacombe stood in the shadows of a doorway in King Street and watched his aunt-by-marriage climb the shallow steps to Almack's unprepossessing entrance.

"Well." Heaving a sigh—of relief or disappointment he was not quite sure—he turned to his companion. "She's gone in—no point in watching further."

"Oh, yes, there is." The words came in a cold hiss. In the past five days, Joliffe's polite veneer had peeled from him. "You're going to go in there, Mortimer, and keep a careful eye on your aunt. I want to know everything—who she dances with, who brings her lemonade—*everything!*" Joliffe's piercing gaze swung to fix on Mortimer's face. "Is that clear?"

Mortimer hugged the doorframe, his relief rapidly fading. Glowering glumly, he nodded. "Can't think what good it'll do," he grumbled.

"Don't think, Mortimer—just do as I bid you." In the shadows, Joliffe studied Mortimer's face, plain and round, the face of a man easily led—and, as was often the case with such, prone to unhelpful stubbornness. Joliffe's lip curled. "Do try to recapture a little of your earlier enthusiasm, Mortimer. Remember—your uncle overlooking your claim to be your cousin's guardian and appointing a young woman like your aunt instead is an insult to your manhood."

Mortimer shifted, pulling at his fleshy lower lip. "Yes, it is."

"Indeed. Who is Lucinda Babbacombe, anyway, other than a pretty face smart enough to take your uncle in?"

"Quite true." Mortimer nodded. "And, mind, it's not as if I've any bone to pick with her—but anyone would have to admit it was dashed unfair of Uncle Charles to leave all the ready to her—and just the useless land to me."

Joliffe smiled into the night. "Quite. You're merely seeking redress for the unfair actions of your uncle. Remember that, Mortimer." He clapped Mortimer on the shoulder and waved towards Almack's. "I'll wait at your lodgings for your news."

Mortimer nodded. Straightening his rounded shoulders, he headed for the sacred portal.

Deep within the hallowed halls, Lucinda nodded and smiled, responding to the chatter with confident ease while her mind trod an endless trail of conjecture and fact. Harry had driven her in the Park on the past five afternoons, albeit briefly. He had appeared every evening, unheralded, simply there, waiting when she descended the stairs to escort them to the balls and parties, remaining by her side throughout but saying not a word as to his purpose.

She had gone beyond impatience, even beyond chagrin—she was now in the grip of a deadening sense of the inevitable.

Lucinda summoned a smile and gave her hand to Mr

Drumcott, a not-so-young gentleman who had recently become betrothed to a young lady in her first Season.

"I beg you'll do me the honour of dancing this quadrille with my poor self, Mrs Babbacombe."

Lucinda acquiesced with a smile but as they took their places she caught herself scanning the crowd—and inwardly sighed. She should, of course, be glad Harry had not arrived this evening to escort them here—that, she was convinced, would have been the last straw.

That he intended making her his bride was patently clear—his likely motive in underscoring that fact publicly was what was dragging her heart down. The memory of his first proposal—and her refusal—haunted her. She hadn't known, then, of Lady Coleby and her earlier rejection of Harry's love. Her own refusal had been driven by the simple belief that he loved her and would, if pushed, acknowledge that love. To hear the words on his lips was something she craved, something she needed. But not, she was increasingly certain, something Harry needed.

She couldn't rid herself of the idea that he was painting her into a corner, that his present behaviour was designed to render a second rejection impossible. If, after all his studied performances, she refused him again, she would be labelled cruel-hearted, or, more likely, as Sim would put it, "dicked in the nob".

Lucinda grimaced—and had to hurriedly cover the expression with a smile. As they embarked on the final figures of the quadrille, Mr Drumcott blinked at her in concern; she forced another smile—a travesty considering her true state. If Harry kept on as he was, when next he proposed, she would have to accept him, regardless of whether he offered his heart along with his hand.

The quadrille ended; Lucinda sank into the final, elaborate curtsy. Rising, she straightened her shoulders and determinedly thanked Mr Drumcott. She was not, she told herself, going to dwell on Harry's motives any longer. There must be some other explanation—if only she could think what it was.

At that precise moment, the object of her thoughts sat at the desk in his library attired in long-tailed black evening coat and black knee-breeches, garments he considered outmoded in the extreme.

"What have you learned?" Harry leaned both arms on the blotter and pinned Salter with a steady green gaze.

"Enough to make my nose quiver." Salter settled himself in the chair before the desk. Dawlish, who had shown him in, closed the door; folding his arms, he leaned back against it. Salter pulled out a notebook. "First—this Joliffe chap is more of a bad egg than I'd thought. A real sharp—specialises in 'befriending' flats, preferably those who come fresh on the town, gullible and usually young, though, these days, as he's no spring chicken himself, his victims also tend to be older. Quite a history—but nothing, ever, that could be made to stick. Lately, however, quite aside from his usual activities, Joliffe's taken to deep play—and not in the hells either. Word has it he's heavily in debt—not to his opponents—he's paid them off—but the total sum amounts to a fortune. All evidence points to Joliffe being in the clutches of a real bloodsucker—a certain individual who works out of the docks. Don't have any information on him except that he's not one to keep dangling too long. A mistake that often turns fatal, if you take my meaning."

He lifted his gaze to Harry's face; his expression grim, Harry nodded.

"Right then—next up is Mortimer Babbacombe. A hopeless case—if Joliffe hadn't picked him up one of the other Captain Sharps would have. Born a flat. Joliffe took him under his wing and underwrote his losses—that's the usual way these things start. Then, when the flat gets his hands on whatever loot is coming his way, the sharps take the major cut. So when Mortimer came into his inheritance, Joliffe was sitting on his coattails. From then, however, things went wrong."

Salter consulted his notebook. "Like Mrs Babbacombe told you, it seems Mortimer had no real understanding of his inheritance—but Charles Babbacombe had paid off his debts annually, to the tune of three thousand at the last. Seems certain Mortimer assumed the money came from his uncle's estate and the estate was therefore worth much more than it is. My people checked—the place can't make much more than expenses. It's apparently common knowledge up that way that Charles Babbacombe's money came from Babbacombe and Company."

Shutting his book, Salter grimaced. "That's all right and tight—and a nasty surprise it must have been for Joliffe. But what I can't see is why he's gone after Mrs Babbacombe—knocking her on the head isn't going to benefit them. Joliffe's more than experienced enough to work that out—some old aunt of hers is her nearest kin. Yet they're keeping constant watch on Mrs Babbacombe—and not as if they've got anything cordial on their minds."

Harry stiffened. "They're watching her?"

"And my people are watching them. Very closely."

Harry relaxed. A little. He frowned. "We're missing something."

"Precisely my thought." Salter shook his head. "Operators like Joliffe don't make too many mistakes—after his first disappointment with Mortimer, he wouldn't have hung around unless there's a chance of some really rich pickings in the wind."

"There's money all right," Harry mused. "But it's in the business. As you know, Charles Babbacombe willed that to his widow and his daughter."

Salter frowned. "Ah, yes—this daughter. A young chit, barely seventeen." His frown deepened. "From all I've seen, Mrs Babbacombe's no easy mark—why pick on her rather than the daughter?"

Harry blinked, somewhat owlishly, at Salter. "Heather," he said, his tone oddly flat. After a moment, he drew in a long breath and straightened. "That must be it."

"What?"

Harry's lips twisted. "I've often been told that I've a devious mind—perhaps, for once, it can be of real use. Just hear me out." His gaze grew distant; absentmindedly, he reached for his pen. "Heather is the one they *could* use to milk the business of cash—*but*—what if Lucinda is Heather's guardian, as well as Heather's mentor? In either role, Joliffe and company would have to *get rid* of Lucinda to get to Heather."

Slowly, Salter nodded. "That's possible—but why try that ramshackle business of sending Mrs Babbacombe to that fancy orgy palace, then?"

Harry hoped Alfred never heard of his ancestral home referred to in such vein. He tapped the blotter with the pen. "That's what makes me so certain Heather's guardianship must be the key—because in order to get rid of Lucinda for such purposes, showing her as unfit to be guardian of a young girl would be sufficient for Mortimer, who is Heather's next of kin, to apply to overturn Lucinda's guardianship in favour of himself. Once that's done, they could simply cut all contact between Heather and Lucinda—and use Heather to draw funds from her half of the investment."

Gazing into space, Salter nodded. "You're right—that must be it. Roundabout but it makes sense."

"And now they've failed to paint the lady scarlet," put in Dawlish, "they're planning to snatch her up and do away with her."

"True enough," agreed Salter. "But my people know what to do."

Harry refrained from asking just who Salter's "people" were.

"Even so," Dawlish continued, "they can't keep a-watching her forever. And seems to me this Joliffe character's one as should be behind bars."

Salter nodded. "You're right. There's been a few unexplained 'suicides' in Joliffe's past that the magistrates were never convinced about."

Harry repressed a shudder. The thought of Lucinda mixed up with such characters was not to be borne. "At this instant, Mrs Babbacombe is safe enough—but we need to make sure our conjecture's true. If it's not, we could be following the wrong scent—with potentially serious consequences. It strikes me that there might well be a second guardian, which would render our hypothesis unlikely."

Salter lifted a brow. "If you know the lady's legal man, I could make some discreet inquiries."

"I don't. And he's very likely in Yorkshire." Harry thought—then looked at Dawlish. "Mrs Babbacombe's maid and coachman have been with the family for years. They might know."

Dawlish straightened from the door. "I'll ask."

"Couldn't you just ask the lady herself?" Salter asked.

"No." Harry's reply was unequivocal. His lips twisted in a grimace. "At the moment, the very last thing I want to do is ask Mrs Babbacombe about her legal affairs. The question of Heather's guardianship can't be all that hard to answer."

"No. And I'll tip my people the wink to yell the instant they sniff any shift in the wind." Salter got to his feet. "As soon as we know for sure what these jackals are about, we'll devise a way to trip them up nicely."

Harry didn't reply. He shook hands with Salter, the thought in his mind that if tripping up Joliffe involved placing Lucinda in any danger at all, it simply wouldn't happen.

When Dawlish returned from showing the ex-Runner out, Harry was standing in the centre of the room, strapping his gloves on his palm.

"Well!" Dawlish opened his eyes wide. "There you be—all tricked out and not at the party. Best I drive you there, then."

Harry looked down, casting a long-suffering glance at breeches he had long ago sworn never again to don. His expression grimly resigned, he nodded. "Best you do."

His knock on Almack's door very nearly prostrated old Willis, the porter. "*Never* did I think to see *you* here again, sir!" Willis raised his shaggy brows. "Something in the wind?"

"You, Willis, are as fervent a gossip as any of your mistresses."

Unrepentant, Willis grinned. Harry gave him his gloves and cloak and sauntered into the ballroom.

To say his entrance caused a stir would be a gross understatement. It caused a flutter, a ruffling of feathers, and, in some, a mild panic akin to hysteria, all fuelled by the intense speculation that rose in feminine breasts as he strolled, gracefully but entirely purposefully, across the room.

Her emotions aswirl, Lucinda watched his approach

with unwilling fascination. Her heart started to soar, her lips lifted—then her earlier thoughts engulfed her. A tightness gripped her lungs, squeezing slowly. Candlelight gleamed on his golden hair; in the old-fashioned attire, he looked less suave and debonair but, if anything, even more the rake than before. As she felt the touch of a hundred eyes, her lips firmed. He was exploiting them all, manipulating the whole *ton*—shamelessly.

As he neared, she held out her hand, knowing he would simply take it if she didn't. "Good evening, Mr Lester. How very surprising to see you here."

Her gentle sarcasm did not escape Harry; he raised his brows as he raised her fingers to his lips and gently brushed a kiss across their tips.

He had done it so often Lucinda had forgotten it was no longer the accepted mode of greeting. The collective gasp that seemed to fill the ballroom reminded her of the fact. Her smile remained in place but her eyes flashed.

The reprobate before her merely smiled. And tucked her hand in his arm. "Come, my dear, I rather think we should stroll." With a nod, he excused them from the two gentlemen who had been passing the time by Lucinda's side. "Gibson. Holloway."

They had barely taken two steps before Lady Jersey appeared in their path. Harry promptly bowed, so elaborately it was almost a joke, so gracefully it was impossible to take offense.

Sally Jersey humphed. "I had meant to ask Mrs Babbacombe for news of you," she informed Harry without a blink. "But now you're here, I need hardly enquire."

"Indeed," Harry drawled. "I'm positively touched, Sally dear, that you should think to take an interest in my poor self."

"Your self isn't so poor anymore, if you recall."

"Ah, yes. A twist of fate."

"One which has brought you once more within the sights of the ladies here. Take care, my friend, else you slip and get tangled in their nets." Lady Jersey's eyes twinkled. She turned to Lucinda. "I would congratulate you, my dear—but I fear he's quite incorrigible—utterly irreclaimable. But if you seek revenge, all you have to do is take him to the furthest point from the door and cut him loose—then watch him flounder."

Her expression serene, Lucinda raised her brows. "I'll bear the point in mind, ma'am."

With a regal nod, Sally Jersey swept on.

"Don't you dare," Harry murmured as they strolled on, his drawl instantly evaporating. His hand rose to cover hers where it lay on his sleeve. "You couldn't be so hard-hearted."

Again Lucinda lifted her brows; her eyes, no longer laughing, met his. "No?"

Harry's eyes searched hers; Lucinda saw them narrow slightly.

Suddenly breathless, she squeezed his arm and forced a smile to her lips. "But you hardly need me to protect you."

Determinedly, she looked ahead, still smiling, her expression as serene as before.

A short silence ensued, then Harry's voice sounded in her ear, low and completely expressionless, "You're wrong, my dear. I need you—very much."

Lucinda couldn't risk looking at him; she blinked rapidly and nodded to Lady Cowper, beaming from a nearby *chaise*. Were they talking of protection from the match-making mamas—or something else?

She got no chance to clarify the point—the mamas, the matrons and the dragons of the *ton* descended *en masse*.

To Harry's irritation, his evening at Almack's proved even more trying than he had imagined. His transparent obsession with the woman on his arm, which he had been at such pains to advertise, had, as he had known it would, doused all hope that he might be struck by lightning and forget himself enough to smile on one of the matrons' young darlings. They had got the point; unfortunately, they had all taken it into their heads to be first with their congratulations.

The very first of these thinly veiled felicitations came from the indefatigable Lady Argyle, her pale, plain daughter still in tow. "I can't say how pleased I've been to see you at our little entertainments again, Mr Lester." She bestowed an arch glance before turning her gimlet gaze on Lucinda. "You must make sure he continues, my dear." She tapped Lucinda's arm with her fan. "*Such* a loss when the most handsome gentlemen cling to their clubs. Don't let him backslide."

With another arch glance and a flutter of her fingers, her ladyship departed, silent daughter in her wake. Harry idly wondered if the girl actually spoke.

Then he glanced down—and saw Lucinda's face. No one else would have noticed anything amiss, but he was now too used to seeing her relaxed, happy. She was neither, now, her features tense, her lips without the full softness they normally displayed.

They sustained two more delighted outpourings in rapid succession, then Lady Cowper caught them. Her ladyship was her usual, kind-hearted self, quite impossible to curtail. Harry bore her soft smiles and gentle words— but as soon as she released them, he took a firm grip on Lucinda's arm and steered her towards the refreshment-room. "Come—I'll get you a glass of champagne."

Lucinda glanced up at him. "This is Almack's—they don't serve champagne."

Harry looked his disgust. "I'd forgotten. Lemonade, then." He looked down at her. "You must be parched."

She didn't deny it or make any demur when he handed her a glass. But even in the refreshment-room the avalanche of felicitations he'd unwittingly triggered continued. There was, Harry quickly discovered, no escape.

By the time the next dance, a waltz, the only one of the evening, let them seek refuge on the floor, he had realised his error. He grasped the moment as he drew Lucinda into his arms to apologise. "I'm afraid I miscalculated." He smiled down into her eyes—and wished he could see in. They were more than misty, they were cloudy. The sight worried him. "I'd forgotten just how competitive the matrons are." He couldn't think of any acceptable way to explain that, when it came to a prize such as he now was, the matrons would rather accept someone like Lucinda, an outsider albeit one of their class, than see an archrival triumph.

Lucinda smiled, apparently at ease, but her eyes did not lighten. Harry drew her closer and wished they were alone.

When the dance ended, he looked down at her face, making no attempt to hide the frown in his eyes. "If you like we'll go and find Em. I dare say she'll have had enough of this."

Lucinda acquiesced with a nod, her expression rigidly serene.

Harry's prediction proved true—Em had also been beseiged. She was very ready to depart.

"A bit like running under fire," she grumpily informed Lucinda as Harry handed her into the carriage. "But it's a dashed sight too much when they start angling for invitations to the wedding." Her snort was eloquent.

Harry glanced at Lucinda, already seated in the carriage; a shaft of light from the doorway illuminated her face. Her eyes were huge, her cheeks pale. She looked tired, worn down—almost defeated. Harry felt his heart lurch—and felt a pain more intense than any Millicent Pane had ever caused.

"Now don't forget!" Em tapped him on the sleeve. "Dinner's at seven tomorrow—we'll look to see you before that."

"Ah. Yes." Harry blinked. "Of course." With a last glance at Lucinda, he stepped back and closed the door. "I'll be there."

He watched the carriage roll away, then, frowning, turned towards his club, just a few steps around the corner. But when he reached the lighted door he paused, then, still frowning, continued on to his rooms.

An hour later, sunk in her feather mattress, Lucinda stared up at the canopy of her bed. Tonight had clarified matters—unequivocally, incontrovertibly. She'd been wrong—no other explanation existed for Harry's actions, other than the obvious. The only thing *she* now needed to decide was what she was going to do about it.

She watched the moonbeams cross her ceiling; it was dawn before she slept.

HARRY DIDN'T LEAVE his rooms the next morning, alerted by a message from Salter and disappointing information from Dawlish.

"They don't know," Dawlish repeated for Salter's benefit when they gathered in Harry's library at eleven. "Both are sure Mrs Babbacombe's Miss Heather's guardian but whether there's another they can't say either way."

"Hmm." Salter frowned. He looked at Harry. "Word came in from some of my people. Joliffe's hired a carriage with four strong horses. No particular destination and he didn't hire any boys with it—paid a goodly deposit to take it without."

Harry's fingers tightened about his pen. "I think we can conclude that Mrs Babbacombe is in danger."

Salter grimaced. "Perhaps—but I've been thinking about what your man here said. You can't go watching them for forever—and if they don't take one, they might take the other. The stepdaughter's still their ultimate goal."

It was Harry's turn to grimace. "True." He stood poised to remove Lucinda from all danger but it was undoubtedly true that, if Joliffe was desperate enough, such a move would expose Heather as Joliffe's next target.

"I've been thinking," Salter continued, "that this matter of the carriage is probably for the best. It means he's planning a move soon. We're alerted—something Joliffe doesn't know. If we can sort out the facts about this guardianship, meanwhile keeping a close watch on Joliffe and his crew, then before they can make their move, we can tie them up with a warrant. My sources are sure Mortimer Babbacombe will talk readily enough. Seems he's in over his head."

Harry drew his pen back and forth through his fingers, his gaze distant as he considered the next twenty-four hours. "If you need the information about the guardianship to obtain a warrant, then we'll have to investigate further." His gaze shifted to Dawlish. "Go and see Fergus—ask if he knows where to contact a Mr Mabberly of Babbacombe Inns."

"Ah—no need." Salter held up a large finger. "Leave that to me. But what shall I tell Mr Mabberly?"

Harry's lips compressed. "He's Mrs Babbacombe's agent—she trusts him, I gather—so you may tell him whatever you must. But he'll very likely know the answer. Or at least know who does."

"Still no thoughts of just asking the lady?"

Slowly, Harry shook his head. "But if we haven't got the answer by tomorrow evening, I'll ask her."

Salter accepted the deadline without comment. "Need any help keeping an eye on the pair of them?"

Again Harry shook his head. "They won't be leaving Hallows House today or tonight." He looked at Salter, his expression resigned. "My aunt is holding a soirée."

IT WAS THE BIGGEST SOIRÉE Em had held in years and she was determined to enjoy it to the full.

Lucinda said as much as, side by side, she and Harry ascended the stairs to the ballroom. "She's positively wound tight. You could almost believe it was she making her come-out."

Harry grinned. The exceedingly select dinner Em had organised to precede her "little entertainment" had been a decided success; the company had been such as to gratify the most ambitious hostess. "She's enjoyed herself tremendously these last few months. Ever since you and Heather joined her."

Lucinda met his eyes briefly. "She's been very good to us."

"And you've been very good for her," Harry murmured as they reached the head of the staircase.

Em was already there, taking up her position to greet the first of the guests who were even now milling in the hall.

"Don't forget to compliment her on the décor," Lucinda whispered. "It's all her own effort."

Harry nodded. When Em waved insistently, summoning Lucinda to her side, he bowed and strolled on into the ballroom. It was indeed a sight—garlanded with purple and gold—Em's favourite colours—lightened here and there with a touch of blue. Cornflowers stood in urns on tables by the side of the room; blue bows tied back the curtains about the long windows. Harry smiled and paused to glance back at the trio at the door—Em in heavy purple silk, Heather in pale gold muslin with a hint of blue at neckline and hem, and Lucinda—his siren—stunning in a gown of sapphire silk trimmed with fine golden ribbons.

Harry decided that sincerely complimenting his aunt would, in this instance, be easy. He strolled the room, chatting with acquaintances, even steeling himself to converse with the few ageing relatives Em had seen fit to invite. But he did not lose sight of the welcoming party; when Em finally quit her position, he was already at Lucinda's side.

She smiled up at him, unaffectedly open, the gesture warm yet with a lingering sense of…Harry gazed down into her softly blue eyes, even softer now, and realised with a jolt that what he could sense was melancholy.

"If the crowds keep rolling in as they are, Em's soirée will be declared the very *worst* crush of the Season." Lucinda placed her hand on his arm and laughed up at him. "I might very well have to plead fatigue from the first."

Harry returned her smile but his gaze remained acute. "Lady Herscult is one of Em's oldest friends; she's charged me most straitly to bring you directly to her."

With a serene smile and an inclination of her head, Lucinda allowed him to lead her into the growing crowd.

As they passed through the throng, people stopped them to chat, all beaming. They discovered Lady Herscult on a *chaise;* she twitted Harry and Lucinda both before letting them escape. Throughout, Harry watched Lucinda carefully; with unshakeable serenity, she turned aside any questions too probing, her smile calmly assured.

The first waltz interrupted their meanderings—Em had chosen to enliven her soirée with three dances, all waltzes.

As, without seeking any permission, Harry drew Lucinda, unresisting, into his arms, he arched a brow. "A novel arrangement."

A gurgle of laughter came to his ears.

"She said," Lucinda explained, "that she could see no point in wasting time with quadrilles and cotillions when what everyone really wanted was waltzes."

Harry grinned. "Very Em."

Lucinda smiled as he whirled her through the turn, her ease on the dance floor a far cry from her first excursion. She felt supple in his arms, fluidly matching her steps to his, following effortlessly, not, he suspected, even conscious that he held her so close. She would probably notice if he didn't.

His lips curved; she noticed.

"Now why are you smiling?"

Harry couldn't stop his slow smile from breaking. His eyes caught hers—he felt he could lose himself in the blue. "I was just thinking what a good job I've made of teaching you to waltz."

Lucinda raised her brows. "Indeed? Can I not claim some small achievement for myself?"

Harry's smile went crooked. He drew her a fraction closer, his eyes a brilliant green. "You've achieved a great deal, my dear. On the floor—and off."

Her brows rose higher. She held his gaze, her expression serene, her smile soft, her lips eminently kissable. Then she lowered her lids and looked away, leaning her head fleetingly against his shoulder.

When they weren't playing waltzes, the musicians had been instructed to entertain Em's guests with gentle airs and sonatas, all pleasing to the ear. As they wandered the crowds, engaging in the usual banter and occasional repartee, without question or, indeed, thought, remaining by each other's side, Harry realised that his siren was indeed calmer, more her usual self than she had been at Almack's the night before.

His relief was telling; he had, he realised, been harbouring a deep concern. Presumably, last night, it had merely been the unexpected gush of semi-congratulations that had shaken her; tonight, she seemed at ease, assured, typically confident.

If he could only discover the cause of the strange hint of sorrow that lay, deep but present, beneath her serene veneer—and eradicate it—he'd be happier than any man, he felt, had any right to be.

She was perfect, she was his—as he had always sensed she could be. All he wanted of life was here, with her, within his grasp; time was all that now stood in his path.

But tomorrow would come—it wasn't what he'd originally planned but he wasn't going to wait any longer. He had completed all the important acts—she would simply have to believe him.

The supper waltz came and went, as did supper itself, an array of delicacies Em's old cook had, Lucinda assured him, been up the past three nights producing. Filled with laughter and repartee, the hours fled past until, at the last, the musicians laid bow to string once more and the strains of the last waltz rose above the sea of glittering heads.

The third waltz.

Close by the edge of the floor, Harry and Ruthven were deep in discussions of a distinctly equine nature while beside them Mr Amberly and Lucinda pursued a shared interest in landscapes. As the music swelled, Harry turned to Lucinda—just as she turned to him. Their gazes locked; after a moment, Harry's lips twisted wryly.

His eyes on hers, he offered her, not his arm but his hand.

Lucinda glanced at it, then looked into his green eyes. Her heart accelerated, pulsing in her throat.

Harry's brows slowly rose. "Well, my dear?"

Her gaze steady on his, Lucinda drew in a breath. Her smile soft and oddly fragile, she placed her hand in his.

Harry's fingers closed tight over hers. He bowed elegantly; Lucinda's smile grew—she sank into a curtsy. Harry raised her, a light in his eyes she had not before seen. He drew her into his arms, then, with consummate skill, whirled them onto the floor.

Lucinda let herself flow with his stride. His strength surrounded her; he was protection and support, lover and master, helpmate and friend. She searched the hard planes of his face, chiselled, austere; with him, she could be what she wished—what she wanted to be. Her gaze softened, as did her lips. He noticed; his gaze fell to her lips, then rose again to capture hers, a subtle shift in the green raising a slow heat beneath her skin, a warmth that owed nothing to the crowds and everything to what lay between them.

With inherent grace, they swirled down the long room, seeing no one, aware of nothing beyond their shared existence, trapped by the waltz and the promise in each other's eyes.

Lord Ruthven and Mr Amberly looked on, smugly satisfied smiles on their faces.

"Well—I think we can congratulate ourselves, Amberly." Lord Ruthven turned and held out his hand.

"Indeed." Mr Amberly beamed and shook it. "A job well done!" His eyes lifted to the couple circling the floor. His smile grew broader. "No doubt about it."

Lord Ruthven followed his gaze—and grinned. "Not a one."

As she leaned back against Harry's arm and let the magic of the moment take her, Lucinda knew that was true. Even while a small part of her sorrowed, she felt elation sweep her. He would ask her very soon—and she knew how she would answer. She loved him too much to deny him again, even should he deny her. Deep inside, her conviction that he loved her had never waned—it never would, she was sure. She could draw on that for strength as she had hoped to draw on his acknowledgement of his love. If it was not to be, it wasn't; she was too prosaic a creature to rail against a much-desired fate.

With the last ringing chord of the waltz, the evening was declared over.

As family, Harry hung back, allowing the other guests to depart. Gerald finally headed downstairs, leaving Harry with Lucinda at their head. His hand found hers in the folds of her gown; twining his fingers through hers, he drew her to face him. Ignoring Em leaning against the balustrade on Lucinda's other side, Harry raised Lucinda's hand to brush a kiss across her knuckles, then shifting his hold, his gaze steady on hers, he tipped her fingers back to place a kiss on her inner wrist.

Lucinda, trapped in his gaze, suppressed a delicious shiver.

Harry smiled—and traced her cheek with one long finger. "We'll talk tomorrow."

The words were soft, low—they went straight to Lucinda's heart. She smiled softly; Harry bowed, first to her, then to Em. Then, without a backward glance, he descended the stairs—to the very last, the very picture of the elegant rake.

Outside Hallows House, lurking in the shadows on the opposite side of the street, unremarkable amid the small gathering of urchins and inveterate watchers who congregated outside any ball or party, Scrugthorpe kept his eyes fixed on the lighted doorway and muttered beneath his breath.

"Just wait till I get my hands on you, bitch. Once I'm done with you, no high-stickler of a gentleman will want to sully himself with you. Damaged goods, you'll be— well and truly damaged." He cackled softly, gleefully and rubbed his hands. In the shadows, his eyes gleamed.

A link-boy, waiting to pick up any likely trade, strolled past, casting Scrugthorpe an incurious glance. A few paces on, the boy passed a street-sweeper, leaning on his broom, his face obscured by an ancient floppy hat. The link-boy grinned at the sweeper, then ambled on to prop against a nearby lamppost.

Scrugthorpe missed the exchange, intent on the last stragglers emerging from Hallows House.

"You'll be mine very soon," he leered. "Then I'll teach you not to give a man lip. Too hoity by half." His grin turned feral. "I'll bring you back to earth right quick."

A thin, tuneful whistle floated across Scrugthorpe's senses, distracting him from his plotting. The tune continued—a popular air; Scrugthorpe stiffened. Alert, he scanned the shadows for the whistler. His gaze settled on the link-boy. The tune continued; Scrugthrope knew it well, even down to the curious lilting catch the whistler put at the end of each verse.

Scrugthorpe cast a last glance at the empty doorway across the road, then, with every evidence of unconcern, headed off down the street.

The sweeper and link-boy watched him go. Then the link-boy nodded to the sweeper and slipped into the shadows in Scrugthorpe's wake.

Chapter Fifteen

The next morning, Harry was flat on his stomach deep in dreams, his arms wrapped about his pillow, when a large hand descended on his bare shoulder.

His response was instantaneous—half-rising, eyes wide, muscles tensed, fists clenching.

"Now, now!" Dawlish had wisely backed out of reach. "I wish as you'd get out of that habit—there ain't no angry husbands 'round here."

Eyes glittering, Harry hauled in a breath then expelled it irritably. Propping himself on one arm, he raked his hair out of his eyes. "What the devil's the time?"

"Nine," Dawlish replied, already at the wardrobe. "But you've got visitors."

"At *nine?*" Harry turned over and sat up.

"Salter—and he's brought that agent of the missus's— Mr Mabberly."

Harry blinked. Draping his arms over his knees, he stared at Dawlish. "I haven't married the damned woman yet."

"Just getting in some practice, like." Dawlish turned from the robe with a grey coat over his arm. "This do?"

Ten minutes later, Harry descended the narrow staircase, wondering if Lucinda would prefer a grander place when they stayed in town. He hoped she wouldn't—he'd been renting these rooms for the past ten years; they felt comfortable, like a well-worn coat.

He opened the door to his study and beheld his visitors, Salter standing by the desk, Mabberly, looking thoroughly uncomfortable, perched on the chair before it.

At sight of him, Mabberly rose.

"Good morning, Mabberly." Harry nodded and shut the door. "Salter."

Salter returned his nod but refrained from comment, his lips compressed as if holding the words back.

Stiff as a poker, Mr Mabberly inclined his head fractionally. "Mr Lester. I hope you'll forgive this intrusion but this gentleman—" he glanced at Salter "—is most insistent that I provide answers to questions regarding Mrs Babbacombe's affairs that I can only describe as highly confidential." Decidedly prim, Mr Mabberly brought his gaze back to Harry's face. "He tells me he's working for you."

"Indeed." Harry waved Mr Mabberly back to his chair and took his own behind the desk. "I'm afraid we are in pressing need of the information Mr Salter has requested of you, in a matter pertaining to Mrs Babbacombe's safety." As Harry had expected, the mention of Lucinda's safety stopped Mr Mabberly in his tracks. "That is," Harry smoothly continued, "assuming you do, in fact, know the answers?"

Mr Mabberly shifted, eyeing Harry somewhat warily. "As it happens, I do—it's necessary for one in my position, acting as the company's representative, to be absolutely certain just whose interests I'm representing." He shot a glance at Salter, then brought his gaze back to Harry. "But you mentioned Mrs Babbacombe's safety. How can the information you requested be important?"

Succinctly, Harry told him, detailing no more than the bare bones of the presumptive plot; Mr Mabberly was businessman enough to readily follow their hypothesis. As the tale unfolded, his open features reflected shock, outrage—and, eventually, a dogged determination.

"The cads!" Slightly flushed, he glanced at Harry. "You say you intend taking out a warrant against them?"

Salter answered. "We've cause enough for a warrant *provided* we can find evidence on this guardianship business—without that, their motive's uncertain."

"So." Harry fixed Mr Mabberly with a flat green gaze. "The question is will you help us?"

"I'll do anything I can," Mr Mabberly vowed, his voice ringing with fervour. Even he heard it. A trifle shocked, he hurried to excuse it. "Mrs Babbacombe's been very good to me, you understand—there aren't many who would appoint someone as relatively young as myself to such an important position."

"Of course." Harry smiled, endeavouring to make the gesture as unthreatening as he could at that hour of the morning. "And, as a loyal employee of Babbacombe and Company, you would naturally be anxious to assist in ensuring your principals' personal safety."

"Indeed." Obviously more comfortable, Mr Mabberly sat back. "Mrs Babbacombe is indeed Miss Babbacombe's sole legal guardian." Again, a slight flush rose in his cheeks. "I'm perfectly sure because, when I first took up my position, I was uncertain as to the point—so I asked. Mrs Babbacombe's always a model of business etiquette—she insisted I see the guardianship deed."

Salter straightened, his expression lightening. "So—not only do you *know* she's the sole guardian—you can swear to it?"

Mr Mabberly nodded, swivelling to look at Salter. "Certainly. I naturally felt obliged to read the document and verify the seal. It was unquestionably genuine."

"Excellent!" Harry looked at Salter—the big man's face was alight, his frame suddenly thrumming with harnessed energy. "So we can get that warrant without further delay?"

"If Mr Mabberly here will come with me to the magistrate and swear to Mrs Babbacombe's status, I can't see anything that'll stop us. I've already got friends in the force standing by—they'll do the actual arrest but I, for one, definitely want to be there when they take Joliffe into custody."

"I'm prepared to come with you immediately, sir." Mr Mabberly stood. "From the sounds of it, the sooner this Joliffe person is a guest of His Majesty's government the better."

"I couldn't agree more." Harry stood and offered Mr Mabberly his hand. "And while you two are tying up Joliffe and his crew, I'll keep Mrs Babbacombe under my eye."

"Aye—that'd be wise." Salter shook hands with Harry and they all turned to the door. "Joliffe's got the makings of a fairly desperate character. It wouldn't hurt to keep the lady close—just until we've got him safely stowed. I'll send word the instant we've got the blackguards in custody, sir."

"Send word to me at Hallows House," Harry told him.

After seeing his guests to the hall, Harry returned to the study and quickly glanced through his letters. He looked up as Dawlish entered with a cup of coffee. "Here you are." Dawlish set the cup down on the blotter. "So—what's the sum of it, then?"

Harry told him.

"Hmm—so that clerk fellow's not so useless after all?"

Harry took a sip of his coffee. "I never said he was useless. Gormless. And I'm willing to accept that I might have misjudged him."

Dawlish nodded. "Good! Last day of this ramshackle business, then. Can't say I'm sad."

Harry snorted. "Nor I."

"I'll get breakfast on the table." Dawlish glanced at the long-case clock in the corner. "We've still an hour to go before we're due at Hallows House."

Harry set down his cup. "We'd best use the time to get all tidy here—I expect to leave for Lester Hall later this evening."

Dawlish looked back from the door, brows flying. "Oh-ho! Finally going to take the plunge, are you? 'Bout time, if you ask me. Mind—wouldn't have thought you'd choose a family picnic to do it at—but it's your funeral."

Harry lifted his head and glared but the door had already closed.

LATER THAT AFTERNOON, Harry recalled Dawlish's observation with grim resignation. Not in his wildest dreams had he imagined playing the most important scene of his life on such a stage.

They were seated on colourful coach rugs on a long grassy slope leading down to the gently rippling River Lea. Some miles north of Islington, not far from Stamford

Hill, the woods and meadows close by the river provided a pleasant spot for young families and those seeking a draught of country peace. Although some way down the low escarpment, their position afforded them an uninterrupted view over the river valley, meadows giving way to marshland, water glinting in the sun. Roads meandered through the marshes, leading to Walthamstow, just beyond the valley. Oaks and beeches at their backs shielded them from the sun; the haze of a glorious afternoon surrounded them. Bees buzzed, flitting from fieldflower to hedgerow bloom; doves cooed overhead.

Harry drew in a deep breath—and shot a considering glance at Lucinda, stretched out beside him. Beyond her reclined Em, her hat over her face. On a neighbouring rug sat Heather and Gerald, engrossed in animated discourse. Beyond them, at a suitable distance, perched on and about a collection of fallen logs, sat Agatha and Em's even more severe dresser, together with Em's coachman, Dawlish, Joshua, Sim and the little maid Amy. In their dark clothes, they looked like so many crows.

Harry grimaced and looked away. Fate had chosen a fine moment to turn fickle.

The instant he had realised that it was Heather's guardianship that was Joliffe and Mortimer Babbacombe's goal, he had determined to come between them and Lucinda with all possible speed. By marrying her, he would assume legal responsibility in all such matters—automatically, without question. It was the one, absolutely guaranteed way of protecting her, of shielding her from their machinations.

But her yesterday had been filled with preparations for the soirée; the household had been at sixes and sevens. He hadn't liked his prospects of finding a quiet moment, let alone a quiet corner to propose.

As for today, they had organised this outing a week ago as a quiet relaxation away from the *ton* after the excitement of the soirée. They had come in two carriages, Em's and Lucinda's, the menservants riding atop; Agatha and Amy had shared Lucinda's carriage with their mistress and himself. They had lunched surrounded by sunshine and peace. Now Em looked set for her postprandial nap; it would probably be at least an hour before hunger again prodded Heather and Gerald to a more general awareness.

So, since learning of her danger, this was his first chance to remove her from it. Hiding his determination behind an easy expression, Harry got to his feet. Lucinda looked up, putting up her hand to shield her eyes. Harry smiled reassuringly down at her before lifting his gaze to her drab watchdogs. With a slight movement of his head, he summoned Dawlish, then strolled back towards the trees. When he was out of earshot of his intended and his aunt, he stopped and waited for Dawlish to reach him.

"Something wrong?"

Harry smiled politely. "No. I just thought I'd let it be known that, when I take Mrs Babbacombe for a stroll in a few moments, we won't need an escort." When Dawlish screwed up his eyes, as if considering arguing, Harry continued, his tone growing steely, "She'll be perfectly safe with me."

Dawlish humphed. "Can't say as I blame you. Cramp anyone's style, it would, having to go down on your knees before an audience."

Harry raised his eyes heavenwards in a mute gesture of appeal.

"I'll tell the others."

Harry hurriedly lowered his gaze but Dawlish was already stomping back through the trees. Muttering a curse, Harry did the same, returning to the rugs on the grass.

"Come for a walk."

Lucinda glanced up at the soft words—which cloaked what sounded like a command. Beside her, Em was gently snoring; Heather and Gerald were in a world of their own. She met Harry's eyes, very green; he raised a brow and held out his hand. Lucinda studied it for an instant, savouring the thrill of anticipation that shot through her, then, with studied calm, laid her fingers in his.

Harry drew her to her feet. Tucking her hand in his arm, he turned her towards the leafy woods.

The woods were not extensive, merely stands of trees separating fields and meadows. They strolled without words, leaving the others behind, until they came to a large field left fallow. The meadow grasses and flowers had taken over; the ground was carpeted in a shifting sea of small bright blooms.

Lucinda sighed. "How lovely." She smiled up at Harry.

Engaged in scanning their surroundings, he glanced back at her in time to return her smile. The trees screened them from their companions and any others strolling the river banks; they were not isolated but as private as, in the circumstances, it was probably wise to be. He gestured ahead; by unvoiced agreement, they strolled to the centre of the field where a large rock, weathered to smoothness, created a natural seat.

With a swirl of her blue muslin skirts, Lucinda sat. Harry noticed that her gown matched the cornflowers scattered through the grass. She had worn a new bonnet but had let it fall to dangle by its ribbons on her back, leaving her face unshadowed. She lifted her head and her gaze met his.

Stillness held them, then her delicate brows arched slightly, in query, in invitation.

Harry scanned her face, then drew in a deep breath.

"Ah-hem!"

They both turned to see Dawlish striding across the field. Harry bit back a curse. "What *now?*"

Dawlish cast him a sympathetic glance. "There's a messenger come—'bout that business this morning."

Harry groaned. "Now?"

Dawlish met his eye. "Thought as how you might think it better to get that matter all tied and tight—before you get…distracted, like."

Harry grimaced—Dawlish had a point.

"Set on seeing you specifically, this messenger—said as that was his orders." Dawlish nodded back at the trees. "Said he'd wait by the stile yonder."

Swallowing his irritation, Harry shot a considering glance at Lucinda; she met it with an affectionate smile. Spending five minutes to acknowledge the end of Joliffe's threat would leave him free to concentrate on her— wholly, fully, without reservation. Without further interruption. Harry looked at Dawlish. "Which stile?"

"It's along the fence a little way."

"We didn't pass a fence."

Dawlish frowned and surveyed the woods through which he'd come. "It's that way—and around to the left, I think." He scratched his head. "Or is it the right?"

"Why don't you just show Mr Lester the way?"

Harry turned at Lucinda's words. She had plucked some blooms and started to plait them. He frowned. "I'll find the stile. Dawlish will stay here with you."

Lucinda snorted. "Nonsense! You'll take twice as long." She picked a cornflower from her lap, then tilted her face to look up at him, one brow arching. "The sooner you get there, the sooner you'll be back."

Harry hesitated, then shook his head. Joliffe might be behind bars but his protective instincts still ran strong. "No. I'll—"

"Don't be absurd! I'm perfectly capable of sitting on a rock in the sunshine for a few minutes alone." Lucinda lifted both arms to gesture about her. "What *do* you imagine could happen in such a sylvan setting?"

Harry glared, briefly, aware she would very likely be perfectly safe. Hands on hips, he scanned the surrounding trees. There was open space all around her; no one could creep up and surprise her. She was a mature and sensible woman; she would scream if anything untoward occurred. And they were all close enough to hear.

And the sooner he met with Salter's messenger, the sooner he could concentrate on her, on them, on their future.

"Very well." His expression hard, he pointed a finger at her. "But stay there and don't move!"

Her answering smile was fondly condescending.

Harry turned and strode quickly across the field; the damned woman's confidence in herself was catching.

Like many countrymen, Dawlish could retrace his steps to anywhere but could never describe the way. He took the lead; within a matter of minutes, they found the fence line. They followed it to a small clearing in which stood the stile—surrounded by a small army of people.

Harry halted. "What the devil...?"

Salter pushed through the crowd. Harry caught sight of Mabberley and three representatives of Bow Street among a motley crew of ostlers, grooms and stablelads, link-boys, jarveys, street urchins, sweepers—basically any likely looking scruffs to be found on the streets of London. Obviously Salter's "people".

Then Salter stood before him, his face decidedly grim. "We got the warrant but when we went to serve it, Joliffe and his crew had done a bunk."

Harry stiffened. "I thought you were watching them?"

"We were." Salter's expression grew bleaker. "But someone must have tripped up somewhere—we found our two watchers coshed over the head this morning—and no sign of our pigeons anywhere."

Harry's mind raced; chill fingers clutched his gut. "Have they taken the coach?"

"Yep," came from one of the ostlers. "Seems like they left 'bout ten—just afore the captain here came with his bill."

Mr Mabberly stepped forward. "We thought we should warn you to keep an especially close eye on Mrs Babbacombe—until we can get this villain behind bars."

Harry barely heard him. His expression had blanked. *"Oh, my God!"*

He whirled and raced back the way he'd come, Dawlish on his heels. The rest, galvanised by Harry's fear, followed.

Harry broke from the trees and scanned the field—then came to a skidding halt.

Before him the meadow grasses swayed in the breeze. All was peaceful and serene, the field luxuriating in the heat. The sun beat down on the rock in its centre—now empty.

Harry stared. Then he strode forward, his expression like flint. A short chain of blue cornflowers had been left on the rock—laid down gently, not flung or mauled.

Breathing rapidly, Harry, hands on hips, lifted his head and looked about. "Lucinda?"

His call faded into the trees—no one answered.

Harry swore. "They've got her." The words burned his throat.

"They can't have got far." Salter gestured to his people. "It's the lady we're after—tallish, dark-haired—most of you've seen her. Name of Mrs Babbacombe."

Within seconds, they were quartering the area, quickly, efficiently, calling her name, threshing through undergrowth. Harry headed towards the river, Dawlish beside him. His throat was already hoarse. His imagination was a handicap—he could conjure visions far too well. He had to find her—he simply had to.

LEFT IN THE PEACE of the meadow, Lucinda smiled to herself, then settled to convert the cornflowers growing in abundance around the base of the rock into a blue garland. Beneath her calm, she was impatient enough, yet quite confident Harry would shortly be back.

Her smile deepened. She reached for a bright dandelion to lend contrast to her string.

"Mrs Babbacombe! Er—Aunt Lucinda?"

Blinking, Lucinda turned. She searched the shadows beneath the trees and saw a slight, shortish gentleman waving and beckoning.

"Good lord! Whatever does *he* want?" Laying aside her garland, she crossed to the trees. "Mortimer?" She ducked under a branch and stepped into the cool shade. "What are you doing here?"

"A-waiting for you, bitch," came in a growling grating voice.

Lucinda jumped; a huge paw wrapped about her arm.

Her eyes widened in incredulous amazement as she took in its owner. "*Scrugthorpe!* What the devil do you think you're doing?"

"Grabbing you." Scrugthorpe leered, then started to drag her deeper into the trees. "Come on—the carriage's waiting."

"What carriage? Oh, for goodness' sake!" Lucinda was about to struggle in earnest when Mortimer took her other elbow.

"This is all most distressing—but if you'll only listen—it's really nothing to do with you, you know—simply a matter of righting a wrong—fixing a slight—that sort of thing." He wasn't so much helping to drag her along as clinging to her arm; his eyes, a weak washy blue, implored her understanding.

Lucinda frowned. "What on earth is all this about?"

Mortimer told her—in disjointed phrases, bits and pieces, dribs and drabs. Totally engrossed in trying to follow his tale, Lucinda largely ignored Scrugthorpe and his dogged march forward, absent-mindedly letting him pull her along, shifting her attention only enough to lift her skirts over a log.

"Damned hoity female!" Scrugthorpe kicked at her skirts. "When I get you alone, I'm going to—"

"And then, you see, there was the money owed to Joliffe—must pay, y'know—play and pay—honour and all that—"

"And after that, I'll tie you up good—"

"So it turned out to be rather a lot—not impossible but—had to find it, you see—thought I'd be right after Uncle Charles died—but then it wasn't there—the money, I mean—but I'd already spent it—owed it—had to raise the wind somehow—"

"Oh, I'll make you pay for your sharp tongue, I will. After I've done, you'll—"

Lucinda shut her ears to Scrugthrope's ravings and concentrated on Mortimer's babblings. Her jaw dropped when he revealed their ultimate goal; their plan to reach it was even more astonishing. Mortimer finally concluded with, "So, you see—all simple enough. If you'll just make the guardianship over to me, it'll all be right and tight— you do see that, don't you?"

They had reached the edge of the river; a narrow footbridge lay ahead. Abruptly, Lucinda hauled back against Scrugthorpe's tow and stood her ground. Her gaze, positively scathing, fixed on Mortimer.

"You ass!" Her tone said it all. "Do you really believe that, just because you're so weak and stupid as to get…?" Words momentarily failed her; she wrenched her elbow from Mortimer's grasp and gestured wildly. "Gulled by a sharp." Eyes flashing, she transfixed Mortimer; he stood rooted to the spot, his mouth silently opening and shutting, his expression that of a terrified rabbit facing the ultimate fury. "That I will meekly hand over to you my stepdaughter's fortune so you can line the pockets of some cunning, immoral, inconsiderate, rapacious, fly-by-night excuse for a man?" Her voice had risen, gaining in commanding volume. "You've got *rocks* in your head, sir!"

"Now see here." Scrugthorpe, somewhat dazed by her vehemence, shook her arm. "That's enough of that."

Mortimer was exceedingly pale. "But Uncle Charles owed me—"

"Nonsense! Charles owed you *nothing!* Indeed, you got more than you deserved. What you have to do, Mortimer," Lucinda jabbed him in the chest, "is get back to Yorkshire and get your affairs in order. Talk to Mr Wilson in Scarborough—he'll know how to help. Stand on your own feet, Mortimer—believe me, it's the only way." Struck by a thought, Lucinda asked, "Incidentally, how is Mrs Finnigan, the cook? When we left she had ulcers, poor thing—is she better?"

Mortimer simply stared at her.

"*Enough*, woman!" Scrugthorpe, his face mottling, swung Lucinda about. Opting for action rather than words, he grabbed her by the shoulders and pulled her to him. Lucinda uttered a small shriek and ducked her head—just in time to avoid Scrugthorpe's fleshy lips. He grunted; she felt his fingers grip her shoulders tightly, bruising her soft flesh. She struggled, rocking to keep him off balance. Her gaze directed downwards, she saw his feet, clad in soft leather shoes, shuffling to gain greater stability. Lucinda lifted her knee, inadvertently striking Scrugthorpe in the groin. She heard his sharp intake of breath—and brought her boot heel down with all the force she could muster, directly onto his left instep.

"*Ow!* You *bitch!*" His voice was crazed with pain.

Lucinda jerked her head up—her crown connected with Scrugthorpe's chin with a most satisfying crack. Scrugthorpe yowled. He put one hand to his foot and the other to his chin—Lucinda was free. She whisked herself away—and Mortimer grabbed her.

Furious, she beat at his hands, his face; he was no Scrugthorpe—she broke free easily enough, pushing Mortimer into a bush in the process. Gasping, dragging much needed air into her lungs, Lucinda picked up her skirts and fled onto the bridge. Behind her, Scrugthorpe, swearing foully, hobbled in pursuit.

Lucinda cast a quick glance behind—and ran faster.

She looked ahead and saw a gentleman striding onto

the other end of the bridge. He was dressed neatly in riding breeches and top coat and wore Hessians. Lucinda thanked her stars and waved. "Sir!" Here, surely, was one who would aid her.

To her surprise, he stopped, standing with his feet apart, blocking the exit to the bridge. Lucinda blinked, and slowed. She halted in the centre of the bridge.

The man had a pistol in his hand.

It was, Lucinda thought, as she slowly watched it rise, one of those long-barrelled affairs gentlemen were said to use when duelling. The sun struck its silver mountings, making them gleam. Beneath her, the river gurgled onwards to the sea; in the wide sky above, the larks swooped and trilled. Distantly, she heard her name called but the cries were too weak to break the web that held her.

A chill spread over her skin.

Slowly, the pistol rose, until the barrel was level with her chest.

Her mouth dry, her heart pounding in her ears, Lucinda looked into the man's face. It was blank, expressionless. She saw his fingers shift and heard a telltale click.

A hundred yards downstream, Harry broke through the woods and gained the river path. Panting, he looked around—then glanced up at the bridge. He froze.

Two heartbeats passed as he watched his future, his life, his love—all he had ever wanted—face certain death. Salter and some of his men were on the opposite bank, closing fast, but they would never reach Joliffe in time. Still others were rushing for this end of the bridge. Harry saw the pistol level—saw the slight upward adjustment necessary to bring the aim to true.

"Lucinda!"

The cry was wrenched from him, filled with despair

and rage—and something more powerful than both. It sliced through the mesmeric daze that held Lucinda.

She turned, her hand on the wooden rail—and saw Harry on the nearby shore. Lucinda blinked. Safety lay with Harry. The rail was a simple one, a single wooden top-rail supported by intermittent posts. Before her, the area below the rail was empty, open. She put both hands on the rail and let herself drop through.

She plummeted to the river as the shot rang out.

Harry watched her fall. He had no idea whether she'd been hit or not. She entered the river with a splash; when it cleared, there was no sign of her.

Cursing, Harry raced forward, scanning the river. Could she swim? He reached the bank just short of the bridge and sat down. He was tugging off one boot when Lucinda surfaced. Pushing her hair out of her eyes, she looked about and saw him. She waved, then, as if she went swimming in rivers every day, calmly stroked for shore.

Harry stared. Then, his expression hardening, he slammed his foot back in his boot. He rose and strode to the river's edge. His emotions clashing wildly, swinging from elation to rage with sufficient intensity to make him dizzy, he stood on the bank and waited for her to reach him.

He had lost Dawlish somewhere in the woods; those of Salter's people who had been near, seeing him waiting, wisely left him to it. He was distantly aware of the commotions engulfing both ends of the bridge but he didn't even spare them a glance. Later, they learned that Mr Mabberly had distinguished himself by laying Mortimer Babbacombe low while Dawlish had taken great pleasure in scientifically darkening the daylights of the iniquitous Scrugthorpe.

Gaining the shallows, Lucinda stood and glanced back at the bridge. Satisfied that her attackers were being dealt with as they deserved, she reached behind her and caught hold of her dripping hat. Tugging the wet ribbons from about her neck, she stared in dismay at the limp creation. "It's ruined!" she wailed.

Then she looked down. "And my dress!"

Harry couldn't take anymore. The damned woman had nearly got killed and all she was concerned with was the fate of her hat. He strode into the shallow water to stand towering by her side.

Still mourning her headgear, Lucinda gestured at it. "It's beyond resurrection." She looked up at him—in time to see his eyes flare.

Harry slapped her wet bottom—hard enough to leave his palm stinging.

Lucinda jumped and yelped. "Ow!" She stared at him in stunned surprise.

"The next time I tell you to stay where I leave you and *not* to move you will do precisely *that*—do I make myself clear?" Harry glared down at her, into eyes that, even now, held a hint of mutinous determination. Then his gaze fell to her breasts. He blinked. "Good lord! Your dress!" Immediately, he shrugged off his coat.

Lucinda sniffed. "Precisely what I said." With injured dignity, she accepted the coat he placed about her shoulders—she even allowed him to do up the buttons, closing it loosely about her.

"Come—I'm taking you home immediately." Harry took her elbow and helped her onto the bank. "You're soaked—the last thing I need is for you to take a chill."

Lucinda tried to look back at the bridge. "That was Mortimer back there, you know."

"Yes, I know." Harry drew her into the woods.

"You do?" Lucinda blinked. "He had some strange idea that Charles had done him out of his rightful inheritance, you know, that—"

Harry let her fill his ears with an account of Mortimer's justification ˙of his deeds as he steered her through the woods. It was infinitely reassuring to hear her voice. His fear that she might suffer from delayed shock receded, lulled by her calm and logical recital, her unflustered observations. She was, he had to grudgingly, somewhat astonishingly concede, totally unaffected by her ordeal. *He* was a nervous wreck. He led her directly to the carriages.

Lucinda blinked when they appeared before them. "But what about the others?"

Harry hauled open the door of her carriage as Joshua and Dawlish hurried up. "We can leave a message for Em and Heather—Mabberly can explain."

"Mr Mabberly?" Lucinda was astonished. "Is he here?"

Harry cursed his loose tongue. "Yes. Now get in." He didn't wait for her to do so—he picked her up and put her in. Joshua was already climbing to the box; Harry turned to Dawlish. "Go back and explain everything to Em and Miss Babbacombe—assure them Mrs Babbacombe's taken no hurt other than a soaking."

From inside the carriage came a definite sniff. Harry's palm tingled. He put a foot on the carriage step. "I'm taking her back to Hallows House—we'll wait for them there."

Dawlish nodded. "All the rest's taken care of."

Harry nodded. He turned back to the carriage, remembering to grab his greatcoat, left on the rack atop, before he ducked through the door. Dawlish shut it behind him and slapped the coach's side. It lurched into motion;

heaving a heavy sigh, Harry subsided onto the seat and shut his eyes.

He remained thus for a full minute; Lucinda watched him somewhat warily. Then he opened his eyes, tossed his greatcoat onto the opposite seat, and reached out and systematically let down all the blinds. The sun still penetrated the thin leather, suffusing the interior with a golden glow.

"Ah..." Before Lucinda could decide what to say, Harry sat back, reached for her and hauled her onto his lap.

Lucinda opened her lips on a token protest—he captured them in a long, searing kiss, his lips hard on hers, demanding, commanding, ravishing her senses until her thoughts melted away and took her wits with them. She kissed him back with equal fervour, perfectly willing to take all he offered.

When he finally consented to raise his head, she lay against his chest, dazedly blinking up at him, with not two thoughts to her name.

The sight filled Harry with a certain satisfaction. With an approving grunt, he closed his eyes and let his head fall back against the squabs. "If you ever do anything like that again, you'd better be prepared to eat standing up for the following week. At least."

Lucinda threw him a darkling glance and reached a hand to her abused posterior. "It still hurts."

Harry's lips lifted. He raised his lids enough to look down at her. "Perhaps I should kiss it better?"

Her eyes flew wide—then she looked intrigued.

Harry caught his breath. "Perhaps we'd better leave that until later."

Lucinda raised a brow. She held his gaze, then

shrugged and snuggled closer. "I didn't plan to be set upon, you know. And who were all those people?"

"Never mind." Harry juggled her around so she was sitting on his knees facing him. "There's something I want to say—and I'm only going to say it once." His eyes met hers. "Are you listening?"

Lucinda drew in a breath—and couldn't let it out. Her heart in her mouth, she nodded.

"I love you."

Lucinda's face lit up. She leaned towards him, her lips parting—Harry held up a restraining hand.

"No—wait. I haven't finished." He held her with his eyes. Then his lips twisted. "Such words from a man such as I can hardly be convincing. You know I've said them before—in reams. And they weren't true—not then." His hand found hers where it rested on his chest; he raised her fingers to his lips. "Before you came along, I didn't know what the words meant—now I do. But I couldn't expect you to find the words convincing, when I wouldn't myself. So I've given you all the proof that I can—I've taken you to visit with my father, shown you my ancestral home." Lucinda blinked—Harry continued with his list. "You've seen the stud and I've shown you the house that I hope we'll make our home." He paused, eyes glinting, lips lifting at the ends as he met Lucinda's gaze. "And I *was* joking about the six children—four will do nicely."

Breathless, dazed, giddy with happiness, Lucinda opened her eyes wide. "Only four?" She let her lids fall. "You disappoint me, sir."

Harry shifted. "Perhaps we can settle on four to begin with? I wouldn't, after all, wish to disappoint you."

Lucinda's rare dimple appeared in her cheek.

Harry frowned. "Now where was I? Ah, yes—the

proofs of my devotion. I accompanied you back to London and drove you in the Park, I danced attendance on you in every conceivable way—I even braved the dangers of Almack's." His eyes held hers. "All for you."

"Is *that* why you did it—to convince me you loved me?" Lucinda felt as if her heart would burst. She had only to look into his eyes to know the truth.

Harry's lips twisted in a self-deprecatory grin. "Why else?" He gestured expansively. "What else could move me to prostrate myself at your feet?" He glanced at them— and frowned. "Which, incidentally, are very wet." He reached down and eased off her sodden boots. That done, he pushed up her wet skirts and started on her garters.

Lucinda smiled. "And you danced three waltzes with me—remember?"

"How could I forget?" Harry returned, busy rolling down her stockings. "A more public declaration I cannot imagine."

Lucinda giggled and wriggled her chilled toes.

Harry straightened and met her eyes. "So, Mrs Lucinda Babbacombe—after all my sterling efforts—do you believe me when I say I love you?"

Lucinda's smile lit her eyes. She reached up both hands to frame his face. "Silly man—you had only to say." Gently, she touched her lips to his.

When she drew back, Harry snorted disbelievingly. "And you'd have believed me? Even after my *faux pas* that afternoon you seduced me?"

Lucinda's smile was soft. "Oh, yes." Her dimple came back. "Even then."

Harry decided to leave it at that. "So you agree to marry me without further fuss?"

Lucinda nodded once, decisively.

"Thank heaven for that." Harry closed his arms about

her. "We're getting married in two days at Lester Hall—
it's all arranged. I've got the licence in my pocket." He
glanced down and saw the damp patches on his coat, close
about her. He frowned and lifted her back so she was
once more sitting upright on his knee. "I hope you haven't
got it wet enough for the ink to run." He undid the coat
buttons and lifted the garment from her.

Lucinda laughed, so delirious with happiness she
couldn't contain it. She reached out and drew his head to
hers and kissed him longingly. The kiss deepened, then
Harry disengaged.

"You're very wet. We should get you out of these things."

Siren-like, Lucinda raised her brows, then obediently
turned so he could undo her laces. He eased her from her
gown, dropping it to the floor where it landed with a soft
splat.

Her chemise, drenched and all but transparent, clung
like a second skin. A soft blush rose beneath it; Lucinda
let her lids veil her eyes, watching Harry's hands from beneath her lashes as, gently yet deliberately, he peeled the
delicate material from her.

Harry sensed the heat rising within her, heard the sudden shallow intake of her breath as he drew the last shred
of concealment from her. She shivered—but he didn't
think it was due to being cold. Drawing in a deep breath,
she raised her eyes to his.

Lucinda looked into eyes brilliantly green, screened by
heavy lids; nothing could hide the desire that burned in
their peridot depths.

She sat naked on his lap. His hands moved gently over
her, over her back, over her arms, languidly stroking, caressing. He leaned forward and pressed kisses to the
bruises Scrugthorpe had left on her shoulders. Lucinda

shuddered. Unbidden, entirely unexpected, a long-forgotten conversation drifted through her mind. Eyes agleam, she chuckled softly.

Harry stared at her hungrily, the siren who had lured him to his doom. Clinging to sanity, he raised a brow in the nearest he could get to languid enquiry.

Lucinda laughed. She caught his eyes with hers, then, leaning closer, let her lids screen her eyes. "Em once said," she murmured, "that I should aim to get you on your knees." Fleetingly, she lifted her eyes to his, her lips gently curved. "I don't think she meant it in quite this way."

The body beneath her was hard, rigid, powerful but harnessed.

"Ah, yes. An eminently wise old lady, my aunt." Gently, Harry lifted Lucinda, settling her so she was straddling his knees, her knees on the seat on either side of his hips. "But she tends to forget that—sometimes—it's very hard for a rake to—er—change his spots."

Lucinda wasn't at all sure about her change in position. "Ah, Harry?"

"Hmm?" Harry wasn't interested in further conversation.

Lucinda realised as much when he urged her towards him and his lips closed gently about one tightly furled nipple. Her breath caught. "Harry—we're in a carriage."

Her protest was breathless. His lips left her; he put out his tongue and rasped her sensitised flesh. Lucinda shuddered and closed her eyes; his hands on her hips held her steady—every time she caught her breath, he stole it away. "You can't be serious," she eventually managed to gasp. She paused—then sucked in a quick breath. "Not here? In a moving carriage?"

His answering chuckle sounded devilish. "Perfectly possible, I assure you." His hands shifted. "The rocking's part of the fun—you'll see."

Lucinda struggled to draw her mind from the sensual web he had so skilfully woven. "Yes, but—" Abruptly, her eyes flew open. "*Dear heaven!*" After a stunned moment, her lids fell. She whispered, a soft catch in her voice, "Harry?"

A long moment of breathy silence ensued, then Lucinda sighed—deeply. "Oh, *Harry!*"

AN HOUR LATER, as the carriage slowly rolled into the leafy streets of Mayfair, Harry looked down at the woman in his lap. She was curled snugly in his greatcoat, dry and warm—he was prepared to swear no chill could have survived the fire that had recently claimed them. Her clothes lay in a sodden heap on the floor; his coat and breeches would keep Dawlish occupied for hours. Harry didn't care—he had all he most wanted of life.

He glanced down—and dropped a kiss on her curls.

He'd been a most unwilling conquest but he was ready to admit he was well and truly conquered.

Tipping his head, he looked into his siren's face, blissful in repose.

She stirred, then snuggled closer against him, one hand on his chest, over his heart.

Harry smiled, closed his eyes—and closed his arms about her.

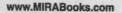

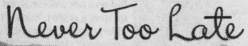

Stephanie Laurens

32175 A LADY OF EXPECTATIONS	___ $6.99 U.S.	___ $8.50 CAN.
32007 THE REASONS FOR MARRIAGE	___ $6.99 U.S.	___ $8.50 CAN.
66661 IMPETUOUS INNOCENT	___ $6.99 U.S.	___ $8.50 CAN.

(limited quantities available)

TOTAL AMOUNT	$ _____
POSTAGE & HANDLING	$ _____
($1.00 FOR 1 BOOK, 50¢ for each additional)	
APPLICABLE TAXES*	$ _____
TOTAL PAYABLE	$ _____

(check or money order—please do not send cash)

To order, complete this form and send it, along with a check or money order for the total above, payable to MIRA Books, to: **In the U.S.:** 3010 Walden Avenue, P.O. Box 9077, Buffalo, NY 14269-9077; **In Canada:** P.O. Box 636, Fort Erie, Ontario, L2A 5X3.

Name: _____
Address: _____ City: _____
State/Prov.: _____ Zip/Postal Code: _____
Account Number (if applicable): _____

075 CSAS

*New York residents remit applicable sales taxes.
*Canadian residents remit applicable GST and provincial taxes.

MIRA®

www.MIRABooks.com   MSL0506BL